Guns of the Yellow Rose

A Clay and Deekie Novel

by

David and Marie Trawinski

David and Marie Trawinski

The Guns of the Yellow Rose

Published by DAMTE Associates.

Cover Image © 2022 David Trawinski. All rights reserved - used with permission. Interior Images © 2022 David and Marie Trawinski unless otherwise attributed. Edited by Deborah Chapman.

Cover Design/Artwork Copyright 2022 by David Trawinski, with images attributed on p. 413.

Special thanks to our friends at the Booth Western Art Museum of Cartersville for the Butterfield Overland Stage Coach image use.

Thanks also to The Roselawn Museum of Cartersville.

All Photos by Marie and David Trawinski unless otherwise noted.

Edited by Deborah Chapman.

Dedicated to

The Memory of

M_r Phillip Chapman,

The Truest & Kindest

Southern Soul

We've Ever Had

God's Grace to Know

The Drovers' Exchange

This novel utilizes a fictional villainous network we have decided to call "The Drovers' Exchange," or as its members more often referred to it as simply, "The Exchange". It emerged in our minds as a clearing house of sorts for cattlemen scouring the Texas landscape for "waddies," "ramrods" and "wranglers," or whatever the cattlemen's needs might be, for those drives of massive herds of longhorn north along the Chisholm Trail in the years 1866 - 1873.

"The Exchange" started out as a way for cattlemen to understand the experience and temperament of those they wished to hire, and especially to stay away from those cowhands who had proven themselves troublesome to other members. In this novel, the Exchange soon morphed into a collective cattlemen network which fictionally took vigilante actions against those ne'er-do-wells that dared to rustle any of their member's cattle, shoot up their ranch hands, or even so much as dare to insult the quality of their livestock brands.

The mark of the Drovers' Exchange was the star within the star, as they viewed themselves as the stealth organization that was the driving force of prosperity within the Lone Star State. They conscripted more than one enforcer, most often ex-veterans from the Civil War, prized for both their loyalty and brutality alike. Our fictional character Cord McCullough is one such enforcer, riding the plains along the Chisholm Trail.

We Never Sleep

The Pinkertons

Whereas the Drovers' Exchange is purely fictional, the Pinkerton National Detective Agency is a remarkably real entity often associated with the Old West. Its founder Allan Pinkerton, a Scottish émigré detective, made his fame by having his female agent, Kate Warne, escort Abraham Lincoln to Washington in 1861. The pair traveled under disguise often due to threats against the President-elect's life. This subterfuge created great fame for his Chicago based North West Police Agency, transforming it into the detective agency bearing his name. It utilized the motto "We Never Sleep," with the logo of an open eye, which many to this day believe to be the genesis of the term "Private Eye". Lincoln later hired Pinkerton's agency for his personal protection during the Civil War.

In 1871, the newly formed Department of Justice contracted out national law enforcement responsibilities to the Pinkertons, making them deFacto federal agents. This arrangement lasted until 1893, when the Pinkertons' efforts in breaking workers became notorious. The Anti-Pinkerton Act was passed into law forbidding any employee of the Pinkerton Detective Agency to also be employed by the Federal Government.

During the twenty-two years between '71 and '93, the Pinkertons were used extensively to pursue outlaws, renegades, and vigilante organizations throughout the West. Our story takes place in the autumn of 1873.

Remembrances & Regrets

He stood in darkness.

Not the heavy, ominous black shadows that had enshrouded him in years past. Virgil Clay-Harris had faced the many difficulties that his young life had presented him, and all these were behind him by the early autumn of 1873. No, these nights were indeed dark, but the onyx sky was mercifully decorated by a light, gauzy cocoon of stars that hung overhead. Amid the night's radiant jewels, Clay hung his own conquests like glimmering well polished trophies.

In the evening, Clay liked to escape the single room shack that he and his gal, Deekie, shared with his brother Truitt to reflect on life. After supper, Truitt, who was by then the County Clerk of the Court, would be planning his next political conquest, while Deekie would be reading her book of stories stretched out in front of the fireplace. Clay instead chose to walk the darkened trail each night that his own footsteps had long ago worn between the cabin and his Maw's grave.

Clay thought the nightly walk to be a transit between the promise of life held in that fire-lit cabin and the certainty of death awaiting them all. Given that truth, Clay liked to thank his Maker nightly for his blessings.

His blessings were many, it is true. First of all, he had survived the tragic *War of The Rebellion* itself, although not without it first having claimed its own due from him. His left arm, nearly up to the elbow, was gone. Only a gnarled stump below the joint was left behind to mark his ever having fought for Dixie.

The townspeople of Cartersville had once hailed him as *"the Savior of Sharpsburg"*, but Clay never had much use for that name's glorification of his killing prowess at Antietam. His piercing stares at the townsfolk drove its use to an early grave, just as surely as his rifle had done to those poor Yankee boys at not only Antietam, but Gettysburg and Chickamauga as well. Clay had killed his share of men, mostly young, a few old, in that war. He was sure after his return that his killing days were behind him.

After the war, Clay and Deekie together had survived the intense drought that echoed throughout the fields of northern Georgia, like a dark shadow cast by the earlier misery of war. It was true that he had been able to save his family's meager farm from burning by the hand of Sherman's invading Union forces, but only to have it attacked anew by the withering dearth of nature's hand. The creek had dried out completely. To grow just enough crops to keep them fed, he had carried leather skins of water for miles from the Etowah River, balanced on a yoke across his back, already scarred from his pulling of a makeshift plow like a beast of burden. The town's folk had also once called him *"the man who beat the drought"*, although that title had withered away also.

Then, finally, he had conquered his worst fear - of one day returning to his killing ways. In 1871, some six years after the fighting of the war had finally ended, Clay had been forced to mount a one-man attack on his friend Willet Blackwell's renegade encampment atop Three Sisters Mountain. He was left no other option than to wipe out all of Willet's marauders. Even after doing so, he had to face the spectre that had haunted his dreams and waking thoughts alike - the killing of his childhood friend, Willet. From that fate Clay was eventually spared, but only in such a way that it still haunted his days.

Blackwell had been raised by his side. The two boys had together plundered the local farms for apples and the occasional peach. So often they found themselves dodging spewed barrels of birdshot from the farmers' shotguns in doing so. Together, as mere boys still, they had left Cartersville to seek glory in war. Willet was now gone forever. The rascal child that Clay had been reared with breathed no longer. Gone was the dreamer who had dragged him into the inviting darkness of every cave in the area, from those under Three Sisters Mountain to the saltpeter cave where Willet would tell him stories of pirates, knights, and something called chivalry. The last word he did not know, but assumed it meant a form of honor. Clay and Willet had been best of childhood friends. And for the past two years, his friend was gone.

Ten years ago, in September of '63, both Clay and Willet had come back from the war after Chickamauga. Both boys were scarred forever by the fighting - both physically and in even more permanent ways. Clay had been determined to salvage his soul through the abandonment of killing, by instead working the land to eke out a living, however meager it might be.

Willet, instead, decided to establish his own band of renegades, pillaging and killing at will in the post-war years. The friends who had been most closely aligned were converted by the wake of the war into polar opposites. Their paths crossed one last time in a final cataclysmic conflict, and Willet was now forever gone.

That was then, two years in the past, in '71. The year of the Lord was now 1873. Virgil Clay-Harris gazed up into the thick swath of stars, their scattered luminescent pinpoints set deep into and across the black velvet night. He was thankful to God that the town had simply returned to calling him by the name they had since he had become his father's first son - merely "Clay". It was as simple and earthy as he was. It, like him, could not carry even an ounce of pretension. That was exactly the trait that had distinguished him from his own father, Clay thought.

His father, Enos, had been filled with the ambition of dreams which were far greater than his abilities to ever achieve them. *"Diddy"*, as Clay had always called him, wore his dreams on his sleeve instead of the emotions of which he never showed a hint. He aspired to one day strike it rich, with as minimum an outlay of effort as possible. Clay's father was a skilled man in many ways, certainly in both blacksmithing and gun-smithing, but he would rather lose himself in his dreams and schemes than put those skills to work. He had used every bit of his life's savings to bribe his way into obtaining this farm along Pettit's Creek when the Cherokee were driven out in '38. Rather than work its fertile fields, Clay's father would merely pan its creek day in, day out, for gold nuggets he was sure would have washed down from the strike in Dahlonega. He did so until the pans went still, and his dreams sieved through his fingers just as had so much of the creek's muddy water.

The other thing that gnawed at Clay's state of mind was the current whereabouts of his father. After the panning for gold had failed him, his father had heard of easy money to be made along the frontier lands of Texas smithing guns just ahead of the war everyone knew was coming.

Clay's *"Diddy"* abandoned his family, leaving only his embittered wife to care for the two young boys. In fact, he would never be seen again, except for the sole night during the war when he mysteriously appeared at the cabin with two guns and a pile of cash to leave for Clay's Maw.

Clay, by that time, had already enlisted in the Confederate Army and was off at war. Enos had told his wife that she could hate him all she wanted, but if she wanted their son to survive the war, then she must use the money to get those two converted Colt Navy pistols to Clay. Enos said that they just might save his life. When she asked her husband what was so special about those guns, he simply produced two large boxes of metallic cartridges - what were being called "bullets" as opposed to the "balls" then in use by conventional percussion revolvers.

"Get these guns and these bullets to Clay. These Colt Navies have been modified so they no longer have to be loaded 'cap and ball' like. They load much quicker from the breech, and that could mean the difference between living and dying on the battlefield. These here guns could sure as hell save our boy's life."

Despite the bitter hatred she held for his abandoning her, she understood the compassion of her husband's intention. Clay's mother could not spite her son over the anger she held for her runaway man. Sure enough, she did as her husband had told her, even though it galled her to have to listen to him. Also, sure enough, those guns did save Clay's life, not once but twice.

To this day, Clay still possessed those guns, even if he no longer had a matched pair of hands to shoot them both together. The blued gun metal with the etched naval battle scenes on their cylinders and their old style octagonal barrels were all he had to remember his father. And, of course, Clay could see the signature of his father's telltale smith-marks on the flat bottom of their trigger guards.

Where was his *Diddy*? Still down in Fort Worth, Texas as Clay had last been told. Was he still with that woman who had accompanied him back to Cartersville that night? Who was this *"Hussie"* his Maw never did get over, right up until her death by the onset of Consumption?

Clay looked down onto her marker, merely a weathered wooden cross that bore her name and the years she had crawled into and crept out of this world. It was here, over her, that Clay liked to come to gaze up into the canopy of stars. Yet despite his need for her being close, Clay would stare up to the heavens because he couldn't bear to look down upon her grave. If he did cast his eyes down, in his mind he could hear his Maw say, *"Virgil, ya' know what ya' needs to do. Git down to Texas, find yer Diddy, and shoot that sonofabitch clean between his eyes for all he's done to me."*

This early autumn night the peace with which Clay looked up into the night sky was taunted by only two thoughts. The first was to find out exactly what had become of his *Diddy*. The second was what everyone was beginning to call the *"Great Depression"*. Clay didn't understand it fully, but as much as he could gather, the flow of money to the bankers and merchants had stopped as suddenly as the rains had during that *Great Drought* that had followed the war. The businessmen were panicking, and once again many folk were losing their livelihoods because of it.

Clay knew one thing for sure, when enough people were out of work, all hell would eventually break loose. Idle hands were the devil's workshop, and those idle hands could prove, sure as the sun would rise, that anything could happen. All that Clay and Deekie and Truitt had worked so hard to build here on this small spit of creekside land could be gone. For just as easily as this modest farm once could've been lost to the flicker of a Union torch, it could now be stolen by the thud of an auctioneer's gavel.

Clay looked back upon the simple shack in which these three had lived for the past few years. The land and structure upon it had been owned by the brothers outright. But when Truitt had become Clerk of the County Court, earning good money, he had convinced Clay to expand the home. Over the summer a project was undertaken to enlarge the one room cabin with two walled off bedrooms. The expansion was by then near enough complete, but with the financial panic, his bank loan was at risk of being called at any time. Thus, the improvements made hung like a razor sharp pendulum over not only the home itself, but the farm's acreage as well. They could be foreclosed on at any time in the near future. Truitt's earnings could cover the loan, but Clay's smaller weekly pay was needed for living expenses for the three of them to survive.

Clay heard the footsteps of another person coming up close behind him. He could sense by the effort put into their stealth that they could only belong to his gal, Deekie.

"Y'already done finished yer readin' by the fire for the night, Deeks?" Clay asked without turning. She had grown fond of reading again, ever since the widow Howell had read aloud to her while Clay recovered from his wounds back in '71. The widow had even given her a finely bound book of a collection of stories by Edgar Allan Poe.

"Damn ya', Virgil," Deekie spat out, using his given name as she had ever since childhood, "one of these nights ya' won't hear me coming and I am gonna sneak up on yer something good. Ya' won't know of it until I done knocked yer to the ground."

"Well, just don't knock me onto Maw's grave," he said, "or it might be like one of them Edgar Allan Poe stories yer are always goin' on about. Her spirit might come through the dirt into me jus' so she can tormen' ya' for another couple decades."

Deekie slipped her arm through his.

"Y'and yer momma and yer *Diddy*, Virgil. When are yer ever gonna accept that they's both gone and neither one t'ain't ever comin' back?"

"The day I accept them terms is the day they will surely come true, Deeks. By and by, I still have hopes of one day finding my *Diddy*."

"Them terms is already true, Virgil," she replied. "Yer Maw's in the ground and for all yer know, yer *Diddy*'s already dead and gone, too. It's been a dozen years since he has showed his face anywhere near his family."

"I reckon ya' could be right about that, Deeks," Clay said, "but what if it's because he caint get back east to us. That's why I been thinking about gittin' on down to Texas to look for him. Settle my mind a bit. All I gots to do is lay my eyes on his marker, and then I'll know ya's right. Then I can focus on other things agin."

"Ya' best be focused on how ya' can keep making enough money to help Truitt pay off that bank note. That's the only marker ya needs to be focused on. Lessen y'do, we all going to be looking to settle more than just our minds. We'll be looking for where to settle our behinds for the rest of our lives."

"Truitt can pay down that note so long as I give him my wages each week from the Gilreath's job. But yer know, I do hear tell of a bunch of money to be made in Texas these days drivin' cattle up north to the railheads in Abilene, Kansas. Bunch of money. Or so I hear."

"Then yer'll go without me, Virgil," Deekie answered sharply. "Yer'll be chasing wild dreams just like yer *Diddy*. I will not cotton that plan of action. No, Sir, ya' need to make yer way in this here town. Now I won't hear no more of this foolishness. Look here, Virgil, I am going back inside by the fire to read a bit more of Mr. Poe before I hit the hay. Ya' git on and say yer goodnights to yer Maw and come inside now. Tell her I says hello and that I'm sure glad she is where she is now."

Clay made a sour face. "That weren't called for, Deeks. I know y'and Maw had yer differences, but them was just plain vicious words."

"That might be true, Virgil," she replied, "but yer Maw always hated me for one reason more than any other. I nursed ya' back to health when she had done given up on ya'. She had given her own son up for dead. Now it's about time ya' came back inside to the living. Ya' done paid yer respects to the dead. Besides, t'ain't like yer Maw is going anywhere."

Deekie then turned so sharply that her field dress twirled like some fancy dancer in a saloon out west. Clay had never seen one - a saloon dancer, either of the Western or Eastern variety - of course, but he imagined that must be how they looked.

The Panic of 1873

The proper word for it was "Calamity".

Things had been rolling along so well after the war that it appeared nothing could slow down the reunified country. But just as the political strength of that renewed union was an illusion, so too was the economic boom that accompanied it. In 1873, a number of things lined up that transformed that economic juggernaut into a plain old fashioned calamity.

First, the situation with the railroads had gotten out of hand. It seemed everyone was speculating on railroad stocks ever since that Golden Spike had been driven at Promontory Summit outside Salt Lake City some four years earlier. Ever since the Union Pacific and Central Pacific were joined there, it appeared to be a race as to who could profit the most on the new railroads that would spawn off of that transcontinental backbone. Thirty-three thousand miles of track had been laid from 1868 to 1873. The United States, along with its banking system, was heavily invested in the lore of the Iron Horse and the rails upon which it ran.

Along with the rampant speculation came the inflation of greed. Too many dollars chased too few goods, so market profiteers raised their prices. The cost of nearly everything rose uncontrollably, especially in the West, where goods were scarcest.

The real trouble started when the banks became over-extended on loans based on railroad speculation. The first signs of the impending disruption came from overseas. In the spring of 1873, banks in Vienna began failing due to their being overly leveraged on railroad stocks, including a significant investment which had been made in the US Railroads. Initially, this was seen as a solely European crisis, and was largely ignored in the US financial markets. But if there was one thing that tied the new world closely to the Old World, it was the fascination with the technology of the Iron Horse.

But even as the European woes came to a head, there was the *"Crime of '73"* which magnified the American vulnerability that was already beginning to become apparent. The United States Congress had passed the Coinage Act of 1873, effectively taking the country off what was known as a bi-metal system. In plain English, it meant that the currency of the country would no longer be based on silver and gold alone. It even allowed lesser coinage of base metals such as nickel and copper.

The price of silver dropped precipitously, for no longer was the nation guaranteeing the lesser metal's worth. Unfortunately this came as overseas demand for silver had also waned. After defeating the French in the Franco-Prussian war of 1870, the newly unified country of Germany in 1871 had decided to stop minting the popular silver Thaler coins in favor of the gold Deutschmark. Their decision hit the silver markets hard in 1873.

The most prosperous silver mines were located in the western United States and were severely affected. This helped stoke the crisis of the railroads, as it was the railroads that hauled the metal ore taken from the ground. The failure of many mines made the bank loans to them all but worthless, and what soon followed was financial pressure on the railroads themselves. When the public realized how overly leveraged the banks were in both the silver mines and railways, nearly all confidence was lost in the country's financial institutions.

In the autumn, the first of the major bank failures hit home in the US. In September, 1873, The Jay Cooke Bank of New York City declared failure over railroad bonds it could no longer find buyers for. It was followed by several other banks, and along with President Grant's policy of contracting the money supply, any companies holding debt found themselves instantly in a very tight squeeze. Railroads, including the Northern Pacific, fell into bankruptcy. Factories closed, and the panic trickled down to nearly all facets of American life. Europe became equally affected. Soon there was a worldwide financial depression.

It became known as *"The Great Depression"* in its time, but ultimately yielded that title years later to the financial tumult of the 1930s. Instead, the Panic of 1873 kicked off what economists today call *"The Long Depression."*

This financial crisis would stretch on until the beginning of the next decade in the US, and longer overseas. It lasted long enough to bore its way into the smallest of towns, disrupting the lives of their common, everyday folk. Those hardworking men and women who had not a penny left over to invest in either silver or rail iron were, nonetheless, affected by the devaluation of both. It was the working man who most took its brunt of this calamity. The *Panic of 1873* clutched hard upon the town of Cartersville in northwest Georgia, and soon wreaked havock on the life of the town's own Virgil Clay-Harris.

***Figure 1 : "Runs" on Banks Became
Common in late 1873
(Source: Frank Leslie's Newspaper, NYC)***

The Unsuspected Effects of the Panic

"Clay!" called out Horace Woodard.

The husky old man was tuckered out from the short jaunt across the lawn of Nelson Gilreath's cottage. He came up to Clay, fishing a small pay envelope from the pocket of his overalls. It was stuffed full of bills and coins.

"Here, son, take this," old Horace said between heavy pants. He leaned over, as if to catch his breath, but in reality he did so to avoid looking Clay in the eye.

"What's this, Horace?" Clay asked as he waited for the man to straighten up. "Payday's not till Friday."

"Aw, confound it, Clay," Woodard said as he finally drew himself erect. "There ain't gonna be no pay this Friday. What I am trying to tell y'is I gotta cut back at Mr. Gilreath's direction. I gotta let three men go, and Clay, I hate to say it, but y'are one of them three." Horace glanced at Clay, as if to measure his response to the news.

"I see," is all that Clay could think to say. Horace's words had pierced Clay, but not as much as the pain he could see it was causing his family's longtime friend to usher them. Horace Woodard was the groundskeeper for the Gilreaths, and it was he who had also gotten Mr. Gilreath to agree to take on Clay as a lawn man when no one else would give him a paying job. Horace also oversaw all the improvements to the cottage. They had recently expanded the one story property with an attic and additional rooms in the rear. Consumed by this, Horace left the care and keeping of the lawn to Clay, and in doing so the grounds and their rose bushes had become the pride of the town.

Clay turned away, not because he couldn't face Horace, but because he wanted to take one last measure of the work his friend had entrusted to him. Clay looked over the lawn that he had tended to over the years and at the matured rosebushes that he had nurtured for Mrs. Gilreath.

"There's a full week's pay in that there packet, Clay," Woodard said, sweating more than the cool autumn afternoon called for. He took a kerchief from his back pocket and dragged it across his brow.

"Well, Horace," Clay said, "I owe ya' more than I can ever hope to repay. Ya' took me on when no one else wanted anything but war stories from a one-armed Confederate. But, I reckon as ya's payin' me for the whole week, I'm of a mind to give ya' a whole week's worth of effort."

"Look, Clay, I know this is bad news…" ol' Horace began.

"It's fine, Horace," Clay interrupted, "we both know ya need able bodied menfolk, especially now that the Gilreaths is making ya' cut back. Ya' need all the hands yer can get. I understand and just…"

"Will ya' hush, boy!" Horace interjected forcibly. "And let ol' Horace here do ya' a big favor. I don't want ya' to work tomorra'. I want ya' to be free to take up another opportunity."

"What might that just be?" Clay asked.

"There's a gambler passing through town. He came to visit Mr. Gilreath yesterday. He shared with the boss that he's carrying a large collection of valuables with him, and is in need of an armed escort for his trip up to Tennessee. He was asking Mr. Gilreath all about ya', Clay."

Clay looked at Horace, his head slightly cocked like a confused dog. "Horace, I believe this gamblin' man may want an armed escort, but I'm pretty certain just not a one-armed escort. Does he not know that I'm crippled?"

"That's just it, Clay," Horace said excitedly. "Mr. Gilreath told him about the handgun and rifle shooting demonstration ya' put on right here on this lawn last summer for the townsfolk. This gambler was very impressed and wants to come by tomorrow for ya' to give him a show of his own. That is if y'are interested."

"Who is this fella?" asked Clay. "Some Yankee travellin' through Dixie?"

"Goes by the name of Jefferson Armistead," Horace responded, "and claims to have never set foot north of the Shenandoah Valley. Claims to be a distant relative of General Lew Armistead."

That last name seemed to sting Clay's memory like an angry yellow jackets's bite.

"Well, I sure hope he wins more as a gambler than his uncle did as a general," Clay said, remembering that he had heard the General went by his nickname, *Lo*, short for Lothario, among his friends. "*Lo* Armistead was a brave enough man at Gettysburg. He cut a fine figure durin'

Pickett's Charge, sho' nuff, wavin' his hat on his sword, gettin' his men to charge across that open field to the Yankees behind their stone wall high up on Cemetery Ridge, only to have himself and all them rebels boys with him wiped out. Every last one of 'em."

Clay knew that was not the full truth, cause it was during this charge that his friend Willet had lost his nerve, playin' possum on that blood soaked battlefield. That open field charge broke Willet's spirit, and it was his friend's passing moment of cowardice that both saved and damned the rest of his life. He was never the same thereafter.

"Ya' say this Jefferson fella was just passin' through town?" Clay asked. "Where exactly would this man be expecting me to escort him to?"

In that instant Horace's old dim eyes lit up like two fireflies on a summer's night. For the first time he thought Clay might just take a bite at this apple.

"Mr. Gilreath asked him just that. Seems this gambler is heading to Nashville to deliver some goods and then on to Memphis to collect on some gamblin' debts owed him. Clay, this is a real opportunity for ya'. I figure ya' could make a year's salary in just a few weeks, if ya' play yer cards right. It could set yer future right."

"I don't figure there's much future in playin' no cards t'all when a gamblin' man is involved, Horace. I just don't trust the sort of man a card sharp must be. Thanks kindly for lookin' out for me, but I reckon I'll just pass on this here opportunity."

Horace Woodard knew his young friend was making a serious mistake. He hung his head in frustration and looked down at Clay's mud splattered boots. The young man before him was as stubborn as a mule and as rigid as the plow it pulled.

"Clay, I know ya got yer pride and all that, but think of all ya' could do for Deekie with that payday. She'd be so much better off than she is now. Why not just come by and show this Jefferson Armistead what ya' can do with a rifle and those Navy Sixes yer Daddy left ya. Hell, boy, ya' been talkin' about going down to Texas to find him for some time now. When ya' part ways with Armistead in Memphis, yer'll not only have the money to do so, but you'll already be halfway there."

Clay looked at Horace and drew a slow breath. The same thought had been running through his own mind, but there seemed to be a filthy echo that chased it. This whole thing seemed to be something akin to what his *Diddy* spent his life chasing - a *"git rich quick"* scheme. Clay knew the right thing to do was to pass on it.

"Horace, as for Deekie, she ain't complaining none. She's happy so long as she has her fancy books to read, and me to tell them about to every night. But if I was to take this job and am forced to kill a man or two defending whatever this gambler is hauling, she'd be complaining up a storm, cause she knows that killin' just don't sit easy with mc. My fightin' days is over, and they should stay so. Some scoundrels are likely to think a one-armed guard is easy pickins. They'd find out otherwise, as I would surely defend myself and protect whatever it was I was paid to do. But then, all my long sleeping demons would arise. Not good for Deekie. Hell, it'd be even worse for her if the attackers was right and I managed to get myself killed."

"Look, Clay, all I ask is that ya' sleep on it tonight," Horace said. "Come tomorra', if y'ain't here at the top of the one o'clock hour, we'll all understand. Not like anyone's gonna call ya' yella or such!"

"They can think me a coward, I don't rightly care. I won't do it, Horace," Clay said. "I made peace over the past two years with the vicious killer who lies quiet inside ma' skin. After the attack on Three Sisters Mountain, I reckon I'd rather just let that sleeping dog lie."

"Just talk it over tonight with Truitt and Deekie. Nuthin' says ya' gotta come by here tomorra', Clay. Hell, boy, even if y'do decide to show off yer shootin' skills, still nothing says ya' gotta take the job."

That night Clay shared the story over a dinner of Brunswick stew with his brother Truitt and his gal, Deekie.

"Any money you made from escorting this gambler could help pay off the bank for the loan we took on to expand this shack, Clay," his brother said. "It's likely you'd never even have to so much as level that Spencer rifle, or draw those Colt Navies from their holsters. Maybe just to wave them around a little, scare folks from doin' something foolish."

"Ya' see, Truitt," Clay responded, "t'ain't how things work. As soon as a man, any man, goes for his gun, all kinds of foolishness can erupt. Men will most likely be layin' dead in the street in a couple of heartbeats, that's all it takes."

Truitt seemed willing to accept his brother's logic, and that stoked the flame that was already burning within Deekie. She reached across the table for Clay's hand, and stroked it to draw his eyes to her.

"Well, Virgil, ya' need to think on doin' it," Deekie countered, "but only if ya was to take me along. I ain't never been to Tennessee before. I'd like to see all the shops and fancy gitups the women are wearing in Nashville and Memphis, not to mention laying eyes on the mighty Mississippi. I don't ask ya' for much, Virgil, but let's git along on this adventure. It'll be good to git on out of Georgia for a bit."

Clay stared at her in disbelief. He was sure that she would have objected to his going after his Paw in Texas, and she surely must have known that was where this was all heading.

"Still, there ain't no offer from this Jefferson fella for yer to tag along, Deeks," Clay said. "Besides, ya' just told me if I went to Texas ya' wasn't coming, remember?"

She had figured he would throw this back in her face. "No, Virgil, I said I would not go with y'if ya' was to take up a job drivin' cattle there. I certainly would go along for a visit..."

"Well, there is no offer from the gambler for yer to come along," Clay repeated firmly.

"Don't worry, Virgil. I'll make him offer," she responded.

"How ya' reckon to do that?" Clay asked. "We're talkin' bout a gamblin' man here."

Deekie grinned a devilish smirk. "Ya' just said it, Virgil, he's a gamblin' man. A gamblin' man is still a man, and I know a little about getting men to do what I want. Besides, Truitt's right, we need to get these extra rooms finished up and get that bank off our backs. Ya' know they won't just take back the materials, they'll take this whole homestead - the shack, the fields, and anything else these grubby bankers can get their grimy claws on to."

"Clay, just go on and show this Armistead fella what you can do tomorrow. What can it hurt? You can still say no after he sees ya' shoot," reasoned Truitt.

"Virgil," Deekie added, "just don't forget yer ain't goin' without me. If ya' do, I won't be here for ya' when yer get back. Now, if ya' boys forgive me, I got some reading to do before it gets too late. Me and Mr. Poe got some further acquaintin' to do."

As Deekie stood from the table, her ragged dress unfurled to the ground and clung to her shapely form. Clay watched as she walked to the shelf to draw her book, and followed her with his eyes as she took a seat by the fire. He did not know what he would ever do without her. He also still did not know if he would take his brother Truitt's advice and show up the next day to shoot.

Figure 2: Gilreath Cottage Circa 1873

Sealing the Deal

One o'clock came and a large crowd had formed upon the Gilreath lawn.

In its center was Virgil Clay-Harris, along with his Spencer repeating rifle and the pair of Colt Navy Sixes. He had decided that there was no harm in showing off what he could do with these weapons. Doing so didn't commit him in any way to taking the position offered. Horace Woodard had set up a series of glass bottles on two benches over a stretched out canvas tarp, in front of a thicket of Hackberry trees that rimmed the back edge of the lawn. Years later a lovely coach house would be built on this spot.

The tarp was meant to catch the shattered glass so that it could be remelted. It was eight years after the war had ended, and glass was still a scarce commodity. *What a shame to destroy so many useful vessels just to prove Clay's prowess,* some of the onlookers must have thought. Some had even already complained to Horace that this demonstration was one of a wasteful extravagance.

Clay was introduced to the gambler, Jefferson Armistead. He was a handsome dark-haired man sporting a finely trimmed mustache. Clay thought he smelled like a barber's shop. His clothes were finely tailored, and the man's boots shined with a gleam unnatural to those of men who worked for a living. Armistead wore a long jacket over a waistcoat with trousers ironed so crisply they seemed to define the man as a straightforward enough sort.

"Mr. Armistead," Horace Woodard conducted the introduction, "this here is the pride of Cartersville, Mr. Virgil Clay-Harris."

Clay extended his hand tentatively, but Armistead took it eagerly and firmly shook it.

"Ah, *The Sniper of Sharpsburg!* Well, Sir, the honor is entirely mine alone," said the gambler. "Having lost my Daddy's brother to the Yankees at Gettysburg, I assure you, Sir, that I recognize that I am in the company of a great man!"

The gambler seemed to be putting on a show for the crowd. He spoke louder than was necessary, smiled more warmly than was natural. Clay pulled back on his arm, but Armistead refused to release his grip.

"Well, Mr. Armistead, that sniper tale is just too tall. More of a myth than fact, mind ya'. But one thing is true, I'll be fixin' to need that hand if ya' wants to see me shoot."

"Truer words were never spoken," the gambler replied with a laugh to the crowd. "Do call me Jefferson. I understand many call you Clay, Do you prefer Virgil or simply Clay?" Armistead still had not released his hand.

"Clay seems to fit me right down to the ground, now don't it?" Clay then yanked his arm hard to free his hand from its imprisonment. "Shall I git on with it then, Mr. Jefferson?"

"Before you do, allow me to ask you, Clay, just exactly how many men did you kill during the war?"

"Is that important?" Clay asked, as if it wasn't.

"For the position I have open, it is quite essential information, I assure you."

"Well, to tell the truth, Mr. Jefferson," Clay said, "I didn't really have much time to keep count."

"Of course not," the gambler chuckled loudly. "So, what then? Twenty or thirty or so?"

"Two or three times that easily," Clay said almost ashamedly under his breath, "between Sharpsburg, Gettysburg and Chickamauga."

"And yet the Yankee bastards were only able to take your arm?" Clay thought the man was pushing him, testing his mettle.

"Them Yankees ain't no different than most men," Clay said, "they don't take lightly to being slaughtered."

"Of course, of course," the gambler relented. "Forgive me for being insensitive to your loss, Clay."

"Why don't we start with the revolvers," ol' Horace stated more than asked, hoping to relieve the tension he sensed stretching between the two men.

"That would be splendid," Jefferson Armistead said. "There are ten bottles on those two benches, Clay. How many do you figure on hitting?"

"All of them," Clay said, "from here, anyhow."

"Then, allow me," said the gambler as he wandered up to the benches on which the bottles rested and walked off twenty-five paces at a brisk, exaggerated gait. He ended up another ten yards further back from where Clay had originally, and still, stood. "Please, show me what damage your Colt Navies can do from this distance, Clay. I suspect you'll find it just a bit more taxing."

Clay walked back to where Jefferson Armistead stood. He looked a stark contrast as he sidled up alongside the gambler. Clay wore his earthen stained work clothes, barely more than rags. Over this he had a thin, ripped work coat and on his head he wore a tattered field hat. As Horace Woodard pulled his friend's gun belt on over his coat, Clay watched the gambler's eyes closely. They were already watching his. Very intently so.

Clay long ago had the gun belt modified so that he could draw both guns with his right, and only, gun hand. After drawing and firing the holster on his right side, he could reach across his body to grasp the second Colt Navy from the holster which Clay had turned rear to front.

Horace buckled the gun belt across Clay's hips. Clay drew the right hand revolver from its holster, leveled it at the first bottle and prepared to shoot.

"Ahem, Clay, that seems a bit pedestrian, doesn't it?" Armistead interrupted.

"I reckon I don't know what ya' just said," replied Clay.

"I'd like you to draw from the holster and fire in one fluid motion, as if someone had moved suddenly against you." The gambler made a motion with his thumb and forefinger as if drawing a weapon.

Clay stared harshly at the man. He thought Armistead every bit the Jim Dandy that he put on to be. Clay returned his gun to the holster and removed his hand to float over it.

"Good, that's more like it. When I say shoot, Clay, you draw that gun and fire at those targets. Then just drop the gun and draw the other and complete shooting all ten bottles. Okay?"

"Iffen ya' say so, Mr. Jefferson," Clay answered.

"Good, because I want to see if… SHOOT!" Armistead screamed the last word as if to startle the man waiting to fire. Clay calmly but rapidly reached down upon hearing the command and came up drawing his right hand revolver. He raised the six shooter fluidly, cocking it with his thumb as he did just in time to line up the sights and fire. The first bottle shattered into a thousand shards. Then Clay methodically pivoted, his eye never losing his sights on the bottles. The next four bottles exploded just as completely as the first had.

After firing off the five shots, Clay knew that he was on an empty chamber. He always kept one chamber empty, for his gun to rest on as he traveled about, in order to eliminate all chances of a misfire. He dropped the blued metal of the gun, its barrel still belching thick smoke that the afternoon breeze failed to whisk away completely.

Clay then reached across his body and drew the backward holstered Colt Navy Six, identical to the first. As he drew it from his left side, the gun's barrel sight snagged the leather just enough to affect his aim. The first bottle on the second bench he missed altogether. The second he hit, but barely so that only the neck of the bottle snapped off. By then Clay had compensated and lined up the gun's sights. The third, fourth and fifth bottles shattered in rapid succession.

"Very impressive shooting, Clay…" the dandy of a gambler said, as he began his assessment.

"Thank ya' kindly…" Clay responded proudly, cutting him off somewhat.

"…but that snag on your second draw could have gotten you killed," said Jefferson Armistead. "Mr. Woodard, would you mind lining up another five bottles on that second bench, Sir?"

Horace agreed to do so. As he did, Jefferson Armistead removed his tailored jacket to reveal a gun strapped under his left armpit. It was only a small 1849 Colt pocket pistol. Armistead removed the gun from its holster and asked Clay if he would like to try it. Clay took the gun to inspect its sights and spin its cylinder, which chambered only five rounds, none were left empty. Instead, the hammer had been resting in the safety notch between chambers. Its barrel was short, only an inch and a half or so, compared to the five and a half inches of Clay's pistols.

"That's what I like to call my Fifth Ace," Armistead said. "If four aces are not enough to convince a clutch of drunken players that I had won, then I have been known to draw that fifth ace a time or two."

"Sounds like a sure way for somebody to end up dead," Clay said.

Armistead eyed the marksman with a flash of hostility. It vanished instantly and was replaced by a smile.

"Never had to come to that, Clay. You see, most men sober up quickly when looking down a revolver's barrel, even a short one like this. Only once did I ever have to fire off a round in the air just to convince them I meant business. Now, Clay, if you take off your field coat, I'll put the shoulder holster on you."

Clay had just retrieved his first Colt Navy from the ground and returned both weapons to their holsters. Clay would never normally drop his weapon to the soil lest it become caked with dirt. He would clean both carefully later that night, a chore he always enjoyed losing himself in. He then awkwardly unbuckled the gun belt using his left stump and right hand so that he could remove the earth-streaked field coat. After he did, Jefferson Armistead strapped the fancy leather contraption across his shoulders.

Clay reinserted the miniature pistol into the holster hanging just below his left armpit. He made the motion repeatedly with his hand to get the feel of the gun's grip.

"I think you'll find that to be a more natural drawing motion, Clay," the gambler Armistead said. "I see Mr. Woodard has completed resetting the targets and is now safely behind us, so Clay, whenever you are ready, draw and shoot."

Clay drew hard across his body, but this time from the weapon under his left arm. The gun drew smoothly and the first and second bottles exploded from hits to their centers. The third bottle only wobbled as the round grazed it, and then the fourth and fifth shattered into a thousand pieces each.

"I like that," exclaimed Clay, as if he had surprised even himself.

"Very impressive, Clay," Armistead said. "Even with that short barreled revolver you managed to get all five. Sure, you only grazed the third bottled, but had that been a man he surely would have been dropped. Very impressive indeed from this distance."

The crowd of onlookers, having heard the gambler's praise, broke out into a round of robust applause, clearly proud of the local sharpshooter's proficiency. Clay blushed red from embarrassment, and only then realized that no one else on this lawn, possibly save Jefferson Armistead himself, had ever killed a man. They did not know that there was no glory in doing so. None at all.

"I reckon ya' want to see what I can do with this here Spencer Repeater," Clay said to Armistead, as Horace passed the rifle to him. It was Clay's favorite, given by his friend Willet, after being taken from a Yankee Captain, stopping his party from torching the family's farm.

"Certainly, Clay," the gambler said, still in his shirtsleeves, right after I get my holster and gun back. I may be needing them." Armistead laughed loudly, once again so the crowd could join him.

"Good as it feels, I wouldn't have a mind to steal it from ya'," Clay stammered, as if he had just been called a thief.

"I tell you what, Clay," Armistead answered with a broad smile, "you take on the job of protecting me and I'll get you one, just like it. I'll have it made when we pull into Memphis. We got a deal?"

"Not yet," Clay answered, "y'ain't seen me work the Spencer."

"In my line of business, Clay," the gambler said, "we never get much of a chance to fire from that far of a distance. But go ahead and show me, anyhow."

Clay took the Spencer and began to walk over to the boarding house across Market Street, but first he stopped to address the crowd of gawkers that had formed behind him on the lawn.

"All y'all need to clear out of here unless y'all don't mind bullets flying over yer heads. Besides, yer crowdin' my rose bushes and they don't take kindly to that. Now git!"

The crowd scattered slowly, like a clan of scolded school children. As the masses parted, an opening allowed Clay's path across Market Street to the widow Howell's boarding house.

On its elevated porch sat the widow Rebecca Howell and several of her boarders, all taking in the show with relish. Clay asked her permission to take aim from the porch on the third round of bottles just set in place by Horace Woodard.

"Oh, of course, Clay," she responded in a flutter. "This is all so very exciting."

Clay then climbed the porch and loaded seven rounds into the tube magazine in the shoulder stock of the rifle. The distance to the targets could not have been more than seventy-five yards, and Clay knew he was a crack shot with the rifle up to three hundred yards or so. He had been proficient at five hundred yards before he lost his left arm in the war, but he could no longer match that shooting from a standing position.

"Now y'all might want to git behind me to where Miss Rebecca is, cause there's about to be some hot metal casings droppin' from this here weapon." With this having been said, the men folk who had proudly stood next to Clay on the porch eked away to safety.

Clay raised the rifle, half cocked the action and worked the lever to load the first round into the chamber. He then rested the forward stock on his left forearm stump. He pulled the hammer all the way back and fired the first shot. As he squeezed the trigger, the first of the glass bottles seemed to vaporize in the distance thanks to the big .52 caliber round and its 45 grain load of powder charge. It was a much larger bullet as compared to the Colt Navy's .36 caliber round, and the massive powder charge imparted much more energy so the weapon could be effectively used at longer distances.

Clay then half-cocked the action, which allowed him to turn the gun to eject the empty casing. After he did, he worked the lever to load another round, pulled the hammer all the way back and squeezed off another round. He did so effortlessly from his muscle's memory as this was his favorite rifle. It had served him well in '71 during his raid on the renegade camp atop Three Sisters Mountain.

The remaining bottles shattered one after the other, only seconds apart. The audience of townsmen and boarders that shared widow Howell's porch burst into spontaneous applause.

Clay turned to thank Rebecca Howell for her allowing him to shoot from her porch. After he did so, he looked down to retrieve the empty casings, only to realize they had all been grabbed up as souvenirs by the men on the porch who had once more swarmed around him.

"Hold your fire, Clay" yelled out an excited Jefferson Armistead as he walked across Market Street to the porch. "We surrender. That's some fancy shooting. In fact, you've given me an idea with that Yankee rifle."

"I like it better than the Henry Repeater, myself," answered Clay, "even though the Henry holds more rounds."

"Another Yankee rifle," Jefferson Armistead replied. "Come to think of it, them Colt Navy Sixes are Yankee handguns, too. Don't you shoot any Southern firearms, my friend?"

"Well," said Clay, "sometimes in life ya' just gotta make do with what yer got. Besides, ya' favor that Colt pocket pistol yerself. It's made up North."

"Well said, my man," the gambler confessed. "I like the Colt pocket pistol because it's the best gun available in its size. I don't give a damn if it is made above the Mason-Dixon line. That's also why I like you, Clay, because as you have just shown, you are the best. In fact, I want you to accompany me up to Nashville *and* then on to Memphis the day after tomorrow. I can pay you twenty-five dollars a day and I'll cover all meals and lodging. Only catch is that I pay you your wages only after we get to Memphis and I collect on all monies legitimately owed me."

"There's another ketch," said Clay as he stepped down off the Howell boarding house porch. "My woman, Deekie, comes with us."

"Absolutely not," said the gambler. "This is no trip for a lady to be slowing us down."

"Then count me out," Clay said. "The only reason I'm even here is cause she ain't never been outside Georgia, and only wants to see Tennessee." Then, he looked over Armistead's shoulder and motioned for her to come over.

"Then, I am sad to say we are at an impasse, Clay," Armistead said, standing his ground. "I cannot and will not budge on this point."

Just then Deekie walked around from behind Jefferson Armistead and strolled up to Clay's side. She wore the fine riding gear that Willet Blackwell had bought for her from Savannah a couple of years earlier. Her riding britches were skin tight, and highlighted every curve of her still young and shapely form. Her riding blouse was tapered at the waist such that it had almost a corset-like effect in highlighting the fullness of her bosom. The riding jacket had a more relaxed fit so as not to restrict the range of motion needed for riding, nor did it restrict the town's men from viewing her ample torso. The few women assembled in the crowd gasped and went on about her "indecent" mode of dress. Deekie had not worn these clothes since that climactic night on Three Sisters Mountain, yet they still fit as well as they had then.

Clay could see Jefferson Armistead's eyes linger on her. The gambler clearly had been expecting someone much less feminine and attractive to be attached to the earthy cripple. Would he reconsider given what he now saw in Deekie? Clay was not sure, but suspected so.

"Mr. Armistead says no ladies allowed on this trip, Deeks, no way," Clay said to her. "So, that's why I'm turning down his offer."

Deekie then turned to the gambler and placed her hands on her hips. "Now that is downright disappointing, Mr. Armistead…"

"Jeff," he said. "Call me Jeff."

"That's a might too friendly, I think. How about I call ya' Jefferson?" she said playfully. "It's a fine name, good enough for Jefferson Davis. Well, now, Jefferson, if I was to convince ya' that I t'ain't really much of a lady t'all, would that change yer mind?"

"Might could…" he played along.

"Well," Deekie replied, "not only am I not ladylike, ya'll find that I am a crack shot myself, too."

"Is that so?" he replied. "Many people are good against bottles and tin cans. Ever shot a man?"

"Matter of fact I have, Jefferson," she teased. "Shot him dead, too. Let me go along with y'all and Clay and I'll tell yer all about it. I'm quite the storyteller, folks say. I'll make the time fly, and make ya' feel just what it felt like on that very night."

Her last words bled with more than a hint of suggestion. A sinister grin unfurled on the gambler's face.

"Then it's all settled," said Armistead. "We take the buckboard and leave for Nashville Saturday at daybreak."

Clay knew Deekie was charmin' this man to get what she wanted - passage to Memphis with the both of them. However, in his gut he felt the twinge of jealousy, something he had not felt since Deekie had once left him to return to Willet Blackwell. He feared now, just as then, that she was playin' a more dangerous game than she even recognized.

"Nothin's settled yet," Clay responded. "I'm not signing on to this job till I see exactly what I'm protectin'."

"You'll be protecting me," Armistead answered.

"Mister Armistead," Clay answered, "y'ain't interesting enough to draw fire, but ya sure are worried over whatever yer got stashed in the back of that buckboard wagon. I want to see what it is, or I'm out."

Jefferson Armistead looked once more at Deekie, lustily measuring the full length on her from boots to bangs. He then joked, "I guess it's just you and me, pretty lady!"

Deekie blushed, then laughed out her reply, "Sorry, Jefferson, even I know better than to travel with a wolf without my own rifleman along."

She wrapped her arms around Clay, as she curled under the stub of his left forearm.

"Very well, Clay," Armistead conceded. "Meet me at the stable behind the Park Hotel tomorrow at noon and I'll show you just what we're carrying."

Later that afternoon, Clay walked into the offices on the town's square of Sheriff Alpheus T. Goff. Clay had gone out of his way to avoid the sheriff ever since the business on Three Sisters Mountain two years earlier, despite that Sheriff Goff had gone out of his way to assure no charges were leveled against Clay as a result of the event.

This meant not only that Clay and Deekie had both retained their freedom, but that the pair had garnered outright respect for ridding the town of the band of cruel and ruthless marauders. Yet, slowly over the months that followed, the town's gratitude had ebbed, until it was once more displaced by the low murmuring of shame shared by these two, the harlot and the cripple, living in sin right out in the open with Clay's brother, the *supposedly honorable* Clerk of the Court, Truitt Clay-Harris.

Sheriff Goff had his face down, reading reports that had come fresh over the telegraph lines summarizing criminal activity in surrounding counties. He raised his head bearing a shock of graying hair and matching mustache to see Clay coming through the door. As he did so, the sun struck off the metal star proudly pinned on his somewhat worn, but clean and brushed suede vest.

"Well, I'll be damned," Goff said, "I never thought the day would come I would see Virgil Clay-Harris walking voluntarily through my door. Yer brother Truitt, sure, with his business regarding the courts and such, but not you, Clay. Figured I'd only ever see you again on some other matter that required me chasing you down somewhere. But then again, I keep forgetting' what a respectable character you have transformed yerself into. What can I do for you this day, young man?"

Clay was somewhat frozen by the question. Or perhaps it had been Sheriff Goff's own transformation that caught him off guard. Alpheus T. Goff had grown old over the past two years. He had packed on weight, not abusively so, but no longer was he the limber and wiry character that had garnered so much respect around town. The hair that Clay had remembered as salt and peppered was now more gray-white like a thick morning's frost, with only remnants of any of the original color of his youth showing under it. The gray had even drained down into the oversized mutton chops he had allowed to grow to join with the thick tips of the mustache that Clay remembered.

"I come to ask a favor of ya', Sheriff…" Clay mumbled as he walked over to the massive oak desk.

"You come to ask a favor of me?" Goff repeated. "You never took the time to thank me for all the favors I already done for yer family over the years, but you got the gumption to come and ask me for a fresh one?"

Clay, who had been nervous, suddenly found himself angered a bit by Goff's response. "Favors y'already dun us? How ya' figur' that, Sheriff?"

The sheriff could not have missed the instant glare his comment had created in Clay's eyes.

Sheriff Goff leaned back in his chair and glanced about the room as if confirming his thoughts. The room was a large space, with the lawman's desk in front of three jail cells, of which it was odd for more than one to ever be filled. This afternoon all three were empty.

"Well, if its an accounting of my deferential hospitality toward yer family, boy, let's start with yer daddy."

"*My Diddy*?" cried Clay.

"Yeah, old Enos Clay-Harris hisself, yer daddy," Goff said. "I should have arrested him the night he had the high brass to come back to town during the war to leave them Colt Navy pistols for you, the same ones you used this afternoon for yer little demonstration."

"Ya' was there? I didn't see y'on the Gilreath lawn."

"Come now, Clay. You should know by now that I have eyes everywhere. It's my business to know what goes on in this town."

Clay looked somewhat confused, but could not help but ask, "What crime was there in his coming back home to leave me these here guns, Sheriff?"

"Well, for one thing, they was illegal conversions," the Sheriff said. "Violated the Colt Company patents."

Clay was quick with his response. "Them patents was protected by the United States. Even I know that at the time *Diddy* dropped them guns off, we was formally succeeded as the Confederate States of America."

"Ok, Clay, point taken. But still yer Maw was over here begging me to go across the square to the Park Hotel and arrest him for sharing his room with that known madame from Fort Worth. I must admit that her name escapes me now, but it was burned like a brand on yer Maw's brain, that much is sure. As a point of law enforcement, I had made a decision a long time ago to look past immorality so long as it wasn't pervasive and dragged crime in on its coattails."

"So, I should be thanking yer for not arresting my *Diddy* and that Madame Fanny Belle cause of their sinfullness?" Clay's dander was stirred now.

"Fanny Belle, that was her. Thank you, Clay. How could I ever forget such a whore's name? What's becoming of my brain in old age? No, Clay, you should be thanking me for not arresting yer father for deserting the conscription. That's why he left town, son, not because there was a fortune waiting to be made in Texas gun-smithin', but so that he wouldn't be called on to fight them damned Yankees. Yer father was as yellow then as them roses in Texas that he took off for."

"So why didn't ya," Clay asked, "arrest him for desertin', I mean?"

Sheriff Goff looked at Clay, and thought him brash.

"Well, for one thing, he had just took off for Texas before you and Willet left for the war. He was not in the conscription age span yet, just a year too old, but he knew it would widen and wasn't about to wait for what was sure was comin'. So, by the time he came back, it had widened and I had every right to hold him, but I didn't. I deferred. Do you know that word, Clay?"

"Sounds like a lawin' type of word. Why would a poor boy like me be expected to know it?"

"It means it was up to me and I decided not to do it," Goff brashly educated Clay. "I deferred, and allowed yer father to wander back to Texas with that Fannie Belle woman yer mother hated so. Even if a few days later I heard they got picked up in Atlanta by that gang he stole the money from. But think on it, son. Yer father had no problem knowin' his eldest son had gone off to be slaughtered by the war, but couldn't wait to skip town so he wouldn't have to do so hisself."

"I didn't get slaughtered, though did I?" Clay now spit back with iron in his tongue. "Crippled for sure, but not near slaughtered, was I, Sheriff?"

"Thanks only to yer kith, Willet Blackwell," Goff seethed in response, "which brings me to the second favor I did for yer family. When you defied my direction and went up on Three Sisters that night, I could have had you arrested for disobeyin' my direct order. But no, again I deferred. Then after you set that mountain afire, I could have stuck any number of the deaths of Willet's men on ya'. But once more, I deferred."

Clay fumed at the rancid reasoning that the sheriff had come to accept as the truth over the past two years.

"More like ya' made a vote gettin' decision," Clay taunted the sheriff, "cause ya' knew iffen ya' charged me, the town would never elect ya' sheriff again. If ya' had the gumption to go up on that mountain with me, in the first place, yer wouldn't have to worry about elections ever again. Yer would have been a hero."

Alpheus T. Goff exploded from the chair, rising so that his eyes were leveled across the desk at Clay's.

"I'll tell you what I'd be," Goff said, "I'd be dead. It's a miracle you weren't killed."

"Miracle or not, I'm here today, t'ain't I?" Clay said. "If I waited for y'and yer posse, Willet and his men would have been long gone, but maybe that's exactly what ya' wanted, Sheriff. To not have to face him. To not have the death of that Irish girl on yer account. Thanks to me not listening to ya', Sheriff, that girl, Ever, lives today, somewhere back up North."

"If you want to call living as her being scarred for life by what she went through," Goff spat back at him. "Clay, you got to think about the results of yer actions before you go busting in and shooting up a situation."

"What else do I not know I owe ya' thanks for, Sheriff," asked Clay, "besides yer advice and yer puttin' things off and all, I mean?"

"I just want you to know, Clay," Sheriff Goff leaned forward so their noses were only inches apart, "that I was all set to arrest yer brother Truitt for throwin' that evidence, that war dagger, onto that northbound train during Willet's trial. It got yer friend off, but Truitt was not aware that there was a witness to his discarding that evidence. Had I not deferred, it could well have caused a retrial and yer brother would have faced criminal charges hisself. Not ot mention losing his job at the court."

Clay stared harshly at the old man. "We heard rumblin's of this rumor. Truitt did no such thing," Clay lied.

"There never was a witness, was they? So, ya' didn't so much as put this off, as ya' lost yer proof? What happened to yer witness, Sheriff?"

Sheriff Goff cast Clay a curious, suspicious look.

"Interesting that you should ask that, Clay. He was a Freeman's boy who had been playing by the tracks that day," Goff admitted, backing away from Clay for the first time. "He disappeared just before the shootout on Three Sisters Mountain. His family said they sent him north to stay with kin. I always thought Willet's boys brought harm to him, and the parent's were afraid for the sake of their other children. I guess we'll never really know the truth."

Clay realized then that Sheriff Goff had indeed regretted many of his past decisions, leading him to say, "Maybe that was yer problem all along, Sheriff. Ya' put things off way too much when action was called for..."

These last words seemed to be a punch to the sheriff's gut. Alpheus T. Goff seemed to have had the wind knocked out of him by the whole back and forth with Clay. It seemed to rip the scars off of old memories that had only freshly skinned over. The old man sank back into his chair, stunned that his emotions had drawn him into this verbal fracas with Clay.

"Clay, what the hell did you come through that door for?" the frustrated Goff finally asked.

"I'm fixin' to take this gambler in town up on his job offer," Clay said more softly, as his contempt muted to pity for the old man who no longer had enough energy for the star he wore. Perhaps he never did. "Do ya' know anything about him? I know it'd be unlike ya' not to run the traps on such a fella'."

"I did just such," Sheriff Goff admitted. "Best I can tell, he's just a gambler from down Macon way. Been arrested here and there throughout the South for minor stuff. Mostly just holding illegal card games. I can't tell you that this Armistead isn't a bad man, son, but he's not got the trail of paper that a truly rotten bastard would have. Just mind yer instincts, boy. They usually serve one well enough."

It was in that instant that Clay realized the Sheriff had always had the best intentions of his family at heart.

"Thank ya', Sheriff Goff," Clay said, now ashamed that he had pushed back so hard against the old man.

"One more thing, Clay," the sheriff said just as Clay had opened the door to exit out onto the square. "Word has it you might be doin' this job just to make yer way to Memphis so you can scurry on down to Fort Worth after yer father. Be very careful should you mind to carry out that dream. That town has earned itself a very notorious reputation. Whatever you do, stay out of the Hell's Half Acre district. I know you consider yerself a man who can hold his own, but there's gangs down there that would just as well shoot you in the back if they thought there was any profit in it. Do you hear what I'm telling you, son?"

Clay thought it unusual he had not mentioned Deekie. He guessed the sheriff had not caught wind that she would be joining him to Tennessee.

"I reckon I'll keep that in mind, Sheriff," Clay said. "Ya' reckon mah *Diddy* is still in that town?"

"I figure so," said Goff, "cause he was last time I checked. Turns out there's a Texas investors group calling themselves *'the Drovers' Exchange'*, who are looking real hard for the gunsmith who is illegally converting them old Colt cap and ball pistols into breech loaders."

"My *Diddy*?" asked Clay.

"The one and the same. Thank the Almighty for these telegraph reports," said the Sheriff.

"Sounds to me like ya' been checkin' up on him from time to time." Clay smiled at the old lawman.

"Well, it's my job to be prepared for anything, Clay. If yer daddy is still foolish enough to be doing that after all this time, he's going to be drawing some heat right soon."

"Whaddya' mean? Like the Pinkertons?" Clay asked.

"No. This Exchange don't have no need for any fancy detectives from Chicago. Word is that they got their own fixer in the field. A vigilante type that roams the plains on their behalf, settling their scores. These men invest a lot of money in everything from cattle to carbines, and anyone who is foolish enough to be cutting into the profits they 'spect to be making is likely gonna get hisself a visit from that fixer sooner rather than later."

"What is this fixer fella's name?" Clay asked.

"Don't know, Clay. Nobody does. Ya see, like the Drovers' Exchange itself, its a great secret."

"Then how is it ya' know about this Exchange, but not its fixer?" Clay found this whole conversation beginning to raise his dander again.

"Well, Clay, it's simple," Sheriff Goff said with a soft smile, "some secrets keep, and some just plum don't."

The Drovers' Exchange

"Well, Clay, it's simple, some secrets keep and some just plum don't."

These last words of Sheriff Alpheus T. Goff would continue to ring in Clay's ears over the weeks ahead. If he had learned any strategy in his life, he had learned it hard in the war. Foremost, he remembered, don't go into a fracas not knowing just what and who you are going up against. Clay didn't know anything about this group and Sheriff Goff knew not much more than he did.

It turns out that the Drovers' Exchange had started out in the late 1860s simply as a group of Texas cattlemen who shared common interests, including information on which cowhands were reliable sorts, and which weren't. As the group became more tightly integrated, it began to share information on the cattle rustlers that plagued their drives along the Chisholm Trail through the Indian Nations Territory up to the railheads in Kansas.

The cattlemen all had the same objectives, to get their massive herds to Abilene, Kansas, where they could be processed and the beef shipped east to the hungry cities of New York, Chicago and Philadelphia, among others. But with each drive of two to three thousand head of longhorn, they all would experience some level of rustling. Sure, it might be only 10-20 head of cattle, but allowing thieves to make off with any of their longhorns at all just did not sit well with these Texans.

The Drovers' Exchange, merely known as *"The Exchange"* among its members, banded together to do something about the rustling. Since most of it occurred in the Indian Nations, where no law other than Federal law ruled, the Exchange decided to take measures into their own hands. One of the more experienced cowboys on one of the ranches knew of a war veteran in Missoura who had just lost his wife and family and was willing to ride the trail and clean out the rustlers - one way or the other. He was meaner than a son of a bitch and quickly proved himself more than capable of rustling up the cattle thieves themselves. One thing was for certain, no federal marshal was going to spend an ounce of their energy in running down cattle rustlers. If the rustlers killed some poor drover in the process, that might be a different story, but a few head of missing longhorns wouldn't be worth a federal marshal's proving his grit over.

The Chisholm Trail could be a truly lawless stretch of land, and not only because it pierced through the territory of the Indian Nations. *The Trail,* as it soon became known, had been worked out before the war by a half-breed trader named Jesse Chisholm. He had the rare ability of garnering trust with both the white and the red man. This indeed was a rare quality beyond the Mississippi.

Jesse Chisholm's trail was nothing more than a series of trading posts that he would work north to south amongst the tribes until he would end up in North Texas. Once there, he would trade the wares he had bargained away from the Indians, and load up on white man necessities that he could then sell on his return trip north. He would end that leg in Southern Kansas. The trail would go on to become far more famous than just for his trading.

While the Chisholm Trail intitially referred to this trade-posts stretching throughout the Indian Territories, in the late 1860s the cattlemen of Texas reckoned they could put it to another use. The railroads had not yet come to Texas in any meaningful way, and the ranchers were amassing great herds of longhorn, far more than the hungry gullets of the Lone Star State could ever hope to consume. Soon the wide open stretches of the Chisholm Trail were tapped to herd great migrations of cattle north to the railheads in Abilene, Elsworth and other towns in Kansas. Once this was proven to be feasible, the trail branched tributary routes deep into Texas into towns like San Antonio, Laredo, and even El Paso. These became the root ball of a mighty tree, whose trunk passed through Fort Worth and the Indian Nations Territory before its canopy unfurled to cover near all of southern and central Kansas. For the Texas cattlemen, this Chisholm Trail would become the tree of life itself.

The drovers who worked the trail committed their own life of spending up to three months a year on the dusty plains of the Indian Nations Territory between Fort Worth and the Kansas railroad towns. Two things were guaranteed, the drovers would let off steam in Fort Worth before setting out and even more again in places like Abilene after ending the drive.

In the former, they would expend their anxiety-driven energies and spend whatever money they had left knowing they would not be in need of it along the trail. In fact, it was safer not to have any coin, less it be stolen or got you into a card game where you might be shot for cheating, deservedly or not.

At the end of the trail, they would most often blow the earnings from the long drive on colorful new threads, fancy grub, better liquor, and whatever female companionship they could afford.

At both ends, there was a healthy amount of hell raising going on. Gambling houses, bawdy houses, and every vice in between were made available. And no place in Texas raised more hell than Fort Worth's red-light district, the notorious Hell's Half Acre. For most drovers, it marked the end of their return from the drive. Unfortunately, for some others still, it marked the end of their life on this earth.

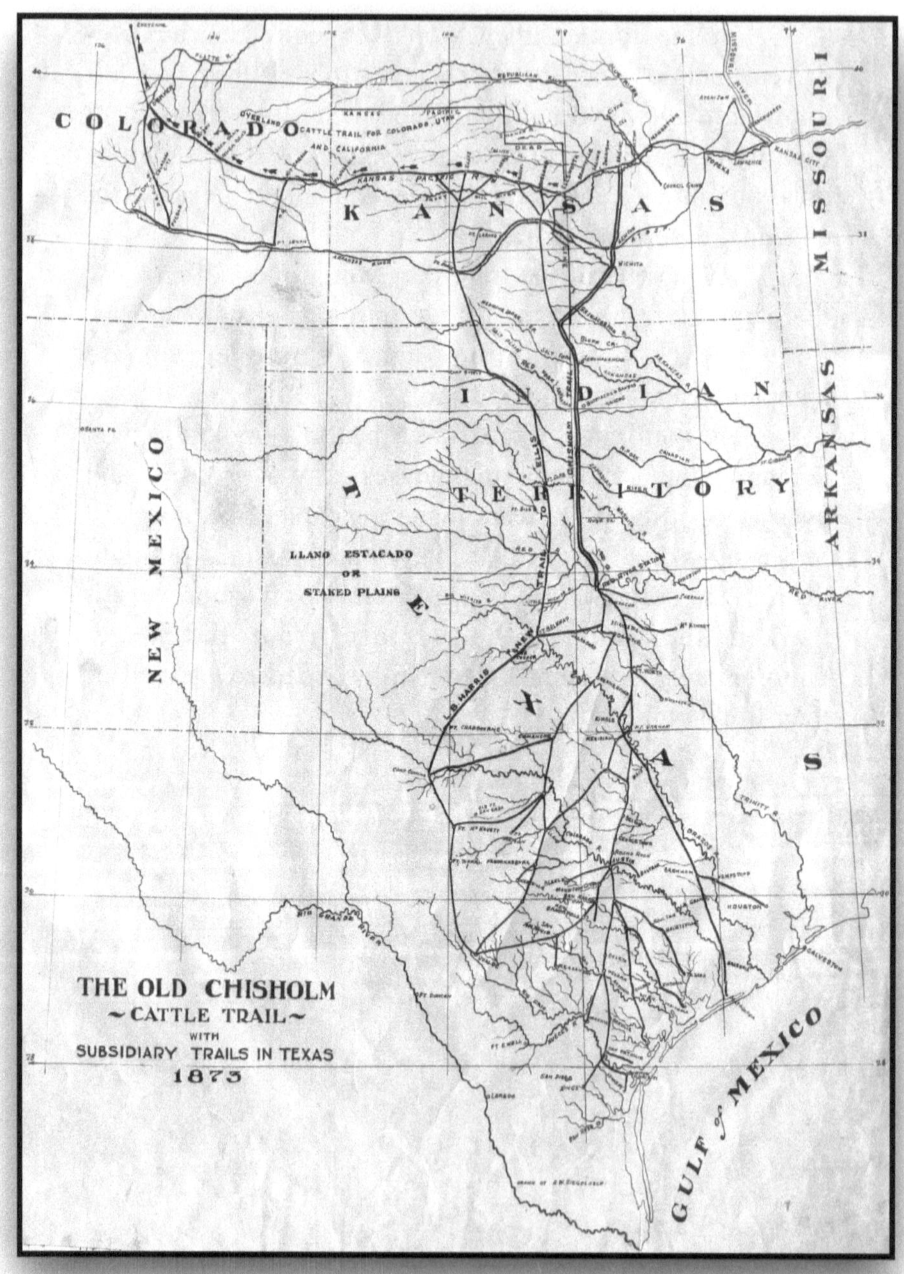

Figure 3: The Chisholm Trail of 1873

A Murder of Crows

The campfire flickered in the night like a jewel hidden in the eyes of a thief.

Despite their trying to hide it, the winds of these open lands west of the Mississippi whipped the flames, giving them a luster and breathing life into their bed of ruby red embers. It wasn't intended to be a beacon, and in fact those gathered around it took great care to assure it wasn't. As for the average passing rider, it would have been hard to sight, but for this man, the fixer sent by the Exchange to search out these rustlers of their precious cattle, the campfire's flames called out like a siren.

"You men in camp, thar," the stranger yelled out, "I'm coming in. I mean y'all no harm. I am unarmed."

The three men around the fire scrambled for their weapons. The last thing they expected this night was an unknown caller. They fanned out to the three points of the triangle that bounded the firepit.

"Come on in, friend," called out their leader, "but with yer hands up where we can see them."

"I wouldn't dare to consider otherwise," said the stranger as he walked in from the stealthy cloak of darkness. "I'm just hoping to catch a cup of hot Joe and a little conversation. It gets a might lonely on these plains, especially at night, with it being Injun' Territory and all. Maybe I'm just a might skittish, that's all."

Two of the three men who had fanned out, drifted behind the stranger as he walked forward, making a problem for this man should any gunplay ensue.

"C'mon boys," the stranger said, "I told ya, I ain't armed."

They looked upon him with great worry. He was a big man, stood some six foot plus. He was beefy, but seemed not to have any evidence of fat upon him. He carried a week's growth of beard, long enough to see the gray whiskers feathered throughout it. Yet, somehow despite this, his face still looked chiseled and alert. The rim of his black Stetson hat had caught the campfire light that bathed the dourness of his complexion. The flicker of its flame cut clear against his face's every detail, and seemed to cast him as the most serious minded sort of individual. Most worrisome was that the smile he wore did not look natural at all. It looked downright forced, and the three men all took that as a bad omen.

"Partner," the leader of the three said, "we've blown away strangers coming in out of the night like that before. Don't you know it ain't taken kindly to out here? Especially this far off the trail."

He referred to their location along the Chisholm Trail just below the Kansas border. There, lawlessness reigned sovereign over man's better nature.

The stranger smiled wider and even more forced as he slowly dropped his arms. "You know what? That's exactly what I thought, too," he said. "Why are these three boys so far off the trail? Good way to get yourself scalped. Now, me, I got my own reasons for straying wide from the trail, but these here boys are trying like hell to just look like some drovers working their way back to Texas after a drive. But why so far off the trail? It's a might curious."

"Ain't none of your damn business, *pahdna*," scowled the second man from slightly behind him with an exaggerated drawl. "You best watch yourself. Curious men end up wondering why they're dead out in these parts."

"Whoa, Whoa!' said the stranger, laughing out loud. "I mean you all no disrespect, but, young fella, you're wrong when ya say it ain't no business of mine. If I'm fixing to join up with some fellas, I want to know a little bit about them first."

The three men looked at each other with a series of strange gazes. "What do ya mean," said their leader, as he reseated himself by the fire, "fixing to join up with? Jesse, check him out."

The second man holstered his weapon and came forward to inspect the intruder who had pulled back his long leather trail duster overcoat. Jesse checked him for a gun belt, of which none was present. No guns were found along his torso, arms, waist and legs. The stranger then released his duster, and it fell like a curtain around his legs. Jesse then checked its pockets, which were empty save for a tin cup.

"He's clean, Quincy, just a guttin' knife on his belt," Jesse reported.

"I told you I was unarmed," the stranger said, "so how about that cup of Joe?"

"A guttin' knife ain't exactly what I call unarmed, pardner," said the leader, a man called Quincy, with minor irritation. But the fact that Quincy then sat back down at the fire with his gun sheathed in its holster spoke volumes. He was confident that his two cohorts had this knife-bearing intruder well covered.

"You three rough and tumble men armed with your revolvers and rifles surely ain't gonna be scared of a lone man with nuthin' but a guttin' knife, now would ya?" the stranger asked in a mock tone.

"Not one as old as you, anyway" snarled the third man over his rifle. Quincy gave a sharp, angry gaze to that gunman, then nodded to Jesse who had re-drawn his revolver and dropped back behind the left side of the stranger. The third hand, still stood with his rifle trained on the man, as he had all along.

"I am looking for a crew to join," said the stranger. "I ain't the first man to rustle cattle along the trail, but it sure as hell is hard to do alone."

"We ain't looking to add to our number just now," said Quincy, "and we sure as hell don't know nuthin' about rustlin' no cattle."

"Even iffen we was to take someone on," said the third man from behind his rifle's sight, "you look a bit long in the tooth for our likes."

"Will you just shut the hell up, Emmit," barked the leader. "Like I said, we're not looking to add to our number."

"Well, I can smell where I'm not wanted," said the stranger, "but you fellas seem somewhat shorthanded with just the three of y'all. Although I do reckon as it's pretty much the end of the drive season, and just the three of y'all can take whatever steer you got penned up in to market."

The stranger then looked over his shoulder in each direction slowly, carefully at the position of each of the armed men behind him before returning his gaze to their unarmed leader.

"Now don't you figure on doin' anything stupid, friend," scowled Quincy. "I don't like that look in your eye I just saw. But you are right, pardner. You sure can smell where you're not wanted." The leader's eyes were riveted on the intruder red hot like the glowing end of a branding iron.

The three figures had this intruder triangulated in the center of them. The stranger in its center ignored the two behind him, knowing they would not take action until their leader, Quincy, gave them direction to do so.

"Well, Quince, - what's that, short for Quincy? - I can also smell that coffee y'all been brewing," he finally said. "How's about I take a cup off yer hands? Just one cup and I'll be on my way out of here."

"Well, now that you know my name, pardner, what exactly do you call yourself?"

"Cord," the stranger said plainly. A heavy second of silence stretched across the four men.

"What, like a cord of wood?" asked the second hand, Jesse, tersely, breaking the tension, after which all three men laughed heartily.

"That's a good one, Jesse," chuckled Emmitt.

"Yeah," the stranger breathed out slowly along with the taste of their disrespect, after the tomfoolery subsided, with no emotion in his voice whatsoever, "like a cord of wood. It's short for Cordell."

"Cord what?" demanded the leader. Quincy had a nasty squint in his eye, one that the stranger, Cord, found rather disturbing.

"Just Cord does right fine by me… So just Cord it is." Cord knew he was taking refuge under the unwritten rule of the West. It was fine to ask a man what he called himself, but asking his name was akin to diving into his past, and that was seriously frowned upon. It was best they didn't know, for Cord's past was darker than any moonless night these three would ever have camped under.

"Well, Cord, you that tin cup wit' ya?"

"Just so happens I do…"

As he reached into his duster's pocket, Quincy looked to his man Jesse who had searched the intruder. Jesse nodded his head, indicating he did have only that cup in that pocket.

"Then sit a spell, have some Joe. After all, we don't want to seem inhospitable, now, do we, to a friend of ours from Texas?"

With that the leader waved down his outstretched palms, signaling to his two compadres to lower their weapons.

"Missoura, actually." The man calling himself Cord fished out the tin cup from within his dusty trail coat, very slowly so as not to cause his three new companions any concern. The leader of the three of them raised the pitcher shaped coffee pot from the fire, and poured Cord a steaming hot cup of trail coffee - where the grinds are dumped right into the pot.

"Much obliged," said Cord as he looked down onto the black specks clinging to the side of his metal cup just above the hot black rim of liquid.

Cord settled himself onto a large rock. No doubt they had picked this location of a ring of small boulders to obscure themselves from passers by. They likely never expected to be found by anyone.

"So. Pardner Cordell," said the leader, stretching out the long form of his name, "what brings you out this way all by yourself?"

Cord noticed that the man, Quincy, after holstering his own gun, had drawn a cup of coffee for himself and settled back across the fire onto a similar rock. Yet he never offered anything to the two men who stayed in the fringe of Cord's peripheral vision, just a couple of steps behind him. Cord figured the leader wanted to keep the other men's hands free, in case unpleasantries might require so.

"Just call me Cord, Quince," Cord replied. "Only my mamma and my wife ever called me Cordell. But to answer your question, a man's got to look for work, don't he? I'm heading down to Fort Worth and thought it'd be safer traveling if I hooked up with a crew and made a little cash along the way. I knew the type of men I was looking for are far too smart to be camping up by the drover trail. So I just swung a little bit wider from it and found yourselves. Like I said, at first I figured you boys to be drovers, but now I can clearly see you're not."

Cord's last words were honed with an edge of accusation.

"Well, that's most interesting," said the leader. His two friends still stood just behind Cord, their weapons lowered but still ready at the draw. "I'm curious, now that you know we're not drovers," Quincy said, "just what exactly do ya take us to be?"

Cord took a deep draw of the coffee and was trying to catch the grinds floating in his mouth with his tongue when he was asked the question. He hated trail coffee, but more often than not, it was all he ever got. He raised his head slowly, and with a slow half-wit smile answered, "I reckon y'all to be nuthin' more than a murder of crows..."

The two men to his side raised their weapons as he uttered the word "murder," but the leader waved them down again. "Well, that's a right interestin' picture to bring to mind, Cord," Quincy said, "and why would you be wantin' to join a *murder of crows*?"

Cord turned his head around to look at the second hand, Jesse, smiled in a devious but knowin' way, before he turned his attention over the other shoulder to the third hand who had been called Emmitt. Then he returned his gaze forward to face Quincy.

"A man sees a lot of unusual things riding these plains," Cord explained. "One day I stopped ol' Trouble, that's my bay mare, and watched a hawk perched on a high dead limb of a tree. Well, for whatever reason they might have had, this murder of crows was set on driving that hawk off that perch. A single crow would fly all around that hawk, buzz its head, and no sooner did the hawk snap at it, that crow would fly off and another would come from behind to do the same. I must have been there an hour or so just watching these crows constantly agitatin' that hawk before eventually it became so perturbed it just flew off and left them crows to take over the perch."

"That's a most interestin' story, Pardner Cordell," said Quincy, "but what the hell is it got to do with us?"

Cord drank the last of the coffee in his cup. The grinds clung scattered to its metal sides like the debris of camp bodies after an Injun' raid. Cord read this to be a good sign. Then he looked up at the leader and shed another forced smile.

"I reckon you boys to be the crows, and the herdsman driving their longhorns to be the hawk. Hell, you all are dressed like crows in all your black dandies. Rustlers, crows, the same thing as far as I can tell."

"Well," Quincy said, "you're wrong on both parts. We ain't rustlers and we sure as hell ain't crows. Crows feast on the dead of others. We do our own killin' when it's called for." His voice had become edged with contempt.

Cord ran his finger inside the empty cup, collecting the telltale grinds. He took his time to respond, knowing it was getting under the skin of the three rustlers.

"You boys nip and agitate," Cord finally said, ignoring his objections, "maybe stealing a head of cattle or two or three here and there from these men trying to make an honest living. Too small for any single herder to bother going after, as their herds number in the thousands on their drive on up to Abilene or Elsworth. They might send some trail hands to chase after you for a bit, but soon enough they'll need them back to drive the rest of the herd north."

Cord saw the tension in Quincy's face tighten like a staked leather hide drying in the sun.

"Well, Cord, like I said, that's real interestin' stuff," replied Quincy, "but let me tell you a thing about your so-called hawks, these herders. Just cause a man calls hisself respectable, it don't make him so. Sure as hell don't make him honest. In fact these herders are some of the most devious bastards I have ever met. So, if we was to agitate them as you say, they are most surely deservin' of it."

Cord smiled, and replied only, "Yup, likely so." He raised his tin cup to drain out the last of his coffee. He then let out a satisfied "Ahh" and said, "That was one mighty fine cup of Joe. I thank ya kindly. Now I'll be on my way."

He turned his cup over and shook it hard three times to shake out the residual liquid. On the third shake it came loose from his grip and fell to the ground at his feet. As he reached down for it, he said, "Maybe Emmitt was right, maybe I am getting a little long in the tooth for all this."

"For all what?" asked Quincy.

Cord reached down slowly for the cup. His hand disappeared into the shadows between his legs. Then he pulled it up with a sudden jerk, a flash of metal reappeared in his grasp. It could have been the cup, but the speed with which it was drawn was too fast to suggest so. He drew up the small revolver hidden inside the lower lining of his leather duster and pointed it squarely at Quincy sitting directly across the fire from him. The other two men drew and raised their weapons but did not shoot, waiting on a signal from their leader.

"Thing about these herders," Cord said, "is that no single one of them is going to waste time coming after y'all. But you rustle enough cattle from the lot of 'em, and they are all going to pony up a stake to get someone to clean you crows out. That someone is me."

"I thought you said you was alone and unarmed?" Quincy calmly said.

"It's just like you said," replied Cord, "just because a man says he is honest, it don't make him so. And I only said I was unarmed, I never said I was honest, now did I?"

"Well, you might not be honest," said Quincy, "but you sure as hell are stupid - one man coming up against an armed gang of three. What the hell is that little toy you're sportin' there anyhow? What's that - a four inch barrel? "

"Colt's Baby Dragoon, Wells Fargo model," Cord responded. "Carries enough of a load to drop you where you sit." He made sure Quincy followed his eyes as he pointed the Colt beyond the dancing yellow fringe of the fire. "I also don't believe I ever said I was alone. Out there in that dark brush is my compadre, Major Rivers with his sights already set squarely on your man Emmitt. So I reckon that evens up the odds somewhat."

Cord could see the leader squinting over his shoulder into the darkness.

"Even were that true, which I doubt it is, that still leaves three on two…" Quincy said. The man looked hard at Cord's face. His chiseled features did not flinch, and this greatly distressed the leader of the rustler gang. *This man is just askin' for us to kill him,* Quincy thought. *Why?*

"Way I reckon, it's two on one," Cord then went on to explain. "You ain't even got your gun drawn yet, which means I got plenty time to take out your fella Jesse behind me and still beat you to the shot."

The leader of the three men measured this stranger with dead, cold eyes. The gun in this intruder's hand was an old Colt Baby Dragoon revolver. The gun had been inside a secret pocket at the bottom of his long leather duster. Cord had pulled it back for Jesse to inspect that he wore no gun belt on his waist, the weapon was not noticed. Nor when his duster's pockets were searched. Cord practiced retrieving it quickly, just for situations such as this.

"You better be not only fast, you better be good." Quincy warned. "That Baby Dragoon you're holding is only chambered for five balls. And I reckon bein' hid in your trail coat, one was empty, leavin' you just four. That's four balls for the three of us. Like I said, I reckon you ain't got another man out there in the brush like you said at all." The crow leader seethed the last words through his teeth.

Cord thought Quincy sounded like a man trying to hide the concern over his situation in the bravado of his comments. He knew the words were less of an attempt to rattle himself, and more an attempt to stiffen the resolve of his two men, Jesse and Emmitt. Cord looked back at the crow leader with a face that was as unflinching as pure but weathered canyon stone.

"Ya know, mister, even when you're right," replied Cord slowly, "I still don't like being called out as a liar."

The moment was taut with strain. Cord kept his gun pointed at Quincy across the campfire, whose hands were raised slightly in the air. The crow leader then began to flutter his fingers hoping to distract Cord, before he said simply, "Go on, Emmitt, kill him."

"I hear him cock that rifle and you're sure as dead, Quincy" said Cord, "I've been listening. He ain't yet."

"Go on, Emmit, cock your rifle," ordered Quincy.

Cord, who stayed frozen with his gun aimed at the man across the campfire, waited for something that had not yet occurred. Cord tilted his head slightly in the direction toward Emmitt, who had raised and sighted his rifle to fire upon the intruder, and snarled, "Emmitt, no sooner you pull that hammer back and River's gonna take you down."

"What was that?" Emmitt asked aloud, as he responded to a heavy rustling in the pitch black brush just beyond the rim of dancing light from the flame's arc. The rustling in that dark abyss was timed to follow Cord's mention of River. "I'm beginning to reckon there is someone out there, after all, Quince."

"Damn it, Emmitt, I said kill him!" demanded the still seated leader, "now git on with it."

Cord then let out a shrill whistle as a response to the repeated threat. As he did so he whipped his gun away from Quincy and turned rapidly to his left side and took a spinning aim on Jesse.

As he did so, a shape flashed from out of the darkness. Both Jesse and Emmitt were distracted as this four legged wolf-like shape emerged between them before it lunged at Emmitt.

The wolf-like creature cut hard to one side when Emmitt pointed his rifle at it, just before it uncoiled its length into a devilish lunge at the man with the rifle.

Emmitt had reacted by jerking his rifle before firing in the direction of the pouncing figure, missing it completely. As he did, Cord continued his spin the other way and fired off two balls at the center of Jesse's body. The first shot went astray, as it was fired before Cord's gun had come to rest from the spin. It did, however, catch Jesse in the non-gun hand, jut before the second ball punched clean through the man's stomach. Jesse dropped his six-shooter, and as he fell to his knees, both hands, wounded and pristine moved to clutch at the excruciating pain radiating instantly from his gut.

In that same moment the wolf-like shape viciously struck Emmitt, whose frantic reflex of a rifle shot had been jerked wide of the beast's lunge. Its large jaws opened and closed like a spring-loaded trap, locking down on Emmit's gun hand and evoking a horrible shriek of pure terror. The scream trailed off into a pitiful mix of his wail and the canine's unending growl, which together seemed to blend with the dense cloud of burned smoke from the rifle, which Emmitt had since dropped to the ground.

The wolfen figure dragging the disarmed Emmitt to the ground, then, with its jaw still clamped about the man's arm, and shook it in the dirt like a little girl's rag doll.

Cord had already spun back to Quincy, who had just drawn his own revolver from its holster. The crow leader raised the revolver to his chest and pointed it at Cord just as the intruder aimed his own gun back at him. Cord locked his gaze onto Quincy's eyes as their guns rose. Then he saw it. The crow leader's focus broke for a mere half a tick to look at Emmitt on the ground under attack from the beast.

Cord knew Quincy's concern was not for the condition of his man, Emmitt, but in case the beast might break for himself. Quincy flinched his revolver, only for a split second, as if to take aim at the canine, thought the better of it, before he returned its aim at Cord.

A shot exploded in the flickering firelight. Cord and Quincy had stood across the fire from another, each man's weapon pointed at the other.

As the echo of the gunshot rang out, a cloud of burnt black powder smoke drifted over the flames. The smoke trailed back to Cord's Colt Wells Fargo pocket pistol. The crow leader's break in concentration had cost him the critical split second that he could just not afford to spare.

Cord's bullet found Quincy in the upper chest. The leader fell back away from the flames and hit the ground with a resounding thud. There was no residual motion. Just a lifeless body of dead weight coming to rest in the cold dirt of the unforgiving and unyielding earth.

Cord watched the man for an instant, walked over and pointed his revolver at his head before deciding that another shot would be a waste. He then lowered his pistol and uncocked it, taking a deep draw of breath. The smell of the spent powder filled his nostrils.

It was then that he had realized he had once again beaten death, even though he had given the spectre a more than even chance at taking his life. Cord knew deep within him that the only reason he was still alive was that he did not deserve to die. Fate had determined that Cord McCullough had still not yet suffered enough in his wanderings to clean the slate of his despicable past sins. Sins so heinous his soul could never hope to be absolved, so instead death ignored his taunts, leaving him to wander the trails of the West like a wayward ghost.

The echoes of the gunplay dinned until the only sounds in the air were the crackle of the fire and the continuing howls that came from Emmitt and the beast. His gun hand was still in the jaws of the canine. Cord cautiously moved toward his partner, Jesse, and found him still alive, but in shock from his gut wound. It produced a mixture of blood and bile which gushed forth from a hole that was placed low, but centered, on his abdomen. Cord knew the man was in for a painful and protracted death.

Cord stooped to pick up Jesse's revolver and took it back to the fire to inspect it. It was a converted Colt Navy sixshooter. He held it up high to allow the flame's light to lick its underside. Cord could clearly see the underside of the guns trigger guard. It bore the marks of the mysterious gunsmith. The same man that the Exchange had ordered him to find and eliminate.

"River, down!" Cord commanded. The dog released Emmitt's bloody arm and sat and growled in front of the man. Emmitt's forearm was torn open in several places and at least two of the boney knuckles of his gun hand protruded through its ripped skin. His forearm gashes bled freely, but Cord knew these wounds, as painful as they might be, were not life threatening, unless they should become infected over the coming days.

"That animal needs to be shot," yelled out Emmitt between howls of pain as he laid on the ground.

"Well, you're in no condition to do so, are ya'? You had your one chance and you blew it, boy. Now, stand up slowly, and then use your left hand to toss that gun in your holster to the dirt in front of me," Cord said in a cold hard voice, his own gun trained on the man, "or I might become inclined to whistle again and ol' River can give ya' a matched set of cuffs."

Emmitt would not take his eyes off the beast. He rose to his feet and made a very tentative movement to his holster by bringing his left hand all the way across his body. The mottled coat of the animal, only a mere dog, looked almost unthreatening, but Emmitt knew otherwise.

"Fingertips only, now" warned Cord. Then Emmitt grasped the gun gently by the grip with his tips of his thumb and forefinger, before tossing his revolver towards Cord.

"What happened to Quincy?" asked Emmitt.

"Which one is he?" Cord asked playfully, already knowing the answer.

"You know, ya bastard. The one ya' been calling that," answered Emmitt. "The one ya' done shot!"

"I done shot 'em both." said Cord, as he carefully squatted to pick up Emmitt's gun, another converted Navy Six bearing the same gunsmith's markings.

"Quincy's the one that's not moving at all," snapped Emmitt.

"I reckon he's dead. Heart shot. I could tell by the way he hit the ground. Who's your other compadre?"

"Jesse? Is he gonna live?"

"For more than he can stand. I figure about another five, six hours or so."

"Why ain't he talkin'?" asked Emmitt.

"He's a might busy talking to the Lord, right about now," said Cord. "Now where did you boys get these contraband hog legs?"

"I ain't gotta answer you nothin," said Emmitt. "Who the hell are you anyway?"

Cord looked at Emmitt, still wincing with every throbbing pulse of his heart as his blood gushed in a synchronized rhythm from his arm in thick red jets.

"I'm just a very bad man sent out to rid the world of other very bad men. Those who sent me decided to fight fire with fire."

"You said you was looking to join up with a crew. That was all a lie?"

"I got all the crew I need in my dog, River, and my horse, Trouble," Cord replied, "but, let me tell ya' something that is surely true. You three boys likely got some horses stashed around here, and probably some rustled longhorn steer penned up as well. Come morning light, I'll find them steer. Then I'll unsaddle and hitch up one or two of your mounts by a lead to Trouble. I'm sure they can carry three dead rustlers' bodies in for the reward just as easy as they can carry two. Either way they can handle it, no problem. We'll send some drovers back for the rustled cattle. So what's it gonna be, Emmitt, you want to ride out of here in the morning piled on top a horse like your compadres? Or would you rather want to be walking out of here alongside their carcasses?"

Emmitt looked at Cord, weighing whether the man could be trusted. Then he glanced down at the dog that growled as it followed his every move.

"What's the point?" said Emmitt. "Them herdsmen will just hang me for rustlin' to be sure."

"Not if I was to tell them there was only two of you," said Cord. "You tell me what I want to know and you can walk on out of here tonight. Now, where did you git' these converted Navy Sixes?"

Emmitt took to pondering the question, still not sure if he could trust the stranger. He answered with a question of his own.

"You some kind of Pinkerton?"

"Now why would you go and ask me that?" asked Cord, as if Emmitt had just unnecessarily complicated everything.

"You gots to tell me," Emmitt said excitedly, as he went on to add, "cause 'iffen you is, it's not proper for ya to shoot a man in cold blood. So answer me that. You some kind of Pinkerton?"

Cord drew a deep breath and then slowly answered the man who babied his gnarled arm and hand.

"Yeah," said Cord, "I am some kind of Pinkerton. Something like that, anyway. Now, where did you and your pardners get these guns?"

"Fort Worth," Emmitt snapped, "down in Hell's Half Acre. The Stone Canyon Gang. Been covertin' these Colt Navy Sixes ever since the start of the war. Got a skilled gunsmith there who does nothing else but."

It was then that the wounded man named Jesse interrupted his communing with the Lord, as well as Emmitt's sudden cooperative streak, to wail out loudly in pain. It was a pitiful, guttural sound that Cord had heard several times before. The man was slowly dying.

It was an unintelligible moaning, as if Jesse's mind had just caught up with the shock of having been shot, and had now come to the realization he had nothin' left to do in this world except to wait to die. Cord knew that the wailing wouldn't stop until the man's heart did, and that would not be for many hours to come. Many insufferable hours of agony awaited him, hours that had to be miserably endured. Cord moved towards him.

"Whadya doing?" screamed Emmitt.

"Well, I sure as hell ain't going to listen to this pathetic caterwaulin' all night."

Cord walked over to Jesse and looked down on him. He saw nothing in his eyes save the small flickering reflections of the firelight. Otherwise, they were lifeless flat discs. Cord slowly raised his pistol and aimed it at him, drawing no reaction from the gut-wounded rustler. He drew the trigger and shot down at Jesse once, placing the ball right between his eyes.

"No! No!" Emmitt screamed aloud. "You can't do that. He was just a kid, damn it."

"He was just another crow," snarled out Cord.

The hound, River, growled menacingly, but did not move from his seated position in front of Emmitt.

"He was a slow kid to boot," continued Cord as he holstered his revolver and stepped back over to Emmitt, "and because he was slow he had to die. But nothing says he had to die slowly. If I was a better shot, he could have died cleanly like your man Quincy over there. So I was just sort of cleaning up my own mess just now."

"He was alive and ya' killed him in cold blood," Emmitt screamed. "You ain't no Pinkerton. Who are ya, mister, really?"

Cord looked into Emmitt's eye and saw nothing there but the rampant flame of terror. "Who am I? I dun told ya', Emmitt. I'm a condemned bastard cursed to walk this earth with a stone cold heart, a fast hand and an even quicker trigger. Watch."

Cord crouched into a shooting stance and drew his pistol on the unarmed Emmitt. His gun hand shot up at lightning speed, leveled the weighty weapon, and pulled the trigger.

Emmitt winced in anticipation of the shot, but there was no thunder of powder, no belch of fire from the barrel. Only a loudly audible click.

The rustler's eyes had grown to an enormous size as the gun was drawn and leveled at his head. Once the click was audible, and he had time to comprehend he was still alive, his eyes shrank to the point they could accommodate his incessant wailing and sobbing. The mock execution penetrated him despite no gun's ball having done so.

"Good for you," said Cord to Emmitt, "that your friend, the head crow, Quincy, was right, ain't it? I keep an empty chamber to travel on, now, just like he said. I dun spent my other four rounds, the last being a mercy shot into your friend Jesse, but likely you might not have noticed while you were playing on the ground with River here."

Emmitt could not respond. Inside him his nerves were shattered, and he lost all control. He let his own guttural scream, along with all the restraint of his being.

"You smell something, River?" Cord said to the cream colored canine mottled with black and brown spots still sitting in front of Emmitt. "Smells to me like rustler piss."

The dog's head cocked and turned toward its master. Cord then walked over to the fire and picked up his tin cup. He slowly reached for the cowboy coffee pitcher and poured himself another cup of steaming hot Joe.

"Another cup for you, Emmit?" he said. "I don't think your compadres are going to object."

Emmitt could not reply. He just shook uncontrollably.

"Emmitt, I suggest you save some of that shiverin' for the morning. Because as sure as I am to turn you over to them cattlemen, they are sure to put a rope around your neck when they find their brands on the steer in your pen. Even if you boys had time to do a brand-over, son, they'll know and you'll have earned that noose."

"I'm done answered your questions, mister," Emmitt stiffened and said.

"I got plenty more," Cord said just before taking a gulp of the hot coffee. "I watched you men for the last several days, when there were six of you. Yesterday the three others mounted up and took off to the south. Where they headed for?"

"You promise me first you'll set me free."

"Oh, I do. I pride myself as a man of my word," Cord replied just before taking a draw of hot coffee.

"Those three were off to intercept the Old Butterfield Stage Coach route near Red River Station, just before it come out of the Injun Nations Territory. You goin' after them, too?"

"My business is my business," Cord answered. "Give me their names." Emmitt did.

After the had sun come up, Cord forced Emmitt, gnawed hand and all, to help him load the two bodies on one of the rustlers' mounts. He then scattered free the other two bandit's horses. He told Emmitt that he best walk out of there before the herdsmen send their drovers back for the penned cattle.

"Why can't I come with you?" he pleaded. "I ain't no threat with this arm as it is."

"Other than River, here," Cord answered, "I ride alone. And if I so much as ever even see your likes again, Emmitt I'll shoot ya' dead, be ya armed or unarmed, it don't matter."

Cord McCulloch rode off to the east into the rising sun, trailing behind him the mare carrying two of her dead.

The Bounty

The smell of the stable was putrid.
At least to Clay it was.

Clay had never spent much time around horses, and here as the speckled light of the noon hour sliced through the spaces between the barnwood slats, the smell of the beasts seemed concentrated and close. Somewhere deep in his memory, Clay recalled the Confederate cavalry dandies, complete with their elaborately sheathed sabres and feathered plumes in their riding caps, sprinting ahead on horseback in front of the infantry column in which he marched. He could still see the dismissive gaze that they would cast upon the foot soldiers when they even bothered to looked down upon them at all.

Armistead dismissed the guard he had been paying to watch over the wagon and its cargo of two large wooden chests. Both were locked with massive padlocks. Through the shank of each chest's lock ran a pig iron chain that was wrapped around one of the stable's center support posts. Even if someone had shot the guard and commandeered the buckboard, these chests weren't going anywhere. It would take two men with a tree saw a half hour to saw through these wooden posts, and if they did, it was likely that the whole stable would have come down upon their heads. Clearly, Armistead had thought this out carefully.

The gambler came up to Clay and extended his right hand. "Clay, even if you decide not to take this job, I need your word that you will not share what I am about to show you with any other living soul, not even your Deekie woman. Come on Clay, I am willing to treat you as a gentleman and take your word along with a handshake."

Clay looked at the extended hand and then up at Armistead. He did not take the gambler's hand.

"Mr. Armistead, no one will ever confuse me for a being a gentleman," Clay said, "but my word stands on its own. It don't need a handshake to make it any more trustworthy than that. I do so give ya' my word."

"Fine, fine, Clay," Armistead said, somewhat defeatedly drawing away his unreciprocated palm. He then reached his hand up to undo the top button near his collar. From under his shirt he pulled a lanyard which, at its end, dangled a single metallic key. Jefferson Armistead then leaned over the cases and used the key to undo both padlocks. As each lock's shank popped free, its pig iron chain fell under its own weight to the floor. Armistead replaced the lanyard within his shirt and opened the first wooden case to reveal a massive collection of revolvers.

"As God is my witness," Clay said, "these is Griswold & Gunnison revolvers. I didn't think there were even this many left after Sherman destroyed their factory down south of Macon in '64. May I?"

"Handle them?" Armistead asked to clarify. "Sure, Clay. Grab one and wrap your hand around it. See and feel its value, after all, it's these lovelies that you'll be protecting."

Clay reached into the case and pulled out the pistol nearest him. He looked carefully at the workmanship, comparing it to his own Colt Navies, of which they were an illegal copy. Of course, during the war Griswold & Gunnison did not have to worry about infringing on a US patent as the Confederacy had declared itself a separate nation, with a separate patent system. Griswold & Gunnison had produced more handguns for the Confederate States of America than any other manufacturer in Dixie. Samuel Griswold, a Yankee from Connecticut, had moved to Georgia in 1830 and started up a factory making cotton gins near Macon. In 1862, along with his partner, Arvin Gunnison, they converted it over to making pistols for the CSA. Unfortunately for them, their factory would later lay right in the path of Sherman's March to the Sea.

"Don't make any sense, Mr. Armistead," Clay said, "with Colt sellin' their new breech loading guns this year, ain't all these cap and ball revolvers just about worthless?"

"Well, my friend, you are a quick study," Armistead replied. "It's true, everybody wants a six gun they can load quickly with the new metallic cartridges from the rear, like Colonel Colt's new gun. Those bullets load a hell of a lot faster than having to place firing caps on each cylinder's nipple and ramming down powder and balls. These cap and ball percussion pistols are *passé*, as you might say, Clay."

"I *might* say that iffen I even knew what the word meant," Clay answered.

"It's a French word, Clay. It means these percussion pistols are antiquated and no longer serve a viable purpose. Everybody wants the faster breech-loading pistols, just like those converted Colt Navy Sixes you enjoy shooting with so much. Even the Colt company has taken to converting their old percussion pistols over to take the new metallic cartridges. With those new bullets, there's no need to ever load a charge of powder and a ball into the chamber from the front ever again."

"Yeah, I hear Colt is making them brand new Single Action Army Revolvers as breech loaders right out of their factory, so why convert their older ball and cap guns at all?" Clay was honestly perplexed.

"For two reasons, Clay," the gambler answered. "First, the US Army is buying up every SAA .45 caliber pistol that Colt can make, leaving them nothing to sell to the public. Second, their factory still has a stockpile of parts to produce old Colt Navies and other front loader models, so why not convert them over to take bullets and sell them to the public? It's what they want, especially out West where the time you save reloading your weapon could save your life. Besides, it also means no more percussion caps to jam up your cylinder while the other shooter busts a cap in your own ass."

"Why ya' think these old cap and ball Griswolds is so valuable?" Clay aimed the pistol in his hand at a bridle harness hanging on the barn's wall and pulled the trigger. Only an audible click was produced, as Clay had already checked to see that none of the gun's chambers were rammed with a charge and a ball.

Armistead decided how much of his secret to share.

"You see, Clay, that what makes this deal so sweet," Armistead said with a wide smile that blazed through even the darkened half-shadows of the stable. "I was lucky enough to get my hands on this lost shipment of these guns. I am selling these revolvers at a huge profit to a gun dealer in Nashville, and he in turn sells them to collectors in the North at another great profit. They don't want them to shoot, hell no! We're talking about rich abolitionists who just want to have them as a sort of trophy for having won the war and settin' all them slaves free."

"What's in the other crate?" Clay enquired.

"Let me show you. You are going to really appreciate this."

Armistead took the Griswold percussion revolver back from Clay and replaced it in the first case. He then opened the second and took out a long gun that was clearly marked Cook and Brother, Athens.

"Cook and Brother rifles and carbines," Clay said taking the rifle from Armistead. He inspected the gun closely. The carbines were basically shorter models of the rifle, generally used by the Confederate Cavalry. "These is the brothers who moved up to Georgia after the fall of New Orleans in '62. I have fired some of their guns during the war. They made a hell of a nice long gun, but they are also all muzzle loaders, ain't they?"

"Again, Clay, these are for sale to them rich Yankee collectors. But not this next beauty," Armistead said. He then reached into the case to pull out a different rifle, much longer than the others. This one had a long tube running off to the left alongside its barrel. "Do ya' know what this is? Be very careful handling this, as it's the only one I have. Just this one singular specimen."

Clay took the long gun and stood it upright on its stock. His fingers felt the opening of its barrel and an instant grin crept upon his face. "I only heard of these. I never reckoned I would live to see one. A British Whitworth Sniping Rifle."

"Once again you are so right, Clay. What gave it away? The precision sight tube?"

"That was the first thing caught my eye," Clay explained, "but it is also the only gun I know that don't have a round bored barrel. When I felt its hex bore with my fingertips, I knew it had to be a Whitworth."

"Then you can guess what's in this box, can't you?"

"Hex balls?"

"Right again, Clay," Armistead confirmed. "Genuine certified Whitworth hexagonal bullets! Although it's hard to call them balls without their being round at all, isn't it now?""

Clay took one of the boxes, opened it and pulled out one piece of the oddly shaped ammunition. "These things are s'posed to shoot dead on. I heard that a good sharpshooter can drop a man with this rifle over a mile away."

"Well, Clay, maybe we can test it out on this trip. I want to give you a chance to see what you can do with this weapon. But not only are these guns very precise, they also are very, very expensive. They sell for well over a thousand dollars new. This one, being so rare, is something I intend to hold on to. Nobody really knows how many survived the war, but it wasn't many. That crazy Brit Joseph Whitworth became so infatuated with making this weapon as accurate as it could possibly be, that he lost sight of just how expensive of a rifle he was making. Priced it right out of what the CSA, or most anyone else could afford."

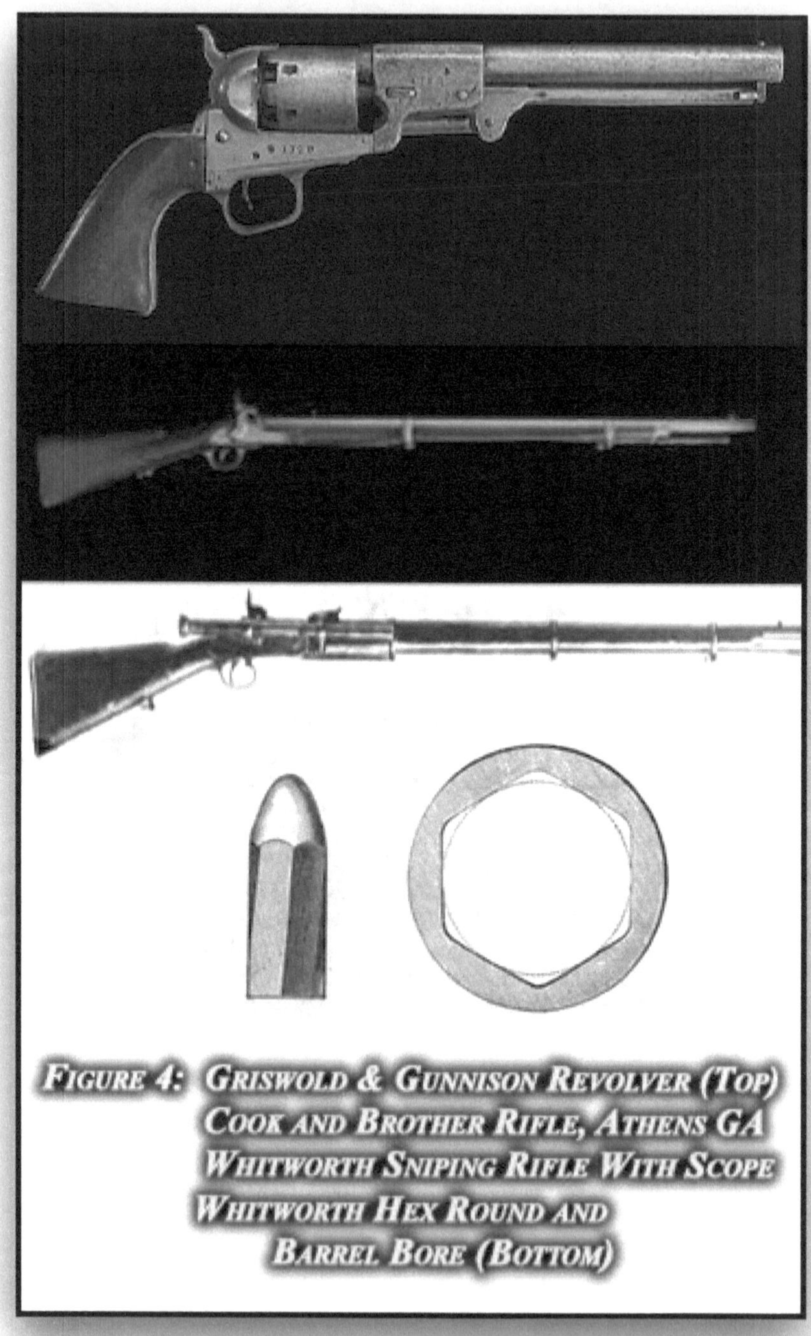

**FIGURE 4: GRISWOLD & GUNNISON REVOLVER (TOP)
COOK AND BROTHER RIFLE, ATHENS GA
WHITWORTH SNIPING RIFLE WITH SCOPE
WHITWORTH HEX ROUND AND
BARREL BORE (BOTTOM)**

Jefferson Armistead repacked the long guns and then was busy rethreading the chains through the padlocks. As he did so, Clay thought hard about whether he wanted to be part of an operation selling Confederate weapons to the Yankees just to become trophies of their conquest of the South. The thought did not sit well with him, but with having lost his employment at the Gilreath cottage, he sure could use the payday. And now, there was something else he wanted very badly - a chance to fire that Whitworth Sniping Rifle, just to see what he could do with it at long range. Maybe he might get that chance, after all.

"All right, Mr. Armistead," Clay said. "I'm ready for this mission."

"Listen to you, Clay," the gambler smirked, "*ready for this mission*. Don't go getting all miltary and such on me. This ain't a mission, it's merely a job. We'll deliver these crates, *sans* the Whitworth, to Nashville. I'll collect my payment and then we'll head to Memphis to make good on a nagging debt due me that a rich gentleman there needs to be repaying."

Clay looked quizzically at him. "Whatcha mean, Mr. Armistead, *sands the Whitworth?*"

"It's French, Clay. It is *sans*, like *sands* without the *d*. It means except for."

"Then why not just say that? In English, like?"

"Because, my young apprentice," toyed Armistead, "in my particular line of work appearances are everything. They can mean the difference between a big payday and a bullet in the back. Your job, my friend, is to watch my back. Are you sure you understand?"

"Yes, Mr. Armistead," Clay responded. "I am sure I understand."

"Well, Clay, then good. This job will serve another purpose."

"What might that be?" asked Clay.

"As soon as we roll out of town, you will stop calling me Mr. Armistead and refer to me only as *'Boss'*. Can you do that?"

"I can, but why?"

"Two reasons," Jefferson Armistead said, the first again being that appearances are everything. The second being that I'm sick and tired of hearing you call me *Mr. Armistead*."

The First Leg
of the Journey to
Nashville

The recurring creak of the wagon wheel slowly counted off the miles.

The three of them, Armistead, Deekie and Clay had left Cartersville just before sun up Saturday. Their goal was to make it north of Chattanooga by nightfall and bunk that night at a farm the gambler's friend owned along the road to Nashville. Jefferson Armistead drove the team of four horses. Next to him on the buckboard's bench sat Deekie in all her fine fitted riding clothes. In the bed of the buckboard Clay sat atop one of the crates, his Spencer rifle held high and in plain sight. This had been suggested by Armistead in order to keep away any curious onlooker types.

They rode further and further north into the mountains of North Georgia, with Deekie chatting up a storm with Armistead. He seemed to be somewhat taken with her, and Clay thought perhaps Deekie was enjoying the attention a little too much. Clay sat quietly, scanning for any signs of trouble that might befall them, but the threat for which he searched never emerged.

Clay's only real participation was an occasional "yes, boss" or "no, boss" to questions posed by Armistead. Clay noticed this mode of response drew odd looks from Deekie, looks that seemed to leach away her respect for him. Clay ignored her glance and continued to call Armistead as he had asked to be addressed along the trail.

After a few hours running along roads painted with the glorious palette of sunlit colors of an early autumn morning, they came upon a rickety covered bridge crossing a wide creek. They enjoyed the coolness of its covered shade, as the morning was just then merging onto high noon and the heat was fixing to become unpleasant. The "clip-clop" of the team's hooves on the bridge's planking echoed like the ricochet of bullets through the cool shelter of the covered span.

As they emerged the bridge, Clay instantly recognized the Lee and Gordon's Grist Mill and General Store. A chill raced through him with the speed of a lightning bolt, nearly paralyzing his muscles, especially those in his tongue. He knew then they had just crossed over Chickamauga Creek and that the battlefield lay just ahead. It was there on those battlegrounds that he had lost his arm and nearly his life, saved only by the dedication of his friend Willet. The same Willet Blackwell who took him back to Cartersville. The same Willet who was by the time of this sojourn gone from this world.

Armistead called for a rest at the general store. The horses were watered for the ride ahead through and beyond Chattanooga. Deekie and Armistead shared a mid-day meal of stewed chicken and cornbread while Clay stayed to watch over the bounty on the buckboard. Besides, the acid churning in Clay's stomach from being there etched away at his hunger. When Deekie and Armistead returned to the wagon, they brought Clay a salted pork sandwich wrapped in butcher paper. Clay thanked them for it, but did not eat.

As they began their afternoon travels, every stride of the refreshed team of horses drew Clay deeper and deeper into his wounded memories of war from almost exactly ten years ago. Time crawled, as Clay's missing lower arm began to ache once more with an excruciating phantom pain. With the rotation of each wheel, it seemed more like another lifetime's passing since they had crossed the covered bridge and stopped at the grist mill. Then as they proceeded north onto the battlefield proper, Clay could once more smell the thick burnt wafts of back powder. He could again hear the screaming wail of overhead artillery that he wished in vain would drown out the howling of the wounded and dying. He could see the boys of the Blue and the Gray as they drained each other's blood, the ground drenched in a crimson spray marking the receding sprawl of where so many youthful lives had been lost.

More than anything, Clay regretted the excitement his heart had once harbored as Longstreet's Army routed the Yankees that day. The Union troops had collapsed into an uncontrolled retreat, and Clay recalled the thrilling satisfaction that this had brought him.

Clay then truly felt the vindication of victory after the withdrawal at Sharpsburg and the merciless three days of fighting in defeat at Gettysburg.

He had felt invincible that day, until that damned assignment for he and Willet to clear out the battlefield farmhouse that had been held by the Yanks. That mission would cost him his arm and Willet his last shreds of morality. After Sharpsburg and Gettysburg, neither of them had any innocence left to lose, but neither man understood just how much more of the promise of life they would be required to squander in that damn farmhouse.

"Virgil," Deekie called, "are ya" fixin' to be sick? Yer looking poorly since we left Lee & Gordon's Mill."

Clay felt his heart race as beads of sweat had formed on his brow. The skin of his face lay clammy and slack, but hung over teeth clenched so tight he feared they might never part again. His tongue, swollen, choked in his throat, made the release of any words nearly impossible.

Clay's gut full of acid was then a churning, roiling sea of bile. He knew this was the curse of returning to the grounds where he had once reveled killing other men, so long as they were dressed out in the Blue.

"Look here, Clay," Armistead called back over his shoulder, the reins in his hands, "if your feelin' unsettled we can stop for a bit. Maybe you can point out to us exactly where you were during the battle." A sneer blanketed the gambler's face.

"Boss," Clay said, but then held his swollen tongue.

"Speak to me, Clay," Armistead said realizing the distress Clay was undergoing as they passed through the beautiful rolling countryside where one would never had guessed the battle had been pitched a decade earlier. "Come now, son, spit it out and deal with it. It's the only way to get over the ordeal of it. Man up, son! Speak to me, man to man."

*Figure 5: Lee & Gordon Mill,
Chickamauga, Georgia*

The words had their desired effect on freeing Clay's tongue. His words uttered forth violently like a sudden stream raging heavy with the flotsam of a dam broke free. The words were not, however, exactly those Jefferson Armistead had hoped to release from his gunman's clenched jaw.

"Boss, maybe iffen ya' break this team into a gallop until we reach Cloud Springs, I can hold off on shoving the barrel of this Spencer up yer hindside."

"Virgil!" Deekie screamed, "that's no way to talk to Jefferson. Y'apologize right now!"

"No apology needed, Deekie," Armistead said with a chortle. "Every man's past is riddled with some demons. Clay's just seem to be roaming freely right now. Let's see just how fast these *hosses* can get our Clay back out of the war and into the present with us once more."

With this, Armistead stoked the team of horses into a full gallop. This was exactly why he had hitched a team of four when two would have sufficed, to outrun any dangers they might encounter on the trail. Yet, he had never expected those grave threats to have appeared only in the tortured mind of his armed escort.

No one spoke any further until they reached Cloud Springs at the northern border of what had been the battlefield. Armistead had been consumed with keeping the team at a full gallop, while Deekie had been holding on to the bouncing, shaking wagon for dear life. Clay was still consumed with surviving the battle replaying in his mind, hoping to recover the shreds of his sanity once more. Clay sat low with his back to the bench that Deekie and Armistead sat upon. They gazed forward on the peaceful, tranquil countryside while Clay was left looking aft at the swell of road dust that had risen behind them like the hot rising smoke of competing cannonades.

"Far too pretty of countryside to be tearing through at that such a frantic pace," Armistead snickered as he heeled the team into a canter and then a fast walking trot. "I hope you'll be feelin' more of yourself now, Clay."

"I reckon I might. I might hope so, anyway," Clay said as he fought to take back control of his mind from its memories of the past.

"Well, I'm just glad you didn't stay suited in the Gray to fight in the Battle for Chattanooga, because we will likely be making that city on the hour or so."

Deekie laughed hysterically at the gambler's broadside upon her man. She had warmed to him along the ride that morning. Armistead's attention to her had made her feel special. She felt a closeness bonding them together. "Jefferson, yer just a plum hopeless rascal."

"The ladies of Atlanta would say, and have said, in fact, that I am incorrigible," the gambler said with a sharp look and an even keener smirk, "but if I am anything I am very *encourage-able*. I can be persuaded to try just about anything, at least once. You'll see."

Deekie blushed at Armistead's pass, but Clay noticed neither. They followed the trail until it dropped down to the Tennessee River crossing. Once they were across, they drove through Chattanooga without stopping, until they picked up the road to Nashville outside the northwest side of the city. They climbed through the low mountain pass, and soon found themselves on the grassy plain edged with patches of small hardwood forests.

Clay's agitation had eased, but not to the point to speak idly, something he was always unaccustomed to do. Instead, he kept to his duty, scanning for trouble in any form which it might take. As if to make up for Clay's silence, Armistead and Deekie lobbed volley after volley of rambling chatter, the theme of which was the story of Willet and Clay. Deekie gave it a full and frenetic voice, and Armistead kept making suggestive remarks as to the role she played between the two men.

"Ya' see, Jefferson," Deekie said, "for all the hullabaloo about Virgil being such a fierce warrior, he is usually a very gentle character. Willet, on the other hand, was anything but. He carried his war dagger which he loved to menace his enemies with, even turned it on me a time or two."

"You mean he stabbed you with it, Miss Deekie?"

"Not as such, but he loved to poke its sharp point into some fleshy pocket of skin. Maybe draw a little blood with the tip of it. Mostly he just craved to scare the days' end out of ya' with it."

"The threat of injury is always more immobilizing than the injury itself," Armistead said. "It's all about keeping your enemies on the point where they still hope they can come away unscathed by bending their behavior to your will. Gambling is sort of the same way in reverse. It's not the winning that keeps the player at the table, it is the *prospect* of winning."

"Willet loved to scare the hell out of his enemies with that dagger," Deekie said, "called it his *Black Raven*."

"Really?" the gambler replied. "Smart, tie an ominous name to further evoke the forboding threat of his weapon."

At that point, as foreign to the moment as if a vulture would have descended from the sky, Clay's voice edged in the conversation for the first time since Cloud Springs.

"Deeks, I spent the better part of three years with Willet in the war," he said softly, "and I don't ever recall him calling that dagger anything but a damn knife."

"Virgil," Deekie replied after the surprise of his voice abated of her, "of course he wouldn't then. It weren't until he deserted from the army and took up renegadin' that he began calling that dagger such. Just ask yer brother Truitt, during the court case that *Black Raven* was the center of all evidence."

"Iffen y'ask me," Clay muttered, "yer reading too much of that Edgar Allen Poe trash. Yer mind done allowed it to leach over into yer memories. Ya' need some help recollectin', girl."

Deekie did not like being called out on the carpet in front of Armistead, who she clearly was trying to impress.

Her distain for her man's interruption then manifested itself in a brutal response.

"Virgil, if there's anyone in this wagon that needs to separate their memories from reality, it surely t'ain't me. I think ya' need to polish up the housing of that Spencer rifle to a mirror finish if ya' want any hope of seeing who needs help along them lines."

"Enough, already," snapped Armistead. "You two might as well get hitched to each other. You're already whipping each other constantly with words like cutting leather strands, so you might as well tie the knot in them strands and maybe that will keep you both from scarring up each other."

Armistead's outburst did not silence the two, but rather send their cutting comments into a stealth of mutters.

"Tying the knot might just make them leather strands altogether more like a cat o' nine tails," quipped Deekie under her breath.

"Better than that cat o' nine tongues I'm forced to listen to every night," Clay whispered in unusual defiance.

"I heard that, Virgil," Deekie snapped, "and this cat don't need to be giving ya' no tail nor tongue at all. Ya' know what I saying, Virgil?"

"If I says no, yer'll just say it eight more times, won't ya'?" answered Clay.

"I said that's enough, the both y'all," said Armistead, raising his voice. "Good God, you sound like an old married couple. We're coming up soon on my friend's farm where we'll be spending the night. I want no more bickering between y'all."

The sun was dropping in the west, and all were tired. The three of the them on that wagon then went silent the rest of the way. The drumming of the team's hooves into the dirt and gravel trail was the only sound to be heard. Finally, Deekie broke the truce.

"Exactly who is this friend of yers, Jefferson?"

"Well, he's more of a partner, really, than a friend. His name is Orrin Fletcher James. He'll give us shelter tonight, all 'cept for you, Clay. I need you guarding those trunks. Never know when someone might try to make their move on them collectibles."

"I take it that tomorra' morn we'll be getting on early to Nashville?" Clay said.

"Not hardly," the gambler said. "The team can do with a day's grazing and watering. Besides Clay, tomorra' we're gonna see just what you can do with that Whitworth Sniping Rifle. This man Orrin has some talent with it, can show you the proper technique. But I am bettin' your skills will surely surpass his own."

Clay said nothing in response. He just allowed his silent satisfaction to unfurl across his face like a triumphant flag snapping atop a hill in the wind.

Remembrances
& Regrets

He was a brute of a man, strong as a bull, with a temper to match.

Orrin Fletcher James dressed in a manner unaccustomed to Deekie. He wore tight gray overalls, tucked into mud slopped, near knee high boots. His shirt beneath the overalls, once white and billowy, was stained with dirt, grease and burnt cinders. The breeze that had once blown through it had been choked out for some time by the great beads of absorbed sweat from the massive blacksmith.

Orrin made quite the contrast sitting at the supper table next to Jefferson Armistead, who had clearly spent the hour or so since they arrived brushing out his vest and jacket. Somehow, inexplicably, the gambler's shirt was still white as the cloud of an autumn sky and seemed about as fresh.

Clay had spent that hour guarding the shipment of valuables chained atop the wagon's bed. He was thankful that the James farm was situated high on the side of a rolling hill. It afforded him a clear view of a mile and a half of dirt trail stemming from the road to Nashville. As Deekie ate at the table with Orrin and Armistead, Clay was relegated still to his duty of guarding the shipment of guns.

"Well, Miss Deekie here is something of a gun-slinging maw herself," Armistead said to Orrin. "She was telling me a purely fantastic story on the road from Chattanooga. How she and some Irish girl were taken captive up on a mountainside by a gang of renegades. Her fella, Clay, out there guarding our shipment tonight, came thundering up the mountain, set it ablaze and killed every man in that gang, except for its leader. Clay had tried to kill him, too, but was unable to do so. So, little Miss Deekie here was forced to do the job. Dropped that man herself. Ain't that right, Miss Deekie?"

While the gambler had been saying this, Deekie had been watching Orrin Fletcher James. His stained shirt was unbuttoned down to the place where his chest met his rock solid stomach and abdomen. His chest muscles were thick and covered with a dense matted tangling of oily black hair. She could not tear her eyes away from looking on it, as it should have disgusted her but surprisingly gave rise to a warmth within her. His chest seemed to ripple with his every move, even though he appeared completely at rest. She caught herself wondering what it would feel like to have those two powerful arms wrapped around her in the midst of passion…

"I said, *'Ain't that right, Miss Deekie?'*," Armistead repeated, as apparently she'd been so lost in her wondering that she'd missed his words completely.

"Yes, yes, Jefferson, just as yer said," she blurted out, flustered. She turned to see the strong man, Orrin, who in turn had been watching her with a slightly mischievous look in his eye. She feared she had been caught in her little fantasy and in her embarrassment, felt herself blush.

"No, Miss Deekie, it's just as *you* said," Armistead countered, correcting her. She seemed lost in her thoughts, and Jefferson had an inkling just what those thoughts might be. "One wonders where your mind might be, woman."

"Oh, I reckon I might just know," Orrin Fletcher James said with a wicked grin just before shoveling another over-heaped forkful into his mouth.

Both men let loose a bawdy laugh, causing Deekie to blush further until her face was as crimson as the bloom of a Crepe Myrtle. She had barely eaten any of the plate before her, when she rose from the table amidst the continuous lewdness of their stares.

"I'm gonna go check on Virgil," she stuttered as she headed for the door.

"Don't ya' want to know where yer'll be sleeping tonight, ma'am?" Orrin called out to her.

"I'll be sleepin' outside next to my man, Virgil," she barked defiantly as she passed through the door.

"Right smart of ya', girl," said the strong man, "let him wrap his arms around ya'. Oh, I'm sorry, let him wrap that arm of his around ya'."

Deekie had been out the door, her heart racing with a combination of her suppressed lust and, even more so, her embarrassment of getting caught lost in it.

Deekie had heard Orrin's last crude joke about her Virgil's arm, and was hurt by the cackling of Jefferson Armistead's laughter that erupted upon hearing it. She followed the beam of light cast from within the house until she came to the wagon. She called out for Virgil, who was still propped up inside its bed, his Spencer ever ready.

"If ya' done brought me something to eat," he answered, "yer a might late as I just got round to etting that salt pork sandwich from the grist mill this afternoon."

"Oh, Virgil," she said with tears in her eyes, "I don't think I like these men at all." She climbed into the wagon, and propped herself next to Clay. "This Orrin fella is just a sow, and Jefferson, for all his dandy and fancy, just rolls around in the muck with him. I have come to see that both Jefferson and Orrin are just downright low brow."

"Hell, Deeks, we're low brow," Clay answered. "It sure seemed ya' were enjoying yerself flirtin' it up with Armistead on today's ride"

"I was not flirtin'," she said, "just trying to make the hours pass."

"Seemed to me that Armistead was making all the passes," Clay scoffed, "and that ya' was rather enjoying his doin' so. Ya' get a bit too easily distracted, Deeks."

"Oh, Virgil," she said, as she wrapped her arms around him, "how many times must I tell ya' that yer the only man for me."

She found her hands unbuttoning his shirt, and spreading out across his chest like a morning's mist on a mountainside.

"Whadya doin', Deeks?"

"Nothing, Virgil, just playin'" she said with a purr. "C'mon and play with me."

"Well, I'm working," Clay said, "I don't want to give Armistead even the least reason to not pay me in Memphis. That's our fare money to Fort Worth. Besides, yer just all riled up from lookin' at that Orrin fella. I saw ya staring at him when we first got here."

Deekie let out a defiant *hmmmpff*. "I done told ya' that this Orrin Fletcher James is nothing more than a pig."

"Might just be so," Clay said, "but the man is built more like a bull. From the way ya' was looking him over, I thought ya' might right could take a ride on that beast."

"Oh, Virgil," she said, "don't be silly, now. Yer lettin' yer mind drive ya' a bit crazy. But, I have to say, since Willet's been gone, this is the first time I seen ya' jealous. I'm startin' to think I like ya' that way."

She pulled his hand away from the Spencer and placed it on her breast. "Come on, Virgil, let's play out here under the stars."

She stared off into the clear cool autumn sky, his hand limp, but still laying upon her bosom. Above them a million shining pinpricks twinkled against the pure black backdrop of the Tennessee night. It was as if the heavens were laid out above them for their pleasure, a pleasure that Deekie now desperately needed.

Deekie unbuttoned her blouse and slipped Clay's hand inside it. It still was not pulled away, but neither did it search out any pleasure for itself.

"Come on, Virgil," she whined, "don't send me back inside with them two ogres. There's a lot wrong with the pair of them."

"Did either of them lay a hand on ya?"

"No, Virgil, they did not touch me a t'all."

"Did they get vulgar with ya in any way?"

"No, not exactly. But they's still somethin' filthy about them. And beyond just that, something's not right. Something's queer."

"Yer right about that, Deeks," Clay said. "Before ya' came on out, I was thinking the very same thing. There's something about all this business that I don't

rightly like. I can't put my finger on it, but I don't like it. No, I do not."

The next morning came and Clay and Deekie awoke in the back of the wagon to a rooster's crow. It pierced their blissful sleep. Deekie had slept in a satisfied slumber while Clay strained to stay awake but failed to do so.

A heavy dew had fallen overnight. Deekie was mostly covered in the blanket that Clay had taken out for himself. Beneath it her hair was wildly mussed, and her breasts hung free in her half opened blouse. Clay was drenched by the dew. He seemed half awake when she spoke to him him.

"Virgil, I'll never forget last night," Deekie said. "Yer was a wild man. I can't 'member the last time yer was so passionate. I think I need to feed ya' a steady stream of things to be jealous over."

"Hell, woman," Clay responded, "ya' just wouldn't let up. I did all that to just get y'off to sleep. What ya figur' was my passion was just yer own dander bein' all riled up."

"Either way, Virgil, I want some more of that."

"Oh, calm yerself, woman," Clay said.

"Well, not right now, Virgil," she said. "But come next time, I want that same treatment. T'ain't been like that for a long time."

Clay rose to stretch himself and to take a survey of the situation that came with the morning light. No sooner had he completed his perusal when out of the house came Orrin. He sighted the pair in the wagon from the doorway, which was elevated slightly above them. He spotted

Deekie, lying on her back the blanket low around her waist. He saw Clay, standing, drenched.

"Looks like the two of y'all had an eventful night." Orrin watched as Deekie pulled the blanket tightly up over her half exposed breasts.

Clay had looked down at her also, and thought she pulled up the covering just a little bit too slowly.

"Open up that case with the Whitworth rifle in it and draw it out. The hex bullets too," said Orrin, "We'll be needin' them just after breakfast."

"Is the boss gonna let me fire it today?" he asked.

"That gambler ain't no boss to me," Orrin said. "Besides, he's still sleeping. After we ett, I'm going to teach ya' how to fire that gun something proper."

"I know how to fire a sniper's rifle," said Clay.

"During the war," Orrin said, "it was said ya' could always tell who fired the Whitworth for the first time by their havin' a black eye."

"Heard that myself," Clay said. "The damn thing has so much kick it was said to drive that scope right back into the shooter's face."

"That's because them fools were using it wrong."

"How so?" asked Clay. "How's a sniper supposed to fire it."

"From the supine position," Orrin said. "Ever do that?"

Clay looked quizzically at the man. "On my back? Naw, cants say I ever done so. Heard about some that did though."

"Well, you'll learn to do so, as that's the proper way to fire the Whitworth. Gives ya' more control," Orrin said. "Ya' can use yer legs to rest the barrel upon. I'll be givin' ya' a lesson in it after breakfast. Then this afternoon, when that damn gambler finally stumbles out of bed, we will put ya' to the test. See if yer sniping is as good as you say."

By this time Deekie rose to her feet, her blouse buttoned but her hair still looking like birds had nested in it overnight.

"I hope you enjoyed being out here in the elements with Clay," Orrin called out to her. "Tonight, when you sleep indoors I think you'll even find that a bit more satisfying."

"I got all the satisfying I need, ya' lumbering ox," she barked back at him.

"We'll good that ya' don't need much," the strong man said, looking at the scrawny, one-armed Clay.

Clay handed Deekie the Spencer and climbed down with difficulty from the wagon. He walked up to Orrin, much closer than was natural, and simply said, "Enough."

Orrin laughed out loud. "Clay, this ain't yer little town. Those tall tales you peppered all over it don't carry no weight this far. If y'expect me to fear yer anger, you gotta earn it."

"I reckon yer best think some more over what ya' think ya' really want!" Clay snapped.

Deekie, still in the back of the buckboard, took Clay's Spencer and half-cocked it, loading a round into the chamber. She kept it aimed low, as to raise it at anyone was a deadly threat. But she thought Orrin knowing it was at the ready was not a bad thing.

"Yer girl's gonna blow her damn foot off, Clay." Orrin said.

"She knows what she's doing with that rifle," Clay responded. "I done schooled her up good on it."

Orrin looked at Deekie standing above Clay. Her face was hard, her eyes steeled, and her stance ready for anything. For the first time, Orrin believed she could actually have killed someone.

"All right. Come with me, Clay," Orrin commanded. "Yer little miss gun maw can stay with the wagon while you and I ett inside."

As the sun rose, Cord McCullough traveled north by east along the fringes of the Chisholm Trail, crossing the Salt Fork of the Arkansas River and then across Medicine Lodge Creek before entering into Kansas. The mare trailing on a lead behind him had no real trouble carrying the two corpses, and on the few occasions when she had resisted continuing forward, a few angry barks from River motivated her to resume. Cord led Trouble along the path to the point where the main trail, the one that led up to Wichita and Abilene beyond, spurred off to a western side trail that led north directly to Ellsworth. Ellsworth, like Abilene, was a railhead on the Kansas Pacific Railroad.

As he approached the split in the trail, Cord knew nearby there was the border town of Caldwell, Kansas. It was a cowtown just west of the Chisholm Trail where he could drop off the corpses and make claim for any bounty that there may be on the dead rustlers. Once he had done so, he figured he could turn south again after the dead men's other three compadres that were fixing to rob the Butterfield Stage Overland Stage Coach line. They might have no more than a full day's lead on him south across the Indian Nations Territory to Red River Station in northern Texas. If Cord moved at a brisk pace, he figured he could catch up with them before they robbed the stage coach, most likely while it was still in the Indian Territory.

"You know, River," Cord said aloud to his canine companion, as he was prone to do, "by my reasoning, it was these dead rustlers being so damn predictable that was their undoing. First, we knew they'd be in the Injun' Nations Territory where they're protected by a lack of local law. Second, we reckoned they'd be close to the Kansas border, so after they finished rustling they'd wouldn't have too far to go to sell the stolen cattle. Likely they burned over the longhorns' brands and sold whatever they had rustled to some dirty dealing butcher along the trail. He'd process them and move the beef locally, or sell it off to the AT&SF in Wichita. Doubt they would be willing to take it as far north as Abilene and the Kansas Pacific. Anyway, once we knew they was in the north end of the Nations Territory, it wasn't hard to figure they be camping along the Red Fork. From there they could easily swing further west and rustle off the Ellis Trail as easy as the main Chisholm Trail to the east. Once we figured all that, six men, careful as they might be, sure leave a lot of tracks."

The dog, yipped, as if replying. "When we get to Caldwell we'll dump these rustlers' corpses and check the telegraph office for any news from the Exchange. Unless we get directed otherwise, we'll head south after those other three rustlers. With a little luck, we hit them before they hit the stage coach. After we take care of them, we'll head down to Fort Worth and try and find that damn gunsmith that's got the Exchange folk all worked up."

They rode their way and made the trail crossing by late afternoon. Everyone called it the crossing, even though it was no more than just a split in the trail. The main trail led to Witchita, a rail stop for the Atchinson, Topeka and

Santa Fe (AT&SF) Railroad. Further north along the trail led to the town Abilene on the Kansas Pacific line.

Alternately, the spur headed directly to Ellsworth, Kansas, which like Abilene, was on the route of the Kansas Pacific Railroad. Whether the final destination of the cattle was Abilene, Ellsworth, or Wichita, in any case all herds came through this juncture.

Soon enough, Cord, Trouble and River rolled into Kansas at *"the Border Queen"* town of Caldwell. This was a cow town that had been founded two years earlier in 1871 by a group of entrepreneurs from Wichita as a provisioning site. From spring to autumn, life in Caldwell was fueled by the influx of drovers from the main Chisholm Trail that it lay astride. The cowboys came into town looking for a little overnight celebration for having cleared out of the Indian Nations Territory unscathed. Caldwell was still little more than an array of mud streets full of boardwalk-lined clapboard storefronts. Like any other cowtown, it had premises to buy overpriced supplies, slam down some watered-down whiskey, or take on the company of an overused trail lady for an hour or perhaps even a night.

Over the next decade, Caldwell would become a particularly lawless place, with more than a dozen town marshals being gunned down or driven off. Its heyday would come in the period 1889-1893, after the cattle drives on the trail had long since ended. Then it served as a launching off point as the Government opened up the adjoining Indian Nations Territory as the new Oklahoma Territory in what would become the country's last great land rush.

Cord went straight to the Caldwell telegraph office, which was no more than a clapboard shack. He sent a message in to the Drover Exchange bringing his employers up to speed on what had occurred, as well as reporting of his present location.

Cord relayed his intentions to go after the other three rustlers in the vicinity of Red River Station. There he would trail them back upstream along the coach's route into the Indian Nations Territory, where they would most likely attack the stage coach. After these rustlers turned bandits were dealt with, he and Trouble and River would work their way on down to Fort Worth.

After sending the telegrams, Cord went to the law office to claim any rewards on the two rustlers, but there was no outstanding paper on either Quincy or Jesse. *Never the mind*, Cord thought, *the Exchange would pay dearly enough for my efforts, especially when they recovered that pen of twenty longhorns I reported back to them.*

Cord then walked into the provisioning outpost and bought more than enough jerky and hardtack to get him across the Indian Nations Territory. He had bought River his favorite treat, dried pigs ears and shared two of them with his canine companion for River's services rendered, but Cord decided to take his own lunch in the warmth of a local saloon. Before doing so, he loaded the supplies into his saddle bags and walked Trouble down to the livery to have her brushed out and fed with grain. Cord made one last stop at the telegraph shack to find a one word reply from the Exchange - "Proceed". He spent the next several hours in the companionship of both a near comely redhead, (a natural no less, he was to find out) and an even more attractive bottle of rare Tennessee whiskey.

Clay had spent the morning learning the art of shooting from the supine position with the Whitworth Rifle along the long dirt road leading up to his farm. Orrin Fletcher James proved to be a decent shot from 500 yards, but Clay, even with his first attempts with the unconventional gun and shooting position was able to match the strong man's scattered spread of rounds piercing the target. On their second set of volleys, Clay was able to better Orrin considerably. His grouping of six shots at that distance, once they had retrieved the target, was nearly tight enough to be covered by the big man's outstretched palm.

"Well, I'll be damned," Orrin said to Clay, "yer as good as them townsfolk from Cartersville bragged on ya'. This is likely the best shooting I've ever seen at this distance."

"I'm sure with another six shots I can get that grouping even tighter," Clay said. "I'm really just gettin' the feel for this weapon."

Clay had come to enjoy the challenge of the new weapon, and the excitement of mastering it so quickly.

"I think we've wasted enough of these hex bullets. They ain't exactly easy to come across. It appears ya've adequately demonstrated that ya' know what yer doing, boy." Orrin smiled broadly as he held up Clay's second target to the sky. "Damn ya' sure as hell do know what yer doing!"

"I'd like to hang on to that target," Clay said as he reached for the sheet of barnwood.

"Oh, no, son. Yer boss done got plans for this here target," Orrin said. "What, do ya' think this be some sort of pleasure shoot?"

"I don't follow…"

"Ya' don't need to follow, Clay. All ya' need to follow is that dozin' gambler's orders."

They returned to the farm house. Once there, Orrin told Clay that he needed to watch while Orrin took inventory of the two chests of bounty.

"Why do I need to watch over ya'?" Clay asked.

"To make sure I don't steal anything," Orrin said. "So ya' can report the same to Armistead when he wakes."

"Ya' mean he don't trust his partner?

Orrin laughed out loud. "Partner? I wouldn't trust that theivin' bastard as far as he casts a shadow. I ain't his partner. I work for the dealer in Nashville he's selling these weapons to. My job is to check out the goods, and make sure Mr. Goodlette is getting what he's payin' for before they get all the way across the Cumberland River."

And Clay watched for the next three hours as Orrin went through the revolvers and the rifles in meticulous detail, writing down each individual weapon's serial number and related specific condition of wear. All appeared to be factory fresh.

"Well, looks like everything's here, as proffered," said Orrin. "I reckon the three of y'all will be on your way at dawn's first light to Nashville."

A little after one o'clock that afternoon, Jefferson Armistead in all his freshly brushed-out finery came out of the house. Deekie was with him and walked over to Clay.

"What time did Jim Dandy finally roll out of bed?" he asked her.

Deekie gave him a stab of a look. "I wouldn't know, Virgil, I weren't in bed with him…"

"Ya know that's not what I meant," Clay shot back at her.

"… as I had already spent the night in the arms of a real man," she went on with a warm, playful smirk.

"At least three quarters or so," he added, deriding his own handicap. "All I meant, Deeks, was that ya' was in the house while Orrin and me was sniping out front. I thought he might have got up earlier and had some coffee with y'or something."

"Oh, we did, all right," Deekie said, "and all Jefferson could tell me was how fine I looked in these resplendent traveling clothes. He told me how Nashville and Memphis have all sorts of shops full of fine lady wear and accessory goods, and how he'd like to deck me out in outfits from New York City if I stayed on with him after this job is done."

"Ya' mean after I'm gone on my way to Texas," Clay said as his face reddened with anger.

"That was the gist of it, I think."

A sadness invaded him, falling like an unexpected fog. "What d'ya say to him, Deeks?"

"Just that I done seen how crazy ya' can get when we was atop that Three Sisters Mountain. It might have been back in '71, and I ain't seen anything so unbridled from ya' since, but I told Jefferson if I was him, I just wouldn't go scratching to see what's below yer surface. Virgil, he's a Jim Dandy all right, but in the end he's just a man, and he mistook me for an easy saddle to climb up into. I set him straight."

At that point, Armistead came over to Clay.

"Looks like your very proficient with that Whitworth, Clay. Good, very good indeed. I'm taking this target and sending it as a message to the man in Memphis who owes me a small fortune. Want to see the message I've scrawled on it?"

He took the wood target and began to hand it to Clay, but Deekie stepped forward and took it instead. She read the inscription Armistead had written on its surface.

"It says, *'I am looking forward to seeing you in a few days as we agreed. Expecting your payment in full. I am traveling with a Confederate sharpshooter who did this grouping at a full mile away using a Whitworth rifle and scope. I expect full payment in gold coin, no silver.'* And it is signed Jefferson C. Armistead."

"What's the 'C' stand for?" asked Clay.

"Clay!" Deekie screamed, "Who gives a damn what the C stands for! Jefferson is clearly threatening this man with yer sniping skills. Wants him to think yer'll kill him if he doesn't come up with what's owed in gold."

"That's about right," Armistead said, "although you'll find it to be an idle threat. I'd never kill a man over money. Far greater things in life to defend than just the love of silver and gold. However, assaulting one's character by holding back payment of a valid gambling debt, well now that *is* a honor worth spilling a little blood over."

"I ain't intending to kill no man in Memphis," Clay said calmly to Armistead, "for neither holding back of coin nor assaultin' of yer character. I done enough killing for one lifetime, and it all turned out to be for naught, anyhow. Besides that, that cluster of shots was made at 500 yards, less than a third of a mile out. I'd be lucky enough to hit a cow at a full mile out, with or without them fancy six-sided bullets."

Deekie was seething as she looked upon Clay and Armistead. Her Virgil was defiant to the gambler, but in a far weaker tone than she would have liked. He seemed to be condoning the man using his reputation as an implied threat, so long as it was understood Virgil would not, under any condition, carry out that threat.

"Clay, my young friend," Armistead said with a sly grin, "this is only business, no more than our upcoming visit to Nashville is. My friend in Memphis just needs to be motivated, that's all. So am I taking a little creative license with the distance? Well, perhaps so. But will the man understand that I am serious about collecting on this debt? Certainly he will. So Orrin here is going to have a rider carry this to Memphis ahead of us. Give the man time to come up with the payment. And you, Sir, don't have to kill anyone. You merely need to look like you have every intention to do so."

Clay could feel the pressure building within Deekie. He wanted to be outraged, but so long as no man was to be harmed, he really didn't care about the situation.

"So, what does the C stand for?" he asked Armistead again.

"Virgil!" screamed Deekie, "Can't ya' see he is just using ya'? And yer ain't man 'nuff to stop him from doin' it. Were it Willet, this gambler would be laid out flat with a couple holes in him."

Clay looked upon her, as she had finally stirred an ire within him. "Well, Deeks, Willet t'ain't here, is he? Ya' done seen to that, now, haven't ya'?"

His eyes were like two cold flat patches of ice, hazily translucent but with no real emotion caught frozen within them. Deekie looked into them, and could feel nothing other than her own want for him to become a real man again, not some push over for a man in a fancy suit with a wagon load full of guns.

"Deekie's right, Clay, I am using you," Armistead said loudly, interrupting the moment between them, "after all, what did you think I was offering to pay you all that money for?"

Deekie turned and walked away in a furor. Clay turned his icy stare onto the gambler, and replied. "Y'ain't paid me so much as a three cent piece yet, Armistead."

"Remember our deal, Clay. You get paid out in full in Memphis. After I get my debts paid." The gambler took the look and the refusal of Clay to address him as "Armistead" and not "boss" as an act of defiance. He knew he needed to de-escalate the situation all around.

"Calhoun, Clay" he then said, almost apologetically, "the C stands for Calhoun. You are working in the proud employ of Jefferson Calhoun Armistead."

Clay looked a second at the man in his finely brushed clothes, his neatly trimmed mustache and freshly shaved face. He was not the kind of man that Clay could ever respect. A part of him understood Deekie's anger at his cow-towing to the man. But to Clay, if he had to swallow some pride to earn enough to get himself from Memphis to Fort Worth to find his *Diddy*, then so be it. It did not mean he had to enjoy being worked harder and with less respect than a rented mule.

"Go ahead, Armistead," he said to the gambler, "Send yer rider and this message on ahead to Memphis. As far as being proud, ya' got enough of that sin in ya' fer the both of us. Just watch yerself, fer my *Diddy* alway's liked to say, *It's the proud nail that gets hammered down first.*"

"Boss," Armistead, tilting his head slightly toward Orrin, "Remember our deal, you're to call me boss, Clay."

Virgil Clay-Harris stared at him for a long second, and a stillness coiled within him.

"I'm done calling anyone boss," Clay spit the words out like a mouthful of seeds. "Y'ain't worthy of it, and I done grown weary of it. If that breaks our deal, then hold yer damn rider to Memphis."

Armistead then snapped his head to Orrin Fletcher James. "Send the rider with the target to Memphis. And as you have already told me you are satisfied with the products I am carrying, we will depart early in the morning to deliver them to your *boss,*" this word the gambler stressed. "Clay, Deekie and I will set off on morning's first light for Nashville to make our delivery to your Mr. Goodlette."

When The Trail Crossed Upon A River

River sauntered ahead of the loping stride of Cord and Trouble.

The man, his horse and the dog made their way south through the Indian Nations Territory toward the land of Texas just beyond the Red River Station. It was a trail they had wandered along many times over the past several years. Up to Kansas, down to Texas, almost always in search of some target of The Exchange. Back in the beginning, it had only been Trouble and he riding together. In fact, they were soon coming to the watering hole where Cord and Trouble had first come upon the canine who was to become the third member of their party of restless wanderers.

The Cimarron River carves a serpentine route, draining down from the elevations of New Mexico, and Colorado, across Kansas, and into the Indian Nations Territory before finally flowing into the Arkansas River. Years ago, just after Cord had first lost his wife and child and had struck out on his own, he and Trouble had come along the trail to this point where it crossed the Cimarron. Before long, he searched along the river's bank looking for a location where it could be forded, when he heard the plaintiff wail of a wounded beast. Cord guided Trouble toward the sound, although the horse was leery to close in on it. As they came over a rock ledge, Cord could see why.

There along the banks of the Cimarron, three coyotes had a large, domesticated dog cornered. It was bleeding profusely, wounded from an attack by the small pack. A fourth coyote already lay dead at its feet, but it was clear that the other three scavengers had already inflicted enough wounds that the canine would be their next meal. The coyotes kept the wild dog trapped up against the waters of Cimarron, too weak to attempt to swim away to safety. The predators waited. Then, as they regained their own strength after what had been a vicious attack upon the dog, they prepared to pounce one last time for the kill.

"Looks like that poor bastard already got the best of one of them coyotes," Cord said talking to Trouble. "Three on one ain't quite no sportin' odds, now is it?" he said drawing his rifle from the saddle sheath, "what say you we even them up a bit?"

Cord took aim on the farthest coyote, the one up the river bank from the dog. He could hit it cleanly without having to worry about harming the dog. He carefully sighted and squeezed off the first shot, whose explosive echo ran up the river's bank and back down the other side.

The coyote was dropped instantly. The other two predators broke into a frenzied scurry, looking frantically for cover. As the one in the center successfully made it to the cover of the brush, Cord cocked his Henry and loaded another round in the chamber. He then drew a bead on the last retreating coyote and hit it on the run, just before it also made the brush-line. It yelped, dropped, and then struggled to rise again, as it then limped with a pulsing spurt of blood cascading from just beyond its shoulder. Cord cocked the Henry and sighted the wounded beast, but held fire. The coyote slowly made it to the brush-line before it collapsed again, with only its hind quarters hanging out in the open.

Cord was satisfied with his shooting. He knew the coyote that escaped had surely been driven off and was no longer a threat to the wounded dog.

"Well, now, Trouble," said Cord, "I would say our part in this drama is played out, but them dead coyotes are surely gonna draw up a mess of buzzards, and if we don't help out that wounded creature down there, they'll just wait around on him too. C'mon, let's get a closer look at him."

Cord guided Trouble down from the rock ledge, through the sparse growth and onto the sand spit where the coyotes had the dog cornered. As they got closer, they could hear the poor thing slightly yelping as it drew quick, frightened breaths. When they drew near, Cord sheathed his rifle and dismounted from Trouble. He reached into the saddle bag and pulled from it some jerky with his left hand. He kept his right hand, his gun hand, free in case this dog that had killed the one coyote on its own might turn on him.

Nothing was more unpredictable than a wounded animal, less that animal be a wounded man, Cord thought.

Cord walked slowly near the dog, holding out the jerky, and called out to it in a slow soothing voice.

"It's OK boy, we're here to help you. Them coyotes bit you up a hell of a mess, but we're gonna fix you up."

Cord tossed the jerky with his left hand. He knew the animal would not eat it in the state that it was in, but also knew the animal would associate the scent of the food offered with friendship, certainly not a threat. The dog licked at the jerky and slowly returned its gaze to Cord, who had stopped some four or so feet away from it.

They stayed in that position for the next ten minutes. Cord assessed during this time just how torn up the dog was, and decided if it was more merciful just to spend another bullet and end its suffering.

Just as Cord had decided this was the most humane proceeding, the dog again licked the jerky up from the sand, but this time began to chew it. Cord then thought that if it was well enough to eat, it was well enough to live. The long shadows of the afternoon stretched across the riverbank, and Cord decided he and Trouble would bed down there next to the wounded dog. He collected up some scrub tinder and dry grass to build a small fire.

That night, after Cord had unsaddled Trouble, he let out his bed roll, a good three to four feet away from the where the wounded dog lay. He had given it several more pieces of jerky, but decided not to advance upon it.

The flames of the fire danced as the curtain of night enshrouded them. Cord lay propped up against his saddle, and watched the beast who never took its eyes off him. Then, as if fearing what might lay awaiting in the night, the dog slowly pulled itself toward the fire and Cord. Its front legs shuffled forth as the animal pulled itself, but its hind legs dragged almost uselessly behind it. Over the course of the next half hour, the beast pulled itself alongside of the reclined Cord McCullough, who vocally rooted it on.

Cord ran his fingers over its bloodied matted fur. He stroked it gently, rubbing out its ears, one of which had been bitten through by a coyote. The dog released a stream of pleasant sounds that Cord found to be one of the most comforting he had heard since leaving home to roam the trail. The dog allowed Cord's hands to flow over it, only wincing with gentle yelps when the stranger's fingers probed the edges of its wounds. The dog drew itself close to Cord, its bloodied hide came to rest upon him as he slept.

The morning light brought with it a glimmer of hope. The dog lay asleep beside him, breathing regular, but shallow breaths. After Cord rose and washed his face, he scooped the wounded animal into his arms and bathed its wounds in the Cimarron. That river was not known as a particularly good river to drink from, as it was full of minerals and salts from the many deposits and flats it passed over flowing down from New Mexico. Yet, those very minerals were known to aide the healing process.

Cord bathed the dog, who he had begun to call Cimarron, after the river. He and Trouble stayed by the dog's side for a few more days, as it slowly healed. Then, when Cord mounted the horse and they returned to the trail, the revived dog followed them everywhere.

Cord kept telling the animal to scoot, to git about its own way. But Cimarron would not listen. It simply endlessly trotted, despite its wounds, after the two of them. Clay soon tired of driving it off, just as he tired of calling it Cimarron, as that turned out to be a mouthful. Instead, he found himself calling it simply "River".

"Well, River, I noticed you never flinched when I fired off them rifle shots," Cord said, "so I figure you to be someone's sporting dog that strayed off. Come along with us, boy. I certainly can use a fellow hunter by my side."

River had stayed by Cord's side ever since. Soon after, Cord had come across an Englishman who knew the sporting breeds, and had told him he was in the possession of a highly trainable German-bred hunting dog. Was it possible it had been brought over by a German settler and had strayed, or been driven off, from that immigrant's homestead?

"Well, in any case," Cord replied to the Brit, "River and me are now a matched set. He stays by my side."

The conversation gave Cord an idea. He began to train the cream and brown mottled beast. This was fitting because with its three quarter brown face mask to which were attached matching solid brown ears, the dog already looked like a bandit. It's huge jaws, those that had killed one of the attacking coyotes, gave it a look that alone could drive fear into a man. River quickly began to learn Cord's commands, even to attack prey on his whistle. He taught it to avoid the pointed barrel of any gun, be it revolver or rifle, and to go for the wrist of anyone who possessed and pointed such weapons at him.

This training had proven itself effective on more than one occasion. Cord was quick to learn that as quick as this dog was to be trained, once turned loose it had a recognizable viciousness in it that proved to be a downright deterrent to anyone looking for a fight. River, as tame as he was on the surface, underneath was nothing more than a wild beast. This was fitting, as the word Cimarron, the name of the river in which its wounds were healed, in Spanish means "untamed".

Figure 6: River, rescued along the Cimarron

The Second Leg of the Journey to Nashville

The three of them rode the next morn in a chilly froth of harshest silence.

Clay, Deekie and Jefferson Armistead took to the Nashville road from the farm of Orrin Fletcher James in the earliest moments of sunrise. The sky was still barely discernible from night, except that the hollowness of the black darkness had given ingress to a subtly tinged canopy of the deepest hues of purple. As they headed north by west, the dark palette overhead slowly crumbled, first into a cobalt blue which soon gave way to alluring pinkish fingers that slowly melted into the rose hues of dawn. Finally, the stabbing full bright rays of the sun seared through that brief but stunningly colorful moment, like the harsh sweep of a sentinel's sword sent to clear away any defiant remnants of the vanquished night.

Clay, as on the earlier leg of their journey, sat amongst the treasured stash of weapons in the bed of the buckboard wagon. His back rested up against the wall that separated the cargo from the wagon bench where Armistead tended the reins and Deekie sat in an eternal silence.

Deekie had remained angry with her Virgil for yielding to the demands of the gambler. She had thought him a stronger man than that. She was equally upset with the gambler Jefferson himself, if not for treating her like nothing more than an object of bawdy desire, than for treating her Virgil like nothing other than an ominous warning and deadly threat to his debtor in Memphis.

Armistead, for his part, had sensed the tension that morning and decided to bluff his hand out to its fullest. So far, he had gotten everything he desired. First there was the conquest of the shipment of guns having been approved by the agent Orrin Fletcher James, who acted as the gatekeeper to the dealer Goodlette in Nashville. All he had to do now was deliver the goods to the dealer's door and collect payment.Those funds alone would pay handsomely enough to cover the expense of his one-armed escort, Clay.

Armistead was also on his way to achieving his second objective. Clay's marksmanship skills with the Whitworth Sniping Rifle had been demonstrated and its results documented. They were sent ahead to Memphis by dedicated rider and that annotated target would arrive there well before they ended their day in Nashville. Armistead knew that the man who owed him a huge gambling debt, an Englishman named Thomasson, would surely pay up, as his cotton export business was heavily tied to the town. He could not merely pull up stakes and run. Having a sniper lurking in the distance was all the incentive needed to assure the gambler's threat would be taken seriously.

The road fell away beneath their wheels and hours passed before they came to the town of Franklin. It had been the scene of intense fighting during the war, so Armistead decided this was as good as any time to strike up a conversation.

"Clay, I know you were out of the war by the Battle of Franklin in November of '64," Armistead yelled over his shoulder, "General John Bell Hood led his Army of Tennessee into one of the greatest disasters of the Confederacy here. It's said that of his 40,000 rebel soldiers, only half survived that onslaught against the Yankee General Schofield and his Army of the Ohio. General Hood attacked one frontal wave after another, throwing as many as twenty thousand men at the Yankees. Hood lost fourteen Confederate Generals, either dead or wounded, in those charges alone. The Yankees repelled the attacks, before eventually they slowly pulled back into Nashville. General Hood followed the Yankees to the capital, only to find there that he was outnumbered two-to-one. The Yankee General George Thomas then routed John Bell Hood's Army once and for all. All that was left when our boys finally retreated wasn't much of a fighting force after that scrape."

Clay listened to Armistead's discourse. It angered him to no end to hear this man, who had never so much as even picked up a weapon in defense of the Confederacy, criticize General Hood who had so valiantly, even if unsuccessfully, led the defense of the South. Let alone the fact that Armistead stood to profit indecently from selling this stash of these very same weapons, those he had never wielded, to collectors in the North. And perhaps, Clay was most disappointed of himself, as he sat amongst this load with his Spencer rifle ready, keeping guard over the arms. *Did this make him no more a hypocrite than Armistead?*

"That Yankee General Thomas was at Chickamauga when I got injured," Clay said. "We was routing them boys somethin' fierce, but Thomas was able to set up a defensive position on what they called Horseshoe Ridge, enough so those Yankee troops could retreat back to Chattanooga. He was a tough bastard, so much so they began calling Thomas the Rock of Chickamauga. So, ya' see, General John Bell Hood had his hands full going up against him outnumbered two to one only a little over a year later."

"Well, one thing is for sure, my friend," the gambler Armistead said. "We will be in Nashville soon enough. Once we get paid for this shipment, I am going to treat you both to a fine fried chicken dinner on Broadway. And once that deadbeat in Memphis pays up, we'll have a grand steak feast to finish off this here trip."

Deekie then chirped in, "I wouldn't go counting either them chickens or them T-bones just yet. Still a lotta things that can go wrong on us all."

"Well, what do you know?" Armistead said. "Our little buttercup here can talk!"

Deekie shot Armistead a glance that would've stopped any other man dead in in his tracks. "Seems to me, Mr. Jefferson, all ya' been thinking about since I joined on this ride was how ya' could spread this little buttercup's petals. I'm here to tell ya' that won't be happenin' anytime soon. Never, in fact."

Jefferson Armistead's rigid face creased with a broad smile. "All right, Deekie, ya' found me out! I am an unrepentant worshipper of beautiful women, it is true. However, you have my intentions all mixed up. I merely want to buy you an outfit from the Broadway shoppes that highlights what a fetching lass you truly are. Those riding britches and that blouse and jacket, even as caked in road dust as they are, are fine enough for some small town tomboy, but in you I sense an elegance that far transcends sheer lust or indecent arousal. I believe I know that the proper clothes would bring out the smart educated woman hiding within you."

"What, me, educated?" Deekie answered, caught in surprise by the flattery of his approach.

"Well, you haven't gotten more than ten feet away from that Edgar Allen Poe book since I met you…"

"Well, I do like to read," she surmised about herself, "it's just that I don't often get a real book to read. We ain't had no money for that frill."

"And now, Miss Deekie, you are getting the experience of travel," Armistead added, "which is widely known to be an education in itself. Not many people get to travel outside the place where they were raised, you know."

"But this is just the first traveling I've ever done…"

"Why on this trip alone you'll get to see Nashville and Memphis, two of the major metropolises of the great state of Tennessee. And if you go on to Fort Worth, as Clay has been saying, you'll likely travel through Arkansas, and into Texas."

"My, that is a lot of traveling, t'ain't it?" Deekie said aloud, almost justifying to herself just what a world trekker she had become.

"If, when we get to Nashville, you allow me to dress you out in true finery from the best Broadway shoppes, I will even throw in any book you like from one of them fancy booksellers there. You can keep it for your own. Get something that tells a story of far away lands you might yourself wish to travel to someday."

"I think I just might could do that, Jefferson," she said dreamily.

Clay interrupted the repartee between the two of them. "Deeks, I know you're weary of them dust strewn britches right now, but with all the smoke Armistead here is blowing up ya' just might as well be wearing a skirt."

"Oh, Virgil," she rebuked him, "yer downright green with jealousy."

"And yer *Jefferson* is as full of lust as a twelve point buck is for a doe in full heat durin' the rut. Don't let them fancy words drippin' off his tongue fool ya none."

"Is that right, Jefferson," she directed to the buckboard driver, "are ya' just out to have yer way with me? Is that what this is all about?"

"If I was, Miss Deekie," he answered, "I surely wouldn't invest upwards of one hundred dollars in dressing you out. I admit I do have an ulterior motive, but it is purely professional. A gambler like myself needs not to have too much attention paid to just what his hands are doing. The best method of distracting the other players at the tables is to have a beautiful young woman standing aside you. And Miss Deekie, I assure you, if you were decked out in what I have in mind, I could make them cards dance on their edges and not a soul would even notice."

"Ya' hear that Virgil?" she turned to spot Clay ever vigilant to assure no one was trailing their wagon. "Jefferson here wants me as a distraction."

"An ever so sweet distraction," Armistead corrected her. "No man could possibly be able to resist looking at you, Miss Deekie, with what I have in mind."

"Good thing he has a cool tongue or yer hind parts would be singed by all that hot air, Deeks," teased Clay.

"Virgil, ya' don't think I could turn the heads of every man at a poker table? Ya' don't give me much credit a t'all, just because ya' take me for granted, Virgil."

"I didn't mean to get yer dander all riled up, girl," Clay said, but it was too late. Deekie had already turned her head back to Armistead, the fullness of her checks were crimsoned flush with anger.

"All right, Mister Jefferson Calhoun Armistead," she said, her voice as excited as her Virgil's twelve point buck, "when we get to Nashville, ya' dress me up like I was one of them Savannah imported dolls from Europe. Ya' know, the kind only them rich little girls have give' to 'em. We can put aside these dusty rags and ya' can dress me up just as ya' see fit."

"I will," Armistead replied, "just as soon as we deliver these guns and get paid for them. Then, I will have you fitted out for taking to the fanciest gaming parlors you ever seen. With every single man watching you, I will have free rein over their souls, not to mention their stacks of chips. We will clean up, darling Miss Deekie, and when we get to Memphis, we'll do it all over again."

"Damn it, Deeks," Clay objected, "can't ya' see he's just intent on using you?"

"Well, Virgil," she snapped, "if his paying a small fortune to show me off to the gazes of a saloon full of men is being used, I could put up with a spell or two of it. Besides, t'ain't nothing wrong with drawing a little attention now and then. I certainly don't draw yer eyes any more. Ya' pay me no attention a t'all."

"Well, girl," he said, "ya' got my attention now and I'm telling ya' yer making a deal with the devil."

The truth was that Deekie was, at that moment, enjoying the notice she was drawing from her jealous beau. She figured she'd play along with Armistead some, and if nothing else, she would get some fancy new clothes, a book and a few nights in elegant gaming parlors out of the deal.

When they came into Nashville proper an hour later, Deekie seemed perplexed.

"Jefferson," she asked, "can ya' shed some light on something for me?"

"If I can, Miss Deekie," he said with a sly grin. "What's bothering your pretty little head?"

"Well, back in Franklin ya' said the Confederates closed in on Nashville. How did them devil Yankees get their hands on the city in the first place?"

"Rivers and rails, girl," he said, "rivers and rails."

"I don't likely follow," she admitted.

"It was somewhat early in the war when Nashville fell. You see, Nashville was a big rail hub, and the Yanks knew if they could take control of it, they could put a chokehold on the movement of goods - food, guns, ammunition - to the Confederate states. So none other than our current President, Ulysses S. Grant, back when he was a General still making something of himself, figured if he could control the two major rivers in Tennessee, those being the Cumberland and the Tennessee, he could control the whole state. So in February of 1862, using Union gunboats and ground troops, he took two forts that protected the entrance to those rivers. The first was Fort Henry on the Tennessee River, and less than twenty miles or so away was Fort Donelson on the nearby Cumberland River. Later that same month, Grant steamed gunboats upriver on the Cumberland to take Nashville without much of a fight. The Confederate troops pulled out of the capital ahead of the arrival of the Yankee troops. Nashville was the first capital of a Confederate State to fall."

"What about them people left behind in the city?" Deekie asked.

"All the civilians were so scared of them twenty or so gun boats and all the destruction they could bring down on their homes and businesses, that they either fled or holed up and hoped for the best."

"The same thing at Chattanooga?" Deekie asked.

"Not quite so simple in that case," said Armistead. Our Southern commanders had learned a thing or two from the undefended Cumberland River that allowed the Yanks a free steam into Nashville. They started setting up fortifications along the Tennessee River. In fact, one of the most vicious fights put up anywhere was near Corinth, Mississippi, but across the river in southwest Tennessee at Shiloh Church. There, old *"Unconditional Surrender"* Grant found out that wasn't what his initials actually stood for. Our boys put up a hell of a fight at Shiloh."

"Yeah, I heard the townsfolk of Cartersville talking about that battle. What was so special about the fighting at Shiloh?" Deekie asked.

"Well, if and when you get to Fort Worth, those Texas boys will tell you the sting the Yankees felt was due to it being the first time the Lone Star troops were in the fight. But truth be told, the Yankees were deep into the South, and it drove the ire of all our boys protecting their homes and families."

"What do ya' mean if and when we go to Texas?" yelled out Clay. "We is going to find my *Diddy*, and nothing ain't going to change that."

"Of course not, Clay" laughed Armistead. "I didn't mean any malice by it. It's just that even our most fervently held plans have been known to change unexpectedly. God's been known to do that to us all, hasn't He?"

"So, this fight at Shiloh Church," Deekie said excitedly, "our boys won that battle?"

"Alas, my darling, no," the gambler explained, "but the boys put up a hell of a fight against the Yanks. So much so that the fight for full control of Chattanooga would go on for another year and a half. The Yankees didn't take control of it until September of '63, but the siege of that city and fighting around it went on until it was finally decided in November of '63. That was right after Chickamauga, where your Clay was taken out of the fight."

The buckboard and its three occupants then entered into Nashville's main business area, which had become quite prosperous in the years that followed the war. Deekie had never before seen anything so amazing as the storefronts that lined the main boulevard of Broadway. She thought no other street on earth could possibly engage in this much trading. There were people everywhere, swarming the shoppes like insects. She caught sight of a beautiful shoppe in whose windows were some of the most elegant dresses and gowns she had ever seen. It was then she first feared Jefferson might renege on his promise. She wanted to be dressed out in such finery so badly.

Armistead led the team of horses to the stables in the rear of Goodlette's gun seller shop. There, he had the trader's men unload the crates while Clay stood guard, Spencer Rifle at the ready. Once inside, the guns were removed from the crates, counted and briefly re-inspected by Colonel Goodlette, who like Colonel Colt long before him, had been awarded an honorary rank by the local militia. Goodlette approved the shipment, relying heavily on the previous inspection conducted by his agent, Orrin Fletcher James. He then paid Armistead in sacks of $20 gold pieces, known as double eagles.

"There sure is a lot of money floating around in this city," Deekie observed as the buckboard, empty except for the several sacks of double eagles, headed down Broadway.

"Yes, and starting tonight," Armistead declared, "with your assistance, darlin' Deekie, I expect to help myself to much more of it from these locals, some who are rather rich. Colonel Goodlette told me that the Commodore has already put up a million dollars of his fortune to establish a local university here in town."

"Who's the Commodore?" Clay asked.

"Only the richest man in all of America, if not the world," Armistead bragged. "Cornelius Vanderbilt made his fortune many times over in steamships and open ocean shipping, as well as railroads. Can you imagine, one million dollars just to have this new university bear his name? That man is shamefully rich, like King Solomon himself."

"As I remember from my Bible learning," Clay recalled, "things didn't work out all that good for King David's son in the end."

"What do you mean, Clay?" Armistead asked. "Solomon was the richest and wisest man on earth."

"King Solomon said before he died all them riches and learning was nothing but vanities," Clay said, sure in his knowledge of this particular scripture. His maw had quoted it often, whenever Clay or Truitt asked why they had so little. "He may have been the wisest and richest of all men, but he likely squandered his soul by leading his people to worship false gods."

"Well, Clay" Armistead retorted, "I sure would like to try my hand at counting his vast fortunes of gold. Not to mention attending to his seven hundred wives and three hundred concubines. That could keep even the most virile of men busy for quite a bit. You see, I know my Bible, too."

"Yeah, yer just payin' heed to all the wrong words in the Good Book. You done missed its lessons."

Late that afternoon in the hotel, the three of them shared a wondrous meal of Nashville fried chicken and all the fixins, as had been promised by the gambler. "If you're enjoying this, wait until we get to Memphis," Armistead said, "for there we will really put on the feast. Now, tonight, Clay, your sole responsibility is to guard this mountain of gold, less the stake, of course, that I'll be taking to dress out our fair Miss Deekie in a high style so she can accompany me to the gaming parlor tonight."

And that Clay did. He sat in the hotel room with his Spencer rifle, extremely bored until Deekie and Armistead came back well after sunset from their shopping excursion. Clay almost did not recognize his gal, as she was gussied up in the loveliest green dress, brocaded with white satin trim around her low-cut neckline. On her head, tilted at what he thought to be a dangerous angle, rested her matching hat behind which she twirled her parasol. Deekie's hair had been finely coiffed and upon her skin wafted a subtle but intoxicating violet perfume.

"Well, I'll be," Clay said, "Deeks ya' look finer than a frog's hair. But why did y'all go and get so gussied up just to come back here in time for bed?"

"Ah, my simple country friend," Armistead interjected, "the night is still in its infancy. We will be setting off for the gaming tables just now and don't expect us back until dawn. I intend to teach Miss Deekie here just how fine the night life of a major Southern city can be."

"Virgil, I will have ya' know that I will be playing the part of Jefferson's beauteous distraction," Deekie said, repeating Armistead's very words. "Less pressure on him so long as the other players' eyes are drawn to me."

Clay felt a slow fury build within him. His instincts told him that Deekie was entering a dangerous realm, yet he held his tongue because he could clearly see how excited she was to be going out into the night in all her finery.

Armistead then counted out several hundred dollars in twenty dollar gold pieces that he intended to be his stake that night at the gaming parlor. He spoke aloud after he completed his counting as he broke down his stack into two equal weights to carry in each pocket of his trousers.

"Clay, despite being out all night," he said, "I'll want to leave for Memphis as soon as Deekie and I can change into our road clothes. Experience has taught me that it serves no purpose to dawdle once you have fleeced the local flock. Too often the losers seek to soothe the sting to their egos in ways not beneficial to my own interests."

"Ya' mean like throwing yer hide in the hoosegow?" Clay snapped back. "Besides, what makes ya' so sure that yer'll even come back a winner from tonight's play?"

Armistead had walked around the bed and moved behind Deekie. He slid his arms under her own and brought his hands together in front of her waist. In each cupped palm there glittered equal heights of gold coins. He raised his chin and leaned forward to rest it on her shoulder, as he said, "With this bounty and this beauty, how could I possibly lose?"

Deekie looked down, then moved his hands with her own forward away from her waist. Initially this pleased Clay as he thought she was rebuking Armistead's embrace, but in the moment that followed his pleasure evaporated as he could see she only wanted a better gander at the wealth of gold, the like of which she had never seen. Deekie's face was painted with a reflection of intoxication.

"Deekie, now, don't yer dare be doing anything untoward in those parlors, like spotting other players' cards for this gambler. Men get shot for such, and if ya' was to get in the way of a bullet, well, I would never forgive myself."

"Oh, Virgil, what kind of hussie do yer take me for?" she replied. "I already told Jefferson I would do no such thing. Really, Virgil, sometimes I wonder if y'even know me at all after all this time."

"Nonetheless, Clay, I am quite glad you said that," exclaimed Armistead as he gently withdrew the stacks of gold coins from around Deekie's waist and placed them softly on the bedside table. "I nearly forgot my openers." He removed his jacket before reaching for his shoulder holster and the Colt pocket pistol which it held.

"Why ya' call them yer openers?" Deekie asked as she took the verbal bait.

"Well, they have more than once opened up a way out of a tight fix for me."

"He means when the players at the table accused him of cheatin'" added Clay.

Deekie's head snapped as she glanced at the gambler with a look that seemed to ask, *"Is this so?"*

"Occasionally, those that lose might make that mistake," Armistead admitted, "but when the intemperance of their accusations draws out the tempered barrel of my Baby Colt, they quickly recognize the error of their words." A sly grin stretched across his face until it seemed to slowly sway like a hammock slung from ear to ear.

"Ya' best watch that pride of yers," Clay retorted, "It can lead to some right nasty things. I seen many a man felled when their chests ballooned too full of themselves. I seen it in wartime, and I seen it since then, too."

Cord McCullough Rides the Trail

Southward he rode as the colors of autumn darkened and crumbled in a foreshadowing of winter.

Cord rode upon his bay mare, Trouble, as the hound, River, ambled alongside. As they moved southward through the Indian Nations Territory, they passed one of the last of the northbound herds making their way to Abilene. Once they did, they followed the trampled width of the trail, as it was the safest route.

However, this also presented its own problem, as everyday Cord had to detour a good distance wide of the trail just to find grazing for Trouble. The Chisholm Trail's grasses had already been grazed out and trodden over by the summer's seemingly unending herds of longhorn cattle.

Being off the trail, even only for a few hours, not only slowed their progress, but made Cord feel vulnerable to whichever of his enemies might be lay in wait for him.

This day he had swayed wide of the trail, until he came upon a creek along which grew a thick blanket of autumn grasses. Cord scouted the surrounding area, deemed it safe enough, but still drew the Henry rifle he carried sheathed alongside his saddle. He holstered a pair of the newest Colt Peacemakers around his waist. They were hard to come by, but as they had been supplied by the Exchange, there was no effort expended on his part in obtaining them. These and the Baby Dragoon he had hidden in the secret pocket at the bottom of his leather trail duster, the same one he had used at the campfire, were now all the protection he would need.

Before he dismounted, he looked down at his saddle's dusty pommel. Wrapped around its horn was his most cherished possession, that which oddly kept him forever moving onward. It was a German made silver crucifix that had once belonged to his mother. She had bought it as a keepsake in St. Louis years earlier. Its argent chain dangled from the pommel like the pendulum from a clock, counting off the seconds, minutes, hours and days of his penance. Alone, forever alone, except for the eyes of Trouble and River whose lives depended upon his own. Every time he had let his mind wander to perhaps taking his own life, these four eyes would peer needly upon him.

Cord unwrapped the chain and the crucifix and slipped both in his left hand riding glove. He stepped hard into the left stirrup, allowing him to throw his right leg over Trouble and dismount. He led his mare to the creek to water her before he allowed her to graze. River had already found the creek's waters and had lapped up his fill.

As Trouble drank, Cord placed the crucifix beneath his left leather glove to feel its burn on his skin. His mother had given it to take along when he left the family home in Missouri with his two younger brothers. Within a year he had given that same crucifix to a young Kansas beauty on the occasion of his asking her to marry him. This was in the years just before the war, during a time in which long festered dark hatreds had raged along the Kansas-Missouri border. It had been the time known as "Bleeding Kansas" just before the war.

Kansas was a free state; Missouri had been a slave state. Kansas had her militant abolitionist "Jayhawkers"; Missouri had her pro-slavery "Border Ruffians" or "Bushwhackers". Cross border raids became commonplace as the war neared. The McCullough brothers believed they had no dog in this fight, as their family had always been Southern sympathizers, but had never owned slaves themselves. Yet all that seemed to change once Cord proposed to a beautiful Kansas lass.

Her name was Callie. She was the most beautiful young woman he had ever laid his eyes upon. Her auburn hair and large brown eyes complemented her tanned farm complexion. Her smile seemed ever-present and shined through with a warm radiance that was instantly infectious.

Cord and his two brothers had come cross-border from their home in Platte City, Missouri into Kansas to work as hands on her family's farm during the summer of '58. The farm was located outside Holton, Kansas near Straight Creek and was owned by the girl's father. It was in desperate need of hands as two of the farmer's own sons had died of smallpox the previous winter. The locals were afraid to work the farm for fear of contracting the deadly disease.

This opened the opportunity for Cordell and his brothers, Conor and Sean, that summer. They made the sixty-five mile journey with the blessing of their parents, who owned only a small home in Platte City, which had no land in need of the boys to work.

Callie was young, just fifteen when Cordell first laid eyes upon her. She often brought him and his brothers food and cool drinks in the fields as they worked. It was her innocence that drew Cordell to her. He immediately felt protective of her, as if she were his own sister, although, in reality, he had none. But his protection was something that she would need, for even then the strains of the border raids was enough to drive otherwise good men to unrighteous acts.

As spring turned to summer in 1858, and the lads settled in to their work, Callie would slowly but steadily find more excuses to spend time with them, especially Cord. He was twenty-five that summer, and knew her to be too young for him, even by the standards of the time. But she wore away at him, and carried herself with a maturity beyond her girlish years. On a Sunday afternoon as the harvest neared, she brought drink to him near the creek that ran through the farm. She sat next to him while he enjoyed it, under the trees of the small family apple orchard. It was there in that tranquil moment, as she asked him about his own parents back in Platte City, Missouri, that his brother Sean called urgently from the house, "Cordell, come quick, something has happened to the old man."

In that instant he saw in Callie's eyes a terror that was not unknown to her. She had lost her brothers just the previous winter, and now something was wrong with her father. They raced up to the farmhouse to find Callie's father upon the kitchen floor, limp and unresponsive.

Cordell dispatched his brother Conor to ride down to the road to Doc Greenier's place and fetch him. By the time he returned with the doctor, the father was dead. Doc Greenier declared it a stroke, but both Callie and her mother knew it was nothing less than a catastrophe. Not only was the family left without a father and husband, but the harvest was ahead of them with the onset of a harsh plains winter just beyond.

Cordell took control of the situation. He planned the burial and wake of the man, and in doing so called on the other farmers of the area to assist the three brothers in bringing in the crop immediately afterwards. The farmers heeded his requests and their generosity flooded the farm with valuable income.

Cordell learned the ins and outs of what could be sold for cash, and what could be canned and put up or stored for the winter in the silos. Cordell raised enough cash to pay off his two brothers, who then returned to Platte City across the border. But he himself could not leave Callie and her mother unprotected in their hour of need. Cordell committed to winter there with them, much to the relief of Callie's mother who wished desperately for a man to remain about the farm.

Christmas came, and Cordell had found himself closer than ever with Callie. She had been mature beyond her years in the summer, but the unexpected death of her father had accelerated her serious nature. Any playfulness that she had once shared with him was by then gone. Yet, Cordell knew that she had drawn herself ever closer to him emotionally, and he to her, over the weeks after her father's death. On Christmas Day, just after saying blessing over the holiday meal, Cordell McCullough presented Callie with the silver crucifix and asked her to marry him.

Callie's mother was delighted, and Callie herself was over the moon with joy. "You have given me the greatest gift I could ever have wished for," the then sixteen year old said to him as she wept.

"And a great joy you have given to me also," added her mother. "May God bless you all your days, Cordell McCullough."

They decided they would marry on the Sunday after her seventeenth birthday in March. They had already planned for his brothers to return in the late winter and begin readying the farm again for the spring planting. Callie and Cordell hoped to have many children, prayed they would be boys, who in time would grow strong and would one day take the place of the Cordell's brothers, Sean and Conor on the farm.

On the last day of January, 1859, the need for provisions took Cordell and Callie into town. When they arrived, all of Holton was abuzz with the fact that the abolitionist John Brown and his group had been spotted on the roads nearby. There had been a three thousand dollar reward put on Brown by the authorities and any sighting of the abolitionist was scandalous news.

Cordell and Callie completed their business and headed out on their wagon to return to the farm. Cordell had driven the team of horses east of town back to their homestead. As they neared it, they came over a slight rise, from which they could see in the distance were two opposing groups of men on horseback. The group closer to them was clearly, even at that distance, that which belonged to the John Brown party and consisted of some twenty or so men, women and children. They were escorting twelve slaves, recently escaped from Missouri to Nebraska, where they would become free men.

Opposing them were a posse of federal marshals including a band of Bushwhackers, numbering over twice that of John Brown's party.

From under the barren limbs of a dormant live oak, Cordell and Callie watched as John Brown charged his party straight ahead at the federal posse, near Straight Creek. The terror Brown instilled in them caused the much larger posse all to turn and flee. Not a single shot was fired. Later, the confrontation would become known as *"The Battle of the Spurs"* after the heated retreat of the federals beat back into Missouri.

Yet, Callie found nothing humorous in this event. It greatly unsettled her, and she called it an omen of disaster. Cordell did his best to console her, but she remained in a state of great agitation. Later that night, Cordell embraced her, and only this seemed to temporarily stem in her the tide of fear for the future. It was in those small hours of that morning, that the soothing of his embrace led to the taking of her virginity, freely given in an attempt to escape the chain of malicious events that had begun with the loss of her brothers, continued with the unexpected taking of her father, and now threatened her future with the ominous events of this day.

Back in the present, Cord had recalled all these events as he had watched his trusted bay mare, Trouble, graze the stalks of grass by the watering hole. He forced himself to stop recollecting the past, and mounted the mare to make their way back to the Chisholm Trail. There they would be safe from adversaries. And with a little luck, Cord would be safe from being drawn back into the dangers of reliving his own disturbing memories. As he always did, Cord replaced the crucifix so it dangled from the saddles horn, ticking off the duration of his penance.

On to Memphis

The orange Sun rose not unlike a peering eye surveying the aftermath of their misdeeeds of the night.

Under its glow, Armistead and Deekie returned in a blaze of their own haste. They entered the hotel room, startling Clay, in an air of frenzied energy.

"Quickly, Miss Deekie, change into your riding clothes. They are on the chair there, as I had the hotel's valet brush them out for you. Come quickly now."

"Oh Virgil," she cried out to her man instead, "what an exciting night we had. Who would have guessed that so much went on while the city slept?"

"I said come now, Miss Deekie," Armistead interrupted her, "you can give him the full regaling once we are underway. Hurry."

Deekie made the frustrated face of a young girl, hunched her shoulders and stomped her feet. Armistead sat at the room's small table and quickly counted out the bank notes that represented his winnings, and set the paper aside the two stacks of gold coins that had been his stake.

"A very profitable night indeed," he said aloud, before he turned to pull his own riding clothes from the closet. Deekie immodestly had already changed into her clothes as if she had known that even her state of undress would not draw Armistead's attention away from his gaming booty.

"I'll wander down to the livery stable and git our buckboard ready for the trip to Memphis," Clay suggested.

"No, Clay," Armistead said, "I will need you to escort us down. Make sure you have those Colt Navy sixes strapped on and fully chambered."

"Just what exactly happened last night?" Clay demanded to know.

"Last night was fine, Clay, it was this morning that stirred up all the commotion."

"What Jefferson is trying to say," Deekie added, "is that the gambling was fine, but as we started to leave the mansion, two young men jumped out of the garden and held held a knife on us."

"What mansion?" Clay asked.

"Oh, the gamblin' was done in the parlor of a most charmin' home in the countryside, t'was truly a mansion. There was so many fancy people. The ladies' gowns were the likes of which I never seen. They wore them so well."

"But none wore them any finer than you did, my dear," Armistead said as he pulled on his road trousers.

"Why thank ya', Jefferson," Deekie said as her face blushed.

"Who pulled the knife on ya' both?" asked Clay.

"Virgil, you should have seen the look on the faces of them ruffians when Jefferson reached into his jacket for his wallet and pulled out that Baby Colt instead. When he fired it over their heads they dropped that dagger and fled like their bottoms would be his next targets. It was so frightenin' at first, but so excitin' after they turned tail and run off."

"I am quite sure it was that man Rollo's doing," Armistead said as he pulled his jacket on.

"Ya' mean that man at yer table who was grumblin' about me?" Deekie asked.

"Why on earth would this fella grumble about ya', Deeks?" Clay inquired.

"He said I was too distractin' when I leaned over to talk to Jefferson, asked me to stop doing it."

Clay thought her drunk, but not from the ferment of grain, but rather from all the attention that had been so quickly doled out upon her.

"Such lassitude!" Armistead objected. "That vile man had neither the energy or the proper reverence to enjoy one of God's greatest views, that being the majesty and beauty of the womanly form."

"Ya' wouldn't had been dealing out the cards whenever Deeks bent over so, would ya' then?" asked Clay.

"Clay, I object to the inference," Armistead barked out, "I most certainly was not."

"And I certainly knew better than to interfere once Jefferson had started to deal," Deekie said, "so I only did so when he would clear his throat while he was shuffling the deck, Virgil. That was his sign to me."

Clay raised his hand to his forehead in disbelief.

"What, Virgil?" Deekie asked innocently.

"Can't ya' see Armistead was using ya' to side track the men at the table while he was stacking the deck? When you'd bend over every man's eyes were surely staring right down yer blouse to look upon yer bossoms, Deeks."

"I'll have ya' know in them society circles it's known as *décolletage.* Jefferson said so himself in picking this dress out for me."

"Come now, you two, time to depart…"

"Wait just one minute," Clay shouted to the gambler, "ya' put my Deekie in harm's way by using her to distract from yer cheating ways. I thought even ya' had some amount of scruples."

"With all the winnings I walked away with last night," Armistead said, "I can buy some when we get to Memphis. Now let's make haste."

"Virgil," Deekie said, "don't be so bitter. Last night was the most fascinatin' night of my life. The mansion we was in was bigger than city hall and the courthouse in Cartersville put together. Bigger than any of them plantation houses along the Etowah, at least the ones still standing. It was so grand, so opulent."

"So what?"

"Opulent, Virgil. It's a word that Jefferson taught me. It means overly fancy. I have never seen such a place, or such a crowd of *hoi polloi* types!"

"Actually, darling Deekie," Armistead said as he handed them each a bag and pushed them both through the door, "that while many people use the term *hoi polloi* to refer to society types, it really means ordinary people."

"Not from where me and Virgil was reared! Anyway, these people was more gussied up than a bride and her groom on their wedding day."

The three of them walked down the hotel's grand staircase tightly bunched, as Armistead sensed trouble might have followed them. The gambler took a heavy black satchel-like bag from Clay's only hand to free it should they be harassed in any way. Armistead then settled his account at the registry counter and had the stable boy bring the buckboard round front for them.

Clay watched, his gun hand freed, as the stable boy threw the bags of clothes onto the bed of the wagon. The last bag he pulled from Armistead's hand and struggled to raise it to the buckboard's height.

"Gee, what ya' got in here, mista, a sack of rocks?" The boy joked. Clay knew that Armistead had loaded the small sacks of gold coins he had been guarding all night into the satchel. Armistead simply laughed and flipped the boy a half dime coin.

"Wow, thanks mista," the young lad said, not expecting such a bounty.

They climbed aboard the wagon, Armistead and Deekie up front on the bench, with Clay at their back amongst the bags.

"Be ready with that Spencer of yours, Clay," Armistead said as he referred to the rifle. "More than a few people here either know or can have guessed that we're carrying that bounty of gold coins. Hell, some of Deekie's *hoi polloi* might just make a play against us using the local police to get their hands on these winnings I took from their elite last night."

"Jefferson, ya' yerself said that one player at our table was the chief of police," recalled Deekie.

"Exactly, Missy," the gambler responded. "Something one learns on my side of the law is that all policemen are corrupt. It's just a matter of how much."

"Ya' mean here in Nashville?" Deekie asked.

"I mean everywhere!" Armistead scowled.

"Well, I ain't shootin' no agent of the law, no matter how crooked they might be bent," Clay stated.

"Just fire over their heads, if you must, to hasten our escape," the gambler said as he whipped the reins and guided his team in the opposite direction of the rising sun. Their escape from Nashville was uneventful, although they would not know that the very next day, a man would come to their hotel inquiring after them.

The Penance of Peace

Three figures - canine, equine and upright spined - loped southwards as constant as the falling rain.

Cord McCullough hated riding in a downpour, although neither Trouble nor River seemed to mind too much, as long as it was not accompanied by any thunder or lightning. Cord had his leather duster turned up at the collar, but every so often, that collar would turn just so, allowing the water rolling off the back of his Stetson hat to drain down inside it. The cold rain trickled down his spine until the inside of his shirt was saturated through with it. The waters which rolled from the back of his hat that did not drain into his duster simply spouted atop of the bedroll that was tied behind the cantle of his saddle.

It had rained all this day, and the bare dirt trail had turned into a muddy mire. Cord wondered how it was affecting Trouble. He looked behind them to see a trail of marks warning that the horse's hooves had been sinking in up to their fetlocks. Had Cord not spent those hours in Caldwell buying the smile of the harlot, Esmerelda, pleasurable as that time was after the hot bath and warm whiskey, perhaps he might have had the luxury to stop and seek cover. But Cord knew if he did, he would have little chance to catch up with the three rustlers before they descended upon the stage coach somewhere along its route to Red River Station. No, he, Trouble and River must continue on, the drainage of the heavens be damned.

So, they pressed forward, and the persistence of the rain lulled Cord into a state of recollection. He had rather it not, but the harder he tried to forget it, the more the image of young Callie danced ahead of him along the trail. He thought of her in late '59, her belly fuller than the barn after harvest with their first, and what would be, only child. He remembered the small hours when she would lie awake in the night, uncomfortable in any position she might try. Cordell would caress her with his calloused hands in the darkness. They would whisper to each other, in an attempt not to wake her mother in the next room, with their plans for the future. Callie told him how she could not wait to deliver his son. Her mother had assured them it would be a boy by the way that she carried the child.

Cordell would spread his hands over her belly, his fingers splayed like the strands of a barn spider's finest web. He would feel the child move and kick and told her how he longed to hold the newborn in his hands, as it cried out with the joys of birth, whether be it a boy or a girl. Either way was God's blessing, he told her.

That came to pass on the second of December. Callie had the birth attended to by none other than Dr. Greenier, assisted by her mother. The doctor delivered unto them a beautiful, healthy baby boy.

Cordell had paced the porch as he awaited the birth, accompanied by his younger brother Sean. The brother had stayed on after harvest given Callie's condition, after their other and youngest brother, Conor, had returned home to Platte City, back in Missouri.

Cordell's child entered this world as darkness fell over fields of freshly fallen snow. As they celebrated inside, all gathered round mother and child, Cordell and Sean were distracted by a commotion through the window. A party of several riders appeared on the road that ran just beyond the farm's edge. They were shrouded in black and bore torches, reminiscent of a funeral procession. Even the horses had been draped in black mourning bunting. The reflection of the flickering torch flames in the ice encrusted snow made for an ominous shimmering effect. The visual composition of black and white was as starkly divided as the nation itself, and they would soon learn just how appropriate that was.

"You stay with your child," Cordell's brother Sean said, "I'll ride out and see just what this all is about." He did so, only for them several minutes later to hear the explosion of gunfire. Cordell moved to the window with purpose in time to see the belch of barrel fire coming from another round of volleys from the procession. He watched as Sean's bay mount returned to the barn, its saddle empty.

Cordell ran up the path to the road, never thinking to take the time to mount up. He found Sean halfway up the snow and ice encrusted path, a long trail of crimson blood streaked behind where he had so tortuously crawled.

Cordell could see his brother was bleeding from several shots through his gut. Sean was alive and fully conscious, but writhing in unbearable pain. They were soon joined by Doctor Greenier who had the wits to ride up on Sean's saddled bay, to which he had thought to quickly tie the farm's crude travois. It was a triangular frame dragged behind a horse as used by the local Indian tribes to move goods, but also to remove wounded warriors from battle. They dragged Sean back to the farm house upon it.

Snow continued to fall as Cordell carried Sean into the house. He cradled his brother in his arms as he paused just inside the front door, drawing the eyes of Callie and her mother. Callie and their son had been laid out in the main room of the house, the warmest as that was where the wood burning stove roared. She instinctively clutched the newborn to her bosom as if to protect it from the horrid sight. Seeing her reaction, Cordell wheeled and carried Sean into the cold stillness of the bedroom, away from the warming heat of the stove and the icy chill of the aghast stares of his wife and her mother.

Cordell was prepared to chase after the funeral party, but was talked out of it by Callie and Doctor Greenier. It was prudent, for when Sean gathered enough strength to speak, he told a tale that while brief was amazing in nature.

"Them damn Jayhawkers shot me up right good, didn't they Cordie?" His brother Sean winced while Doc Greenier unbuttoned his vest and shirt to examine the wounds. As the doc did so, the flop sweat on his brother's face seemed to Cord to turn into a bath of frothy anguish.

"What reason might they have?" Cordell asked.

"I 'sume none other than just for us being from Missoura…" he winced as the words drained out of him.

"I don't understand," said Cordell.

"They was mourning the hanging of that abolitionist John Brown in Virginia." Sean winced again in pain as Doc Greenier explored the three wounds. The smell was foul, a toxic mix of the bitterness of bile, the foul stench of excrement and the metallic sweetness of blood. The doctor looked up to Cordell only to shake his head as there was nothing he could do for the young man. Cordell followed the doctor out onto the porch, out of earshot of both Sean and Callie.

"Your brother's done been shot clean through the lower gut in three places. His descending intestines are punctured and I can't do nothing for him as I am no surgeon. Closest one is in Lawrence, as Doc Whiteford in Topeka is back east through the holidays. Sean might not be dead before we got there, but he sure wouldn't be strong enough by then to undergo the knife. It'd be best you say your goodbyes now before I fill him up with laudanum. Believe me when I tell you that what's in front of him is a most terrible way to die."

Cordell wiped away the tears that had formed in his eyes. He rushed back into the main room of the house, ignored Callie's call, and into the bedroom where his brother still writhed in excruciating pain.

"Doc Greenier is goin' to take care of you, Sean boy," he said to his brother.

"Tell me straight, Cordie," Sean pleaded as he grimaced, "I'm dying, ain't I?"

The look of fright that had overtaken his brother's face had tightened into an unyielding rigidness that even Sean's deluge of sweat failed to soften.

"Tell me straight, brother." Sean beseeched him. "You never lied to me that I knew of."

Cordell could see death creeping onto his brother's face. Outside in the snow, when he first got to him, Sean's eyes peered through a mask of shock. That had been supplanted by a terror as Sean read the doctor's face as he explored his wounds. But now, his brother's face was awash with nothing other than the resolute look of a man who faced his own imminent death. Even the reaction to the pain seemed to have faded away. Cordell knew Sean just wanted his brother to confirm that which his body and soul were already telling him was true.

"Doc can't do anything but help with the pain," Cordell leveled. He figured the words must have stung Sean's ears with the weight of their finality. A quiet lulled between them both. What must Sean be thinking? *What's to come next? What about my sins? What happens to my body?* .

"Thank you, brother," Sean's said. Somehow, the rigidity of his countenance had been released by hearing Cordell confirm the certainty of his dire future. His face melted into another tortured grimace as the searing pain returned. Sean had to drive away excruciating agony to collect his next few words. Cordell feared they might be his brother's last.

"I counted eight of them Jayhawkers," Sean said excitedly, his voice trembling with weakness. "They called me a *'bushwhacker'*, so they must be from these parts nearby. I didn't even so much as fire a shot at any of them a t'all."

"Calm yourself, Sean boy!" Cordell said to him as his own eyes filled with tears. "Rest. Rest on up now, brother."

"I can't rest… not until I know I'll be avenged… take vengeance on my undeserved death," Sean whispered.

"I will, Sean," Cordell said as he leaned forward and kissed his brother on the cheek, as he whispered in return, "I will see that they pay for what they have done to you. Measure for measure."

"I am so cold and thirsty," Sean whispered in his brother's ear. "I'm afraid to die, Cord." He choked out between gasps, "Pray for the deliverance of my soul."

"I will, brother," Cordell said, "I will. Now rest."

Doc Greenier entered to tend to his brother as Cordell left the room to check on Callie and the newborn boy. She had fainted with all the commotion. Doc Greenier had tended to her and said she was fine, but best to let her rest. In her hand Cordell found his mother's crucifix, that which he had given her. It had been removed from her neck to comfort her during her laboring, but Callie had refused to depart from it completely. She had grasped it so tightly that it left an imprint in her left palm.

Cordell then kissed their baby boy, nodded to her mother watching over them both, before he gently drew the crucifix from her grasp. Cordell kissed it first and then his slumbering wife immediately afterward. He hoped his lips would spread the cross' blessings upon her. He put the crucifix in his pocket, rose and then walked to the kitchen hearth, above which hung his shotgun. He took it down and filled his pockets with extra shells. He also took along the percussion revolver which he slowly and painstakingly took the time to load.

"Cordell, you owe it to your wife to stay here," her mother whined. "You can't make her both a mother and a widow on the same day."

"As much as I do owe it to her to stay, I owe it more to my brother to go," he responded. "She'll be here when I return, but he won't be, even if I stay."

"You mean *if* you return…" her mother added. "You don't even know where that party might have gone to."

"I know exactly where they were headed," he replied. Cordell went outside the house and freed the crude travois from Sean's bay. He then mounted the still saddled horse and rode off to where he knew the Jayhawkers traveled - Straight Creek, where he and Callie had witnessed the *Battle of the Spurs*.

As he rode through the crisp air of the darkened night, his blood pumped through him with the destructive vengeance of the rage of waters unexpectedly released from a freshly burst dam. But instead of brush and limbs being swept away by its fury, the loss was of his logic and sensibilities. A fury raged through him as he had never before felt in his young life.

The snow laden fields seemed to consume all sound, even that of the hooves of his mount. He soon came upon the tracks in the snow of the Jayhawker party which led to the very same rise where he and Callie had seen John Brown charge the federal marshals. He watched the mourning party in the distance, still under the glow of their own torches. Cordell waited and watched as the Jayhawkers mourned there in that spot that they must have held sacred. Cordell reckoned they would have to come past him to return to Holton. He removed the silver crucifix from his pocket, kissed it once more, and whispered, "Lord, protect my Callie and my newborn son should I not return. Please take mercy on Sean's soul."

He walked his brother's bay mare to hide it in a nearby copse of trees. He then returned to the dormant live oak and let its trunk shield him from the Jayhawkers view. Soon after they slowly headed his way in making their return.

Cordell had no problem with their honoring the death of John Brown, although Cordell considered him to be nothing more than a murderer himself. John Brown had raised his own "army" and had taken over the federal arsenal at Harper's Ferry on the morning of October 17th. He had hoped to free and arm the local slaves in order to continue his rebellion, but instead the local militia pinned him down at Harper's Ferry until the federal forces under Colonel Robert E. Lee and his adjutant, J.E.B. Stuart arrived.

Lee had quickly attacked the engine house in which Brown and his men were sheltered. Brown was captured and two of his sons were killed in the fighting. John Brown was charged with treason, slave insurrection and murder by the state of Virginia. He was found guilty in an expedited trial, only to be hung earlier on this day, the same that Cordell's son was born and his younger brother murdered.

Cordell McCullough pressed his body tightly up against the live oak as the eight riders of the party passed under the barren canopy of the tree's limbs. He brought up the double barreled ten gauge and instinctively aimed it at the back of the largest figure as they passed. They all wore black hooded capes over their clothes, with the hoods pulled up over their heads. Cordell stepped forward, sweeping the gun's double barrels side to side.

"Which of you cowards took the life of my brother?" he said plainly after they had passed. They turned their mounts to face him, but not one of them dared to reach for their guns. Their faces were framed by the darkness of their capes and hoods, but Cordell thought that those masks were not near so black as the recesses of their hearts.

"I said," Cordell repeated, "who shot my brother?"

"Whadya know, another Bushwhacker,..." said the shrouded face of the largest man. "I don't mind us killing another of your kind..."

The blast from Cord's shotgun ripped open the massive man"s chest, blowing him clear out of the saddle. His mount whinnied and reared. Cord spun to the next largest fellow, who was already in the process of drawing his gun. The second barrel of the shotgun belched a thunderous roar, and he also fell. Cord then dropped the shotgun as the bark of the tree next to him exploded. The shot had just missed his head, but in no way diminished Cord's concentration. He drew the revolver from his waistband, as he did not own a holster. Its first ball quickly found the chest of the man who had just fired upon him, spooking his mount in the process. That third Jayhawker teetered atop his horse before he also fell clean from the saddle.

All the horses were rearing in terror from the explosions and the thickening cloud of black powder smoke. This gave Cord a distinct advantage as those who aimed for him fought the erratic movements of their mounts. Another shot fired found and exploded more of the bark of the live oak, but it did not find Cord, who returned fire and shot a fourth man in the chest. He missed the fifth jayhawker as the animal he was upon lurched. His next shot found its target, just before his next two shots from his revolver felled two more riders.

The last rider was still in his saddle. He was clearly a young boy, somewhere between twelve and fourteen years by Cord's reckoning. He was frozen in terror, except for his face which cried out like a toddler after its first fall.

None of the fallen had moved. Their horses had run off, one dragging a corpse, its foot lodged in the stirrup.

Cord pointed his revolver's barrel at the last one, the crying child.

"Quit yer caterwaulin', boy," Cord said as he retrieved his shotgun. He cracked open its breech and ejected the two spent shells. When he reached in his coat pocket for replacements, the point of the silver crucifix jammed into his finger, reminding him of his need for mercy for the child. He loaded the shotgun and snapped close its breech. He returned the revolver to his waistband and pointed the shotgun at the youngster.

"Which one's yer kin, son?" Cord asked the boy. He pointed down to the big man, the one Cord had shot first.

"He's my Paw," the child said, sniffling between words, before correcting himself. "He was anyhow."

"Which one killed my brother back at the farm?" demanded Cord, still aiming at the boy.

His finger moved as slightly as if it had been a leaf on the wind. It stopped at the third man Cord had killed, the one he had missed at first.

"Take off that shroud your wearing, less you want to be buried in it," Cord yelled tersely. The child yanked it off as quickly as he could and threw it down at Cord's feet. Without it, he looked even younger than Cord had guessed. It was then that he thought about his own new boy's life that cried out to him from back home. Would he not look like this child in ten years or so?

"You know your way home, son?"

The boy nodded.

"Don't come back here. If you do, I'll shoot you deader than your daddy. You understand?"

The boy nodded again.

"Now go on and git," Cord said as he fired his shotgun into the air.

The horse reared and the boy spun him around and took off at a full gallop down the road. Cord walked off into the distance to retrieve the corpse that had been dragged by its mount. He pulled it back to the live oak and placed it in the snow alongside the road. Cord then checked the other bodies. Only one had any sign of life within it, although it was unresponsive and breathed in and out with a deathly rattle in its chest. Cord got on with pulling the other corpses under the live oak alongside the first. Finally, he pulled the wheezing body alongside the others knowing it would also perish soon enough.

He then collected up the weapons to show the law that they had all been fired upon him. He wrapped them in the boy's shroud and returned to the farmhouse.

Doc Greenier was still there. Callie still slept as her mother watched over her and the child. Cord turned to the doctor and asked simply, "Sean?"

"Gone," said the doctor solemnly, before adding, "I might have *accidentally* administered too large a dose of Laudanum."

"Good," admitted Cord, "although I would have liked him to know I killed the man who killed him."

"Which one was it? Which one did you get?"

"I got them all, save a boy some ten or twelve years old," Cord said, not bothering to say that one was alive when he left him. "The seven bodies are all out under a live oak near Straight Creek."

Cord laid out the weapons on the kitchen table, knowing the law would come round in the morning.

"Are ya' filled with pride now, son?" Callie's mother asked Cord as he returned the crucifix to his wife's palm.

"No, I am not," Cord confessed. "I am drained of all emotion. My body is completely empty, even of its soul."

Cord walked out the front door to unsaddle the bay. He patted it lovingly on the neck. "Sean always said you was nothing but trouble, though you gave me not a bit this night. My brother is gone now, and you are mine. Out of respect for Sean, I will call you Trouble, girl."

In the morning the sheriff came, inspected the weapons, and conversed with Doc Greenier about the shooting of Cord's brother, Sean. It was clearly deemed to be cold blooded murder.

"As for your killing them seven Jayhawkers, I'm not going to take you in as you're the only man left to protect these women and your son. I would surely have had to if you had killed that boy, but thank God you didn't. You still might have to face trial for the others, but we'll settle on that later. Just don't run off, Cordell."

"Cord, Sheriff" he corrected the lawman. "Cordell died with Sean boy. From now on its Cord, just plain Cord."

The doctor interceded to draw attention away from the highly agitated Cord. Greenier spoke to the sheriff after drawing the lawman aside.

"Sheriff, is it true what they are saying about John Brown's last words before the hangman's trap was sprung on him?"

The Sheriff gave the doctor a troubled look. "I am afraid it is. Came across the telegraph late yesterday. The outlaw even went to the trouble of writing out the words so as not to be misunderstood if his voice choked with emotion. He handed them to the executioner just before the noose was laid around his neck. It read:

'I, John Brown, am now quite certain that
the crimes of this guilty land will never
be purged away but with blood.'

Gives a man chills to read that, don't it, Doc?"

Doc Greenier looked upon the lawman stoically. He dropped his head slightly and spat out the following words:

"Sheriff, from my perspective as a man of medicine, I have come to believe that bloodletting only begets more bloodletting. No sins or crimes are ever purged by it, although many more are often inspired by it."

The Bluff City Blues

The city of Memphis lay before them naked atop a bluff along the shore of the mighty Mississippi River.

The city of 50,000 souls seemed deserted as they entered it late the next day. There were very few carts or horses in the streets, and even fewer folk shuffling about by foot.

"Why is this town so deserted?" Deekie asked Armistead. "I thought ya' said Memphis was a bustling river town?"

"I am afraid, Miss Deekie, you have just answered your first question with your second. You see, Memphis was indeed a bustling river town. Riverboats travel all the time either up to St. Louis or come up river from New Orleans. Well, earlier this year one of them coming from

N'awlins stopped off in Vicksburg where they was having an outbreak of the Yellow Fever. Brought it here. Now them that could have left town have already done so, and them that can't are hunkered down for fear of catching the fever."

"Ya' knew all this and still brung us here?" Deekie was incensed.

"Miss Deekie, you and I won't be here long enough to have to worry on that. Besides, my surprise for you and Clay is that I am putting you both up in a suite in the finest hotel in town, the Peabody. They have not had any reported cases there, so we will be fine."

"Just how bad is this outbreak?" Deekie asked, still frightfully concerned.

"They have had several outbreaks here over the years," Armistead said nonchalantly, "only a few hundred deaths."

"My God! Virgil did ya' hear that."

"I'm afraid our protector and rifleman drifted off a ways back," Armistead reported. "Let him sleep, after all he allowed us to do so last night when we pulled off the road.. I know I slept better knowing he was watching over us. He deserves the rest, and it's been a quiet and pleasant enough journey from Nashville. Besides, while he does so I have a little proposition to run past you."

The word "proposition" caught her attention. "And what, pray tell, might that be?"

"Well, Miss Deekie, let me start by saying that in Nashville, you took to the gaming parlors like a duck to June bugs. You must admit you enjoyed those fancy clothes and all those men's eyes pouring over you in them."

"Maybe," Deekie said coyly.

Figure 7: The Original Peabody Hotel

"Well, I would like you to offer you that life on a permanent basis. Oh, I know Clay has got his sights set on chasin' after his daddy down in Texas, but that don't mean you gotta go with him."

"But, Jefferson, I'm Virgil's gal!"

"I don't see no ball and chain! Instead of bein' his gal, be my partner. Tomorrow, Clay and I will collect on the debt owed me and I'll be as flush in cash as I ever been since the end of the war. Tomorrow night you and I will go to the parlors once again, but when we get back the following dawn, all you gotta do is say goodbye to Clay and step aboard the riverboat with me heading to St. Louis. We can work the gamblin' boats up and down the Mississippi, and all the gaming halls from New Orleans to Cairo, Illinois. You'd get to see half of America."

An uneasy silence abruptly descended upon the conversation. The seconds were counted off with only the *clop, clop, clop* of the team of horses on the city's cobblestone paved roads.

"I don't know, Jefferson," she finally said. "I'll need some time to ponder on that request."

"But you *will go* gambling with me again tomorrow night?" he asked, knowing that if she said yes, it was more certain to lure her into a long term arrangement. She agreed to one more night of such.

"Fine, thats enough for me," Armistead said, "for now."

It was then that the gambler reached behind him and rousted Clay. "Hey, look lively back there. We're coming into downtown Memphis, could be trouble brewing."

Clay roused himself from a deep sleep, and was amazed to gaze around at the deserted streets. "Only trouble I see is trying to find a soul to ask the time of."

"They got an outbreak of the Yellow Fever goin on here, Virgil," offered Deekie as if she had known all along. "Jefferson says its allright, cause he's puttin' us all up at the best hotel in town."

As she said this, Armistead led the team of horses around a corner onto Main Street. "The Peabody Hotel, in fact, dead ahead there on the corner of Monroe Street. It's only four years old. They paid out sixty thousand dollars to build it. Named it after George Peabody, a fat cat Yankee who helped raise the financing for it. He died just as they was opening her up. Costing me a small fortune to stay here. Can't get any of its seventy-five rooms for any less than four dollars a night, but there's gas lighting in every room. Only the best for the three of us while we're here."

"Lucky for ya' I'm protecting a large fortune back here," Clay said. "And y'ain't even collected the debt owed ya' here yet. I reckon ya' can cover it."

"Well, I sure hope that Yellow Fever can't cover the cost of a room here," Deekie said snidely.

"It hasn't been able to yet," Armistead quipped in reply. "It's why I settled on this joint in the first place."

The trio soon enough found themselves in the elaborate lobby of the grand hotel, with Clay carrying the heavy satchel of twenty dollar gold pieces, while Armistead had the porter look after the other bags.

They were led to a fine suite of two bedrooms adjoining a common sitting area. Armistead tipped the bellman with a paper note, not wishing to advertise the wealth of gold coins he carried.

"Iffen ya' don't mind, Mr. Armistead," Clay was still refusing to call him boss after the fuss that Deekie had made, "I'd like to go downstairs and ask about passage to Fort Worth."

"You go right ahead, Clay" Armistead replied, "while Miss Deekie and I freshen up. You have that fare added to my account, and we'll settle out in the morning after I pay you your pay for the trip."

Clay walked down the grand staircase to the lobby where he asked about travel at the registration desk, who then referred him to the concierge. Clay told him he needed the fastest passage possible for two to Fort Worth.

"Well, my good fellow," the concierge said sarcastically after noting the dusty field attire adorning Clay, "as it is, getting to that part of Texas presents some problems at the current time. You do have options, just none of them very direct or expedient. You can take the riverboat north to St. Louis and ride Missouri Pacific trains west, until you intersect with the Katy Flyer south again."

"They named the train after a woman?"

"Not Katie, Sir," the concierge corrected him, "the K-T. The Kansas-Texas Flyer. But that line currently stops at Dennison, Texas just after crossing over the Red River. You might be better served taking the Overland Stage Coach to Ft. Worth. They're talking of shutting it down soon. Once the railroads finally make it into Fort Worth, these old stage lines will become obsolete."

"I see," said Clay, although he was not familiar with the last word, but guessed at its meaning. "Yeah, that sounds more like what we're after. I'll need two tickets for the day after tomorra'."

"I'll contact them to hold two seats, in what name? I can have the front desk bill it against your room folio."

Clay gave the man his name and suite number, which caused the concierge to arch his eyebrows in unexpected respect. The concierge then handed him a slip of paper as a receipt, and warned him, "Be here no later than eight in the morning the day after tomorrow. The coach awaits you across the river. Passage on a riverboat ferry is included. But don't be late, lest you be left behind."

Clay thanked the man, but did not know to tip him, drawing a seething scowl from the concierge behind Clay's back. He went back to the room to return to Armistead and Deekie. The gambler sat resting at the desk, disassembling his Baby Colt to clean it, while Deekie sat in a winged back chair reading her book of short stories and poems by Edgar Allen Poe.

"Deeks, I thought Armistead said he was going to buy ya' some other story in Nashville. Ya' surely have read that book cover to cover and back again."

"We merely ran out of time, Clay," the gambler interceded, "as Miss Deekie got herself all absorbed in trying on nearly as many gowns as the dress seller had to show. In any case, there is a first rate bookseller in the lobby of this establishment, so while you and I are collecting a long overdue debt tomorrow, Miss Deekie can pick herself out a new book downstairs and spend the rest of the day plunging its depths."

"I can't wait to do so, Virgil," Deekie added, "I can have his beautiful suite of rooms all to my own while I read my new novel. I hope it'll be a story that will carry me around the world. Take my mind to places I am likely never to live to see. Jefferson says the bookseller downstairs has a a bunch of books second to none to choose from. He says they got stories from over the world down there."

"I see," was the only thing that Clay could think to respond. All he saw was that his Deekie was falling hard for all the luxuries Armistead had to offer. Yet there was one thing he knew she loved that he could afford to provide. "I reckon I'll stretch my legs downstairs a bit."

"Good idea, Clay," Armistead said to him, "but don't leave the lobby of the hotel. With the Yellow Fever goin' about, it's not prudent."

"I reckon not," Clay said, feeling as if he had just been scolded by the gambler. He was anxious to get both Deekie and himself away from here. Only tonight and tomorra' was left, and the following morning the two of them would catch the ferry to the stage coach across the river, before rolling on to Texas.

"I'll walk with y'in the lobby, Virgil," Deekie said, and started to rise from her chair.

"Deeks, best ya' not," he answered, "as I got some serious thinking to do. I won't be long, just got some knots in my mind to untangle."

Clay left the room and headed once more to the main staircase.

"Well, that sure was rude of Virgil," Deekie said aloud for Armistead to hear, "and not very much like him, a t'all."

"*Hmmmnf!*," the gambler replied, not looking up from his gun cleaning task.

"Just what's that supposed to mean, Jefferson?"

"Well," he said, dropping the disassembled parts of his gun and turning to look at her, "did you ever stop to think that perhaps he's off to ponder just what he's going to do with that windfall of riches when I pay him his earning's tomorrow? Ten days at twenty-five dollars per works out to be one-quarter of a thousand dollars. That much money, likely more than he ever held in his hands at one time before, can make a man more than a little crazy. Did you ever think that just maybe the knots he's trying to untangle are if he should go on alone to Fort Worth? He'd save on a full fare. It's not as if you're not going to be a third wheel anyhow once he finds his Paw."

"*Diddy*..." she corrected him.

"What's that?"

"He don't call him Paw, Jefferson," Deekie explained. "His father has always been his *Diddy,* "

"It don't matter if he calls him Daddy, Poppa or Padre, I surely can see that you're the one who is going to get ignored, Miss Deekie. And don't be surprised if Clay comes back just to tell you that the two of you are through. Why not get the drop on him and tell 'em you're going to be joining me on the riverboat to St. Louie in a couple days time? I know you been thinking on it."

Deekie closed her book. She had been thinking on his proposition. Not so much as something serious, but more as a savory daydream made all the more attractive by the possibility that it *could* actually come true. She thought it not unlike a church raffle, that so long as one held a ticket, she could hold onto the possibility of a dream, as unexpected as it might be, to come true. She didn't wish it to, but loved the dream of seeing the world.

Yet, she knew in her heart that her Virgil would never abandon her, as she had once him. For that reason, along with the fact that she loved her man, she knew she would turn down the gambler Jefferson Calhoun Armistead's offer. But still, that could wait until after one more night in a beautiful dress by his side during a bout of all-night high stakes gambling. She would keep him waiting, and keep her dream alive for a few nights more.

"Yer right, Jefferson, I am thinking on it."

In the lobby, the hotel bookseller prepared to close up his shop just as the dinner hour approached. As he arranged a shelf of titles behind the counter, he heard someone enter the still open doors of the store from the lobby. He could hear the heaviness of the footsteps, and knew without looking that this interminably late customer was a man.

"I will be with you in just a second, *Suh*," came from the clerk, his arms still high over his head behind the counter. Having finished his rearrangements, he turned to see the one-armed Clay in his dust covered road clothes in the space where he thought he might find an actual customer. The man looked as lost as the Biblical Adam himself.

"Might there be something that I may present to you, *Suh*?" He hoped that any sarcasm in the last word was not readably noticeable.

"Well, not for me, mind ya'," Clay apologized, "on account I never had much schooling, but my gal loves to read. At least lately, as she now has some time for it. I want to get her a book full of exciting foreign adventure and such."

"I see, *Suh*, and what writers does the young lady prefer?"

"Well, she is currently reading stories and poems by Edgar Allen Poe," Clay answered, "and really taken a likin' to them. Well, to be honest, I think she has read them many times over by now."

"I see," said the bookseller, "and thus the need for a new tale of lore. Foreign travel, adventure and a bit of mysticism, perhaps? I may have just the thing."

The bookseller raced his fingers along a shelf and stopped on a book, finely bound in leather. He pulled it from the shelf and announced apologetically, "Mr. Poe was was born in Massachusetts, although was known to spend much time in Richmond and Baltimore, where he died. Like him, this fellow is also a Yankee author, I hate to say. But this book is extremely good, and tells the tale of a one-legged sea captain chasing a white whale halfway across the world. It's called *'Moby Dick, or The Whale'* and was written a decade or so before the war by a fellow named Herman Melville. Unlike Mr. Poe, this author is still alive living somewhere up New England way. I am quite sure your lady will enjoy it immensely. But I have to ask you to decide quickly or I will have to request you to come by tomorrow. I am expected by the hotel to be closing just now so as not to interfere with the dinner hour."

"A one legged sea captain?" Clay said, massaging through his shirt sleeve the fleshy stump of his left forearm, "I wonder what took yer mind to that? Still, it does sound just like the sort of story she might enjoy," Clay said, taking the book into his own hand. The bookseller watched as the crippled customer held it as delicately as if it were made of the finest porcelain. Clay handed the book back to the man, as he said, "I'll take it, how much might it be?"

The book seller looked at Clay just as he pulled out an unexpected large wad of bills from his pocket, the remnants of his final pay from Horace Woodard, the groundskeeper at the Gilreath cottage. The bookseller could see it was more than enough to cover the cost of the novel several times over, so he generously quoted Clay a price only twice that at which the book would normally sell. When Clay agreed without reservation, a shadow of guilt overcame the bookseller, and in order to suppress it he agreed to wrap the book in his finest violet foil paper at no charge, even finishing it off with a beautiful yellow silk ribbon and the best bow that his greedy fingers could tie.

Clay returned to the suite and was able to hide the gift of the book from Deekie. The next morning, he was to accompany Armistead to collect the debt in the countryside just outside Memphis. With Deekie still asleep, he lay the magnificently wrapped book on the night table next to her just as they departed.

They stopped at the front desk and Armistead registered his satchel of gold coins for storage in the hotel safe. He thought it much safer there than leaving the coins in the room, even though Deekie would be there throughout the day until their return. It certainly was safer than taking the small fortune with them upon this day's journey.

Clay soon had the unusual sensation of riding up front on the buckboard next to Armistead. He had no bounty to guard, except for the reputation of the Whitworth sniping rifle that Armistead demanded him to bring along. After about an hour's travel, they rested upon a hill overlooking a farmhouse situated on a vast, sprawling tract of land.

"Clay, do you see that farmhouse down there? I figure it to be about a half mile from here, wouldn't you say?"

"I'd reckon closer to two-thirds or so," Clay replied. "It's mighty fine a building to call just a farmhouse."

"And fine it is, Clay. Let's call it a manor house, then. And we'll agree it sits at two-thirds of a mile off. That man living there owes me a small fortune from gambling that he's been finding every excuse not to pay. I want you to stand here with this Whitworth rifle upright by your side, where he can see you, that's all."

"So this is the man ya' sent that target to with the note scribbled on it," said Clay. "Yer wantin' him to think that I can easy shoot him dead from this spot. What he don't know is I wouldn't do that even if ya' was to hold a pistol to my head."

Armistead gave his protector another wicked glance and said, "It is exactly that last bit that he has no need to know, now isn't it?" Armistead watched Clay awkwardly lower himself from the wagon, and then he whipped the reins and pulled away, leaving Clay all alone.

Clay waited and watched until the buckboard pulled up to the manor house off in the distance below him. A well dressed figure, no mere farmer at all, came out of the impressive structure wielding a shotgun and appeared to be threatening to shoot Armistead if he did not drive off immediately. Then Clay saw the gambler point his arm in his direction and the landowner held a cupped hand over his eyes, for the morning sun was coming up behind Clay.

Clay could see Armistead, his arms waving gently as he talked to the man, like the branches of a willow tree on a spring breeze. The man slowly lowered his shotgun. Clay guessed that the gambler had told him that he would leave his sniper on that hill if he did not pay. That if he did not pay this day, he could be struck down when he least expected it, anytime he might egress from his fine abode.

Armistead must have explained that it wouldn't matter if the man was able to somehow get a message to the law. That his sniper would merely hide in the underbrush of the terrain until the opportunity arose to settle the debt on his behalf with a deadly accurate six sided bullet.

The man from the manor house turned and walked slowly, defeatedly into the house. After perhaps fifteen minutes, he returned carrying a weighty wooden box. When Armistead inspected its contents, he began to object vehemently. The man carried the box back into the house, and after a long delay re-emerged, again carrying the box.

Upon his second inspection, Armistead seemed pleased. He closely inspected whatever the box contained, meticulously inspecting its contents. Then, Armistead transferred the contents from the box into another satchel which was identical to the one in the hotel safe. After doing so, the gambler reached out his hand to shake, which the landowner refused. Armistead then jerked the reins and the team of horses pulled the buckboard off the property and out of Clay's sight.

After a lengthy delay, Armistead returned in the buckboard to collect Clay. His face was hard creased with a self-pleasing smile. He could barely contain his glee.

"Clay, I knew my investment in that Whitworth and your keen firing of it would pay off handsomely. I had all but given up on getting that money from that guile bastard. He had the nerve to try and pay me off in silver coins, until I made him go back inside and make payment in gold, which he finally did. This satchel is full of eagles, double eagles, even quarter and half eagles. Likely only loose change for this miserly merchant. But he did come up with payment finally after seeing you perched upon this hill."

"I am happy for ya'," Clay said.

"It's all thanks to you, Clay. He greatly desired to avoid the fear of having a sniper potentially taking aim upon his Brit carcass every time he walked out of his magnificent country manor house."

Clay pulled himself up onto the bench of the wagon with his one hand and one good arm. "I thought ya' were pretty sly yerself setting this whole thing up so the man would have to look up into the sun to see me. Not much chance at that range and under those conditions he'd notice I only had one arm. Were it?"

"Clay, he didn't need to know that at all," said Armistead, "but even if he did, I would have told him that even with one arm mangled, such as yours is, you still made that pattern of hits in that target I sent ahead."

Clay added, "But not at the distance ya' said."

Armistead snapped the reins and the team of horses were underway. "Clay, could you or could you not have dropped the man next to my wagon from this hillside? Yes or no?"

"Yeah, I reckon I could," said Clay, "but I wouldn't. Armistead, y'ain't nothing but a user of people. Y'used me here this morning to get yer gold. Y'used Deekie the other night to hide yer cheatin' ways. No tellin' how many ways y'used other people all along in yer life. Sooner or later, that's gonna catch up to ya'."

"Well, Clay, tonight I'll use sweet Miss Deekie one more time as my angel of deception, and tomorrow morning I'll settle up with you and then our paths will separate forever."

"I'll be glad when that comes to pass," Clay said.

No, not really, thought Armistead, *for tomorrow morning you'll watch as the lovely Miss Deekie boards that Mississippi Riverboat with me.*

A Near Miss or Two in Memphis

They strutted along the riverfront promenade in a cocoon of excitement that glistened with the rising sun.

"Oh, Jefferson, what an exciting evening that was," Deekie said. "I think ya' did real good tonight, although not quite as good as on our first night's outing together in Nashville."

"Well, so many of the big money folks have left Memphis because of this dreadful Yellow Fever business. Yet, I assure you, Miss Deekie, with you all dolled up in these fine clothes as you are, especially in this delightful yet elegant gown, I assure you we have nothing ahead of us but many evenings of joint and continued success."

As he said this, Armistead reached over to play teasingly with the frilly shoulder of her green gown. "You really are quite a lovely woman, Miss Deekie, and those men I was playing against tonight had no choice but to smother their gazes upon you."

"Well, Jefferson, that may be, but it seems to me that these men y'are playing against are catching on to yer bag o' tricks. I mean telling y'along with the invite to leave yer under the shoulder gun back at the hotel. One of these days yer going to find yerself outnumbered and overpowered."

"Deekie, I may have left that pocket pistol and the shoulder holster with Clay back at the hotel, but I still have a few tricks up my sleeve. Don't you fret none about me. All you need to worry over is how to cut your Clay loose when we get back to the hotel and then you can get on that riverboat with me later this morning. It'll be moored just ahead up here along the river in another hour or so."

"Is it even wise for us to be walking back to the hotel down here along the river with the fever about?" Deekie asked her companion.

"Do you see anyone about to catch the fever from?" Armistead grinned as he shared his reasoning.

"No, there's not a single soul on the streets," Deekie said, feeling somewhat reassured, "at least at this hour."

"Nor near any other," Armistead's grin expanded, "and for that reason it could not be any more safe, my girl."

"But these mosquitos are biting me up to no end."

They had been strolling along the riverfront promenade, when Armistead escorted her across the street. There they walked alongside the length of fine cedar fences that marked off the yards of some of the finest riverfront homes in the city.

Soon they came upon an alleyway that yielded access to the coach houses of these fine domiciles. Armistead slipped his arm through her own as he lied, telling her the alley was the shortest way back to the hotel.

Deekie stopped hard in her tracks just as the line of fences gave way to the rear alleyway. "Don't be foolish Jefferson. Just a little further down Front Street we can turn onto Monroe and the hotel is only a block or two east.

Armistead, sensing her hesitancy, used his hand to firmly grasp the soft flesh of her upper arm just below the shoulder. He turned her abruptly so that she again faced across the road to gaze out upon the river beyond.

"Jefferson," Deekie protested, "please be a little more gentle in yer handling of me. If I didn't know ya' was a gentleman, I would swear yer gittin' a little too restless with me. "

"I am becoming more than just a little restless with you, Miss Deekie. For the past several days you have told me how much you wanted to see the world. Well, woman, that river is the gateway to it all. Never been to *N'awlins? St. Louie? The Caribbean? Across that sea to Mexico? Cuba?* These river waters can take you on to anywhere on this earth. Let me show you a world you will never ever come to know as long as you stay with Clay."

With having said this, Armistead turned her again to face him, once more with a bit more force than she cared for. He then leaned in, his lips in search of hers.

Deekie put her outstretched palm on his chest and pushed as strongly as she could to arrest his advance. "I have been perfectly clear wit' y'all along, Jefferson, that I am Virgil's woman. He may not be able to take me across the seas, but I am sure that even if he did it would only teach me that my only place is by his side."

The gambler's eyes collapsed into cold black hollows, as if he had finally recognized that he had utterly failed in his quest to convince her to join him. He had lost his main wager, but now he only wanted to cash in a side-bet that Deekie wasn't even aware she had made.

His hand swung up rapidly, grabbing the wrist of the hand that Deekie had been pushing into his chest. He yanked it down violently. "Let's see just how much your Clay wants you back after I'm finished with you, woman. He pulled her forcibly into the alley, and with his other hand tore at the front of her dress so violently that the material ripped, partially exposing her left breast.

She instinctively clutched her arms high to cover her nakedness. A primal, sheer panic raced through her. How quickly this gentleman had turned predator on her. She then realized that all Armistead had to do was to take her by force in this deserted alley, after which he could leave her there, beaten senseless perhaps, before escaping aboard that riverboat in only a few hours.

"My God, Jefferson, have ya' lost all yer senses? What about Virgil?" Deekie struck at him with the arm opposite her ripped bodice.

"I am gonna teach you just how much a real man with two hands is capable of pleasuring a woman," Armistead snarled. "But don't you fret none, darlin' Deekie, after our little tryst is over, when you change your mind, you can still come aboard that riverboat with me."

He pushed her violently against the wooden doors of a finely crafted carriage house. His one hand clutched firmly at her neck as he reached down with the other to grab a fold of the dress between her knees. He pulled it up, and exposed the soft creamy flesh of her thighs, where her black silk stockings abruptly ended.

Armistead then slipped his finger under the garter of the corset where the dark and light tones met. He plucked the strap like a banjo string. Its spanking strike upon the tender skin of her thigh produced a wave of fear in her that was surpassed only by her foolish shame for ever having allowed this situation to come to pass.

"You see, girl, one way or the other you gotta pay for these fine clothes," Armistead seethed.

She could only think of Willet Blackwell and how his temper had so quickly changed just before the abuses he had rained down upon her. She had told herself never again. She bolted her knee as swiftly and as violently as she could in an attempt to inflict severe pain upon Armistead's manhood. But the gambler had anticipated this move and merely squeezed her knee with his own thighs and in doing so, slowed her attacking stroke rendering her attempt futile.

Armistead then pressed himself against her and brought his lips to land upon hers with an unnatural force. His eyes were flooded with a mixture of rage and lust. From the corner of his mouth, his lips still pressing hard upon hers, he said, "I have been looking forward to this, girl, by hook or by crook, since I first laid eyes on you. You passed on the my offer's hook, now you'll get the crook."

She could feel his lower hand as it explored the smoothness of her thighs. His finger taunted her by again digging under another of the garter straps, and pulling it taut until it snapped hard once more. "There's of plenty pleasure coming just ahead to erase that pain, Deekie."

Armistead then slid his hand up under the bunched canopy of her gown to her most sensitive and private areas. His other hand remained clenched around her neck, its tight grasp intended to choke her into submission. But Deekie refused to submit.

"Virgil...will...kill...ya'," she gargled through his chokehold.

"Well," Armistead snickered, "it just so happens your one-armed sharpshooter isn't here to save you."

Just then, she felt Armistead being violently ripped off of her and thrown to the ground. The shock of the reversal overtook her. She instinctively slid down into a protective crouch and for what seemed an eternal spell sucked in as much air as possible through her freed, but bruised, throat. She attempted deep draws of sweet fresh air, each she hoped would restore a calm to her senses. Instead, she fought razor sharp edges in her pitched breaths, which horridly honed the slicing pangs in her aching lungs.

When Deekie regained some semblance of control over her breathing, she looked up expecting to see her Virgil, who had miraculously come to protect her from the climax of her foolish decisions with Armistead. Instead, her eyes at first did not recognize the huge hulking figure in front of her. She knew it was not her Virgil by its bulk, but especially when it used two powerful hands to pick up the muddied Armistead from the slurry of dirt and morning dew draining from the center of the alleyway. Then, one meaty hand held him up, as effortlessly as the gambler had held her against her will, while the other formed a fist that pummeled him relentlessly with heavy thudding blows.

"Armistead, ya've been a very nasty fella'," the hulking figure said. It was upon hearing his voice that Deekie recognized the blacksmith, Orrin Fletcher James.

"Thank ya', Orrin," Deekie called to him, panting.

"Ya' stay where y'are, girl," the blacksmith snarled, "when I am done with him, I'll finish what he started. I 'member how ya' stared at me back at the farm. Ya' won't have to wonder 'bout what ya' missed out on much longer."

The words were spoken with a force that both terrorized and froze her. Deekie stayed crouched against the door of the carriage house, afraid to move. Orrin continued to pummel away at Armistead, every blow he threw was accompanied by words of accusation that he spat aloud.

"You thought you could pass off those counterfeit Confederate guns on Mr. Goodlette? Make me look like an ass? You thought he'd not find out? You took his gold and figured you'd sail away on the Mississippi never to be seen again? You was wrong, Mr. Jefferson Calhoun Armistead. Now, you'll pay for it. You'll pay with everything you got."

Deekie stood to break and run up the alley, but Orrin the blacksmith released Armistead's throat and moved to cut her off. The gambler fell to his knees, wheezing for breath.

"I told you I ain't just done with you yet, girl." He threw her back hard against the carriage house doors.

In the short bit of time it took Orrin to do this, Armistead, still on his knees in the dirt, had fished into his vest pocket for something. As Orrin turned to renew his assault on the gambler, Armistead pointed a miniscule Derringer at the blacksmith. Orrin reached for the gun, and grasped the gambler's hand just as its first shot rang out. The ball found the fleshy area just above the blacksmith's hip. The shock of it drove the blacksmith backward.

Orrin quickly shook off the jolt of the shot and lunged forward at Armistead. He wrestled for control of the toy-like gun before the gambler could freely complete his aim for the blacksmith's heart. Orrin crushed his hand, pressing it hard into the small, but unyielding gun's metal. Armistead's finger somehow found the trigger, and the second ball found the strike of hot powder and shot upwards and lodged into the blacksmith's meaty shoulder.

Orrin Fletcher James flinched, but nothing more. He released Armistead's hand, knowing the gun had expelled its only two rounds. Orrin then slid both his hands around Armistead's neck and raised him from his knees as he drove him back violently against the carriage house doors.

Deekie had moved out of the way just in time before the gambler's body slammed into the door's frame, causing the whole structure to shudder and quake. Deekie slowly backed up the alley toward the river as she watched Orrin Fletcher James continue to choke the life out of Armistead. Deekie thought she could even hear the fine bones of his neck snap, one by one. The gambler's bulging eyes went from registering an unrelenting terror, yielded to a debilitating shock, before finally expressing recognition that the end had come indeed from Orrin's overwhelming force. Then, still open, they melted into lifelessness.

The blacksmith did not loosen his death grip on the gambler, even after he felt the body go limp. Orrin's face was overcome with an ungodly ecstasy that could have almost been mistaken for carnal lust. Perhaps this was bloodlust, Deekie thought, although there had been barely any letting of that most precious essence of life. Orrin was clearly savoring the choking of life from his prey. Did he relish the sheer advantage of power he held over most men? With no other weapon than his own hands, he could kill anyone he so desired. But how often did he have the actual opportunity to do so? It clearly brought to him a rush of ascendant dominance, of contested superiority, of utter eminence. She could see this painted sickly upon his face, yet no sooner than the gambler's last breath was expended, Orrin's luminous state of bliss began to slowly fade. Deekie could see that more than his greatly enjoying this, he needed it. Then Deekie feared his needing more of it.

Perhaps Orrin's comment about finishing off what Jefferson had started, she thought, would culminate in his strangling the life out of her body. She could still feel the grip of the gambler's grasp around her neck, and thought how much more terrible would be that of the strong man. Her fear spiked within her. It crippled her, especially when Orrin turned his head to look at her with his death-crazed stare.

"Come over to me, Deekie girl" he panted.

She slowly began move backwards, one step after another out of the alleyway.

"I said come here," demanded Orrin. The blacksmith dropped the lifeless body of the gambler, so that it fell face first into the fetid dirt, already soiled with his last release of bodily waste fluids. Deekie watched the dead fall of Jefferson's corpse and envisioned her own falling later alongside it. It was then that she finally bucked up enough courage to overcome her terror. Deekie spun round and bolted back to the riverwalk.

Orrin made a brisk movement to catch Deekie, but as he did so the ball wedged in his hip caused a lightning bolt of pain to wrap around his legs like a vine of thickets, tripping him up as he fell into the wretched slurry of dirt, wetted with the gambler's filthy last release of death.

"That's all right," he said under his breath, "I know where she and that one-armed cripple are heading - Fort Worth, Texas." Then, he thought to himself as he crawled over to Armistead's body to relieve it of the gambler's overnight winnings, *This gambler was too wise to ever say exactly where his next stop was to be, but those other two couldn't keep their mouths shut. Goin' to find Clay's "Diddy" in Fort Worth, where I'll be waiting for them. I'll get Goodlette's gold back from them in that cowtown.*

Deekie ran all the way back to the Peabody Hotel. She clutched her exposed breast in the crook of her elbow, covered with her opposite hand. The Peabody was just atop the bluff that front street climbed and a short distance to the east on Main and Monroe. As she shot across the lobby, the day clerk, having just come on duty and seeing the frantic jerk of her movements, yelled out from his desk, "Miss, are you in distress? Can I assist you?" Deekie ignored him and ran up to the suite, where she banged on the door, flailing with both hands. Clay opened the door as soon as he had heard her voice screaming from the hall. He pulled her into the room.

As he did her torn dress fell open, once again exposing her breast.

"What in the world happened to ya', Deekie?"

"Virgil, I am so sorry. Armistead wanted me to leave ya' for him," she was panting heavily. "When I said no, he tried to force himself on me."

Tears were streaming from her eyes. She looked through them to see a plume of anger rise in him.

"I'm gonna kill that son of a bitch," Clay seethed, his face red with fury. "When I get through with him, he'll wish he was already dead."

"He *is* already dead," Deekie cried out, loudly, as she began to sob. Clay pulled her close to his chest and blanketed her in the tight embrace of his arm.

"Ya' killed him?" Clay whispered into her ear. He certainly knew she was capable of it.

"No. Orrin, the blacksmith from the farm south of Nashville pulled him off me and strangled him. Right before my eyes, Virgil. I could hear the bones in his neck snap. It was awful."

Clay tightened his embrace of her. His anger had peaked, yielding just as his curiosity was piquing.

"Serves Armistead right. But why would Orrin Fletcher James be here?"

"Looking for Jefferson and us..." Deekie murmured from her face buried deep in the safety of his chest.

"Us?" said a startled Clay. "Why would he be looking for us?"

Deekie fought to control her hysteria. She felt protected in the arm of her Virgil, and soon got herself under control.

"He said them Confederate guns Jefferson and yerself sold to Orrin's boss were all fakes. Orrin means to kill us all to get Goodlette's gold back."

"Fakes," Clay said with surprise. "Well, that Armistead sure is a sneaky bastard."

"Ya' mean *was* a sneaky bastard," corrected Deekie. "I know Orrin thinks we're all in on this together. We gotta leave here right quick like. Ya' don't understand, Virgil, that man enjoyed chokin' the life out of Jefferson. I mean he really enjoyed it. Ya' didn't have to look at his face like I did. I hope ya' never do."

Deekie pulled herself from Clay's embrace and immediately began to change out of the green dress. When she had, she threw the unwanted gown vengefully into a corner. Almost as a final act of rebellion, the gambler's gift of the gown filled full of air, ballooned in flight and landed haphazardly.

"Come on, Virgil, let's git," Deekie yelled in panic.

"All right, we'll git the hell outta here." Clay looked upon Deekie's bare back, and noticed a large red angry welt that ran across her shoulder. "Did Jefferson do this to ya'?" he asked, as he moved forward to touch her.

"What," Deekie replied just before Clay's fingernail scraped across her welt. "No, that's from those darn mosquitoes down by the river. We walked through what must have been a swarm of them last night on our way to the gambling house. Damned thing itches like crazy. I couldn't stop scratching at it all night long. I guess I tore up the skin back there. Now, will ya' get yerself together already, Virgil?"

"Allright, Deeks, we'll check out of here and make straight across the river to the Overland Stage Coach and be on our way to Texas. Am I gonna have to keep my Navy sixes ready for that Orrin fella?"

"I don't think so," Deekie replied. "Armistead put two Derringer balls into Orrin before that blacksmith strangled him. That should slow him down. Last I saw he was wallowin' in the dirt like the swine he is."

Clay watched as she dressed into her riding clothes. They were still dusty from the journey through Tennessee. It felt good to have the old Deekie back.

"Well, well! That Armistead was sure slicker than deer guts on a doorknob," Clay said, "but two Derringer balls in a man as big as Orrin ain't gonna do much more than slow him down, lessen they pierced his heart."

"We're not nearly that lucky, Virgil," Deekie scowled.

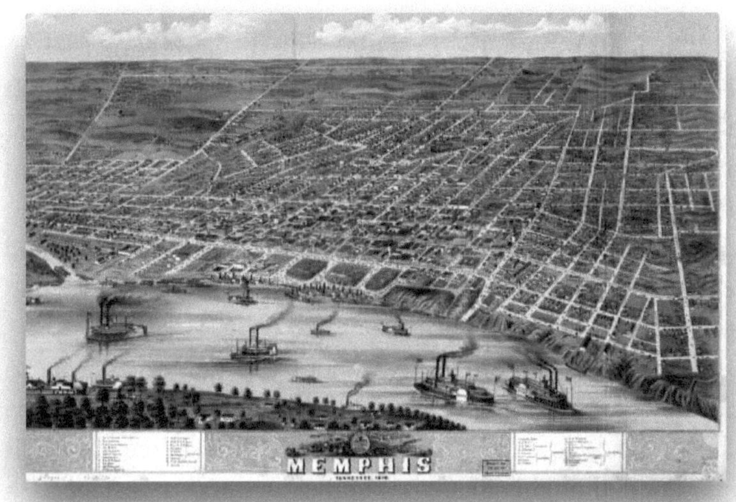

<u>*Figure 8: Memphis on the Mississippi, circa 1870*</u>

Another bit of luck had avoided them as well. For while it was true that Memphis had experienced multiple outbreaks of Yellow Fever before and since the Civil War, that of 1873 would be the worst yet, killing over 2,000 of the city's 50,000 population. Only an outbreak five years later in 1873 would prove more lethal, killing some 5,000 souls.

What was the greatest sin of the disease was that it had not been understood how it was passed to the population. They did not realize it was carried by mosquitoes. In fact, the disease had been delivered to the South from slave ships, carried aboard by West African mosquitoes, which then spread aboard other ships as they passed up and down the Mississippi. Yellow Fever thrived on long, sultry, wet summers followed by mild autumns, when the insects could breed unceasingly. It proved to be passed readily among the congested riverside towns, with outbreaks in New Orleans, Vicksburg, and Memphis. In 1873, even the distant town of Dallas, Texas had fought an outbreak of Yellow Fever that fall.

In Memphis, the first outbreak of the fever struck in 1828, affecting 650 and taking the souls of 150 residents. It re-occurred again after twenty-seven years later in 1855, infecting 1250 and killing some 220 townsfolk. It emerged once more in 1867, with a renewed vengeance, causing 2500 cases and 550 deaths. By the time the 1873 panic had begun, few who could afford to leave the city dared stay behind.

The pattern of the fever that had emerged over those years proved it to infect white town dwellers, at least those who had not left the city, in much higher percentages. It was later thought that the higher natural resistance to Yellow Fever in the former slaves and their offspring was due to the generations of their ancestors that had survived along the African coast. Despite this fact, many of the freemen city dwellers died also from the outbreak. While their infection rates were lower, the fact that most blacks had little or no resources to leave the city added to their desperate situation.

Yellow Fever would manifest itself in severe pain in those affected. The inflicted could, on several occasions, be seen running through the streets like lunatic madmen suffering from their overwhelming distress. Often after an initial fever, a slight remission could follow after which the affected might evidence a telltale blackish vomit. After this, failure of the liver and kidneys could lead to death in as little as two weeks, after painting the afflicted with the yellow jaundiced color associated with the disease's feared telltale name.

End
of
Part 1

Figure 9: The Mighty Mississippi

Reflections on Crossing the Midpoint

Crossing the river's flow as it scours distant shores,
Its currents etch away all things left loosely moored,
The dignity of life subsides, as the ferry harshly oared,
Defiles with cruel uneven tides, its blight be ne'er restored,
Like fate itself, its flow abides,
and remains thus forever scored.

Crossing the midpoint hides a bevy of dangers unaware,
Turbulent, murky waters chide, yet defiantly never spare,
Once purest souls, so full of pride, of sinful acts most err'd,
No rest, no solace, nor hope survives,
cast before a mercy impaired,
Left unreconciled to silent strides,
in which they suffer dark despair.

The river bends crooked, muddy, upon itself, true,
As even the straightest of men are oft prone to do,
Despite serpentine lives, they still side-wind through,
Matched gates of Sunset, Sunrise, each as God paints anew,
And yet, these lowly souls can never aspire to pursue,
Shelter from the flagitious acts their hands known to do,
Amidst the shores of youth,
its shadowed trails once more renewed.

Figure 10: The Old Butterfield Overland Mail and

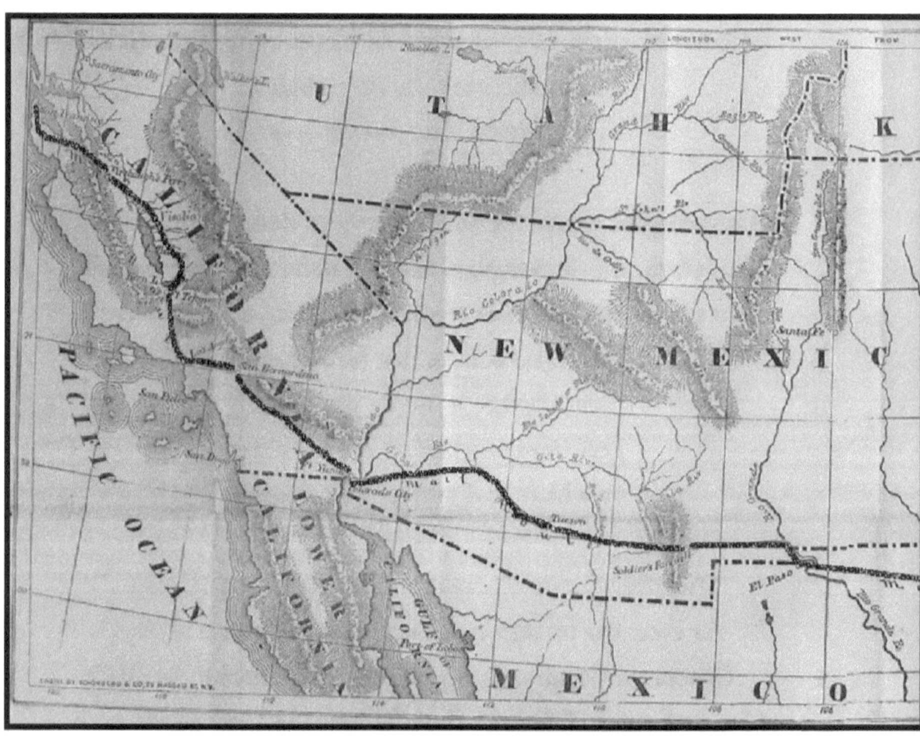

Passenger Stage Coach Trail
(The Ox Bow Route)

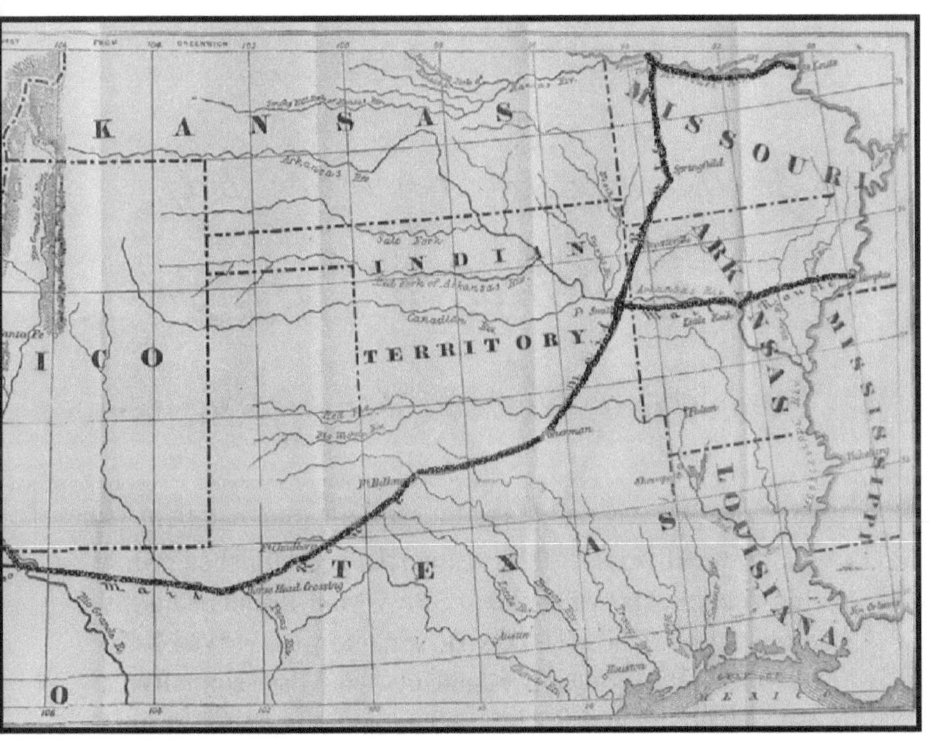

The Way Across

Stretching out like temptation itself, the Ox Bow Trail called out to those who sought adventure and purpose.

Way back in 1858, with the country in dire need of an overland mail route, John Butterfield established what would become known as the Ox Bow Mail Route using his line of stage coaches. The Ox Bow name was derived from the shape of the route. It began in two Mississippi River towns, Memphis and St. Louis, and came together in Fort Smith, Arkansas. From there it travelled westward through Texas, New Mexico, the Arizona Territory and finally into Southern California. Between Arkansas and Texas, a lawless corner of the Indian Nations Territory (modern day Oklahoma) was transited.

The entire journey from the Mississippi River to San Francisco was 2800 miles and could take up to 26 days to traverse. The route was laid out as southernly as possible to keep it mostly free from snow. Butterfield's Ox Bow Route became a logistical enterprise which ran twenty-four hours a day with a multitude of stations supplying fresh teams of horses and the skilled teamsters to drive them.

Passengers paid handsomely to travel on the coach along with the mail, as the realization of a transcontinental railway was still another decade off. A typical coach would accommodate nine travelers. Any additional passengers would require adventurous ticket holders willing to travel outside the coach, often atop the rolling, shuddering wagon.

The vast distances traveled made the coaches and their passengers easy targets for desperados. Coach robberies became commonplace until the coach service was interrupted in 1861 by the Civil War, which drew the direly needed stock of men and horses east to the conflict.

After the war, the Butterfield Overland Stage Coach Line was reconstituted in part by David Butterfield (no relation to John), but shifted the route further north near his business interests in Denver. Attacks by stage coach bandits and hostile Indians persisted and proved entirely too disruptive for the business to survive. By the end of 1866, most national coach lines were consolidated into a single entity known as Wells, Fargo & Company.

After the completion of the transcontinental railway in 1869, only fragmented sections of the coach lines existed to service areas where no railroads had yet reached. In the fall of 1873, with the emergence of the Long Recession, one town that had been earmarked for rail service, Fort Worth, Texas still awaited the trains that would not arrive until three years later in 1876.

Given this, travel to Fort Worth became highly dependent on the remaining segments of the Old Butterfield Stage Coach Line. In early October, 1873, Clay and Deekie took passage on that line from Memphis to the emerging frontier cowtown.

Before the war, the original Butterfield Line had run west of the town to Fort Belknap before continuing on to west Texas and points beyond. However, as Fort Worth grew from a mere military installation to a small, but critical stop for Texans to intersect the Chisholm Trail, the stage coach line was rerouted to service Fort Worth. The frontier town adopted the slogan *"Where the West Begins."*

Clay and Deekie had crossed the Mississippi River by riverboat ferry to the marshy shores of Arkansas that chilly gray morning and boarded the stage coach. The coach was one of the newest Concord Coaches, quite elegant in its near pristine condition. It was manufactured by the Abbott, Downing Company, in Concord, New Hampshire and bore the number thirteen upon its doorpost.

The interior of the coach was a cramped affair. There were three rows of seats, each meant to accommodate three passengers. The forward seat faced the rear, and the rear seat conversely faced the carriage's front. Both were sized for three passengers so long as they were not much beyond average proportions. Each seat was also notoriously tight on headroom, so much so that anyone above average height would have to ride the third row, a removable bench with no back installed off-center between the other two seats, but closer to the rear. When the bench was in use, a leather strap, called the back-brace, was hung across the interior to keep the center-benchers from falling back into the laps of those riding in the rear seats behind them.

The center bench was bolted into the carriage floor, but both of its ends were hinged about a third of the way in. That way, either of these two extensions could be flipped up to accommodate loading and unloading at either of the coach's side doors.

Clay and Deekie had thrown their few meager belongings collected in a single ragged bag under the heavy leather tarp which covered the rear of the wagon known as the boot. Clay carried the Whitworth Sniping Rifle inside the carriage. It was, other than the two matching satchels holding the dual fortunes of gold coins, his most guarded possession. Clay had already wedged these satchels beneath the rear seat, well before the other passengers approached the coach. He dared not leave these twin fortunes in the rear boot where it could readily be stolen or pilfered from, nor placed in storage under the driver's box. Clay was much more comfortable knowing them to be safely hidden behind the wall formed by his worn and dusty boots. After all, men were known to kill for much less gold than this.

When Clay helped Deekie board the coach, he noticed she lacked her usual energy and excitement that such an adventure would normally arise in her. Clay feared she still was terribly affected by the trauma of her near rape at the hands of her "friend" Jefferson Armistead. Or possibly she could not shake the horror of her being "saved" only to watch his last breaths strangled from him by the brute Orrin Fletcher James. Or perhaps it was the blacksmith's taunt to finish off what the gambler had begun, or all three terrors combined. Surely the safety of crossing the river into Arkansas must have allowed her to release her angst. He had not considered that Deekie's malaise might just be the function of another, more natural, physical cause. One that originated from the river itself.

After Clay and Deekie had taken their places in the coach rear seat, they were joined by three other passengers. The two Georgians faced forward, while the other three passengers took the front seat that faced back at them. The center bench and back brace were not installed at that point. The trio in the front seat consisted of a prim and proper husband and wife, dressed out in their finest traveling clothes, along with a much rougher looking passenger adorned in well worn fringed buckskin. Clay guessed the couple to be from the East, perhaps Pennsylvania or New York. The buckskin clad fellow, he dared not reckon t'all.

"Now, you folk don't go gettin' used to all that room inside now," yelled out a large burly man as he walked around the coach one last time. "We'll be meeting up with the Saint Louie line in Fort Smith, after which this here coach is gonna be full as a tick. Might even have some hangers-on topside, we'll see."

"And who just might you be, my good man," the prudish Easterner, the husband, asked of the coachman.

"You can just call me *Brother Whip*," answered the strapping man as he continued his inspection.

"He's the driver," explained the young man in buckskin, whose blonde hair was long, covering his ears and neck. His beard was full. Every bit of him was dirty and trail ridden. "That wiry fella' walking alongside *Whip* with the scattergun will be riding shotgun up on the box."

Brother Whip and his shotgun wielding companion then moved forward to make final adjustments to the team of four horses. The coach rocked softly as they did, then jostled more prominently as the two men climbed aboard its frame and up to their perch atop the driver's box overhead. For a brief second, all was still.

"And we're off, folks," yelled out the shotgunner as *Brother Whip* let out a ferocious *"Hiiiyyyyaa!!"* as he snapped the reins of the horse team.

The coach jolted forward and then rolled westward along the flat rutted marshland roads of eastern Arkansas as the morning sun rose behind them. The motion first lurched the carriage, suspended as it was over the coach's frame on a series of leather straps called "thoroughbraces". The carriage rested on these as might a weary body slung across a hammock. The result was a swaying, bounding ride. The passengers instinctively grabbed at any part of the structure to hold on. All except the buckskin clad young man, that is.

"Gonna be as full as a tick?" Clay repeated what the *Whip* had said. "Only is the one seat left in this coach."

A sly smile drew across the face of the buckskin clad passenger. "They got themselves a center bench they'll wedge on in when we git into Fort Smith," he said.

"It's already far too cramped in here even without even any sixth rider," complained the wife, who they would come to find was named Cora. "There is no room for another bench. No room for more passengers but the one."

"Ma'am," Buckskin replied, "enjoy the space whiles you got it. You'll come to know whoever rides those three center seats on that bench like long lost kin."

The five passengers then tried to relax if only to synchronize the momentum of their bodies to the swaying cadence of the carriage. Clay and Deekie sat in the middle of the rear seat aside each other, the Whitworth Rifle propped up by Clay's side. They faced the husband in the opposite center, who separated his wife, Cora, at the front right window from the buckskin clad man at the window on the left.

As they rolled and swayed along, Cora, seemed to be taking the full measure of the odd pair of Georgians opposite her. She did so with what she though to be discreet glimpses, but Clay could feel her scour them with every glance she so critically cast. Although, had this priggish moralist of a woman known just how much the two had so stealthily stashed in the two matching bags under their seat, her sense of superiority and probity would likely have been stripped away from her as easily as husks from ears of corn.

The man in buckskin was far less critical and far more easygoing. As much as Clay could see, he carried only a large Bowie knife on his belt. With the recent rash of holdups, the stage lines no longer allowed passengers to carry guns inside the coach, lest they themselves prove to be insiders working with the bandits. That was a risk the coach lines could no longer afford to take.

Buckskin, as Clay came to think of him, stretched out his long legs. He wedged the tip of his boot under the corner of the rear seat, uncomfortable close to the two black leather satchels full of gold coins. This drew a nervous look from Clay that was not lost on the man. He raised his eyes to Clay and opened his mouth to speak, projecting that voice that by then Clay had determined to be thickly strung with an unmistakeable Texas drawl.

"No offense meant, my friend," Buckskin said, "I just figured hooking my toes under the bottom of your seat was more neighborly than insulting you by showing you the soles of my boots. It's just far too long a ride for me not to stretch out these horse-bowed legs o' mine."

Clay, caught red handed in his nervousness, attempted to hide his concern over the stashed gold. He flashed a brief acknowledging smile at the man, but then waited several seconds before responding.

"Fix yerself however it best pleases ya', Mister, I ain't one easily offended," Clay said in slowly drawn response. As unflustered as he wished to appear, his hand fidgeted with his field coat, and accidentally drew it back, exposing his empty holster belt. He meant nothing by it, but the movement was taken otherwise.

Buckskin then replied to Clay, "You don't have to show me your not carrying friend. I saw them Navy Sixes you was sportin' as we was crossing on that Mississippi River Ferry, but I already done noted their no longer being on your waist anymore."

Clay looked at Buckskin and once more said nothing for a second or two. Then, as if he had measured the man and found him to be worthy of answering the unusual comment, he responded in a slow, but firm voice.

"The coachman made me pack them away in the boot. They must have figured even a one-armed man was too much of a threat with twelve chambers loaded. Well, ten if ya' figure for the one chamber I always leave empty in each pistol for traveling."

"Well that's plum too bad, Pardner," Buckskin said, "cause I doubt that fancy long-gun o' yours ain't goin' to do you much good should we get set upon by renegades."

"Surely not with all of its cartridges and bullets in the boot," Clay admitted. "They wouldn't allow it in the cabin else wise. Must be afearin' one of us inside here might he'p any bandits that might *'set upon'* us, as ya' say."

"Nobody is going to be *'set upon'* by anybody, not on this short of a ride," interrupted the husband harshly, in an effort to console his wife. "We have a full day's ride to Fort Smith, then, after we take on more riders, down to Red

River Station and finally down into Fort Worth. It'll be over before anyone has a chance to do much of anything."

"I sure hope you're right, Mister," Buckskin said. He shot a glance to Clay which indicated he did not believe so. "It's that stretch in the Injun Territories, between Fort Smith and the Red River that tends to draw the trouble."

Buckskin then used his thumb and forefinger to cooly rake through the thick golden mustache that drained like a creek down into the pond that was his unkept, shaggy beard. The flat, black round-rimmed hat he wore, set far back on his head, bore semblance to a leather sifting pan.

Buckskin's eyes found and hung onto Clay's. The dusty and somewhat kindred souls shared a thought, knowing what the husband and wife did not - that trouble would not stay away just because any of them hoped it so.

Deekie had fallen asleep as she leaned into Clay's side. He was worry on her, but tried to write it off simply as her resting, safe after all of the morning's commotion.

"Hey, Long Gun, you mind my asking how you lost your arm?" Buckskin asked insensitively.

"The name's Clay, and I lost it in the war at Chickamauga," he regretted answering a bit too quickly.

"Was you in with the Blue or Gray?"

"Confederate Infantry, under Longstreet," Clay answered proudly.

"Good for you, Brother. I fought with the Texans under Kirby Smith at Shiloh, myself. Ain't right fair, is it? I mean you boys whip the Yanks there and you loose an arm, while we lose to them Bluebellies and I come out whole."

Clay looked back Buckskin and with no reservation said, "If war done taught me one thing fer sure, it's that life has absolutely no sense t'all about being fair. That's where luck comes in. On the battlefield, yer better off going forth with a little luck, more than a mountain of fairness. After Sharpsburg and Gettysburg, luck just plum gave up on me."

"But you can still shoot that long gun with just your one arm?" Buckskin prodded.

"More so than yer might reckon," Clay answered.

"From how far off?"

"I'd say three-quarters of a mile, maybe longer," Clay replied, just short of bragging.

"Well, that's some might' fine shootin', that is. I'd like to see that for myself someday."

"Be careful what yer might wish fer, fella..." Clay warned, "...ya' don't wanna find yerself in my sights".

Buckskin merely smirked in response. "Gawd, no. You ain't never said nuthin' truer. Whaddah meant was I'd just like to watch you fire that contraption, but, never from in front of its muzzle, even a mile off. Gawd almighty, no!"

The conversation fell off and they rode in silence for a long stretch. It was during this period that Clay caught Buckskin from time to time casting stealthy glances at the two black bags under his seat. As soon as Buckskin noticed he had drawn Clay's gaze, his eyes would dart back out the window. Clay did not like the feeling this produced in him.

For the first time, Clay felt threatened. Had the that buckskin clad Texan somehow come to guess about the gold stashed in those bags? Had Clay somehow through his own actions given it away? He had no weapons with which to defend them, as far as this man knew. But there was the sole exception of Armistead's pocket pistol, that which still dangled beneath Clay's left armpit. Clay could only hope it was still unknown to Buckskin.

The gold had already become a major problem for Deekie and Clay. It had to be attended to constantly, like a beautiful small children, lest someone figured to run off

Figure 11: Butterfield Stage Coach
(Coach Image Courtesy of Booth Western Museum
of Cartersville GA)

with them. After rapidly settling the hotel bill in Memphis, Clay realized his only option was to take the bags of gold with them to the stage coach. He had to carry the two fortunes in his sole hand's grip while Deekie was forced to haul the bag of possessions and the Whitworth rifle. The two loaded satchels, side by side, was almost more than Clay could carry. Now all were safely stored aboard.

Together, the two bags bulged with an amalgam of the funds paid out by the gun dealer Goodlette in Nashville, melded with the monies collected outside Memphis under the implied duress of Clay's Whitworth Sniper Rifle. That much combined gold could draw an awful lot of attention. Clay knew the heaviness of what he carried could draw the darkness out of almost any man.

Another thing Clay was sure of was that while he knew that the gold was not theirs to keep, he and Deekie could not simply leave that much of a fortune behind.

On the other hand, Clay and Deekie knew by taking the fortune they would most likely draw exactly the sort of trouble they wished to avoid. For even if, as they hoped, no one else was to come to know of their dual fortunes, they were aware that Orrin Fletcher James would come after it, and do whatever was necessary to recover at least Goodlette's gold. He had proven that with the murder of Armistead.

The road to Fort Smith was long and boring. No trouble was anticipated and none was found. As the road stretched on, Deekie collapsed more fully into her fatigue. First, she had leaned hard against Clay's frame, before the jostling rhythm of the coach slowly slid her down, until her weary head resting finally in his lap.

"We'll, Mister Clay," said the staid Easterner's wife, "it appears your young lady friend is rather exhausted…"

"Cora, now that's none of your business," warned her husband.

"She's such a sweet thing to be so exhausted this early in the ride," the wife went on, ignoring her husband.

"She's just tuckered out, Ma'am," Clay attempted to explain. "She's done had a rough couple of nights lately. I figur' to let her catch up on her beauty sleep after them long nights in Memphis. She'll be fine after a spell."

A flash of shock erupted on Cora's face.

"You spent time in town at Memphis?" the woman seemed to accuse. "Tell me you both were not fool enough to lodge overnight in town there."

"Cora!" objected the husband. "Enough Already!"

"Just the last two nights, Ma'am" said Clay despite the husband's protest. "Stayed at the Peabody Hotel. Finest place in town, if not in all of Dixie."

"So near the river?" An edge of panic seared her words. "That hotel is right on main street, near the river!"

"Cora, stop your snooping right now," her husband demanded. "Excuse my wife, Mister."

"Chester, the town of Memphis has the Yellow Fever in a very bad way," yelled his wife. "Their hotel was so near the river and the riverboats that brought the sickness to town. His lady friend could be quite sick with that dreadful fever. We could all be at risk because of her."

"No, Ma'am, nothing to fret over wit' my Deekie. She ain't gots no fever," Clay said, "just too much excitement out gamblin' all night, that's all. Like I said, she's just plum tuckered out. She just needs her rest."

"Seems healthy enough a gal to me," said Buckskin, still looking off in the distance out the coach window. "Let her get some shuteye. The air and the ride'll fix her up."

Deekie slept soundly while Clay and his other three companions rattled along the trail's route. A succession of stops came and went, all of which Deekie slept through: Plumer's Station, followed by Pottsville and later Dardanelle, Stinnett's Station, Paris, Charleston and at 2:00 a.m. the next morning, the coach at last entered Fort Smith.

"Your woman has been sleeping for the entire time we've been in this coach, Sir," Cora said, staring at the sweat drenched countenance of Deekie's face in Clay's lap.

"Cora," her husband resumed his protests, "mind your manners. I warned you about your busy-bodying."

Yet Clay was in no way put off by her comment, but her husband seemed to anticipate that his wife's digging into their fellow passengers' business had just begun.

"I know she's got the Yellow Fever," the woman turned to whisper to her man. "These two were fool enough to stay in the city, Chester. We may all yet catch that filthy swamp rot disease from her."

"I don't care," her husband whispered back clenched teeth, "there's nothing can be done about it."

Clay could hear every whispered word and gently jostled Deekie. She had to be famished, he thought, having missed the dinner meal stop from the Potts Inn at the Pottsville stop. Buckskin had kindly brought out plates for the two of them. She had no appetite, so Clay ate both.

At Stinnett's Station, a team of mules had replaced the horses to get the coach over the rugged Boston Mountains on the way into Fort Smith. The mules pulled the Concord Coach into that town, coming to rest aside a second Concord Coach which had traveled earlier from St. Louis and was awaiting the arrival of the Memphis coach. As soon as they pulled in, that coach departed back East.

After their coach came to a stop in Fort Smith, the other riders quickly got out to stretch their legs. Clay took a handkerchief from his pocket and wiped the damp sweat nearly dripping from Deekie's furrowed brow, then gently leaned the back of his hand against the tender skin of her forehead. She was burning up. Only then did Clay admit to himself that the woman Cora had likely been right all along. However, he knew he could never admit openly to it, lest both he and Deekie be denied permission to continue on to Fort Worth. Clay used his good right arm to cup Deekie's shoulder and raise her to a sitting position.

"Virgil," Deekie said groggily, "I just don't right feel like myself. I am so tired I can't but raise my head. I seem to have the sharp edge of a peach pit stabbing in my stomach. My bones hurt. My whole body aches."

Thankfully, Clay and Deekie by this point were the only two souls left in or near the coach. Buckskin had leapt out as soon as the coach came to a stop and walked off. The married Easterners, Chester and Cora, were by then already on the prowl to size up the other four souls from the St. Louis coach who would be joining them on to Fort Worth.

It was then that *Brother Whip* called for Clay to gather up Deekie and exit the coach. "Come on, now, fella, I need to get in there and install the center bench and its back-brace before we leave for Fort Worth. I got asses paying for these seats, and as such you gotta get yer and her hides outta that coach. Now!"

Despite her having talked to him, Deekie seemed still to be floating in and out of a deep sleep, or under a spell much like it.

"Come on, Deeks," Clay said, "let's git ya' some fresh air. Walk off this weariness ya' been carrying around within ya', git yer blood pumpin' a bit."

Clay lifted Deekie to her feet, and then helped her to the ground outside the stage coach with *Brother Whip's* help. She stumbled with her first step and crashed hard onto Clay's chest just inside his good arm. After that, she was nothing more than dead weight pulling straight down on him. Her weary body seemed to fight against his, as if it only wanted to drain into the earth like some shapeless liquid.

"Damn, girl, work with me here," Clay snarled.

Deekie seemed not to even hear him at first, then at last acknowledged his speaking so harshly to her.

"Virgil, I'm sorry," she said, her eyes floating in unshed tears, "I'm sorry I done played along with Jefferson and all that gamblin' business. Sorry I ever got all worked up over his fancy dress, or the attention of all them gamblers' eyes staring at me in it. I'm sorry I hurt ya' that way, it weren't right."

"Come on, Deekie," Clay said softly. "It t'ain't but nuthin.' Come and walk with me, girl.'"

"Ya' never deserved any such treatment," she went on. "All y'ever been was good to me. I can see that now."

Clay looked at the sickly girl he almost did not recognize. Her face was gaunt and had already become soaked again in sweat. Her eyes had a paleness to them that he had never seen before. Most of all, a weakness had crept in and overtaken her being. He was scared for her, but dared not allow it to show.

"Deeks, just stop yer gibberin'," Clay said. "It t'ain't like yer not gonna be here by my side much longer. It's nothin' but nonsense. Yer thinking ain't straight, girl, not a t'all." He hoped the cool night air would revive her somewhat.

Clay watched inside the coach as *Brother Whip,* assisted by the shotgunner, installed the center bench they had brought out from the station. Next they strung the leather back-brace strap above that third bench seat. It stretched from one side of the coach's interior wall to the other, and hung from smaller leather straps which dropped from the ceiling overhead.

Deekie found the energy to raise her head to look at Clay as he studied the coach's conversion. She knew he was staying within sight to assure the two men did not find the gold in the black satchels under the rear seat.

The driver had spotted Clay as he studied them. "You like watchin' other fellas work, Mister?" *Brother Whip* yelled out to him.

"T'ain't never seen a stage coach converted over, before," Clay stated, as if it were fascinating him.

"If you wasn't an on-board payin' hide, I'd take you out and kick yer one-armed ass." *Whip* said angrily.

"I meant no offense," Clay said, but continued to watch the two at their chore like a hawk.

"I don't deserve ya', Virgil," Deekie finally confessed, causing Clay to turn his head back to her.

Clay looked down upon her gaunt face, beaded with sweat. "No, gal, ya' gots it all wrong. If there was ever one thing I did not deserve in this life, Deeks, it is the love y'ave showered upon me."

"Why?" Deekie asked weakly as she searched the warmth of his eyes, and this action alone seemed to exhaust her. "Why do ya' love me, Virgil? I just keep goin' on and runnin' 'way from ya'."

Clay stroked her face compassionately with the back of his hand. "And yet, Deeks, y'always find yer way back to me. I've come to know those is the sweetest moments, and it's them that I have come to live for."

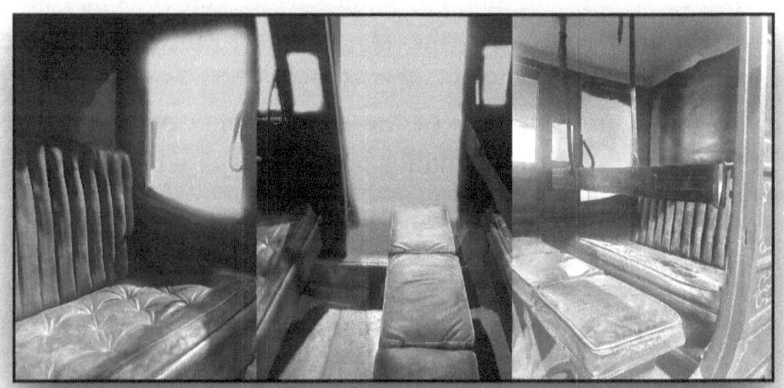

Figure 12: View of the Concord Coach Interior, with Front Seat (Left), Bench Installed (Center), and Rear Seat with Bench and Backbrace shown (Right). (Courtesy Western Museum, Cartersville, GA)

Following A Hunch

The Red River snaked between the wild lands of the Indian Nations and the law bidin' shores of Texas.

Cord McCullough had tracked the three rustlers south through the Indian Territories. The trail had gone cold several times, but each time Cord had convinced himself that he and River had once more picked up the trail made by the outlaws. Upon approaching Colbert's Ferry, the Red River crossing for the stage coach, Cord was bothered by a nagging thought. Three men. Only three men. This was just not a large enough group to effectively rob a stage coach. With one man tending to the driver and his shotgun partner atop the coach's box, only two would be left to subdue the full load of passengers. Figuring more then half of those to be men, a lot could go awry with two men against five.

For one thing, the stage would likely be full and some passengers might be secretly bearing guns. Generally, the stage line operators tried to prevent this, as they feared a passenger might himself prove to be an inside operative for any highwaymen. But they could not frisk every man or women each time as they boarded and re-boarded at the many stations along the route. If even only one passenger was carrying a weapon, the advantage of the robbers could become precariously thin.

Cord, Trouble and River crossed on the ferry over into Texas and made their way down to Red River Station on the off chance that the three renegades had also done so prior to making their play on the coach. Neither Cord nor River picked up any sign of the three rustlers on the Texas side of the river. They pressed on to the station where they learned the coach had left Fort Smith in the early morning hours was expected on time. No one had seen any three strangers at that stop. Cord became angry with himself as he figured that the three outlaws had never crossed over into Texas. Why should they? To get food or supplies? Not likely, for here they would face Lone Star justice, known to be harsh, immediate, and in the case of cattle rustlers, horse thieves and coach robbers, near always permanent.

Cord had Trouble watered, then hung with a feed bag of grain as he found himself a hefty steak, the meat and bone of which he shared with River. Then they rode out and double tracked back to Colbert's Ferry where they crossed back into the Indian Nations Territory. Then, it was just a matter of tracking eastward along the stage coach route, but Cord sensed they were likely too late. It was nearly noon, and with the coach having left Fort Smith in the early morning hours, they surely were already deep in the lands of the Choctaw Nation by then. *Damn my folly,* he thought.

"Well, River," Cord began another conversation with his canine companion, "only three of them to rob a full coach. That just don't play! I figure either they met up with some others bandit, or they got somebody planted inside that coach already. Likely, the plant, I best figure, as that way he could take the measure of all the men onboard as to who might become a threat, as well as size up which passengers might be carrying the most valuables."

The dog trotted alongside Trouble and looked up occasionally at his master, as if considering every word with his full attention.

"It's likely we won't make it there in time to prevent the coach robbery," Cord admitted, "but we won't arrive too much afterwards. Them rustlers turned bandits will be in a hurry to get out of there and in their haste will likely leave a trail behind that a blind man on a dark night could follow."

Cord looked up at the climbing morning sun, and secretly wondered just how much of a head start the rustlers might make for themselves after the holdup. He also wondered just how many dead and wounded they might leave behind for him to attend to.

"We'll catch up with them renegades somewhere in the territory. By then the coach line will have a hefty reward on their heads. We'll collect on this from both ends. Both the Exchange and the coach lines will pay us when we bring in their bodies. I just hope none of the good folk aboard that coach get killed or maimed in the robbery. I shouldn't have taken us into Red River Station. I hate to think some one might pay for my mistake with their life. "

The number thirteen Concord Coach had rumbled out of Fort Smith well before sun up. It slipped along its route as the hues of the onyx night as slowly transitioned into the dark gray mists of morning. The stagecoach entered into the Indian Nations Territory and each of the nine passengers jammed inside knew that this forthcoming part of the journey was likely to be the most dangerous.

Dangerous, but not at all from the hands of the tribes of the Choctaw Nation. These were generally peaceful Indians, and had been ever since they were relocated west from their ancestral lands in Mississippi. They had been forced to come to the newly formed Indian Nations Territory by the Treaty of Dancing Rabbit Creek in 1831. No, the dangers of passing through the Territory came not from its inhabitants, be they Choctaw, Chickasaw, Cherokee, Muskogee or Creek Indians, but from the savage actions of renegade white men who also roamed its lands.

So peaceful were the Choctaw that the coach robbers never even bothered to disguise themselves as members of this tribe. Such a ruse would never have been believed by any of the federal lawmen assigned to cover this territory. But had the stage coach made it through this part of the Ox Bow Route before the war, it would have continued westward beyond Fort Belknap and into west Texas. Real threats would have come there from other tribes, including the Comanche. Further west still were tribes such as the Apache and the Yavapai. Just two years earlier in 1871, there had been the Wickenburg Massacre in the Arizona Territory of six passengers and crew who had been descended upon by fifteen Yavapai warriors. Given these attacks, everyone aboard Concord Coach number thirteen consoled themselves by remembering that they would travel no further west than Fort Worth.

Those more serious threats to stage coach operators, mostly along and beyond the western borders of Texas, were one of the reasons that by 1873, only fragments of the once famous route still existed. And in 1873 this short surviving segment of the Ox Bow Route ended in Fort Worth. As long as the coach made it across the Red River, into Texas, its passengers would be perfectly safe.

But in that relatively short stretch of the Indian Nations Territory, the white man was the most feared. Among them were the fiercest number of cutthroats, thieves and killers. They would take full advantage of the relative lack of law enforcement, as it was a large expanse of land where only few federal marshals had jurisdiction.

Inside the Concord Coach, nine passengers watched as the black night sky slowly lightened. There was no majestic painting of the heavens with vibrant hues this morning, only a gradual transition from one tone of gray to another. The night had already given unto a slate gray dawn which later rendered into a woolen gray morning sky.

Between Fort Smith and Colbert's Ferry across the Red River were eleven stops known as "stands". Each stand offered little more than to swap out the tired team of four horses with a fresh set. Each stand was operated by different full-bred or half-bred Choctaw or Chickasaw Indians, and served as an impromptu trading post. A distance of roughly twenty miles or so separated the stands.

They had just left the third stand at Holloway's Station. The next stand, eighteen miles in front of them, was Riddle's Station. Between the two lie the Upper Brazil Creek and an area known simply as "The Narrows" that had to be crossed. So far, all had gone well and the passengers were comforted since the veil of darkness, under which evil reigned, had already been lifted.

Crammed in the coach were Clay and Deekie, the married couple of Chester and Cora, the "Buckskin Kid", and four others that had joined their coach in Fort Smith. Whereas the Memphis coach typically drew passengers from the South and East, the St. Louis coach drew more midwesterners, especially those from Chicago.

Those four new passengers were made up of a haberdasher and his wife, an opinionated old geezer, and a preacher dressed in the grandest finery of Chicago. The last man's clothes seemed to have been dyed in competing tones of gray, as if to match the morning sky. Everyone had taken this man to be a Methodist minister because of the wooden-boxed Bible he carried on his lap. Yet, for a minister, he wore an unusually expensive looking and well attended to Dakota style Stetson hat.

Clay and Deekie along this stretch were taking up the rear left corner and center seat. Clay manned the middle, and Deekie he had propped up into the left corner using his shoulder. The haberdasher's wife took the last open rear seat on the right hand side.

The bench seat that had been installed to accommodate the other three new passengers was quite a Spartan ride. It was merely a wooden and leather bench, separated in thirds by two hinges. These allowed either end to flip up in order to ease the loading and unloading of passengers. It was offset from the true center of the coach more towards the rear seat, leaving only a minimum of legroom for any of the nine passengers. Those in the rear also had the annoyance of the bench's back-brace. It was nothing more than a leather strap that hung from the ceiling and was secured to the coach's side interior walls. It was used to catch the backs of the bench riding passengers and keep them from falling into the laps of those in the rear.

On that bench sat the haberdasher (directly in front of Clay), and on his left was the chatterbox old man, who would not stop talking even though everyone around had long stopped engaging with him. Opposite him on the right edge of the bench sat the Dakota Stetson wearing minister.

The space inside the coach seemed as confined as putting multiple bodies into a single pine coffin. The distance between the bench seat and the rear seat was barely enough to accommodate the legs of those who rode the latter. The bench riders were jolted rearward into the hanging leather back-brace, Their shoulders and backs only inches from the faces of those in the rear seats. So much so, Clay worried for Deekie's ability to draw a fresh, unused breath, despite her being aside the open window.

Perhaps those on the bench had it even worse. They faced the passengers on the front seat, often with their knees interspaced with each other. As the cabin swayed and lurched, it was impossible not to brush or bang legs.

"I tell y'all, this world's going to hell in a hand basket, and in a hurry," the old man rambled on, a wobble in his voice, talking to no one and everyone at the same time. "Giving all this prime land to them Injuns. We gotta stop serving them everything up on a silver platter..."

"Sir," interrupted the minister, his ability to resist engaging this babbler long wore away, "these Indian Nation tribes have already been driven from their homelands. The Cherokee driven here from Georgia and the East, the Chickasaw and Choctaw from Mississippi, the Creek from Alabama and the Muskogee from the Tennessee River Valley. The platter they have been served is anything but silver. In fact, they have not been given silver at all, only slivers. And yet still greedy, sinful men like yourself wish only to steal what little has been left to them."

"Well, pardon me, Padre," the old man reacted, "but it seems to me that all these savages just keep taking whatever they can get from our government. I think that the only thing they truly deserve is the pointy end of a bayonet as the US Army drives them all the way down to Mexico."

"That certainly is not a very Christian way of thinking, let alone acting," replied the minister.

"That's just it," the old man prattled on, "there ain't a Christian soul in any one of them red savage chests. They are heathens, through and through. Not like all of us here."

"So, you consider yourself to be a God fearing man, then?" asked the minister.

"Only a fool would tempt the wrath of the Lord," came the prattler's answer in quick response.

"And yet you do exactly this," said the Minister.

"How you figure, Padre?"

The man in gray with the fancy Dakota allowed the question to hang in the tight quarters of the coach's cabin for emphasis. Then he slowly replied.

"You would rather banish these non-believers from our land than spread God's Word unto them. Teach them about Jesus Christ, our Lord and Savior. I tell you, my friend, you are tempting the wrathful red right hand of God Himself."

The old man was silenced, if only for a second. "You just might have something there, Padre," he finally said. "If the likes of your kind could convert all these heathens to worshiping Our Lord as we do, then they would no longer really be Injuns at all, just poor Red Christian Men. We could then cheat them out of their lands like we do any poor white man. That just might work for these five mostly peaceful tribes, but I think the Apache out West and the Sioux up in the Dakotas are gonna be a tougher sell."

Clay tried not to pay any mind to the old chatterbox as he droned on, which might have been harder to do had Deekie's condition not worsened. It commanded all of his attention. Clay had her propped up against him such that her face was as close to the open window as possible as she frequently needed fresh air. Her face was continually drenched in a clammy sweat, upon which had settled a film of road dust. Despite her being wrapped up by him in an oversized blanket, Deekie's frame had begun to shake as she surely battled a series of internal torments. Clay was unsure whether anyone could see her shivering as Deekie was hidden in that back corner behind the old chatterbox.

Clay knew deep in his heart that the woman Cora was right; she must have picked up the Yellow Fever in Memphis. If he could get Deekie to Fort Worth where she could rest under a doctor's care while he searched for his father, Clay figured, there would be no sin in using some of that gold fortune still beneath his seat for her care.

Clay felt her body shudder. He thought about the gold, and the Whitworth Rifle that was still propped upright against the window frame. What good was all this, the gold, the guns, even finding his *Diddy*, if it resulted in him losing his Deekie? He realized she meant more to him than anything else in the world, including his own life. Yet, it was his own weakness, his failure to say no to the world's trappings, that had brought Deekie to this perilous point, even if these things he sought merely for her benefit.

The coach had been lurching along the trail when it came to the shallow waters of Upper Brazil Creek. It forded its way across with little difficulty. Soon after they approached a tight pass snaking in between two opposing rocky bluffs, known as "The Narrows". It was here that the day's troubles would begin.

A loud gunshot rang out from the surrounding countryside. The coach veered as the driver reined in the team, fighting the horses' instincts to flee in panic.

"See, see, we're being attacked by Injuns," yelled the old man in a frightened pitch.

"Hardly," said the Dakota preacher more calmly. "This is surely going to be a hold-up by highwaymen. They'll stop us here and get us all out and rob us of our possessions and the coach of its strongbox and valuables it might otherwise be carrying. Don't resist these men, they are likely to be very dangerous. Do as they say."

Clay looked suspiciously at the man. He thought the sureness of his statement was that of someone planted by the robbers themselves. What better cover than that of a minister? Clay watched his hands carefully, as he thought the man might be reaching for a hidden gun. Clay had been forced to store his Navy Sixes along with the Whitworth's cartridges under the boot's tarp, but best as he could tell, no one knew of the hidden pocket pistol still hanging under his left armpit. He touched his hand to it when the coach veered as *Brother Whip* fought for control of the team.The wagon came to a stop just before the narrow rocky pass.

No doubt we just heard a warning shot fired from atop them rocks, Clay thought. *That would have been the location I would have sought out.* Then, he noticed two figures creep out from the surrounding scrub brush, one on either side of the coach. Both wore bandanas over their faces; only their eyes showed under their hats. The one on the left hand side carried a rifle. Clay recognized it to be a Henry, which could hold some fifteen rounds.

"Whip," the first robber wielding the Henry rifle yelled out to the driver, "don't go and do nothing stupid like, ya' hear? Nobody needs to get hurt here today."

"Yer shooter done blown a hole in the chest of my man riding shotgun," the driver called out, "without so much as a warning shot. He's been blasted clean through and he needs some quick 'tending to."

"He needs to have found another line of work," laughed the second robber from the coach's right side, "but it's a little late for that now." This callous renegade had no rifle, like his compadre, but sported a gun belt that held two revolvers, one which was already drawn. Clay thought they looked like his guns, converted Colt Navy Sixes.

"Real careful like, *Whip*, go on and kick down his scattergun," said the first robber, an edge in his voice "and r'memba, our sharpshooter up in them rocks by now has yer chest plain in his sights, so don't get any foolish notions up there. Sooner we get done here, the sooner you can get on yer way and get yer friend some tending to"

"He's already dying, damn it," the driver yelled in anger. "He ain't never gonna make it all the way back to Holloway's Stand."

"The scattergun, *Whip*, kick down the damn scattergun." A second later the shotgun fell to the dirt. The second robber holstered his revolver and retrieved it.

Clay could hear every bit of this tense talk. *So much for my guess of a warning shot. Calculated. Disable the shotgunner and leave the Whip able to stop the team. These men had blown a hole in the chest of the shotgunner with no call. They were cold-hearted killers. They'd just as well kill all the passengers as let any live. No mouths left to tell tales.* Clay kept watching the gray Dakota preacher, as he was more sure than ever that he was in on the robbery.

Clay glanced at the kid clad in buckskin, and with his eyes motioned to the minister. Buckskin nodded his head slowly, as if to say, *I got your back, my friend.*

"OK, *Whip*, good," the first robber called up to the driver. "Now throw down the strongbox. Don't forget my sniper's got you in his sights. Yeah, don't forget that. And I guarantee you don't want me to have to climb up onto that perch to come after ya, 'cuz that'll put me in a real cross mood. I'll only do it after he plugs you, understand? So go on and git to it."

As Clay listened, he detected the nervous speed with which these taut words were parlayed. Then to his surprise the door next to the gray minister was yanked opened by the callous second gunman, by then wielding the shotgun. Not on the traditional left side where Clay sat, but on the right side where the preacher sat. It could only mean Dakota was indeed in on all this. Clay watched the robber as he waved the barrel of the recovered shotgun in a menacing fashion.

"Everybody out," he bellowed, "through this door. You use that other door and our sharpshooter takes you down like a twelve point buck. You first, Preacher man…"

He pointed the shotgun at the chest of the Minister and backed away a couple of steps. The minister stepped out of the coach. The haberdasher was next on the bench, and leaned behind him for his wife, just before the robber forced the minister to reach in and pulled him out alone. Then followed the old geezer, unusually silent, followed by the husband and wife Easterners on the front seat. Finally the haberdasher's wife emerged. Just then, up front on the other side, the strongbox crashed into the dust on the coach's left side.

"OK, *Whip*, get yer fat ass on down here," said the first robber, "and bring me the key to open this beauty."

"What about my partner?"

"You said yerself he was dying, so let him die."

The passengers no sooner crawled out of the coach before they were forced to lie on the dirt, one aside the other, making a human corduroy road of sorts.

Clay had not yet moved from his seat, as he had been trying to stir Deekie. She was still burning up with the fever and wanted only to stay in that left corner. Only Buckskin sat across from them, all the others lay in the dirt.

"C'mon, Deeks, we gotta git," Clay pulled at her.

"If you all don't git yer asses outta that coach in the next ten seconds," the shotgunned robber cursed, "I'll be pulling the three of y'all's corpses out in twenty."

Despite the tough words, Clay still heard an uneasiness in his voice. These robbers sounded awful nervous, if not outright scared, Clay thought, and that was nothin' but dangerous for all the passengers. He looked again at Buckskin, who nodded his head in return. He watched the kid reach for the Bowie knife at his side, just as Clay nodded back. They would act together.

"My gal is sick something fierce," Clay shouted.

"I'll fix that if you don't git yer and her asses movin', cripple. None o' all y'all will ever get sick again!"

Clay pondered the odds of drawing the pocket pistol and shooting from inside the coach. He might kill the second robber, but the first was still up front on the other side of the coach. Also, the sniper was still high above them among the rocks. Clay decided he would draw his weapon but not fire it until he was outside the coach. He had finally gotten Deekie roused to her feet, although she still seemed out of things. She complained of great pains in her gut. Just then, Buckskin rose and began to squeeze past him and Deekie with his Bowie knife unsheathed but by his side. Clay decided he would do the same, draw his gun, and hide it behind Deekie's back as he helped her off the coach.

Clay gently leaned Deekie forward against the bench seat's hanging back-brace and slowly began to draw the pistol from the holster under his arm.

It was then that he felt a strong hand snap onto his wrist and drive it forcibly back against the seat next to him.

"The cripple's got a gun," yelled out Buckskin, "and he's been hiding something real valuable in them bags under his seat in here. Been protectin' them like a momma goose over her baby goslings ever since we left Memphis."

"Ya' bastard," Clay seethed through his teeth, "ya' been part of this all along." Buckskin raised the bowie knife to Clay's face. He circled it menacingly inches away from his eyes.

"Sorry, Clay. I guess you figured me and you was 'bout to roust up some trouble, didn't ya'?" He smiled broadly showing his full set of grimy, yellowed teeth. "I guess if you had another hand, you'd have it around my throat right about now, wouldn't you?"

Buckskin's lips sneered before they formed to release a mocking laugh. Deekie stood only inches away, hunched over the leather bench back strap. She stirred in agitation, moaning loudly.

"Stop yer caterwaulin' and git that pair of them on out of there, now," the shotgunned robber called into the coach to Buckskin. Clay could clearly hear the panic in his voice. *Were these thugs robbing their first stage coach?* He wondered. *Buckskin is likely the only one to have been through all this before.*

"Hold your horses. Just let me git the gun from this one-armed bastard," Buckskin sneered. He laid down the Bowie knife on the end of the bench seat and reached with his freed left hand for the pistol in Clay's pinned right. He feared not Clay's other arm, a useless withered stump.

"And I do believe that bitch lady was right," Buckskin said under a snide laugh to Clay, "I do believe your woman here is aflame with the Yella Fever."

Upon his saying this, Deekie lurched toward them from her standing position clutched leaning over the leather back-brace. She let out a horrendous cry, which was immediately followed by an uncontrolled gagging reflex, which in turn was succeeded by her bellowing out a thick blanket of pale black vomit. She spew it all over Clay and the buckskin clad passenger turned robber.

Buckskin's reaction was to pull back from the dark upchuck, although his right hand did not to let go of Clay's wrist. With his left he reached blindly back for the knife.

Clay took the opportunity of Deekie's spewing to wrestle away from Buckskin before collapsing himself into the opposite corner where the haberdasher's wife had just sat. He pulled Buckskin along with him. He had hoped to break his grasp in doing so, but Buckskin's grip still held fast. Clay, could see Buckskin feeling blindly for the knife.

It sat on the hinged extension of the center bench. Clay kicked up his leg as hard as he could, sending the bench seat's extension rotating wildly up and over its hinge. The Bowie knife was sent flying, and Clay could hear the *thwang* of, but not see, it sinking its tip into wood. But Clay could see that the bench extension was up and out of his way. He kicked his leg high, and planted his boot's sole hard onto Buckskin's chest amidst the fringes of his jacket.

Clay then thrust his leg forward as hard as he possibly could. Buckskin was driven away from him. In the process his grip on Clay's wrist slid down to the Georgian's forearm. Its skin had become slick with Deekie's bile-laced vomit. Buckskin's grasp slipped away, freeing Clay to aim the pistol as Buckskin fell backward.

"Aw, shit," screamed Buckskin as he recovered to make one last pathetic lung for the Bowie knife, by then stuck in the left hand window frame. Clay's first shot rang out at point blank range into Buckskin's chest. He crashed backward against the front wall of the coach, before sliding down, smearing a bloody veil of crimson on the leather seat. Clay then fired a second shot into the pathetic worm-like writhing of the wounded Buckskin.

It was as Clay caught his tortured breath that he heard his life come to an end. Or so he thought. Two rapid explosions of gunfire came from the right hand open door. All time seemed to slow to a cruel crawl. Clay knew that the shotgun bandit surely had a clean aim at him once Buckskin was driven back away. Clay waited for the impact of the buckshot. All time was frozen, yet as it thawed Clay realized that the explosions were too small to be point-blank shotgun blasts. They sounded more like revolver fire. That realization snapped everything back to real time.

Clay turned his head to see the second robber dropping the shotgun into the dirt as his body was riddled by two bullets finding their way into his back. Crimson clouds of blood and raw mangled flesh instantly pierced through his shoulder and chest. Clay watched as the robber fell to his knees, where in shock he teetered like a lone cottonwood against the vicious onslaught of winds from a prairie storm. A final shot from Clay's five shooter convinced the marauder to collapse into the dirt, where he fell lifelessly, but ever close to the corduroy road of live passengers. Those men and women jumped to their feet in panic. They scattered in horror like storeroom cockroaches when the day shutters are thrown open to allow in the full cleansing burn of afternoon sunlight. They soon took cover hunched behind the stage coach's rear leather boot.

Where had those shots come from? Clay wondered, *Who was firing on these bandits other than me?*

Clay looked up to see a smoking revolver in the grip of the gray Dakota preacher. At his feet lay the discarded wooden Bible box and cottonwool in which had hidden his piece all along. Dakota nodded at him, then moved to recover the still unused shotgun from the dirt.

Clay looked to his left and thought Deekie to be safe enough as she had fallen back into her corner amidst the spewed blanket of her vomit. Buckskin was alive, although barely so, not moving, only moaning. He posed her no risk. Clay knew they all were still in great danger with the sniper and the gunman with the Henry rifle still in play. He rushed past Deekie, pushed open and threw himself out of the left door of the coach. He hit the ground with a dull thud. As the dry soil dusted up around him, he remembered the threat of the sniper above. He rolled as quickly as he could under the shelter of the coach, just before a sniper's bullet kicked up dirt where he had landed.

From his position under the coach, Clay took notice of all the pairs of boots that he could see. He could make out up front those of the driver facing tip to tip with the first robber but could not tell which was which. They were engaged in a struggle, he thought. Clay also could make out far to his right the gray dyed boots of the man in the Dakota Stetson.

Then a rifle shot cracked the sky overhead. Fired from above the rocks, Clay's dilemma up front was solved as *Brother Whip* fell to the ground on his side. His chest bore a spreading crimson stain of blood. His face stared at Clay with a lifeless gaze. Clay took aim on and fired at the remaining set of boots to *Whip's* left, and watched as one exploded into a red meaty splatter at calf height.

The gunman fell to the dirt alongside the driver. Unlike *Brother Whip*, the robber was very much alive. He clutched his bloody calf muscle with both hands, having dropped his Henry rifle just under the front of the coach.

Clay knew his pocket pistol was now empty. He had started with the five shooter on an empty chamber for safety. His weapon now exhausted, he scurried on his good arm and knees forward to retrieve the Henry rifle.

Still writhing in pain on the ground, the robber spotted Clay crawling under the coach and reached to pull his revolver. Clay froze, just as another pair of shots rang out from the sniper above, but these shots resulted in nothing, their rounds found no one. Clay thought the sniper might be panicking, and then realized as the coach began to roll forward that his intent was to panic the team of horses by firing over their heads.

As the robber in the dirt drew his piece from its holster, and the stage coach began to move, he had to roll to his left to clear the path of its wheels. Clay lay as flat as he could on his stomach as the coach rambled over him. He looked back to see a leather strap dragging in the sunlight as it neared him. Clay tossed aside his empty pocket revolver, and reached up just in time to grab with his only good arm the leather strap hanging down from beneath the boot. No doubt someone had attempted to retrieve weapons from the boot and had unstrapped it.

The coach dragged Clay forward just as the wounded robber recovered his position and took aim. Behind him, the newly exposed passengers scattered into the brush fearing the sniper's fire. Even with being dragged by the coach, Clay was exposed and unarmed, hanging out in the open, aft of the boot, like a sitting duck. If the wounded robber didn't shoot him, the sniper surely would.

Then, as the coach picked up speed and cleared the line of sight of the calf wounded gunman, a blast boomed out. It sounded more like a ten gauge than a revolver. In the open stood the man in gray sporting the Dakota. His shotgun was leveled, bluish-gray smoke wafted from its barrel. The gunman, who had been readying his aim on the dragged Clay, lay still on the ground. Dakota then aimed upward at the sniper's position and emptied the scattergun's other barrel. He threw down the shotgun and walked over to the wounded gunman. He drew his revolver and emptied two rounds into the buckshot riddled man's heart and head.

Clay let go of the accelerating coach's boot strap and rolled over to the Henry rifle dropped in the dirt by the dead robber. All that was left to do was to take out that sniper. Clay looked up in time to see movement among the rocks. *It was the sniper scurrying to his getaway*, he thought. *After Dakota's upward buckshot volley, he must have become fearful of being the last man standing.*

Clay took the rifle and scrambled as best he could up that rocky bluff. He was afraid his one-armed climb had wasted far too much time. When he got to the top, he could see the dust being kicked up in the distance by the fleeing sniper's horse. Clay took the recovered Henry rifle, dropped prone on the ground and rested its barrel on a large stone. He sighted on the rider who he feared was already approaching the limit of the gun's range. Or even worse, the limit of his own skill. He must not let him escape.

Clay steadied his nerves and squeezed off a round. He waited a beat. The rider was still in a full gallop. Clay had missed. Once more he sighted on the rider, made a correction for windage and fired. He waited, and on the second echo of the shot, the rider swayed in the saddle and fell from the horse, dropping like a rag doll into the brush.

"I'll finish him off," yelled out Dakota, the man in gray who had climbed up the bluff behind Clay. The man ran forward after the fallen sniper. He carried only his pistol as the shotgun, having expended all of its buckshot, still lay in the dirt back below them where the coach had been assaulted.

Clay turned back and looked below him for the coach. The panicked runaway team had pulled it forward through the rocky gate of *"The Narrows"* and about a half mile up the trail. He saw it flipped over on its side there. A broad swath in the dirt of the trail suggested that the team had dragged it the last hundred yards or so on its side.

Until he saw the wreckage, Clay had completely forgotten Deekie was still inside it. He climbed down the bluff and raced up the trail toward it, the Henry rifle still in his hand. He feared that she may have been seriously wounded when it flipped. Then, he remembered the dying Buckskin and the Bowie knife. Even if that bastard was too badly hurt to wield it, that knife could have become dislodged and gored her when the stage coach overturned.

As he neared the wreckage, it became clear that as the team of horses sped away, the coach had swung wide of the trail, struck some rocks, caught a rut, and flipped.

The team of horses was still hitched to it, upright but racked by their twisted bindings. Clay climbed up on the overturned coach and looked down into it from atop through the window what had been the right hand door.

He saw at first only Deekie. There was blood everywhere. He opened the door and scrambled down to her. She was breathing heavy and had some major scrapes, but otherwise seemed unharmed. Clay's immediate concern was that he could not locate Buckskin. *Had he somehow found the strength to pull himself clear?*

It was then that Clay heard a gunshot off in the distance. He assumed it was Dakota, the man in gray, finishing off the sniper.

Now where had the wounded Buckskin gotten to? Clay returned his attention to Deekie. She still appeared sicker than a dying dog, but was no worse physically except for some bloody minor scrapes, wear and tear from the jostled runaway ride. But there was far too much blood to be from these wounds. *Where was buckskin, and where did all this blood come from?*

As he slowly began to move her, both Clay's concerns were instantly answered. Clay realized she had avoided major injury only because as the stagecoach flipped, she had fallen atop the wounded, bloody body of Buckskin. As Clay began to raise her, he could not stomach the sight of the man's corpse. The window frame must have broken when the coach struck the rocks. As it flipped, it trapped him between the broken window frame and the ground. Buckskin was dragged face down, gravely wounded, but still alive, against the ground, scraping away layers of his skin and muscle. Embedded in his shoulder was the blade of the massive Bowie knife he had pulled on Clay. His wounds had flowed a red river of his own blood, which only stopped along with the beating of his heart. Clay realized most of the blood on Deekie flowed from the wounds of his flayed skin.

Try as he might, Clay was unable to raise Deekie by himself to get her out of the coach. He tried lifting her over his left shoulder, and using his right arm to pull himself up along the uprighted coach. Each attempt proved useless, and he damned himself for the loss of his left forearm. He became frustrated, but resigned himself to wait for help to find him.

Several minutes later, Clay felt the wreckage jostle from the weight of another person climbing its exterior. The face of Dakota, the man in gray, the false minister, soon emerged in the opening above them.

"You all right, Mister?" he asked.

"Yeah, so is she, but she's sick as a dog," Clay yelled up. "Yer might not want to git yerself close to her just now."

"It's OK, I'm coming down to help ya get her out."

"She's likely got the Yella Fever," warned Clay.

"Well, I ain't gonna leave you both down there to rot. Not after all that you did back there."

"Who the hell are ya', anyway?" asked Clay.

"Just a fellow traveler, friend," he answered.

"Well, *'Traveler'*, ya' got a name?"

The man in gray cocked his head, almost like a dog as it looked at something it did not understand. He cleared his throat before answering, "Is this your first time west of the Mississippi, friend?"

"As a matter of fact, it is," responded Clay.

"Here's a lesson for ya' that becomes more important the further west you wander. Don't ask a man his name. It's the same as asking where he's from, or what sins he might be running away from. Men don't take kindly to it out here. They come to think you might be hunting them down. Instead, ask them *'What do you call yourself, friend?'* It puts them at ease and allows them to recreate themselves in any fashion they care to with their answer."

Clay could never fully understand the concept of a man running away from his past. Yet, he could wrap his mind around the notion that should a fella' feel the need to do so, the West was where he'd likely run to. It was a land full of fella's recreating themselves in some fashion.

Although Clay had still not yet seen them, he knew the West's huge tracts of land offered a space easy to lose oneself in. These vast landscapes offered a baptism, a forgiveness, of both the open air and the sealed past.

The gray Dakota faux minister climbed down into the overturned coach. He came to stand aside Clay, and looked upon the one-armed man in a kindly way. The two of them then carefully extracted Deekie from the wreckage. They laid her gently on the ground alongside the upturned undercarriage, in order to block the wind which still licked at them.

"What if the man I am speaking to ain't my friend?" asked Clay playfully.

"What?" Dakota said.

"Ya' said to ask, *What do ya' call yerself, friend?*"

"In the West," Dakota replied, "everybody is your friend until they prove otherwise. The trick is to never allow them to prove it so. Now, other than her sickness, your gal appears to be unharmed. A few scrapes, I'd say, nothing more. But her sickness is bad..."

"Should we pull that dead young fellow in buckskin out of the carriage?" Clay asked.

"Ain't no such thing as dead young or dead old, only dead and alive," Dakota replied. "Leave that coward where he lies. He was their inside man on this robbery, so leave him inside. He nearly killed you, but you bested him, didn't you? Besides, his being pinned under that coach will make it harder for the turkey vultures to get at him."

Clay looked up into the morning sky and saw nothing. "I don't see no buzzards."

"Not yet, you don't." The man in gray followed his gaze upwards, "But don't worry, they'll come, if not for him, for his three dead friends. Now let's see to your gal."

The gray traveler's hands quickly explored the bones in her arms, ribs and legs, then felt her forehead.

"Like I said before, best I can tell, she seems all right from the carriage flipping," he said, "but she sure is in a bad way with that sickness."

"It's the Yella Fever," Clay admitted. "We was in Memphis for a couple days."

"We gotta get her to Sulphur Springs right away," the traveler said. "They got mineral springs there famous for healing any number of afflictions. Can you ride?"

"On a horse?" Clay asked.

"Well, we just happen to be fresh out of zebras and camels," the man in gray laughed.

Clay couldn't help chuckling at his quip. "I ain't barely ever been on a horse."

"Then I'll take her in my saddle, you can follow alongside. I can tie a lead to your mount, if need be."

"I don't reckon ya' noticed, but that team of horses, t'ain't a one of them has a saddle on it."

"We leave the stage coach's team of horses here," the traveler said, "they'll need them once the stage line's rescue crew arrives."

"They don't even know what has happened to us."

"Don't matter," Dakota said, "once we don't show at the next station, they'll send a party out from Red River Station looking for us. Your girl here is so sick we just can't wait around hours for them to show. We got to get her to Sulphur Springs right away or she won't make it."

"And what do we do for horses?" asked Clay.

"We got three dead bandits, don't we? I don't figure they all rode out here on that sniper's horse. His mount done run off, but it figures there are at least two other horses hitched up somewhere around here, don't it?"

"And we just gotta find 'em," Clay followed his logic. "But before Deekie and I go anywhere with you, I got one question to ask of ya'."

"And just what might that be?"

"What do ya' call yerself, friend?"

The man in the Dakota laughed aloud. "Good, you're learning. Just call me 'Travis'. I guess I can't call you *"friend"* forever…"

"I'm Clay and she's Deekie."

"Well, let's get moving with your Deekie. Time is not our ally, I'm afraid."

"Why ya' doing this, Travis?" Clay asked.

"First off, and most importantly," Travis said, "it's the right thing to do. You'll never find your way to Sulphur Springs from here. I can. Second, I ain't got time to sit around waiting for a rescue party. I got places to be."

"They got a dead driver and shotgunner back there," Clay said, "don't yer think we should stay here to explain to the stage coach rescue folk what went on."

"They got five other witnesses over there. We'll tell the others where we're headed and why. The coach line folk and the federal marshals can always find us there. Look, besides the two coachmen's corpses, there's also the four dead bandits, counting our half-flayed buckskin wearin' friend back in the wreck. If we wait for the rescue party, I guarantee your Deekie girl will be as dead as all six of them combined. Now, you stay here with her for the moment, while I go rustle up those bandits' mounts."

"Can ya' grab my pocket pistol from out the dirt?"

"Sure, it has served you well." Clay watched Travis walk off at a brisk pace. He could hear his voice echo in his ears. *"In the West, everybody is yer friend until they prove otherwise. The trick is to never allow them to prove it so."*

The Race to Sulphur Springs

The increasingly concentrated smell of sulphur overpowered Clay and Travis as they neared its namesake town.

In the golden hour of deep afternoon light, they passed along a field of cotton over which were scattered hundreds of crows. On that sea of white, the black birds stood out like the pips set on gamblers' dice. Clay could only pray this wouldn't prove to be an omen sent by Armistead's ghost that he and Travis were too late and it was waiting to collect Deekie's soul. Clay knew if she succumbed to the fever it would be his own fault. He had tried at first to ride fast alongside Travis, but was unable to do so. He had told Travis to ride ahead with her, but the man refused.

"No, Sir, we've been through enough, the three of us, we stay together," Travis said. So, they rode all night.

The town of Sulphur Springs, Texas was soon enough upon them. It had originally been established in 1854 as Bright Star, Texas but in May of 1871, the Hopkins County legislature had decided to relocate the county seat there from the town of Tarrant. They also took advantage of the move to change the town's name to Sulphur Springs, after the increasingly popular mineral water treatments that were taken there.

"The closer we git the more it reeks of rotten eggs," Clay complained to Travis.

"Well, it may smell like hell, but those waters are known to be heavenly," Travis answered. "They can cure almost anything that ails a person, including Yellow Fever. Some say that sulphur water is a modern day miracle."

"For the sake of Deekie, I sure hope they ain't just out drumming up visitors wit' them words. How is she?"

Travis had her in his saddle upright in front of him, his one arm around her waist. All she did was moan and burst into hacking coughing fits from time to time. He moved the back of his rein hand to her forehead, as he said, "She's as hot as a pistol barrel. We need to find her a sulphur bath and a bed pretty damn quick. How are you doing with your little problem?"

Clay reached down to where his thighs joined to meet the saddle. They had been jostled and rubbed raw for the many hours they had been bouncing in the saddle.

"I am as raw as a freshly slaughtered side of beef," he answered Travis. "I don't know how ya' can ride the same distance as me and not be."

Travis laughed out loud, remembering back to the days when he had learned to ride.

"It's because I actually do ride my mount," Travis ribbed him, "whereas you just allow yourself to be bounced around in that saddle."

"All I knows is that once I git off this damn horse," Clay responded, "I ain't never gettin' on another. Not unless Deekie's life requires me to do so."

They trotted their mounts into town and on the square asked after the closest mineral bath. They were directed to one establishment near the springs, to which they headed with no delay. Almost immediately, they booked two rooms which Clay insisted on paying for. Within the hour, Clay escorted Deekie, still barely conscious, into the bathing treatment.

As he settled into the bath with Deekie, Clay felt a stinging sensation burning in the raw, chapped areas *"of his undercarriage"*, as he would later say to Travis. After a few minutes, the stench of the waters seemed to revive Deekie, even if only to break out hacking into another coughing spell. But as the treatment went on, Clay thought he could see in her eyes, which had recently shone no life at all, a flicker, just the slightest flicker, of her revived spark.

"Oh. Virgil, I am sick like I have never been in my whole life. Where are we?"

"We are in Texas, Deeks. A place called Sulphur Springs, on account of these stinking mineral baths. S'pose to be the best thing for anything that ails ya'. So we brought ya' here."

"Who's we?" she asked.

"Me and that fancy pants fake minister from the stage coach. The one that was all dressed out in gray. Calls hisself Travis. He helped me with y'after it was robbed."

She was weak, and appeared weaker still when the cloud of confusion crowded crossed her brow.

"Robbed, what yer talking about?"

"Ya' don't 'member the stage coach being held up? All the shooting? The coach being flipped over? With y'in it?" Clay was amazed.

"No, Virgil. Not a t'all. The last thing I remember was crossing the Mississippi, cuz even then I was trying not to throw my guts up. I don't remember much about the stage coach other than my being jostled all 'bout. And being so sick, with every ounce of energy sucked out o' me, only to fill back up with near every ache and pain I had done ever felt. All I could think was that I was dying. I still feel that way. Am I dying?"

"I won't let ya' die, Deeks. I'll spend every piece of gold in them bags back in the room if I has to and make sure yer by my side for a long, long time."

"Virgil, I am tired like I ain't never been. Can we go back to our room now?" Deekie was fading fast.

"In another quarter hour or so, Deeks. Ya' need this sulphur treatment to be sure. We needs to git ya' stronger now, gal. T'morra', I'm gittin' ya' some proper treatments here at the clinic."

After first treatment was over, Clay carried Deekie, wrapped only in a white robe, back to the room. There he found Travis sitting on their bed with Clay's saddlebag full of gold coins next to him. Clay had found the leather bag on one of the two bandits' horses. He emptied the satchels into it while Travis spoke one last time with the survivors.

"Clay, you and me gotta have a talk." Travis said tersely. "And we gotta have it now."

"Move yer hide so I can lay her down," Clay said as he held her under the shoulders with his good arm, and under the knees with his weak stub arm. "T'ain't exactly easy doin' this with jus' my arm and a half, yer know."

Travis moved quickly from the bed as he grabbed the saddlebag with one hand and pulled back the blankets with the other. Clay laid the dozing Deekie down and pulled the sheets and blankets up over her. She slept and Clay could tell it was a more peaceful rest than the tortuous darkness into which she had earlier drifted. He felt her head, it was still hot, but he thought not so badly as before. He hoped her fever had broken.

"I gotta gets her a doctor," Clay said.

"Not until after we talk. You got yourself a small fortune in this here saddlebag. How'd you come by it?"

"Ya' theivin' from me, Travis?"

"I'd be two counties away from here by now had that been my intention. Me and this saddlebag both. But I'm here, ain't I? Go ahead and count it. It's all there. I'll wait. Then you're gonna tell me where you got all this."

"Why? What's it to ya'?" Clay declined the offer to count the coins. He wasn't sure he could even if he wanted too. There were just too much gold there.

Travis looked somewhat uncomfortable with the question. "It ain't me, Clay, it's the people I work for. They don't take kindly to me helpin' out criminals."

"Well, first thing, Deekie and I ain't no criminals. We might be poor, but that ain't no crime, is it?"

Travis emptied the saddlebag creating mountains of gold double eagles and such on either side of Deekie's ankles. "This ain't exactly what poor looks like, Clay."

Clay was the one who looked uncomfortable now, and took the opportunity to change the subject.

"All right. I'll tell ya' the whole affair, but first ya' gotta tell me exactly who it is that yer working for. Ya' sure as hell ain't no minister of any kind, not as familiar as ya' were with killing them robbers back at the coach."

Travis reached into his pocket and pulled out a black fold of leather. He flipped it open to reveal a shield shaped badge that read "Detective Travis W. I. Brooks, Pinkerton National Detective Agency."

Clay inspected it closely. Then he looked up at Travis and embarrassingly asked, "What's it say?"

"You mean to tell me that you can't read, Clay?"

"I reads a little, but anything with that many big words Deekie would read for me. She reads right good."

"It says, *'Pinkerton National Detective Agency.'* We are out of Chicago. You've heard of us, haven't you, Clay?"

All of a sudden, Clay felt as guilty as Eve's first bite of the apple. He had to convince himself that he really hadn't done anything wrong.

"For sure, for sure. Ain't y'all the guys who snuck that damned fool Abraham Lincoln into Washington town setting off the War of Rebellion?"

"That was us, but it wasn't no guy. That was our agent, Kate Warne, who travelled with the President in disguise to deliver him safely to the Capitol Building for his inauguration. Now, our agency works under the auspices of the Federal Government."

"The *aw-what of what*?" Clay looked confused.

"Auspices. Means we work for the Federal Government."

"Well, why didn't ya' just say that to 'gin wit', Travis? Yer a long way from Chicago. What ya' doing all the way down here?"

"I am here to break up a vigilante group that has a hired gun passing himself off as a Pinkerton. I'm heading down to Fort Worth to find that bastard and bring him to justice. Then, from what we learn from him, we'll go on and break up the group of cattlemen he works for. "

"Fort Worth? That's where I need to be headed. I'll make a deal with ya. I'll tell y'everything, but if it all checks out just fine, and it will, then ya needs to take me along wit' ya to Fort Worth."

Travis looked at his fellow traveller with a measured glance. "OK, Clay, if everything checks out. And I *will* have the agency check it out. I'm just surprised you'd even consider leaving Deekie here alone."

Clay had forgotten about Deekie in all his excitement. He looked down at her, to see if she had heard any of the conversation, but she was in a deep restive sleep.

"It all begun back home in Cartersville, Georgia," he said, "when this gambler named Armistead come to town. Jefferson Calhoun Armistead. He was looking for an armed escort to Nashville and Memphis…"

What Travis Brooks had failed to share with Clay was that their both being on that same stage coach to Fort Worth was no mere coincidence. Only days before, a Pinkerton agent in Nashville had busted a dealer in town selling counterfeit Confederate guns and confiscated a shipment that had just arrived. In investigating the complaint, the agent had heard of a one-armed Georgian who had talked about traveling to Fort Worth to find his gunsmith father. That Pinkerton knew Agent Travis Brooks in Chicago was working on bringing down a band of cattlemen known as the Drovers' Exchange. He had remembered Brooks reporting a connection to a gunsmith in Fort Worth that *"the Exchange"* was known to be wanting to have killed.

Travis Brooks realized that if he could track down this Georgian, he might lead him to the Exchange's enforcer. The Pinkerton only knew that man by the code name, Major Rivers, under which he sent his telegraph messages to the Drovers' Exchange. The detective had for some time been listening in on the Exchange's wire traffic. He knew this Major Rivers had been tasked with killing the gunsmith, but that was about all they knew of the man. Track the Georgian, find the gunsmith, find Rivers. Simple.

Brooks had checked the manifests of the stage coach in Memphis, and while he could not make it there in time, he was able to make it to Saint Louis. He caught the stage coach there that was scheduled to join up with the Georgian's coach in Fort Smith.

The robbery and its resultant firefight had been unanticipated, but fate had used it throw the two men closely together. Now, Travis Brooks, Pinkerton, merely had to refuse Clay's requests to join him to Fort Worth until the Georgian finally wouldn't take no for an answer.

Cord McCullough came upon the overturned coach late in the day of the robbery. The sun was just beginning to set when a man in fine eastern clothing walked towards him from the huddled mass of still frightened passengers.

"Thank God you're here," Chester, Cora's husband said to him. "We been out here all day. Are you the federal marshal? You must be. We got the stage coach strongbox over here. I assure you it hasn't been touched. I'm Chester Wells, from Trenton, New Jersey."

Chester eagerly held out his hand to shake. The smell from the coach was already raising up a powerful stench. Cord dismounted Trouble and passed his reins to Chester's outstretched hand to hold as River trotted up from behind the horse.

"Well, I'll be! I have never seen a marshal with a dog before…"

"Have you ever seen *any* federal marshal before, Chet?" asked Cord. He thought the man to be on his first trip west from his clothes, speech and mannerisms.

"It's Chester, actually. No, not really."

"Well, out West, Chet, we all got dogs. Use them to sniff out rattlers and track bandits…"

"Well, I'll be damned!" exclaimed Chester.

Cord McCullough laughed to himself at the man's gullibility as he climbed off Trouble and instantly up the exterior of the overturned stage coach. He peered down from its top to find the half-flayed, buckskin-clad corpse. The putrid stench of the body's decay rose like smoke through a chimney - concentrated and overpowering. After Cord had peered into the coach from overhead, he had to turn his head, not so much to look away, but in the hope to draw a fresh breath of air. That hope went unanswered, as the reek lingered in his nostrils. He yelled out, "Any of the other passengers killed or injured, Chet?"

"It's Chester, Marshal," replied the increasingly perturbed Easterner. "No. No other passengers were hurt. Not so much as a scratch. Just a lot of rattled nerves. We can say that only thanks to the two passengers who killed all these would-be robbers."

Cord took one more look into the wagon. He then began to climb down the coach's undercarriage. He jumped down the last few feet, kicking up a cloud of dust.

"Just how many of these bandits did these two men kill?" Cord asked.

"All four, Marshal."

"Four?" echoed Cord.

"Well, really just three ambushed us, but that buckskin-clad bastard was a passenger and he was in on it. He got shot and then was trapped and dragged to his death when the runaway carriage overturned. Wore the skin off his underside, I'm told. I can't imagine a more sickening sight in my whole life."

"I figure that's about what he deserved," said Cord.

"For bein' in on the robbery?" asked the Easterner, still holding Trouble by the reins.

"No, for wearin' buckskin," Cord quipped. "I wouldn't be caught dead in it myself. Looks like he was. You said this fella was in on the hold up?"

"Yeah, he got on the coach with us in Memphis. But I'm sure thankful that the Georgian took care of him all right."

"And just who might this Georgian be?"

"Clay, the man with just the one arm," said Chester.

Cord looked at the man as if he were joking. Certainly, there were many veterans from the war scattered about the country with amputated limbs, but for some reason finding one involved in the winning side of a stage coach shootout seemed odd. "Well, take me to him, Chet. I'll need to speak to your one-armed defender."

"Well, one and a half, really. His left arm was cut off just below the elbow. I couldn't see it, but I figure he had a stump of a pad by the way he was moving around that sniper rifle's. And it's Chester, Marshal."

"Sniper's rifle, you say?" The idea of his being a sniper instantly made him dangerous in Cord's mind.

"Yes," the Easterner went on, "he seemed real proud of that thing. Wouldn't let the coachmen put it in the storage boot. You would of thought it was made of gold. He had said we was on his way to Fort Worth to see his father. Said his '*Diddy,*' as he called him, was a gunsmith there."

"Well, now I am really eager to chat with him." Cord tried not to show his surprise. He figured this man well could be chasing the same gunsmith as he had been ordered to kill by the Exchange. Cord thought himself lucky. All he had to do was follow this man to Fort Worth and let him find his paw. It couldn't be any easier than that.

"I'm sorry to tell you that he is long gone, Marshal. Took off to get that sickly girl of his to Sulphur Springs in Texas along with that other passenger who saved us. That town's supposed to have some healing mineral waters there. I don't go for all that natural healing gibberish. May as well take snake oil from a traveling salesman, either way you're throwing your money away. My wife, Cora, is convinced that the girl was suffering from the Yellow Fever. Figured she caught it in Memphis. That other man, all dressed in gray and pretending to be a preacher of some sorts, went along with him, to show him the way there. Had it not been for the two of them, God only knows where we would all be right now."

"When did they leave?" Cord asked.

"Pretty much right after the attack," Chester said, "they took their things out from under the boot and rode off on the dead bandits' mounts. Been gone for well over eight or nine hours, I'd say."

"Damn it," Cord muttered under his breath. "Show me where these robbers' bodies are. While we walk tell me how this all went down. And don't leave out the slightest detail, Chet."

"Chester," corrected the Easterner. "My name is Chester, Marshal. By the way, what is your name? Marshal who, exactly?"

"Rivers. Marshal Cole Rivers," Cord fed him his alias. "Now get on with your story…"

"Sure, but before I do, how are you planning to get us all out of here?"

"The wagon from the stage coach line should be here any minute," Cord exaggerated somewhat, but he knew the wagon would have been sent from Red River Station and would be there sooner rather than later.

"Good, Good. We only got a few pistols and this shotgun, but we ain't exactly eager to use them. What do we do if all these corpses draw coyotes or wolves? The driver and his gunman's two bodies are over there under that leather tarp to keep the buzzard's away. I'm guessing you're going to wanna see them."

"I'll look at them later," Cord said, having no interest to do so, "but first show me these three dead bandits before it gets altogether too dark to see anything."

The Easterner did so, and told him his story as Cord inspected them. The dead men fit the general description of the three rustlers he'd been tracking.

Cord was tempted to take off then to Sulphur Springs but realized these passengers would be in dire straits if the rescue coach failed to show. He used the day's last light to collect tinder, kindling and firewood. He built up a roaring fire. It served to keep them warm, drive off vermin, and serve as a rescue beacon all in one. Cord questioned the remainder of the passengers one by one.

The sun set, and the pitch black sky soon swallowed up all the light scattered by the roaring flames when the rescue coach pulled up alongside that overturned carriage.

In a rush of thanksgiving, all the remaining passengers ran up to it, greeting the four riflemen who rode on horseback alongside it. When Chester, in his role as their spokesman, told the rescuing coachmen about the federal marshal and his dog, the riders all laughed out loud.

"No, it's true." said Chester. "They all have dogs to track the renegades. Just ask him. He's right over there…"

"Mister," the lead rider said, "there ain't no lawman any of us ever met that would bother to travel with a mangy mutt. I don't know who ya' been talking to, but he sure as hell weren't no federal marshal."

"But this dog wasn't mangy at all," Chester answered. "It had a beautiful cream colored coat speckled with a lot of big brown spots and a full mask of brown fur over its head and face. Looked like a fine hunting dog, like ones I'd seen back East. Come on, I'll find them for you. You can ask Marshal Rivers for yourselves…"

"Did ya say '*Marshal Rivers*'?" asked the lead rider. "We ain't never heard of any lawman by that name in these parts, federal or otherwise."

"Marshal Cole Rivers!" Chester insisted.

"Cold Rivers?" The rider laughed. "Mister, ya' been drinkin'? Can't say as I blame y'after what y'all been through."

"Oh, come on, the marshal's right over here…"

Chester's offer came too late, as Cord had slipped off into the night with Trouble and River. He had no need or desire to get all caught up with these stage coach riders. He had decided he would rather, under the cover of darkness, put some distance between himself and them. Tomorrow, after first light, he would report his findings back to the Exchange as soon as he came to a town with a telegraph office.

Then Cord would proceed on to Sulphur Springs to find the two men who had killed these three rustlers, just to assure they were in no way connected to the robbery. Yet, he already knew they weren't, as the stage coach's strongbox had neither been taken, nor had it been opened. Its seal was still intact. Also, none of the passenger's possessions had been taken.

Cord felt he needed to find those two men who had risked their lives to take on three, no four, armed and dangerous men. Cord had to admit to himself that his sidetracking over to Sulphur Springs might really be just to see what these two men were made of. *They were too damn much like me,* he thought. *After all, Sulphur Springs wouldn't be too far off my trail ride west from here to Fort Worth.*

Besides, Cord convinced himself, *that one-armed Georgian could lead me to his Paw, who just might be the same gunsmith I'm after down there.*

The Curative Properties of Brimstone

The devilish glow of the match soon ignited a translucent blue halo around the bright yellow rock.

It became engulfed in an eruption of Biblical fire. The coarse yellow rock was soon fully consumed in an eerie bluish halo, not unlike the flames rendered from settting pure alcohol aflame.

"It's this very yellow sulphur rock that gives these waters their recuperative powers," Travis said. "In the Bible, they called it 'brimstone'. Hellfire and brimstone was brought down upon Sodom and Gomorrah it says in the Good Book. Yet, once dissolved in these waters, these stones of hell transform to heal the afflicted of the earth."

Clay stared intently at the burning rock, never having seen anything quite like it before. "The good Lord surely works in mysterious ways," he mumbled.

"Well said, Clay," Travis went on. "These springs have an amazing power to restore good health. More than one preacher has said that the Lord is the everlasting water, the very fountain of life and in His waters even the devil's brimstone is converted to something not only useful but miraculous. After all, it has been only one day and your Deekie appears to be already improving."

Clay continued to watch the yellow stone burn, as its odor filed his nostrils with its repugnant smell. "I can't argue with them men of the cloth none. Deekie seems to be getting better a bit, I reckon, but how many more of these baths is she to have before she's back to being herself ?"

Travis looked at Clay patiently. "Give her some time, friend. Have faith in these waters, for just as no soul is washed clean with one dunk in the creek if it has no true belief in the Lord, no body is cleansed of all sickness with only a day's treatment in these springs. Perhaps never if the powers of the waters are questioned. I figure a week here might make her right. Just be patient."

"And yer still fixin' to leave in the morning to go on to Fort Worth?" Clay asked, probing the plans of the Pinkerton agent.

"Yup," answered Travis simply. "especially after talking to that stranger who was already here to heal his mangled hand and arm. His knuckles were ripped all to hell from an encounter with a wild beast of some sort. He said it was a cross between a wolf and a coyote, and that it was fierce as hell."

"What did what he say to git yer to move along so soon?" Clay asked.

Travis searched Clay's eyes. The two men had become close after foiling the stage coach robbery together.

"Oh, it wasn't the story with the beast, Clay. It was what he said about that fella who walked into his camp and shot down his two partners. He said that man had a saddle marked with sign of the star within the star. That is the mark of the vigilante group called the Drovers' Exchange. I have been sent to disrupt them, and the key to doing so is to apprehend that same particular man. He's their fixer, their killer out on the range. Anyway, that Emmitt fella only convinced me not to waste any more time here. Told me that the vigilante passed himself off as a Pinkerton Detective. He's the man I'm after, all right. Emmitt said he asked about where he and his friends had gotten their illegally converted Colt Navy pistols. Emmitt told him Fort Worth, and so I figure our killer is headed there to hunt down and take out that gunsmith."

An icy chill ran through Clay on hearing the last sentence. His own *"Diddy"* had been doing that very bit of gun-smithin' ever since he left Georgia.

Could it be a mere coincidence? Clay reached his hand out and cupped it around the burning yellow stone, as if its flame would drive away the chill of Travis' revelation.

"What would this vigilante fellow want with a lonely old gunsmith?" he asked.

"It's not him that has the feud with the gunsmith, Clay. It's the outfit he's working for. The Drovers' Exchange is a group of rich cattlemen. One or more of these men has a reason for wantin' that gunsmith gone. They might have had a man or two lost to guns bearing this gunsmith's mark. So they tell their fixer, this vigilante fella', to git on down to Fort Worth, find him and kill him."

"Kill him? Dead?" exclaimed Clay.

Travis laughed out loud. "Ain't any other way to kill a man, Clay. If he ain't dead, he ain't killed. And this man, this enforcer, who acts for them, is one bad soul. Said to have left a trail of death everywhere he travels. That Emmitt fellow saw him kill two others with his own eyes. Hides a Baby Dragoon Wells Fargo in his leather duster trail coat. Thanks to Emmitt, I now also know what he calls himself - Cord."

"Cord what?" asked Clay.

"The man never gave up anything more than that. It's likely his name isn't Cord at all. Even that might be just what he goes by on the trail."

Clay could not bring himself to look at Travis as he spoke. Instead, he just watched the flickering of the near transparent blue flame that slowly, but steadily, consumed the sulphur stone.

Clay could not get the image out of his head of his father being shot down by this unknown vigilante killer called Cord. Not before Clay could find his *Diddy,* and have so many of his questions answered by him. *Why did ya' leave the family in the first place? Why did ya' come back with them guns? Why didn't ya' stay then? Why did ya' never say even so much as "so long, son"?*

"Well, Travis, thar ain't no tellin' what mischief that Emmitt fellow and his partners was up to. But why would this Cord fella go after a poor old gunsmith in Fort Worth? For just covertin' over some cap and ball guns?"

"Hard to tell, Clay," Travis said, "I just know he is. The fact that this killer is going to be asking questions all over Fort Worth about this gunsmith should actually help me find him first. Fort Worth is just a cowtown and like any cowtown, it's not all that big a place. He'll find that gunsmith fast enough. Unless I find him first."

So either Travis was to find and likely kill this vigilante, or he'd fail to find him and the vigilante would be free to go about killing my Diddy, Clay thought. He knew he could not allow his father to be forever silenced before he himself could find him. Clay knew then that he had to go to Fort Worth with Travis. He reckoned Travis would lead him to his Paw, one way or the other. Clay knew he had to get there to make sure no harm came to his *Diddy*.

"What if I was to go along with ya'?" he finally offered to Travis after fighting a loud, angry battle within the peaceful silence of his own conscience.

"You can't go with me, Clay," Travis said. "You gotta stay here with Deekie until she's feeling fit to travel."

"No," Clay argued, "that's not the way I see it, a t'all. Ya' yerself said she was already improvin'. They wouldn't even let me go in during her last treatment at the springs, or stay in the room with her afterwards lessen' I was to git the Yella Fever. That Negro woman attendant at the springs, Jolene, is already doing all the caretaking of her. I got enough money to pay for Deekie's treatments in advance. I can pick her up here in a week or two on my way back to Georgia."

"I don't know, Clay," Travis hesitated for effect.

"That money is not illegal, I swear," Clay argued, wanting to believe his own point but not entirely doing so.

Travis glanced at him critically. "Well, I did contact the agency in Chicago by telegraph last night. They validated that story about Memphis. Got the response on the telegraph wire just an hour ago. Sure enough they confirmed that the gambler Armistead was indeed found dead in an alley by the river, like you said. His windpipe was crushed, the poor bastard. They're in the process of confirming your story about the gun dealer in Nashville…"

"I swear it's true," Clay snapped. Travis already knew it was, but he already had his fish hooked, and now wanted nothing more than to reel it in slowly.

"I don't know, Clay? A dealer buying fake Confederate weapons from you all? Sounds a little suspect to me. Even so, I guess I have no legitimate reason to confiscate your little fortune just yet. But even given that, you would dare to even think about leaving your girl here alone? When she does feel well enough to keep her eyes open for very long, you'll be nowhere to be found. Then what's she going to think? "

"I reckon ya' could he'p me write a note for her. She's real good about understanding. And she reads as good as any Yankee y'ever met."

Travis reflexively let out a hearty laugh.

"I don't know, Clay, You think too highly of us Northerners. I've known a bunch of illiterate Yankees in my day," Travis smiled. "Besides, your ass is still chapped something raw from the ride down here. You couldn't take another couple of days in the saddle if your life depended on it."

Clay had thought through this problem as well. "I can't argue that, but it t'ain't exactly my backside that's rubbed raw. In the morning I'll buy us a good hearty wagon that we can hitch to them horses. Maybe a good pilla' or two as well. That way, I won't have to chafe my manhood no further along the trail."

"Clay, you got an answer for everything," Travis said. "Tell me, though, what's drawing you so desperately to get to Fort Worth, anyway?"

Clay broke his solitary gaze at the burning yellow rock. He turned his head to look Travis in the eye. As he did something told him not to give up the whole truth.

"Let's just say, my Paw is in a bad way. I gotta get to him before he succumbs to a worse fate. Deekie will survive without me, but most likely, my *Diddy* will not."

Travis clenched his jaw, to make Clay think he was considering declining his request. What Clay had not realized was that Travis initiated this entire discussion with the intent of pulling him along to Fort Worth. After all, Clay had still been stuffing that saddlebag full of gold coins when Travis had his discussion with the busybody woman, Cora. She had told the Pinkerton that on the stage coach run from Memphis to Fort Smith that Clay had several times mentioned that he and his gal were on their way to find his gun-smithin' Paw in Fort Worth.

Travis had deliberately let loose the tale of the vigilante looking to kill the gunsmith, if only in the hope it would get Clay's dander up. It had. Travis knew that if Clay would ride with him to Fort Worth, together they would have a better chance finding his father. He figured Clay could lead him to his Paw, the gunsmith, hopefully before the vigilante, Cord, found him. And then, Travis could simply lay in wait for this Cord fellow. Even if the gunsmith got killed by Cord before they arrived, so be it. At least Travis would then be hot on the vigilante's trail.

Travis eased his jaw. "All right, Clay, you done won me over! Tomorrow we will buy that wagon and set out for Fort Worth. Together. My only stipulation is that once we get there, we do things my way. You understand?"

"No, I do not understand. Especially if yer gonna use fancy words like *stip-u-lay-shun*."

"We do things my way, or not at all," Travis repeated firmly.

"I reckon I can accept them terms," Clay agreed. "So long as we find my *Diddy* as soon as we can."

That very night, even as the two men spoke, the "vigilante" Cord McCullough worked his way across the upper plains of Texas. He, Trouble and River had earlier come to the very edge of the Indian Nations Territories when they reached the Red River at dusk, but the ferryman insisted his raft was closed for the evening. Cord thought about convincing him at gunpoint, but instead merely pointed to the insignia of the star within the star branded into the leather of his saddle.

The ferryman knew what it represented, for his face went as pale as the creamy white fur in River's speckled coat. Most people here knew of the Drovers' Exchange, and they feared its reach. The ferryman, without saying a word, boarded the man, his horse and his dog, and delivered them across to the other bank that was the Texas border.

As night fell, Cord thought about making camp, but quickly decided he would instead travel slowly by the light of the harvest moon. He wanted to reach Sulphur Springs as quickly as possible to find the one-armed man from Georgia. After all, that man's father was most likely his next target assigned by the Exchange.

Somewhere along the way, Cord might even thank the Georgian for dispensing of the three rustlers turned robbers. Saved him from having to do so himself. Cord understood that the Georgian was assisted by another traveler, and this caused the Missourian some concern. A man carrying a gun in a hollowed out Bible case, the other passengers had said. Cord did not know quite what to make of this, but sensed it could be big trouble.

River and Trouble followed the trail as Cord fought off the fatigue of the full day's ride. It would not be the first time he had caught forty winks in the saddle. The three of them would trundle along the trail all night that way, riding harder once the sun came up in the East. Cord figured for one rest stop for the mare, and with a little luck they might still make Sulphur Springs by an hour or so after midday.

The next day, Deekie awoke late in the afternoon alone in a room in the town of Sulphur Springs. She was totally exhausted, as played out as if she had been drug by a team of horses over rock-studded terrain. Every joint ached her, but they were no longer on fire as they had been during the stage coach ride. Her stomach was a hollow pit, a muddle of brine, but the wrenching pain within it had faded. Her head still pounded, but the vice that had threatened to crush her skull had eased.

The harsh daylight stabbed at her eyes. She was parched. Her mouth was bone dry, as was her mind. She did not know where she was. Her limbs felt like lead, and it was hard for her even to lift her head from the pillow. She tried to call for her Virgil, but no sound came forth. Her tongue, thick and dry, was cemented to the roof of her mouth.

Where was she? Her head pounded as she tried to think. She felt a trickle of spit crawl through the desert that was her mouth. With great effort she freed her tongue.

"Virgil," she moaned softly, "Where are ya', Virgil?"

There was no answer. A gust of cold autumn breeze blew in through the window, making the white lace curtains flutter into a frigid dance. It raked across her arm's still heated skin. Yet, while Deekie was herself warm, she no longer felt aflame as she had the day before. She came to realize all but her arms were under a heavy goose down comforter.

Deekie also came to see that everything in the room was awash in white. The comforter, the walls, the ceiling, the few pieces of furniture: a chair, a small bedside table and a cedar chest. The paleness of it seemed to be in drifts all around her, as if a snowstorm had brewed up magically in the room. The only thing not completely white was the unlit oil lamp which sat atop the bedside table. It was brass and had a delicate glass lampshade upon which a scene of the local dairy had been hand-painted.

A thought occurred to Deekie. Could this all be done so that any blood or bile from her could be rapidly identified, and even more quickly cleaned up? The thought sent a shiver through her. Was this an infirmary or where Clay had sent her to die?

Just then the door flew open and in walked a young Negro woman, herself also all dressed out in white. The contrast could not have been greater against her warm brown skin. She walked slowly over to Deekie's bedside. "Good, Chile, ya' finally be awake. I thought I heared just the softest o' stirring in this here room."

The Negress attendant laid her hand gently upon Deekie's forehead.

"Take yer hand off me, Miss…" Deekie protested in a feeble, withered voice, but quickly realized that would have to be the limit of her objection. She was too weak to do anything else.

"Jolene," the woman answered, ignoring the protest. "What?"

"Miss Jolene," she said, as if finishing Deekie's original sentence. "I'm the attendant who been looking after ya', honey. Good, I do believe yer fever has done broke."

Jolene picked up a cool compress and gently patted her patient's forehead. At first Deekie resisted to being attended to in this way, but quickly came to appreciate the comfort from the Negress' care. Jolene's soothing touch allowed Deekie to relax and soon she ceased her resistance altogether and rested her heavy, weary head into the plush softness of the pillow beneath it.

"Jolene, where's my man, Virgil?"

"I have a note at my station outside for ya' from a Mister Clay Harris. Is that him?"

"Yes, Virgil Clay-Harris. One and the same."

"I'll bring it right in with some cold water for ya', honey."

"Jolene," Deekie murmured ever so softly, "why is the window kept so wide open?"

"Yer in need of the air, dearie. Ya' done come down with the Yella' Fever. Ya' needs to get yer lungs cleaned out. Nuthin' better than a warm blanket and cold fresh air."

Deekie took a long breath. The cold air stung just a little as she pulled it deeply through her nose and into her lungs. It burned in a gently refreshing way, not in the acrid manner that she remembered from the rancid air of the coach. It was then that she realized that she was on the mend, although she was still weaker than a newborn. She knew she had to let this woman continue to tend to her.

"Jolene, please have my Virgil come to me…"

"Sweetness, he can't come to ya'. Ya' got the Yella Fever. You be in quarantine. Thank God above that he got ya' here in time for that sulfa' spring water to be curin' you of that disease. But neither yer Virgil nor no one else can come in here to see ya' just now."

"Then how come yer in here? Ain't y'afeard of catchin' the fever yerself?" Deekie was angry and thought she had caught the woman in a trap.

Jolene just laughed in a knowing way. Her manner was such that she was neither offended nor frightened. She was confident in her comforting skills and had faced many a hostile client in her days.

"Honey, I done had it. The Yella' Fever, I mean. Years ago, when I was just a young thang and lived outside Baton Rouge. I knows exactly what yer going through. I been where ya' been, where y'is now. Doctor says I can't gets it no more, so I am the one who tends to anyone coming here who has it. Just like me, once ya' come through this, ya' won't have to worry about catching it again, neither. And I'm sure yer already on the road to getting back to where yer need be. Now, 'scuze me, honey, I'll be right back with yer man's letter."

She left the room and after a short spell returned with a tall glass of cold water and an envelope. She would not give the letter to Deekie until her patient drank every drop of the water. Deekie protested, but then realized Jolene would not yield on this point. She swallowed the water all down, but noticed a slightly unusual taste. Deekie thought it was a tincture of some sort, perhaps a test to see if she could keep it down, which she did. Only then did Jolene hand the wax sealed letter to Deekie.

"Shall I read it to ya', honey?" Jolene asked.

"No, thank ya'. I can manage." With these words, Jolene left her alone, saying only that she'd be back soon.

Deekie examined the wax seal. It bore an imprint that had only the image of a single open eye upon it, below which it was stamped the word "Pinkertons". She broke the seal with her finger. She unfolded the thick fibrous stationary from the local hotel and read the note written in a fine cursive hand that was definitely not Virgil's.

Deeks,

Everyone tells me you are improving with each passing hour. I am not allowed to be by your side, or else I would be so. I can't wait until you are better and we can go home together. I have had enough of seeing the world if it continues to bring you only pain and sickness.

I figure you won't remember much of the stage coach or the attack, but the man who helped me ward it off also helped us make it here to Sulphur Springs for your healing. Without him, I don't know where we'd be. His name is Travis.

Travis is taking me along with him to Fort Worth. Since I can't be with you here, I hope to find Diddy there. By the time you'll have read this we will be well on our way. I know you are too sick to travel, even too sick for me to visit you, so I will double back for you in a week or so. In the meantime, you get yourself better real quick. When I see you next, Diddy will be with me and we'll all be fixin' to head home to Cartersville together.

Forever your Virgil

"Son of a bitch," Deekie muttered under breath. Not only was this not his handwriting, for Virgil could barely read or write, these were not even his words. *Forever your Virgil!* Might as well say, *With Love,* or some other such nonsense that her man would never utter. *That bastard left me here on the verge of dying just to go look for his good for nothing Diddy.*

Just then Jolene returned to the room, and took Deekie's wrist to measure the rate of her pulse. Deekie whipped her hand away from the Negress, who only took it back more forcibly.

"Now, honey," the Negress said with a bit of impatience, "if you gonna play the chile on me, I am gonna be forced to treat y'as such."

"Jolene, when ya' take my pulse consider I am running more than a little bit hot. My blood is boiling from that jack ass man of mine leaving me here all alone."

Jolene looked at her with a tender caring expression. She knew just how this disease could corrupt one's thinking.

"Y'ain't all alone, honey. Jolene is here wit' ya,"the Negress comforted her. "Yer Mista' Virgil Clay done made sure o' that. Don't let that letter upset you none."

"Don't let it upset me none!" Deekie exploded. "My man just run off and left me here in a strange town. Damn right I'm upset."

"It's OK, Miss Deekie. This town may smell a little strange to ya, wit' the sulfa' and all, but its the best place for ya' to be. He paid your account up a full month in advance. He'll be back. Anybody running away from ya' would have only paid for a day to two and never come back. Believe me, girl, I done seen it all before. Them men figur' you are gonna die and run off quicker than a jack rabbit, just so they don't have to even watch. But in yer case, I am sure as tomorra's sun'll rise that yer Virgil will come back to sweep you off yer precious little feet. We just gotta get ya' well enough to stand up on them pretty little feet again. Besides, y'already got another man in town asking after ya'."

"What do ya' mean?" asked Deekie, not understanding her. "What other man?"

"He said he just rode in this afternoon. Wants to ask ya' a few questions about the stage coach robbery. I fussed at him something fierce that there was no way that was gonna happen today."

Deekie's thoughts turned to Orrin Fletcher James, and his assault on the gambler, Jefferson Armistead in that Memphis alleyway. A fright ran through her. "Was he a big bulky man, with a round muscular body and face and black hair like a raven?"

Jolene thought on the question long as if she had to draw her memory from the room next door. She hadn't expected the news to rile her patient so.

"No, no. He was muscular all right, but tall and lean, not bulky in any way. He was certainly quite rugged looking, but no way was his face round. It was squared off and covered with the beard of a man who had been riding the trails. Ya' know, only a week or so's growth. And his hair was sandy, not even a dark brown. The man had a smell, though. Ya' know, that trail smell. I dunno about his needin' them sulfa' springs, but that man surely be in dire need of a plain old hot water bath to sep'rate the trail from his hide. He did have the cutest dog I think I done ever seen with him, though. It was all creamy white speckled with brown spots and a matching brown face. It followed him round like a noontime shadda'."

Deekie breathed out a sigh of relief, before feeling a wave of dizziness come over her. She laid her head down again and could feel herself drifting into a deep sleep as the heaviness of fatigue returned to race through her once more. "I think I'd like to sleep some more now, Jolene," she said.

"Don't ya' worry, honey," the attendant said, "that's just the laudanum in the water I done given ya' startin' to take effect. Yer gonna have a good, deep sleep now. Don't fight it. Jolene'll be here when you come round. And she'll be hoverin' over ya, watchin' out every minute in between."

The next morning, Deekie awoke in a groggy haze which slowly burned off like a morning fog. When it did, she felt more refreshed than at any point since leaving Memphis. True to her word, Jolene was at her bedside as she opened her eyes. By the time her haziness had left her, Jolene was bathing Deekie's face from a pan of soapy, warm water.

"We gots to get ya' looking propa' for yer gentleman caller," she said lovingly, almost motherly, to Deekie.

"Yer gonna allow him to come into this room, as sick as I've been?"

The warm cloth came to an unanticipated rest on her chin as Jolene froze before she answered. "No, Miss Deekie, that would not be propa', now would it, chile? In fact, I told him to go away and come back next week, but that man bucked up like I was standing in the way o' him and the Lord's second coming…"

"Why is he so fixed on talking to me at all?" Deekie asked. "I can't recall much of anything since Memphis."

Jolene rubbed her own head, as if the question pained her. "As I recollect it, he was more interested in yer man Virgil, though he called him Clay, and why he was going to Fort Worth. Said something about a gunsmith. I told him to go away, but he was persissen', sayin' time was urgent, and that he was on official Pinkerton business."

Deekie seemed confused at that last comment. She recalled the Pinkerton seal on Virgil's letter. She had thought that the man Travis who Virgil traveled with must have carried a signet ring with that embossed in it. "Why would a second Pinkerton Detective be riding the trails of Texas, and with a dog, no less?" she asked. "He could surely be lyin' bout that. Did he show yer his badge?"

"No, and I didn't ask for one," answered Jolene, "but ya' can ask him to see it yerself when he comes in ten minutes time or so. Now sit up in this chair so I can brush out yer hair. It looks like a rat's nest gone wild."

Jolene helped Deekie, who was weak and sure to be uncertain on her legs, stand for the first time. They moved slowly from the bed to the chair alongside it. Jolene covered her with a warm, thick shawl. As she began pulling the brush coarsely through the thicket that was Deekie's matted hair, she said, "I done seen less tangles on the fur of Fido's butt."

Deekie heard her, but opted to act as if she had not. Looking pristine for this caller was the last thing on her mind at that point. *Why had Virgil deserted me? How can I ever hope to find him again? Who was the man Travis that Virgil had left with? Was he really a Pinkerton? Or was he just someone who wished to rob her man of the small fortune they were carrying?*

"I can't believe that this man will even risk coming into this room," Deekie finally said aloud to Jolene.

"Oh, no, Honey," she responded emphatically, "yer still be in lockdown." The last word snapped in two as though she had been gored by a bull halfway through. "No, his hide is gonna be on the other side of that glass winda over yonder. It's closed now after you been all aired out yestaday. Now stay still so I can finish my brushin' o' your hair. Then we gotta move this chair over yonder by that winda pane. And if ya' get too tired while he's hounding on ya', just start clutching yer hand on the leg of this chair. I am intent on stayin' here in this room right behind y'and if I see ya' do that, then I'll cut him off like a quarter horse. You understands me now?"

"Yes," Deekie said, "and thank ya', Jolene, ya' been so kind to me."

"It ain't kindness, chile. It's mah job, now ain't it? And I am sure good at mah job…"

"Ya' most certainly are," admitted Deekie.

Cord McCullough strode toward the window with a wide, confident gait. He hated losing even a single day on the pursuit of the one-armed man he had come to know as "Clay". He and the other fella, Travis Brooks, had left for Fort Worth before Cord had rode into town. Cord was eager to catch up to the pair. He sensed they would lead him, knowingly or not, to his gunsmith.

Cord McCullough had decided to put the lost day to good purpose. He had bathed, taken a shave and a haircut before emptying out half a bottle of some decent Tennessee whiskey. The other half he would take on the trail with him after he questioned Clay's girl. Whiskey was always a welcome escape to bring on sleep on those lonely nights so often haunted by memories of his dead wife.

River trotted alongside Cord's boots as they kicked up small dusty clouds from the street's dirt in their haste. Cord would spend the next hour getting a description and any relevant information on this "Clay" so that he could spot him in Fort Worth. He had just about decided to leave the day before and forego the calling on this Deekie gal. *After all,* he thought, *how hard could it be to find a one-armed man in that town who is looking for a gunsmith?*

The one thing that Cord knew for sure, with no exception, was that the Exchange wanted that gunsmith dead. He didn't know why exactly, and had offered just to rough up the man pretty nastily to scare the living daylights out of him. Break a few ribs so that they healed real slow like, along with his memory. But no, the telegraph message was as plain as the midday sun - any daylights still living in that man, Cord was to snuff them out. No exception.

Cord was unsure what this gunsmith had done, but reckoned one of his pistols must have robbed the life of one of a cattleman's hands. Cord knew what he had to do. He had used his old ruse of being a Pinkerton Detective to gain today's access to Deekie, despite the Exchange having warned him off that tactic. Seems word had gotten back to Chicago, and the real Pinkertons were not too pleased. *Well, so what?* Cord thought, *Chicago was an awful long way off from Sulphur Springs and Fort Worth. If they want to fuss over it, they can send a detective down here.*

As he left he dirt of the street, Cord's boots clattered on the wooden boardwalk that surrounded the structure in use as the infirmary. The soft fall of River's paws on the planks clattered rhythmically to fill the emptiness between each of his own steps. As he approached the window for his visit, Cord thought that he would get a description from this woman, immediately after which he would gather Trouble, River and the other half bottle of whiskey and start heading to Fort Worth. Cord would pursue Clay so that he could lead him to his father. Then he'd kill the gunsmith, and if needed, finish off Clay too. *After all, how much trouble could a one-armed man be?*

Cord sidled up to the window, in which he found the large framed woman Jolene with whom he had talked the day before. Her girth blocked his view into the room.

"Alright, Mista' Detective Cordell *Whoever You Are*, I am giving you no more than thirty minutes with Miss Deekie. If she tires of ya', it will be even less, so mind yer p's and q's. I will be right here in the background the whole time, so don't ya' go try and shoo me off. Y'understands me clearly?"

"All right," Cord said plainly, "let's get started. And its McCullough, Ma'am, Cord McCullough."

"Ain't yer forgettin' something, Mister Cord McCulla'?" Jolene said, refusing to move from the glass.

"What's that?" Cord asked.

"It's customary to remove yer hat in the presence of a lady," the Negress Jolene scolded him.

"I ain't even in her presence," Cord argued, "I'm just standing out here in the cold."

"Don't matter none, Mista'," Jolene said. "Duff the hat or ya' might as well just go back to whence ya' come. If ya' stay here ya' be talkin' to a drawn curtain."

Cord reluctantly removed his trail-dusted black Stetson and held it in front of his belt. He then blushed as if holding it there was the most unnatural act of his being.

"Uh - huh," Jolene said in victory as she moved away from the window. "I figur' yer'd see it mah way."

What came next was a thunderbolt for which Cord McCullough was totally unprepared. In the space vacated by Jolene sat the familiar frame of a woman whose head was dropped. When she raised her face to the window, Cord McCullough's breath was stomped from his chest as if he had fallen flat in among a stampede of rattled steer.

"Callie," he only half whispered under his breath as he stood frozen in a still panic before the glass.

The woman sitting before him was the spitting image of his departed wife and twin lightning bolts of remorse and loneliness raced along his spine. Tears gathered in the corners of his eyes, which he steadfastly refused to shed. With the back of his hand he wiped them away along with the cold sweat that had frosted his forehead.

"Not Callie. My name is Deekie, Mr. McCullough," she corrected him. She had barely heard him, but noticed his inability to say anything in response to her. Deekie paused before she asked, "Are ya' feeling quite right, Sir?"

Cord drew a deep breath and sucked out the sand of the chilled morning air that had filled his lungs. His heart fell, as if God had truly reunited him with his deceased wife. His mind raced like a stallion thinking this could not possibly be happening.

"I'm sorry, Ma'am," Cord eventually brought himself to say, "it's just that you bear a striking resemblance to someone I once knew. Caught me a little off guard, that's all."

"Well for as bewildered as y'appeared to be," Deekie said, "I reckon it must have been someone might close to ya'." After saying this she smiled warmly at him. The smile penetrated Cord in a most unusual way.

She even sounds like Callie, he thought. His mind began playing tricks on him, as he swore he could faintly smell the sweet fragrance of her scent, although he knew no scent was possibly penetrating that thick pane of glass. He then clutched nervously at the brim of the Stetson in his hands, until he noticed she was watching him do so.

An abyss opened within him. It was a feeling like none that he had ever felt. A sour sea of regret sloshed within it in frantic waves, but still could not fill the vast emptiness there. He could not quell the emotions that rolled upon their breaking crests. In an instant, he was lost in his tragic past. He was held captive by the guilt he had hoped to subdue, but never was successful in conquering The remorse of Callie's death overwhelmed him as it forged a weight of repentance heavier than any mass of iron chains.

"I am so sorry," Cord finally stuttered, "it's just that for a moment, just a moment, I thought you were my wife."

His words shook Deekie to the core. They stunned her with both their candor and their tenderness.

"It is I who am sorry, Mr. McCullough," she replied. "Are ya' searching for yer wife? Is she somehow tied up in all this business involving my Virgil?"

The words echoed as if spoken by Callie's ghost. The voice was his wife's own, and each word that sprang forth was formed in her same manner. It was far too much for him to comprehend. If not for the voice's slight taint of a deep Southern accent, Cord would have sworn this was a window into the realm of heaven itself. Or worse, into the past from which he ran away as far as he could each day.

"No, Ma'am," he replied, "I am sorry to say my wife passed on several years ago. It's just that you resemble her so much that, I'm afraid, I lost my train of thought."

River pawed at his thigh, as if to say, *Git on with it.*

Cord could see this Miss Deekie was somehow flattered by his admission in the way she adjusted how she held herself. He thought she had relaxed just a bit as she leaned forward in the chair.

"Mr. McCullough, ya' got no reason to apologize. I never been mistaken for another man's wife. Ya' clearly must have loved her dearly to be affected so."

Cord looked upon her. She sat on the chair near the window wrapped in an all white body shawl, in front of a background of the blanched, cloud-like room. Only the attendant Jolene stood in contrast near the door. *Callie rests in heaven,* Cord thought, *this is her way of telling me so.*

"Ma'am, you can't imagine how dear she was to me," Cord said, as he choked on the emotions he fought not to release from his throat. He took a deep breath as he could see Deekie recognize his inner battle. Finally he said, in an attempt to leave the sting of his feelings behind, "I need to just ask you a few questions, Ma'am, following up on the stage coach robbery in the Injun' Territory."

"I'll be glad to answer yer questions, Mr. McCullough," she responded, "once yer so kind as to tell me under who's authority yer asking. Jolene said ya' told her ya' was a Pinkerton. If that is so, I should like to see yer badge."

"Ma'am," Cord hemmed and hawed, as he felt himself unable to lie to her. "I am not a Pinkerton. I just said that to get Miss Jolene here to allow me this time with you. I work for a group of cattlemen tracking down rustlers. I was on the trail of those men who tried to rob your stage coach the other day. Just didn't git there in time. Now, if you accept that explanation, I will get on with my questions. If not, then I'll be on my way."

Cord thought he should not have offered that last bit. The last thing in life he wished for at that instant was to be separated from this woman. To be separated again from *his* woman, *Callie.*

River again pawed at Cord's leg.

"Ya' go right ahead wit' yer askin'," said Deekie. "It looks like yer friend down there is in a bit of a rush."

"Oh, yeah. This here's River," Cord explained. "We been through quite a bit together. Now, back to business. Well, it appears your husband, Clay, and another man killed all three robbers, four if you include the man crushed in the coach itself. It seems that …"

"Ya' got that all wrong," she interrupted him, "Virgil's not my husband, Mr. McCullough. He's just my man. We ain't hitched, though might as well be. Most call him Clay, but I prefer Virgil, the name his folks give 'im."

"Apologies, Ma'am, but please feel free to call me by my given name. It is Cord. Mr. McCullough is a bit too much a mouthful for a simple saddle bum like me."

"OK, Cord, but only if ya' call me 'Deekie' and not that awful 'Ma'am' business. Cord McCullough, it's a strong name. I like the name Cord - that's a nice Irish name, ain't it? Is it short for Cordell?"

Hearing his name "Cordell" thrown forth from her lips was like a spear he could not dodge. It was Callie calling out to him from another realm, in the only form of his name she had ever used - *'Cordell.'* At first, the recollection was pleasant enough, until his wife's last words burned in his ears and heart: *Oh, Cordell, what have you done? What have you done, Cordell?*

"Yes, Miss Deekie, it is Irish," he pressed on. "So, who was this other fella that your man Clay was with? The man who brought you both here to Sulphur Springs?"

"I am of no help to ya' there, Cord," Deekie replied. "Ya' see, I caught the Yellow Fever in Memphis. Last thing I remember since leaving there was bouncing around in that dang stage coach, trying like all git out not to puke up my guts. To no avail, I am told. Virgil said that other man brought us here. I vaguely recollect being hoisted up on a saddle riding through the night with him. I rememba' cause I was watching Virgil bounce along as he rode through the night, but even them memories is like something out of a thick fuzzy fog."

Just like the fuzzy fog I'm battling my way through right now, Cord thought. "So this man that brought you here, the one that left for Fort Worth with Clay, do you know his name?"

"Only because Virgil left me this note. Said he was traveling to Fort Worth with a man called Travis. He said that he trusted Travis, enough to allow him to ride me in his saddle to git here. That man of mine can barely keep his own butt in a saddle, t'ain't no way he could handle me too, ya' see. But this Travis fella' I'm told had not a problem with me t'all. I don't reckon Clay even knew this Travis' last name when he agreed to let him bring us here."

"That's all right," Cord said. *I can have the Exchange check up on the stage coach manifest and I'll know who I am dealing with soon enough.* "Anything else about this fella Travis you can share with me?

"Well, just one," Deekie teased. "Virgil left me this note that was not in his own writing. I suspect this Travis wrote it fer him. The envelope was sealed in wax with a Pinkerton's sealing wax stamp."

Aw, damn it, ain't that just a kicker, thought Cord. Once more he tried to hide his surprise. "I was told your man, Clay, was going with him to Fort Worth to track down his Paw."

"His *Diddy*," Deekie corrected him. "It is his Paw, all right, but Virgil always called him *Diddy*. It's a back country thing. His *Diddy* ran away from the family just before the war. Came to Texas to make money gun-smithin'. Something about converting pistols to be breech loaders. Gave a pair to Virgil. He left one for me - Jolene, can yer go and fetch that Navy Six Shooter that Virgil gave ya' to hold for me."

"Sure, Miss Deekie, I'll get it," Jolene said, as she saw the conversation between them had settled into a civil discourse. As soon as Jolene walked out the door and Deekie heard the door click shut, she leaned as close to the pane of glass as she could get.

"I don't know what business it is of yours, Cord McCullough, but if you're going after my Virgil and this Travis fella, then I am sure as all damnation going with ya'. As long as yer ain't scared of catchin' this fever I'm gittin' over. But I ain't givin' ya' no description of Virgil to help ya' find him lessen ya' take me along. Just give me one more day to get ma' strength back full."

"Well, Miss Deekie," Cord said, "I sure as hell ain't afraid of catching no fever." He thought, *If I was to catch anything to kill me, it would only be Callie drawing me close to join her in the afterlife and end my suffering on this earth. Even if we was on opposite sides of that afterlife, cause I sure ain't earned any trip to paradise with her.*

"You think you'll be strong enough to ride by tomorrow?" he asked Deekie. "I don't want to be responsible for you fallin' back into that sickness."

"I sure as hell ain't going to sit here taking sulfa' water baths and being locked up in this here cotton-white jail cell of a room any more. Yer going to wait for me! Tell me ya' will, swear on it now. Swear to me on yer late wife's soul."

He could see the tempest brewing within her. In this way she was totally unlike his Callie. His wife had been reserved, quiet, always willing to be told what to do. And that trait had cost her life in the end, and the life of another as well. But even in her weakened state, this Deekie was as spirited as a mustang, he could see that. She was independent. His own feelings were lifted by her offer to ride with him, like a hawk rising on a fresh spring wind.

"OK, Miss Deekie, I'll wait for you," he conceded, "if you can get yerself extracted out of this infirmary. I'll be staying at the hotel up on the town square."

"Don't ya' worry none, I'll be comin' soon enough," she said, "and there ain't to be no more '*Miss Deekie*', just plain old Deekie. Y'understand? Then say so."

"Yes, ma'am," Cord said sheepishly. "I understand."

"No more of that '*ma'am*' stuff, either. I done told ya' that. Yer gonna wait for me, Cord?"

"I already said I'll wait for you, Deekie." he replied, as a small flame of anticipation was lit within him.

Just then, Jolene returned with the converted Navy Six. She handed the pistol over to Deekie. Cord had her turn it up so that he could see the underside of the trigger guard. It bore the same gunsmith's mark as the revolvers he had taken from the rustlers around the campfire. There was no doubt about it now. Clay's *Diddy* was the same man he was ordered to kill by his masters at the Exchange. The only question left was, *Who exactly was this Pinkerton named Travis?*

Arriving in Fort Worth

Their wagon wheels carved fresh ruts deep into the muddy slop of its streets.

"If we're gonna pick up any sign of your father, Clay, we best start up here near Main Street. Then we'll work our way down to that rat-infested third ward known as Hell's Half Acre. If your Paw is here, that district is full of the local scum who'll know of him, or the people he's working for."

"Ya' been here before?" Clay asked Travis.

"A time or two, Clay" the Pinkerton answered, "enough to know my way around a bit."

They had just passed through an open square square with a wooden courthouse from which rose a high spire, the face of whose clock cowboys were known to shoot full of slugs as they left town. Travis mentioned that it had been started in 1860, but not finished until after the war in 1866. Clay looked up at it as the wagon slowly slogged forward, the horses fighting the resistance of the muddy roads.

Figure 13: Fort Worth, 1876

"If this town be called Fort Worth," Clay asked, "where in blazes is the fort?"

Travis answered with the authority of someone who had studied the town carefully.

"We just rode through it," Travis answered, when we came up and over that bluff, back there where the courthouse now stands. The actual fort had been built in 1849 down along the Trinity River as one of a line of ten proposed forts stretching south from the Rio Grande up to the Red River. Their purpose was to protect settlers from the dangers lurking further west, including hostile Comanche Indians, as well as the disreputable renegades and opportunists who would dare to profit from supplying them with guns and liquor. They only ended up building seven of the forts, abandoning that one to rebuild it atop this bluff above the Trinity. But even that reconstructed fortification had been deserted by the army by 1853 for a line of new forts built further west, including Fort Belknap. With the fort itself abandoned, all that was left were the buildings to its south that had grown in as the core of this town. I guess the folk here kinda liked the name Fort Worth cause they kept it."

"I reckoned there'd still be a fort here, even if the army had done pulled up stakes," Clay responded. "There's just no trace of anything to bear out it had ever been here."

"As I said, that fort was abandoned some twenty years ago, Clay. I guess over those two decades the locals stripped it bare. All those wooden stockades would have been easy pickings for firewood. It gets pretty cold up here in North Texas come wintertime. Freezing cold, in fact."

They continued south of the courthouse, where a density of businesses stood, most servicing the courts.

"What are all these other places?" Clay asked.

"Well, this area is called," Travis said as he pointed with his outstretched arm. "Mostly businesses that sprang up around the fort back in its day. This saloon is one of the few in uptown, as most are down in the Acre. I think we'll stop for a beer. It's been a long day of traveling already."

Travis guided the team to a spot where the horses and wagon could be hitched to the post in front of the saloon at Main and Third streets.

"What's the Acre?" Clay asked.

Travis raised his head quickly. "Damn, Clay, I keep forgetting you know near next to nothin'! Hell's Half Acre is this town's *Entertainment district*. That is, if you find entertainment in disreputable acts. The Acre's full of saloons, dance halls, sporting houses and gamblin' joints. It makes up most of the third ward I was talking about earlier. Caters to the cowboys, the cattle drovers. There is a stretch there where all the longhorn of Texas pass on their way north to the Chisholm Trail. Lots of drovers, looking for one last good time before spending two or three months on the trail, are separated from their cash in the Acre.

"Just what might be a *sporting house*?" Clay asked.

"Hell, Clay, you really don't get out of Cartersville much, do ya? They're bordellos, you know, whore houses."

"Ain't never had need of one, myself," Clay responded, as if justifying his lack of knowledge.

"Lot of drovers and wranglers been coming through this town since the cattle drives began in '66," Travis explained. "Look ahead there, see that fancy stone mansion way up ahead?"

Clay looked southward, squinting into the sun.

"Yeah," Clay said, "it looks a bit out of place there surrounded by all those run down pinewood shopfronts."

Travis had by then gotten down from the wagon and hitched the horse team.

"That's Madame Mary Lee Parker's parlor house, just around the corner from Rowdy Joe's Red Light Saloon. That's pretty much the beginning of the Acre down on tenth street. Back when the fort was still here, the Army declared there could be no liquor served within a mile of it, so that was where the Acre sprang up, exactly one mile away. So, right up front is Madame Parker's Parlor House, but folks round here got to calling her just Momma. She runs the most respectable bordello in the Acre. Gets the best clientele who spend top dollar on her fillies. Some are said to get five dollars a night. So it's right up front, after all, can't have all them fine gentlemen of this town wandering too far into the Acre among all them drunken cowboys."

"Ya' seems to know quite a bit about these places," Clay observed.

"The kind of people I chase after don't exactly spend their time in churches, Clay. A man in my profession does have to blend in somewhat. Therefore, I have to look like I been there before, don't I?" Travis smiled broadly at Clay.

"Well, them fancy gray threads make ya' look like ya' should be visiting a church instead of Momma Mary Lee's, even with all the trail dust on them."

Travis then led Clay up onto the wooden boardwalk in front of the Club Room Saloon on Main Street. He explained to Clay, "This saloon opened after the fort had already pulled up stakes, so that's why it's closer in than the others in the Acre."

The two men walked out of the stark and somewhat offensive October sunshine and into the dark, cool confines of the saloon and ordered themselves a beer.

"I'm thinking we can start off trying to find that woman that come back to town with *Diddy*," Clay said, "I got no idea what she looks like, but if we can find her, she can lead us to him. My Maw always said she was nothing but what she called a strumpet, a cheap whore."

"Yeah, Clay," Travis smirked, "I know what a strumpet is, no need to explain."

"Hell, I myself had never heard the term before my Maw started wearing it out," Clay admitted. "She was hotter than a dry August creek bed at my *Diddy* over her. Right up to the day she died she called her a cheap whore."

The two men had already walked through the establishment's wide open wood and glass doors, and then passed through the batwing doors positioned just inside. Clay seemed unable to control his excitement as they planted themselves on wooden stools at the massive oak bar that stretched the saloon's length. The barkeep came over to them, and they each ordered a beer.

"Welcome to Fort Worth, Clay," Travis said as they waited for their glasses. "This is a town with a multitude of places to find cheap whores. We got many places to check. After all, this is where the West begins."

"I figured that might could be Dallas," Clay replied.

The barkeep served them up quickly, and as he did, overheard the end of their discussion. "Hell, there ain't a man tough enough in all of Dallas to rope a steer or get bucked from a bull. Fort Worth is where the West begins, all right, but Dallas ain't nothin' more than where the South peters out."

Clay and Travis laughed, cautiously, such that their smirking would not be loud enough for any other patrons to think was at their expense. The last thing they needed to provoke after a long ride was somebody's short temper.

"I gonna wander out to the jakes," Travis said, after draining his glass. Clay knew the term referred to the outhouse. "Don't you go and wander off. I don't want to be troubled with havin' to come looking for you."

Travis wandered to the back of the saloon. After several minutes Clay caught the barkeep's attention. "Another round for both of us. Say. Mista, where's the railway depot in this town?" He had forgot there was none.

"Ain't no damn trains in this town, son, and I sure as hell hope they never get here. They's all our politicians and business men can bring themselves to talk about. *'It'll bring prosperity.'* I say it's all a bunch of bullshit."

"Well, it'd be a hell of a better way to get here than by stage coach," Clay said. "That's getting to be nothing more than a chance for a fella to donate all he has to them highwaymen and bandits. We just had a taste of that."

"You don't say?" the barkeep bit back with an air of mock concern. "Just the same, I hope that those damn trains never make it to this town. Soon as they do, it'll kill off the cattle drives and our business with it. The drives are all but over for this year now, but if you came in here this time of day just a couple of months ago, we'd have been wall to wall full of waddies, wranglers and ramrods."

Travis returned just in time to explain the last three words to a confused Clay. "Those are all just different types of trail cowboys."

"All with money to spend and bellies to fill with whiskey and beer," added the barkeep. "Dallas got the railroads this year and the only thing they got to show for it was the Yellow Fever being shipped in with all the people coming west from New Orleans and Vicksburg. I heard just recently they been turning the trains back or making passengers go into quarantine. Who needs all that!"

"Right you are, my good man," Travis agreed, after starting off on his second draught, "but if the railroad did come here, them longhorn herds would still be driven up from all over Texas to Fort Worth where they could be slaughtered, butchered and loaded onto the trains over ice blocks for shipment to Atlanta, Philadelphia, and even New York. You'd still have plenty of cowboys to fleece."

"Mister," the barkeep said to Travis, "my experience says that the railroads always bring something to a town that would kill our type of business - respectability. Just look what they did in Chicago and Saint Louis. The railroads bring in respectable businesses and the businessmen to mind to it, who then bring along their wives and children. The next thing you know, these very families want to run our types right out of town on them same rails. No thank you, I'll keep things just as we got 'em, nice and dirty, just like our customers."

"Friend, I have to tell you that I just came in from Chicago," Travis said, "and I can attest that they still have more than their fair share of whores and card sharps. And in St. Louis it was much the same. Any respectability those towns have is as thin as the clapboard walls of these Main Street storefronts." He then changed the subject asking where they could find themselves some accommodations.

"Depends on what type of accommodating you might be looking for," the barkeep said as he measured their interests with an indifferent eye.

"Just a room, friend, for a couple nights or so," Travis said, insinuating the company of the local ladies was not required.

"Well, there's the Commercial Hotel just up the road, it's respectable enough," the barkeep replied. "And there's any number of fleabags in the Acre itself."

"Y'ever heard of a whore woman named Fanny Belle around here?" Clay asked out of nowhere. The question was asked in such an unexpected manner, it drew a sharp look from Travis for Clay's being just a little too inquisitive.

The barkeep noticed the wayward glance from his friend, but answered none the same. "Most everybody from here either heard of, knew of, or was trying to forget about Miss Fanny Belle. Many in a quite kindly way, if you understand my meaning."

"Where can we find her?" Clay asked excitedly.

The bartender looked at Travis, as if to gage whether he should respond. His eye seemed to measure whether or not these men were to be trusted.

"It's OK, friend," Travis said in a softened voice, "my partner here is just trying to find his Paw. He was last seen with her."

"A lot of men been last seen with her," the barkeep said and then laughed slyly. "Well, if you're trying to find Miss Fanny Belle, you might try Mississippi, Alabama and Georgia."

"Which one?" Clay asked excitedly.

"All of them," the barkeep smirked, leaning as far forward across the massive oak bar as it would allow him. "Local rumor has it that the Stone Canyon Gang left a trail of her body parts strewn from a train window as they was returning from Atlanta. She's said to have made the mistake of running off with a pile of their money. But that well could be just a tall tale. Only thing is no one has ever again laid eyes on her since she done fled with that fella."

"What fella?" Clay asked excitedly, as he remembered Sheriff Goff having said Diddy and her were picked up by some gang in the Atlanta train terminal.

"I don't know," said the barkeep, "she was supposed to have run back East with some fella who was making them a small fortune convertin' Colt Navy six-shooters. They were said to have killed her. Her fella was said to have been brought back and chained up somewhere by the gang as their slave of sorts. They kept him to gunsmith them pistols. Been chained up for ten years now, the tale goes. It's likely just a story, cooked up by them Stone Canyon Gang boys just to keep people from pryin' into their business."

"Where can I find this Stone Canyon Gang?"

Clay's question was interrupted by the loud slamming of Travis' glass on the oak bar.

"Commercial Hotel, you say, friend?" Travis repeated, intending to cut off Clay's overeager questioning.

"Fifth and Rusk," replied the barkeep.

"Thanks, much, I think we'll head over there now." Travis threw a handful of coins on the bar to cover their beers. He pulled Clay from the establishment into the autumn sky, which was quickly filling with layers of dark gray clouds.

"Clay, you can't be so damn direct with your questions," Travis said. "You're gonna draw people on us like buzzards on a day old carcass and they are likely not to be the type of people we are ready to see just yet. We gotta be more discreet about gaining this information. We don't want to tip our hands. Not quite yet."

The Escape from Sulphur Springs

The morning light had not yet pierced the infinite blackness of the night sky.

Deekie was eager to flee under its shroud of darkness. The confinement of the room had choked and stifled her. It was textured in tones of charcoal and ash under the moonlight, but would soon alight of the dazzling Texas sunrise, tempting to fade away all its slightly soiled hues of white.

The soft lunar glow penetrated the window and called to her like that of a lighthouse guiding a ship at sea. She had never seen such an alluring beam, but had read about exactly such a signal in her books. Specifically, the book that her Virgil had just given her, *Moby Dick*. Deekie had read for days after she had tired of sleep. Time had come to follow that beacon's light to her love, to her Virgil.

Deekie would use this man Cord to follow her Virgil's trail, even though he had abandoned her for the company of the mysterious Pinkerton known as only as Travis. She would, in turn, depart with the equally unknown and mysterious man, Cord McCullough. Together they would seek out her Virgil among the wild town of Fort Worth.

It had been two days since Cord had first come to visit her. He had returned the next day and she whispered through the glass that she needed one more day of rest. The sulphur spring water treatments were helping her greatly, but she still felt weak. The day after that she told him to be ready before the next day's dawn. She could no longer stand the restriction of her confinement and finally felt she had enough strength to manage her escape.

In the moonlit darkness before dawn, she went to the cedar chest, opened it and found her riding clothes. She slipped into them as quietly as she could, not wishing to wake Jolene who she knew would be sleeping on a cot just outside her door. Then groping deeply into the dark recesses of the cedar chest, her touch found the hard steel of the Navy Six revolver that Clay had left for her. She had asked Jolene to leave it with her, and her attendant compromised by placing it, unloaded, in the chest under her other things.

Deekie then moved to the window, threw up its sash, and lifted her leg through the opening. She grasped the window frame to steady herself, as a slight dizziness came over her in clearing the sill. She still was not fully herself, but could wait no longer for all her strength to fully return. She feared that Cord would tire of waiting and leave for Fort Worth without her. She did not then realize the full effect that she had over this man.

Deekie made her way to his hotel and was surprised to find Cord coming out, with River trailing close behind, from its livery stables to meet her. He had waited all night, knowing not exactly when she might come to him, only that it would be in darkness. He led out Trouble and another horse saddled and ready to ride.

She leaned over to pet his dog who was at her feet, its tail wagging excitedly.

"You've met River already," Cord said in not much more than a whisper, "and this here is my mount, Trouble."

"Hello, Trouble" she said slowly stroking the horse between its eyes. "What do ya' call the other?"

"I don't right know," Cord told her. "Just bought her for ya'. The man called her Sheila. I thought that a might' odd name for a horse. She might be stolen, who knows?"

"Then Sheila it'll be," Deekie said. "Let's git outta town before warden Jolene discovers my empty bed."

"First things first," Cord said. "You sure you can ride, Deekie?"

"Of course." She had always been comfortable around horses. Loved them, in fact. "My family had horses when I was small, before everything got destroyed during the war. I grew up riding, and that's something a girl never forgets how to do."

Cord raised his hand and placed his palm ever so gently against her forehead. It was the first time he had touched her. It sent a small burst of excitement through him.

"I didn't mean that," Cord interjected. "It's just you been so drained by the fever. I don't want you to overly strain yourself. A fall might just kill ya', now."

"Oh, hush yourself," she replied, and pulled away his hand, "I'll be fine, but ya' might help me mount up."

Deekie then approached the horse, a sorrel mare, and grasped the pommel to pull herself up. She threw her leg up, but failed to throw it hard enough to clear the saddle's cantle. She felt herself become faint and falling backwards. She then felt the power of Cord's strong hand through her riding britches under the curve of her buttocks. He lifted her effortlessly until she was upright in the saddle.

"Excuse my lack of manners, Ma'am," Cord said, "for being a little too familiar with yer hindquarters."

"Don't be silly, Cord," she replied, "I asked for yer help, didn't I? And knock off that Ma'am business. I done told ya' that."

They rode out, side by side, just as the pink streaks of dawn stretched overhead. And true to her statement, her ability to ride came effortlessly back to her. They rode west and south throughout the brightening morning, stopping only to water and graze the horses. She felt weak, but invigorated by the landscape that opened before them. They rode for two hours before settling aside a creek for a watering break.

"You ride good for an Easterner," Cord said. He had trailed her most of the way in order to keep an eye on her, in case she needed to stop and rest. She hadn't.

"Y'all boys west of the Mississippi think yer the only people ever to climb atop a horse, but I have to admit, ya' ride pert well, too," she said, as if in refusing his compliment he'd not think less of her in any way.

"Well, I reckon I should, Cord quipped, "for being nothing more than a saddle tramp."

"After she died, ya' mean?" Deekie said without thinking. The words hit him with the force of a runaway bull.

"Yeah," he said, hanging his head, "after she died."

Deekie then instantly felt great sorrow for having let loose her tongue so coarsely. She could sense the sorrow that it raised in him.

"Ya' loved your wife greatly, didn't ya'?"

"Callie?" he said, slowly raising his head. "Like no one or nothing else I've ever loved in this world."

"I thought that was the name ya' muttered under your breath that first day when ya' saw me. Do really I remind y'of her?"

"In ways I can almost not quite stand," he said, "and in other ways you are totally her opposite."

For the first time she sensed the full measure of effect she had upon on this man. It was more than just her supposed uncanny resemblance to his dead wife. There was something else in their connection, something that lurked much deeper within him. She was determined to find out what it was.

She reached out and placed her hand on his arm, just below the shoulder. "How did she die?" Deekie asked as tenderly as she could.

He seemed to wince at the question, as if it were the very thing he feared the most. Not dying as it would be for most men, but having to to recall the death of his wife.

"Perhaps some other time I'll tell you," he said. "For now, we need to resume our ride. We're burning daylight."

And ride they did. They rode hard for the rest of afternoon, until Deekie unknowingly let signs of her fatigue show. Cord, still trailed her still and watched for signs of her weakness. When they appeared, Cord, rode up beside her. "That's enough for one day, Deekie," Cord said, "Trouble and River are in need of a good rest. We'll camp along the river just ahead."

Truth be known, Trouble and River could have gone on for hours more, but Cord respected her fatigue. They made camp that evening by the banks of the Trinity.

Deekie rested there, thankful that spoken aloud or not, Cord had recognized her stores of energy had been fully drained from within her. All the while the dog, River, lay protectively by her side as Cord unsaddled, watered and allowed the horses to graze. When they had grazed enough he brought them nearby the firepit he had constructed from river stones and using long strips of rawhide hobbled their legs. Then, just before nightfall, he gathered enough wood to get them to morning.

It was late in October and the daylight faded quickly. The temperature, which had been refreshingly cool during their day's ride, dipped to a bone penetrating chill as the night fell hard upon them. Deekie and Cord sat around the flickering flames, taking in its warmth and sharing the camaraderie that was generated from a day's ride. It was a pleasure that had special meaning to Cord.

"Deekie, I have to say," he began, "that I am more than a might impressed with your riding skills. Especially with your just gettin' over the fever and all."

She looked at him, and with his gaze upon her, wondered if in the firelight she reminded him even more of his dead wife. *How many fires had they sat across? How many tender looks were passed? How deep was their love before she perished? Just how had she died?*

They had a feast of jerky that Cord had purchased in Sulphur Springs, and chased it with deep swigs from his bottle of Tennessee whiskey.

"My Callie would never touch this stuff. I always figure if it don't cure you of what ails you," he said, "it will at least make you feel a hell of a lot better on the way out."

"I'm feeling pretty good already," Deekie admitted. "Are we safe here, Cord? Aren't there Indians in these parts?"

"Indians?" Cord scoffed, "we are just ten miles or so past Dallas. Ain't been an injun in these parts for some years now. Tomorrow, with any luck, we'll ride into Fort Worth by day's end and sleep in a nice bed. Now if we was to proceed west from there across the open prairie, then we would have something to consider since that is still land claimed by the Comanches. But here we are more than safe, and besides all that, we have the best watch dog in the world in River. He's never let me down yet."

"Ol' River is the best, aren't ya?" Deekie said in a hushed voice as she took the dog's face in both her hand sand worked her fingers massaging its jowls. "How in the world did y'ever come across him?"

They chatted in the dancing light of the flames as Cord told her the story of rescuing the dog from the coyotes. Deekie was intrigued.

"And while we are yappin' over it," she said as he finished the tale, "howd'ya' come to name your horse? Ya' said Sheila was an odd name for a mount, but what about Trouble?" That is quite a queer name for a mare."

Feeling the warming glow of the whiskey in his gut, Cord told her the story of the night of Callie's giving birth to their son, and his brother's death at the hands of the Jayhawkers. She was riveted as he did so, and while Cord wanted to leave out the details of gunning down the party of Kansan Jayhawkers in revenge, he found that he just could not do it. He admitted every bloody detail to her.

"Ya' was in a rage, Cord. They took yer brother's life for no good reason a t'all. Thank God ya' had Callie to pull ya' through such a bloody, unnecessary tragedy."

Cord swallowed another sip of the whiskey, and gazing into the fire, answered, "Yeah, she pulled me through all right. Wasn't but a few months after that when her Maw died, so I hope I pulled her through that a bit in return."

"I'm sure ya' did," Deekie said reassuringly. "Still, it must be tough riding yer brother's horse all this time. I would think every time ya' mount up on Trouble, she must remind y'of yer brother Sean."

"No, I think of Trouble as bein' all mine, now. Besides, Deekie, the memories of Sean are some of the best that I have. I'm honored to ride his horse day in, day out. It keeps him close to me. He gave his life protectin' us all. It's the other memories that I have to fight from coming back into my mind."

"Callie?" she asked, as gently as she could.

"Yeah, Callie," he said morosely, the whiskey by then having taken its deeply rooted hold on him, "Callie and Sean…"

"Yer wife and yer brother?" she asked, incredulously. "Did they betray y'in that unwelcome way?"

Cord looked at her as if her head had grown a third eye. Then he began to laugh sweetly.

"Naw, Deekie, my brother would never have thought to wrong me that way. I meant my wife and our son, little Sean. After my brother Sean died, we named my infant son after him. Callie and little Sean," he repeated with an echo of heaviness.

"Oh, I see," she gasped, "I am so sorry. I was indeed very, very confused."

"Confusion can be a terrible thing sometimes," Cord said, as if the statement had a special meaning to him.

"Where is little Sean now?"

Cord didn't answer right away, just took another, pull from the bottle, noticeably harder this time. He let it spread within him, before he finally answered, "Gone with his Mama to Heaven, it saddens me to say."

Deekie thought she saw his eyes fill with the weight of unshed tears. She wondered how long he had lived with these miseries, the ones that remained, as yet, untold to her. She got up from her place by the fire and walked slowly over behind him. She knelt and wrapped her arms comfortingly around his neck.

"Cord," she whispered, "y'ave to unburden yerself. These memories ya' carry round like a sack of stones, they are not just bruising ya' with their weight, they are tearing away at ya'. Ya' continue to wallop yerself with them. The only way to shed them is to get them off yer chest. Why don't ya' go ahead and tell me what happened to Callie and little Sean?"

She watched as he bit his lip, fighting the emotion swelling inside him.

"You look so much like her," he said with the slightest of slurring of his speech. "You sound like her, 'specially when your voice is soft like that. You even ride like her. But, girl, you are also so different from her. Callie would never be as direct as you can be, never quite so bold."

She began to stroke his face. He started to raise his hand to take hers away, but stopped midway.

"Tell me more about her, Cord. What was Callie short for?" Deekie thought if she could get him talking about his wife, he might tell her the full story of what happened. Her curiosity burned like a fuse within her. She simply didn't realize the pain it would unleash in him. She thought him strong enough to take it. She had to know.

"Callista," he said, allowing the name to roll gently from his tongue wrapped in the nostalgia of cherished memories. "It was a family name, her grandmother's name. They said every other generation had to have a girl called *Callista*. She loved when I called her by it. *Callista*. She said it reminded her of her daddy calling out to her. I never understood that fully until I met you. When you say my name, it is like her calling to me."

She was by then haunched over him from behind. Her hands dropped from his face and were rubbing hard into the tense knot of muscles where his rough neck met the spread of his strong shoulders.

"Ya' really loved her so much, didn't you?" Her breath was warm and moist in his ear. She knew what she was doing, knowing it might make him think of her, and share with her the story of his wife's demise.

"I loved her like no one else in this world," he said, modifying his statement earlier that day. He said this so tenderly that Deekie could almost feel in her hands the recollections rising up in him in a trembling tension.

"It's all right, Cord. Whatever happened to her and little Sean wasn't yer fault. Let it go…"

It was then that she felt a tremendous shudder explode within him, as if his core had released all its grief in one fell swoop. It rose violently within him. He turned to look into her eyes, and said in a bitter, whiskey-stained voice, "We both know it was *all* my fault, *Callie…*"

His eyes watered but he stubbornly fought the shedding of tears. Deekie reached to once again take his cheeks in her hands as she repositioned herself from behind him to just aside. She leaned into him, pressing hard.

She used her thumbs to massage away the moisture collected in the corners of his eyes.

"Stop blaming yerself," she felt compelled, as if from another dimension, to say to him. His reaction was to shudder again, but this time almost continuously.

What she did next even she could not have anticipated. She brought her face forward and kissed his rough-skinned cheek, not in a sensual way, but more in a motherly manner, in hopes of calming him.

His response was to reach up his hand behind her neck and pull her head closer to his. He placed his weathered lips on the smoothness of hers, and although she resisted, the shuddering in him abated. Deekie felt guilty as she had initiated this, had unfurled pure torment in this man. She knew what she had to do to make up for it. She relaxed and pressed hard back into his kiss. However, when his hands waterfalled down to just below her shoulders, she pulled away harshly.

"Cord, I can't," she said, again softly, but firmly. "I just can't. I'm Virgil's gal, and I wouldn't be able to live with myself."

He sat dejected as she moved away, scooting back to her spot still held for her by the loyal River.

"I understand, Deekie." Cord said with not an ounce of emotion in his flat voice. "I'm sorry I lost control of myself. I know a lot about not being able to live with yourself. It's not a burden you ever want to carry around, I can guarantee you that. It never goes away. Never."

She then cursed herself for having pulled away so abruptly. She felt as if she had just succeeded in opening him up, lowering his defenses, only to have him retreat once more behind his high wall of seclusion.

"Ya' really need to share yer grief with someone. Whatever happened to yer wife and child, Cord," she re-engaged, "whatever happened, it was not yer fault…"

Cord did not respond at first. He merely gazed into the midst of the flickering flames, as if something lived there, something he desperately wanted to hold, but knew it would burn his touch unless it was first extinguished. In that way, he gave into the pause of reflection. It was as if the pattern of the red ember coals were a puzzle he could never solve, so his fate was to roam the unforgiving plains and peer into a thousand other fires; to raid a hundred other rustler camps, until one of those being raided was finally successful in putting him out of his misery.

"What happened, Miss Deekie, was *exactly* my fault," he eventually murmured, not raising his eyes. *"You see, Ma'am, I killed them both."*

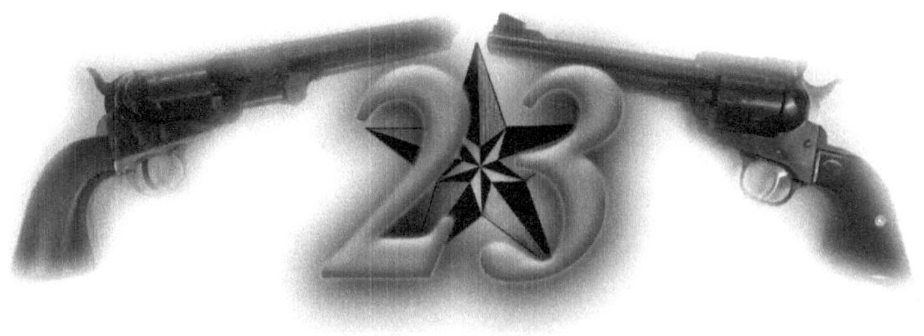

Hell's Half Acre

They had visited every ruinous crook of the Acre's decrepit sprawl. Yet, the truth they sought evaded them.

Clay and Travis had covered every bit of the Acre over their first two days in town. As they explored the saloons, the gambling houses and dance halls, Travis took over the role of the questioner in an attempt to teach Clay how to do so in a more relaxed and less threatening manner. But even that took a concerted effort. for Clay was absolutely bustin' to find his *Diddy* and take him back to Cartersville.

Within the area know as Hell's Half Acre there were a score of places a man could find drink, a card or dice game or half an hour's company with a *"sportin' gal"*.

"I told you about them fancy parlor houses," Travis had explained to Clay on their first foray into the Acre proper. "They're full of elegant furniture, the best whiskies to be found in all of Texas, and likely the prettiest and least used-up whores, too. Now, these other places calling themselves ladies' boarding houses are nothing more than lesser bordellos, a solid notch below the parlor houses. Most of those places are all in the Acre proper. And most of that district's saloons will also accommodate any lonely, homesick drover looking for female companionship in their backrooms. Those girls from the boarding houses or saloons are likely to cost a dollar or so a roll."

"And them little shacks we're passing along?" Clay asked of Travis.

"Those are called cribs, Clay. Those are the lowest rent places some girls can get. Crib girls make only two to four bits a roll. As you can imagine, they ain't too much to look at, compared to the girls in the bordellos and parlor houses, but they still get plenty of business. Seems to be no end to the demand for it."

"And they sure got plenty of saloons here in the Acre, as well," Clay said. "Rowdy Joe's Red Light ya' done told me 'bout. What are some o' the others?"

"Like you said, Clay, plenty. There's the Tivoli, the Club Room, the El Paso, the Occidental, The Empress, The Emerald and the Palace Saloons to name a few. Oh, yeah, there's also the Waco Tap Room."

"Too many saloons," muttered Clay.

"Hardly, friend," Travis answered. "See how wide this street is? This year alone them drovers ran some five hundred thousand head of longhorn steer through here on their way up to the Chisholm Trail. That means plenty of thirsty cowboys with money to spend…"

"…and company to seek," Clay added. "That I get. I just can't imagine my *Diddy* involved in all this."

"On the contrary, I think what's really bothering you," Travis answered, "is that you actually can see that. From what you've told me, the man would fit right in."

Since that discussion, they had visited most of the saloons in town. Travis took the lead in asking of anyone he could where a man might get his hands on a pair of breech-loaded six-shooters, preferably old Colt Navies. He did so earnestly, as he figured if he could unite Clay with his father, he could then wait until local gossip of the reunion would draw out the vigilante Cord, who he was really after. Travis figured he would personally share that gossip by his asking after the guns in every watering hole within the Acre. It would spread from there on its own quickly enough, he figured, and before long, the Exchange's trail riding enforcer, the man known as Cord, would track down Clay. And Travis would be waiting for him.

It happened on their third afternoon in town. They were in the saloon known as the Waco Tap Room, when Travis was approached by an old wrangler wearing trail-dusted chaps, a worn, tanned leather vest and a sun faded Raffia straw hat. Its side brim edges were rolled up like a pair of tongues licking out at the air, tasting for danger, or maybe seeking out opportunity. His beard was unkept, his teeth yellowed, and the bulbous tip of his weathered nose bore a branched network of spidery red veins. The ridge of that same nose seemed to be broken in all directions, like the twisted branches of a mesquite tree.

"You fellas appear to be new in town," the wrangler said to Travis instead of introducing himself. "Word in the Acre has it y'all been asking around about getting yer hands on some repeaters…"

"Breech loaders," Travis clarified. "We got no call for cap and ball guns. Hear there's someone round converting old Colt Navies. A pair of them would do us nicely, friend."

"You got some might unusual and particular needs, don't y'all?" the wrangler said.

"No, nothing unusual about it," Travis replied, "We just know what we want, and what we don't."

The wrangler had screwed his face into a tight coil before relaxing it. "We'll as it so happens, I might could be able to fix you both up," the stranger said, "with something like this here revolver, of course assuming you got the cash for such a purchase."

The wrangler handed Travis a Colt Navy 1851 sixshooter that had been converted. Travis looked it over, then passed it on to Clay who recognized it immediately. It was just like the one he had shoved within the holster of his gun belt under his field coat. Clay turned it upside down to inspect the trigger guard. He could see nothing in the dark saloon light, so he walked over to the closest oil lamp.

"What in blazes is he doing?" asked the old man.

"I guess he's just making sure you're not selling us a pig in a poke," Travis replied.

"I could easier just taken him outside and fired it a few times."

"Oh, I'm sure he thinks it works just as you say," Travis baited the old wrangler, "but he wants to make sure it was made by a reputable gunsmith."

Clay was by then inspecting the gun, upside down, under the glow of the oil lamp, drawing more than a few odd looks from the saloon's other patrons.

"Who cares who converted it so long as it works?" the old buzzard asked in disbelief.

"Well, friend, it appears my partner does…"

Just as Travis had said these words, Clay marched back to where they stood.

"How does two hundred in double eagles sound?" Clay replied. The offer drew a look of rebuke from Travis, which Clay saw, but ignored.

The stranger looked at them both, his eyes flickering from one to the other like the tongue of a serpent, before saying, simply, "Allright. Two hundred. Each."

"Each? You can't be serious," Travis erupted. "Two hundred is far too much for even the pair. You're trying to take advantage of my young friend, here."

The wrangler's old trail-worn faced did not flinch.

"Fine. Then you boys can simply wait until Samuel Colt's company stops selling all their new .45 caliber Peacemakers only to the Army and starts offering them to the public. Or you can travel up to Connecticut to plead with Colonel Colt to sell y'all a pair of them factory converted Navy Sixes. But if you want a pair down here in Texas, the price is four hundred dollars in double eagles."

"Convincing Colonel Colt might be quite the task as he's been dead for some eleven years now," Travis quipped. "Therefore, I guess my friend here will be forced to acquiesce and avail himself of your stated price."

"Acqui- what?" The wrangler said. "You sure talk a might too fancy for these parts, Mister."

"Ya' got 'em here? I wanna to see them first," Clay blurted out.

"Oh, we got 'em, all right," answered the wrangler. "Just not here in the Acre. I'll take a ride to our camp tonight and I'll have them here tomorrow noon for ya. But you gotta pay me now." The demand fell flat on the stale, dank air of the saloon.

"No way," said Travis, "What do we look like, a couple of greenhorns from back East? We give you payment now and we'll never see hide nor hair of you again."

"All right," conceded the old stranger, "I'll bring the pair in good faith, so long as y'all agree to the price. Four hundred in gold. Thats twenty double eagles. Got it?"

"Deal," said Clay, "but only so long as them guns bear the same gunsmith's marks."

"Don't you worry, sonny. These will be as legitimate as the gun I'm carryin'." The old coot smiled broadly, knowing he had just struck a cracker of a deal. "And if you want more for the same price, I can get that same gunsmith working on them right away."

"No, the two is all we need," Clay said.

"Hold your tongue, partner," Travis said. "If he can make them fast enough, I'll take four more, but I'm only willing to offer six hundred for the four revolvers."

The old man's eyes widened like a child on Christmas morning. "How long you boys gonna be in town?"

"Just five more days," Travis answered, confusing Clay as to what he was doing.

"Well, that will be a rush job, but I'll see what I can make happen. I'll have the first two guns noon tomorrow and an answer on the other four. Deal?" The old wrangler reached out his calloused and rope-burned hand to shake on its closure.

"Deal," said Travis, thrusting his hand in into the old buzzard's. Then, the wrangler reached out his hand to Clay, who extended his own hand more tentatively than had Travis. As they shook, the old geezer grabbed Clay's limply hanging left sleeve with his free hand and squeezed.

"Sorry, fella," the old wrangler said, "just had to know if you really had lost yer arm or was just playing me in some way. In the war?"

"Chickamauga," Clay responding in an insulted tone, as he was tiring of answering this seemingly never-ending question. He looked down on the hand squeezing the sleeve where his forearm had once been. The old buzzard released the empty grasp of sleeve as he noticed Clay's irritated glance.

"OK, fellas, meet me here tomorrow noon and we'll get on with business," the old wrangler said. "I got me a little drinking to do before I head out tonight." With that he turned and walked away from Travis and Clay.

"What was all that business about buying four more guns?" Clay asked Travis. "All we need to do is follow him to take me to *Diddy*."

"No, all he had to do was to go wherever they might have had two of your *Diddy's* guns already stashed," Travis explained, "but now, he smells a thousand dollar payday, and want's every penny of it. The fact is that now he has to check to see if his gunsmith, your Paw, can turn them other four guns around in five days. This means he is sure to go to wherever they are holding your Paw against his will."

"I dunno, Travis," Clay said, "he seems too old to be a member of a gang. Not much of a rustler, is he?"

"Just an old one," Travis answered. "He's just what we call a front man for the gang, someone they trust, to a degree, and use so they don't have to come in town where they'd be recognized themselves. That way they don't get arrested for gun-runnin' by some over zealous marshal who might have come into the Acre chasing some other outlaw, or maybe just to have himself a drink or two."

"So what do we do now?" Clay asked.

"How many of them double eagles you got with ya, Clay?" Travis asked in a whisper.

"I counted out five hundred dollars worth before we put the rest in the hotel safe," answered Clay.

"Keep your voice down," snapped Travis in a stern rebuke, although it was no louder than a murmur, "or we're gonna have every drover who ever even thought about being a robber laying in wait to bushwhack us. Five hundred is good. That gives us a enough of an excuse."

"Excuse for what?" asked a befuddled Clay.

"We're gonna wait till he leaves and then trail him. Must be a good way from here or it wouldn't take him overnight to get back. We follow him, find where they're holding your father, and work up a plan to get the drop on them all. I figure he'll nurse a beer or a whiskey or two until sunset so he can travel in the darkness. But we'll still track him, don't worry."

"And the five hundred?" Clay said in a hushed voice.

"Our excuse if we get caught. We changed our minds and wanted just to get the two Colt Navy Sixes tonight."

"All right, Travis, but what was that bit about grabbing my coat sleeve?" Clay asked.

Travis smiled to himself, "I guess he wanted to make sure he knew how to recognize you, Clay. Either that, or he wanted to see just how much of a threat you might be in a gunfight. Or he might just be curious why a one-armed man needed a *pair* of Colt Navies…"

The Confession

*Cord and Deekie traveled the next day
in an icy state of silence, each of them
burdened by the awkward night before.*

They were just two to three hours outside of Fort Worth, following the trail along the meandering Trinity River. It was then that Cord suggested they stop and water their mounts one last time before making the final press. Even River seemed to agree, for as soon as both riders dismounted their horses, the dog laid down and sprawled itself out in the tall grasses by the river's edge.

Cord took out his canteen and offered a cool drink to Deekie, who took it from him in what was their first real communication of the day. He offered, and she accepted.

After taking a deep draw from the canteen's depths, Deekie handed it back to him. When he reached for it, she grabbed his arm. She couldn't take the stone cold silence from him anymore.

"Cord, I'm right sorry about last night," she said gently. "Ya' was so caring and unselfish in sharing yer world of hurt with me, and I was just nosing like a busybody so painfully into yer past with *Callie*. Forgive me, but it's just somehow I feel connected to her, ever since that special way ya' first looked upon me."

His stubborn, sullen solitude slowly eroded. Cord glanced at her as a softness eased across his hard, chiseled face.

"No, Miss Deekie, I am the one who needs to apologize. Whiskey and memories are a dangerous combination. I'm sorry but the more I drank the more you began to look like *Callie* in that firelight. It won't happen again, for tonight we won't be sleeping in our bedrolls, but on real mattresses in each of our own rooms in town."

"How can y'afford that, Cord?"

"I got some money due me from the men I work for," he said. "A good bit, actually, for past services."

She still did not really know the services he spoke of, or what kind of work he did. She felt embarrassed to ask him, as she felt she had plied too far into his business the night before. She regretted asking him so much about his past. *He had said he killed her, and their son. It couldn't possibly be, could it?* She became choked with an overpowering guilt, over which was layered the fog of confusion. *What did he mean saying he killed them both?*

She walked away from him toward the river to hide her flooding emotions. "It just hurts me so that I remind ya' so much of her…"

"Well, like I said, you do and you don't," Cord replied, following after her. "You may look and sound like her a bit much, but you certainly don't act like her. In that way, the two of you differ like night and day."

Deekie blushed, not knowing how to take his words. At least he was talking to her again, and that was a major improvement over hearing only the wind whispering in her ear all morning and early afternoon.

"I'm getting a might hungry, Cord," she said, changing the subject.

"Well, we done finished the jerky and hard tack that I brought along," he said, "but if you can wait a few more hours, I'll buy you a big steak dinner in Fort Worth."

"That sounds good," she said, "I can wait." She smiled, then added, "Last night ya' said yer just a saddle tramp. Winter is coming, is that when ya' go home?"

"My home is the open range, Deekie," he said.

"What about yer house? Where ya' lived with yer family?"

"Gone. Burned to cinders," he said, his as his jaw tightened. "Nothing left but a few foundation stones."

"Indians did that?" she asked. His words were tight, and more taught with each question she asked. But somehow she could not stop herself. She needed to know.

"Jayhawkers," he responded after ponderin' on it.

"Last night ya' said ya' killed them all, 'cept the young boy."

"There's a lot of them damn Jayhawkers in Kansas, girl," he said.

Deekie held up a bit. She could see him fighting the pain of his memories, but still he seemed determined to bare his guilt fully to her. She was probing him again, yet he did not shut her down.

Deekie was determined to find out what exactly this man had suffered through, and why he still endured the torture of its open wounds. She was about to press further, when he spoke.

"Have you ever heard of what went on at Lawrence, Kansas, Deekie?"

"No," she said, uncertain what it could have to do with their conversation.

"Like I said last night, that Kansas-Missoura border was aflame with the Free State Jayhawkers battling against the Slavers from Missoura. There were raids on both sides of that border. Had been even before the war for more than a decade or so. So much so they called it *Bleedin' Kansas*. When the war finally came, I signed up for fighting as an irregular in the battle of Shiloh, in western Tennessee, but I got so fed up with all the unnecessary and brutal killing, I jumped from the Confederate Army and went straight home to Callie and little Sean. However, I picked a bad time to make it back that way, getting there just before the raid on Lawrence."

"I don't know what that was, Cord," she said.

"It was a massacre," Cord explained, "plain and simple just a slaughter. A bloody damn slaughter that didn't need be. There was a group of Jayhawkers there, called themselves Red Leggers, who had been raiding the Missoura farms that summer, setting them on fire and freeing their slaves and taking their goods back to Lawrence. Well, a group of Confederate irregular soldiers under a Captain Quantrill retaliated by raiding that town of Lawrence in late August of '63. Killed up to two hundred men and boys, and if you listen to the Jayhawkers, wives and widows too. They butchered a mess of them Red Leggers just to make their point."

"'Ya' said ya' were an irregular - were ya' part of that business?" Deekie was aghast.

"No, I was in hidin' for running off from the Confederate Army at Shiloh. It was in the week after the Lawrence Massacre that a handful of riders were kicking up a ton of dust coming up the road to our farmhouse. I thought they were Confederate Home Guards who had tracked me back there. Figured they was comin' to take me back to the war, so I grabbed my rifle and made to the woods. I watched from there, but I soon figured something was wrong. They pulled little Sean and Callie out on the front porch. There was four of them, although from the distance one appeared to be nothing but a teenage boy."

Deekie knew this was it. Cord was about to unload his mass of regrets onto her. She hoped she could handle the torrent of sorrows that were about to flow.

"Two of them searched the farmhouse," Cord continued, "and came out with a few things in their hands, then went around back and lit bottles full of kerosene or some such liquid and threw them on to the house. It was then that I had a good look at the boy. He was none other than the same boy I had let live years earlier when I had killed them Jayhawkers who had gunned down my brother Sean. These weren't Confederates at all, they were Jayhawkers out to even up the score after Quantrill's raid on Lawrence. That boy had led them straight back to our farm. I knew then I should have killed him the first time."

"Oh, Cord, tell me ya' didn't..." Deekie sighed.

"My first two shots took down the two of them men who had set the farmhouse aflame. The boy came running up towards them, and the anger in my blood boiled over, telling me to drop him, and so I squared him up in my sights..."

"Oh, no, Cord," Deekie gasped.

"I squeezed off that round, and he fell dead in his tracks. Then there was just the one last Jayhawkin' bastard left. I searched through my sights back to the front of the house, which by then was fully engulfed in fire. The smoke clouded my view. Just then, a stiff breeze parted the fumes, and that big fat fella stood with his back to me. He had a gun on Callie just beyond him. She was pleading with him, waving her arms at him and such. I wasn't about to watch him kill her and as he raised his revolver to shoot, I took aim on him with my rifle and pulled the trigger. Hit him clean in the back, near his shoulders. I knew the shot was enough to drop him, but somehow he stood and wavered as though something was holding his weight up against what should been him falling to the ground. Then he finally went down on his side. Callie was hysterical and ran straight toward him. I thought, *No woman, run away, not at him. Why would she do that?* Before I could get another round off, that bleedin', dyin' Jayhawkin' son of a bitch shot her, dropping her to the ground. A rage rose up within' me. I had heard men say they saw red, but at that moment everything in my eyes swam in a crimson sea. My nerves seemed to be jumpin' outta my skin as I pumped another three rounds into the center of his fat back. It was then that I saw them both."

"The Jawhawker and Callie?" Deekie asked, "Ya' said she had already fallen." Cord was looking out over the river, but when he turned to face her, his tears flowed freely from his eyes. Cord could not bring himself to answer her. She feared what words he would speak next, but knew she must draw their sting from the wounds of his mind where they had festered for so long. "Tell me, Cord," she said as she moved to embrace him. He pulled away from her.

"No, not Callie and *him*. That fat bastard Jayhawker had fallen atop my little Sean, who he had been holding all along in his clutches. I couldn't see my boy through the broad back of that Red Legger son of a bitch. That's why she ran towards him, he had our little Sean. She ran to get our boy. Our poor, defenseless child. After she was shot, from where she lay, she watched as my last rounds went right through that Jayhawker and into my sweet little boy. I could see the horror and sheer agony on her face I killed my own son in pourin' out my vengeance on that last damn Red Legger. Callie was forced to watch every second of it."

Deekie's hands raised aghast to her mouth. *No wonder this man had wrestled so with the carnage that was his memories. No wonder his soul was in such turmoil.*

"Ya' didn't know, Cord. Ya' couldn't possibly have seen him." Deekie was crying picturing the scene in her mind. Tears cascaded down her cheeks, mirroring his own. She looked away from him, out over the Trinity's flow. Its endless waters swept past offering no hint of absolution.

"I raced out to little Sean," Cord continued, "but he was already gone as his bullet-riddled, bloody body lay there on the ground. The child hadn't lived to be six years old, because of me. I then ran over to Callie, who was frantic. Her screams were like nothin' I ever heard out of her, ripsawed with terror and hysteria. She had tried to get to Sean, but being shot in the chest, she could only lay on the ground spittin' up a fountain of blood. It sprayed forth with every pitiful wail she made. Only this kept her from finding the words to condemn me. When I looked into her eyes, they silently cursed me. *Cordell, your killing ways have caught up to us all. You killed that poor Jayhawker boy and the Lord made you repay his life with our Sean. Damn you, Cordell. Damn your ways. Damn you to Hell.*"

Cord began to tremble as he paused from giving voice to the memories that had haunted his life's every moment since then. His eyes still flowed, and he made no pretense to shield this from Deekie.

"Was she able to speak to y'at all?" Deekie asked.

"I held her in my arms in front of the inferno that had been our home," Cord said, "And all she would say to me was, 'Bring my boy to me.' I said to her, 'Callie, Sean's gone.'" But she would only repeat to me, 'Bring him to me, I want to die with him in my arms.'" Which of course I did, despite how riddled Sean's body had become with my fury. Callie was fading fast. I placed Sean's tortured body in her arms. She clutched him to her bleeding chest, but her bloody lips could only spare me the words '*Oh, Cordell, what have you done? What have you done, Cordell?*' And after she fought to speak these last words, she died. Just as I wrapped my arms around their entwined lifeless bodies."

He dropped his head, heavy with gravest shame.

She turned her back on the Trinity to face him. "Cord, I am so sorry," Deekie said as she wept openly in front of him. "I am so sorry to remind y'of her, and make ya' think back on that terrible way that ya' lost her."

He stood before her, his chin driving into his chest.

"Deekie, you didn't make me recall it," Cord said, his eyes averted as he talked, "for not a single day has gone by as I rode through these lands that I haven't thought about that moment. It's just that last night, under the flickering light of the fire and the warmth of that whiskey in my gut, I somehow figured if I could just kiss you… just kiss *Callie*, one last time in front of the blaze of our crumblin' homestead, amidst our dreams turned to ash… that she might just somehow find it in herself to forgive me. I apologize for my using you in that silly, drunken way."

Deekie moved close to him. She took her palm, cupped his chin, and raising it said, "Ya' was brave enough to speak the truth to me, and you'll see, it'll set ya' free."

She covered his lips with hers and kissed him passionately. She felt him resist, as if he could not accept her pity. She then pulled back to whisper in a her softest, most comforting voice, one from another time, another realm, the simple words, *"I forgive you, Cordell."*

He wrapped his arms around her and pressed himself hard into her. Their mouths merged into one, and in this way their souls were joined. There was no flicker of of campfire flame to tempt them, no burn of liquor to confuse their intentions. The moment raged, and then passed between them. They both knew when it had done so.

Deekie then pulled back slowly from his lips, then paused before she kissed his cheeks. Then she whispered ever so affectionately into his ear, *"Cordell, Callista forgives ya'. I feel it washing over me like the descent of a distant spirit. She forgives ya', Cord."*

Cord lowered his head upon her shoulder, as if he might cry like a child. He then reached in his pocket and from it pulled out the silver German crucifix. He undid its clasp and raised his head, and ever so gently placed it around her neck. As he did, Deekie took the cross into her hand and gazed down on it.

"It's beautiful," she said. "Was it Callie's?"

"It's all I have left from her," Cord replied.

"I can't take it," Deekie said, "It wouldn't be right."

"Wear it for me, just for the next few days…"

"I just can't…"

"Let me see it around Callie's neck for just a few days more." Cord pleaded. "Allow me this one last bit of pleasure."

"All right, but yer taking it back when I leave," she said firmly.

"Thank you, Deekie," Cord said. "You have no idea how much this means to me."

Tracks of the Old Buzzard

Travis and Clay trailed the old wrangler westward to a small enclave called White Settlement.

From there, the old man continued west along the road that soon devolved into nothing more than a grassy trail. He was easy enough to track in the moonlight, as he made no effort to check his tail to see if he was being followed.

The trail cut into the open prairie. They could see, even in the soft glow of the moonlight, its sage bushes and long grasses swept ever so gently by whispering winds. It was completely different countryside than they had ridden through coming into Fort Worth. For the first time, Clay came to understand the town's motto, *"Where the West Begins."*

After some time, perhaps two more hours of gentle riding, the trail wound itself through a hilly, rock-strewn stretch of countryside that unbeknownst to them was known as Stone Canyon. The sun was just beginning to rise and the light had a streaky rose-colored hue to it. The trail crested over a hill and then descended down toward a creek, when Clay asked, "What in the world is that?"

A tall bird streaked across the road just in front of them. Its head had a tall crest spiked with a fan of prideful feathers. It moved in quick but in herky-jerky strides. In its mouth wrestled a small snake or lizard fighting unsuccessfully for its freedom.

"That's a road runner, Clay," Travis explained. "They eat snakes and such. Plenty of rattlers out in these parts for them to feed their young ones on. And likely even more cottonmouths and water snakes down there ahead in the creek. So mind where you set yourself down."

The two men found that in paying their attention to the road runner, they had lost sight of the old wrangler. They pressed onward, following the winding, descending trail. It wrapped round the base of a bluff. They thought the wrangler had merely made a turn out of their line of sight. It was then that a single rifle shot rang out from just behind and above them. Bark exploded from the closest cottonwood tree, as a voice in front of them called out.

"I know you fellas are likely thinking that our rifleman is a pretty bad shot to miss you both so widely. Let me set your minds at ease that he is not. That was a warning shot, but the next rounds will find themselves true in the centers of your backs. So git to throwin' down your weapons on the trail. NOW!"

Clay and Travis knew then they had followed the old wrangler straight into a trap.

Clay and Travis then abided the voice's instruction, even though it remained unembodied. They tossed down their revolvers into the grass-strewn dirt. Clay did not throw down the pocket pistol he had taken to wearing in the shoulder holster under his field coat, figuring they might not detect it, and he might use it to make a play.

"Stay on your mounts," commanded the voice from the shadows that had not yet been driven off by the rising sun. As it instructed them further, a youthful figure, unattached to the voice, emerged to take up the surrendered weapons.

"All right, y'all can go ahead and dismount now," the voice from the shadows directed, "but no sudden movements, or our rifleman above y'all will prove to ya' just how crack a shot he is."

After they had gotten off their horses, the man behind the commanding voice from the shadows emerged into their sight. He was a balding fellow, going on forty years old or so, Clay figured. He carried a rifle of his own. He walked with a slight hop in his gait, likely from an old bullet wound. He signaled them, by sweeping the barrel of the rifle, away from the horses.

"Hey, Seth," the second more youthful gunman said, "this one is already carrying a converted Colt," He yelled out to the leader, who by then had hobbled up to inspect the gear still saddled on their mounts.

"Pretty fancy rifle you got sheathed here," the man called Seth said to Clay as he inspected the Whitworth. "Why didn't you throw it down when I called for it?"

Clay said nothing.

"I asked you a question, fella…"

"I never took it out of the sheath, I figured that's akin to throwing it down." Clay's words were tight.

"I guess you didn't much want to ruin that fancy sniping scope on it. Now don't you fellas go and do nothing stupid like," Seth said again. "We're going to walk from here on in. It ain't very far to our little *hacienda*. You boys been awful busy askin' around the Acre the last few days about our gunsmith and his works, so it just so happens your gonna get to see what you come for."

Seth let go of the Whitworth and allowed it to drop back in the saddle sheath. "Ol' Hank says you boys might be carrying a mess of gold coins, is that right?"

They didn't see the old wrangler, but figured he had passed by his hidden companions. Both Travis and Clay took him to be the "ol' Hank" that this man, Seth, spoke of.

"I got five hundred dollars worth in my pockets," Clay said, hoping this fact would keep them alive.

"And a hell of a lot more than that back in our hotel safe," added Travis to insure it did.

Clay and Travis then followed the lead of the hobbling renegade, Seth, who swung the rifle in his two hands in wide arcs for balance The other man, barely more than a boy, followed them with his rifle raised. They passed around a bluff, the same from atop which the still unseen rifleman followed their every move through his sights.

Clay could smell the fire as soon as they cleared the bluff. The scent was powerfully strong, and instantly provoked memories of his childhood. Clay by then realized it came from a large Spanish style stone cabin complete with a terra cotta tile roof set within the protective surrounding of a natural horseshoe-shaped bowl of rock that was the bluff. Surely this was their so-called *hacienda*. Nestled safely within the rocky overlook on most every side, its only opening, a massive oaken door, was aligned with the narrow opening of the rocky horseshoe.

They were escorted inside the stone house through that great wooden door which swung open wide into the structure. The interior was one open massive room, with sparse furnishings. A bed, a table, a makeshift privy chair. Upon crossing the threshold, Clay was assaulted by an overbearing wave of heat. It rolled on him, threatening to pin him under, it was so intense. This was because the room was dominated by a great hearth, more than six feet high and ten feet in width.

Clay simply looked into the raging blaze inside. It gave off a great shower of flickering ruby sparks popping up from its ember bed, along with the smell that Clay recognized instantly from his boyhood. The scent of molten metal that he still associated with the sounds of tongs, anvils and hammers clamoring in the night. Those memories were from much happier days when he was just a boy and his Paw had still attempted to earn an honest living as a blacksmith and gunsmith.

Inside the *hacienda* were two other figures, already present. The first was the old timer they had met in the Acre and trailed here. The radiant glow of the fire from the hearth, as well as its reflection off the interior stone walls, painted his face with the flickering color of a circus clown. He wore a proud smile across it, one that threatened to burst like the rising sun into the full fledged laughter of a clear western morning.

"Damn if you two ain't a matched set of *idjets*," he said as Clay and Travis emptied their pockets onto a wooden table by the door under gunpoint. When Clay laid down out the twenty-five double eagles, ol' Hank's demeanor changed suddenly. "Damn, y'all wasn't pulling my leg about them gold pieces, was ya'?"

"That's only a small part of it," Travis added.

"So you've already said," Seth said.

"We changed our mind and just want to git the two Colt Navies. Thought we could square up tonight and be on our way.

"That must be why you were layin' back so far behind ol' Hank, instead of catchin' up wit' him on the trail," Seth said as he poked his rifle's barrel into Travis' back. "Now you both git on in there. We need for young Garrett here to tie you both up.

As they were pushed further into the large open *hacienda*, Clay made out the second figure standing aside the hearth. He was chained by the ankle as a dog might be. In the flickering firelight, the man looked old and haggard, thin and frail. But there was no mistaking it was the very same man he remembered from those days before the war.

There was no doubt it was Clay's *Diddy*.

Clay was overcome with elation on seeing him. He ran across the room to embrace his Paw, and failed to heed warnings to stop by Seth and the second gunman.

"For God's sake," Travis shouted, "don't shoot him,.Your gunsmith is his Paw. Give him a second."

Clay hugged his *Diddy* tight. "I so reckoned ya' might be gone. That I'd never see y'again!" He whispered into his father's ear.

"Is that so, Enos?" Seth asked aloud. "This one-armed fella is yer son?"

Enos Clay-Harris extracted himself from his boy's embrace, and said simply to Seth, "Yeah, he's my eldest."

"Anything else you want to tell us, Enos?"

The old man thought for a second, then looked at his son and whispered "Sorry, Son", before returning his gaze to Seth. "Yeah, he's carrying a pistol up under his left shoulder."

A Second Introduction to Hell's Half Acre

Deekie cleansed her face from a washbowl; River watched from her bed.

All she had left within her had been given to the day's ride, she thought. Or was her the fatigue she was feeling from the emotional ordeal of Cord's confession? In either case, in the comfort of this hotel room, she yielded to it. A weariness seemed to start in her bones and then spread like the stain of a thief's greed through her. A slight nausea persisted. Deekie hoped it was not the fever returning.

She laid herself down on the bed next to River, who instantly rose to circle atop its covering to find the most comfortable spot to bed down. It turned out to be in the crook between Deekie's body and her arm. The warmth of River's touch comforted her. It coaxed her to give in to the lethargy that had arisen in her. She needed its safe respite.

The slow pace of the dog's rhythmic breathing, along with the beams of afternoon sunshine slicing through the moth eaten holes in the dried out, musty shade, somehow relaxed her nerves. She had pushed herself hard to keep up with Cord as they crossed the open range and now she was content give in to the demands of her body.

Perhaps she had left Jolene and Sulphur Springs too soon. She was no longer violently ill as she had been in the coach or even in the first days at of her treatments, but she was still unbearably weak. It was as though every last ounce of energy had been sapped from her, as if all her blood had been drained from her veins. Over the past few days, her life seemed to be running only on her fierce will and rigid determination. Those were no longer enough.

Knowing that Cord had the room next door also comforted her, even though he had just left to walk down to the telegraph office in town. She could not think of anything other than how emotionally scarred this bold and powerful man was. *How had he managed to pen it all up for long? With all he had been through, was the wicked life he led a surprise? Was his retelling to her of his wife's and son's deaths the first time he had ever done so? Did it bring him the least bit of relief from his grief to confess it aloud?*

I killed them both, he had said the night before, and Deekie was sure that in his mind he held himself accountable. But how could Cord have known that last Jayhawker who was threatening his Callie was blocking little Sean's body from his sight? How could he possibly be responsible for what happened to them both? He had not pulled the trigger on the round that killed Callie, yet he still blamed himself. Deekie harbored a tremendous pity for Cord within her heart, and something inside her wanted desperately to absolve his soul. *But then there was Virgil.*

Deekie knew what must for years have run through the rugged man Cord's mind, over and over again. It surely wore out ruts so deep his guilt would never be able to claw its way out of them: *If I had only killed that Jayhawker boy under that live oak near Straight Creek the day that Sean was born, I would not have had to drop him the day my Sean died. I might have seen that fat Jayhawker grab my son, and not fired. There was no need for my pure innocent boy to die other than my rage.*

Deekie knew that his mind wretched back and again between these two misdeeds regarding that boy. The first was an act of compassion that Cord should have never granted, but in doing so it set up the later vengeful act that he should never have allowed himself to give into.

She was sure that somewhere, beneath Cord's tough as nails exterior, was a kind and gentle soul. She had seen glimpses of it in his eyes. She had felt it in the kisses that he had driven so forcefully into her lips, wishing and hoping her to somehow be his Callie. Not for a night, but only for a moment of absolution. She felt the quivering of his mouth, the gentle trembling of his touch. In those moments she had wished she could have given herself fully to him, if just for that one night, to calm his eternal unrest, but she did not because she was her Virgil's gal.

What ripped through her own mind was a single question that she had asked herself over and over again since that riverside confession earlier that day - *If Cord had told me that whole damned story amidst the firelight and whiskey the night before, would I have given myself to him out of sheer pity?*

Cord McCullough walked through the muddy streets of Fort Worth wrestling with a conflict brewing inside him. Could he even kill the gunsmith when he found him as he had been ordered? What about his being the Paw of Deekie's man, Clay? He put it aside as he entered the telegraph office and penciled out a quick message to send:

ARRIVED FORT WORTH WITH GIRL STOP WILL FIND HER MAN WHO WILL LEAD US TO GUNSMITH STOP WILL BRING GUNSMITH BACK FOR QUESTIONING STOP REPEAT WILL CAPTURE GUNSMITH FULL STOP

Cord then waited for a reply, one he prayed would simply read PROCEED. Instead, it came ten minutes later, short, but not quite as short as he had hoped.

GUNSMITH TO BE SEPARATED NOT CAPTURED STOP REPEAT SEPARATED WITH NO QUARTER STOP ACKNOWLEDGE FULL STOP

Cord looked down upon the code word SEPARATED, which in their not so subtle cipher meant separated from this world. The term WITH NO QUARTER simply meant don't give the bastard a chance, no matter how he pleads for his life.

Cord thought of Deekie and felt a tremendous guilt. She had no idea he was using her to get to her one-armed man, Virgil, who would in turn lead him to the gunsmith. Yet, even without Deekie's role in all this, it had been the first time, in all the killing he had done for the Exchange, that he had questioned whether the target had truly earned the fate the ranchers had decided for him.

For the first time the conscience of a jurist had entered the executioner's mind. He had these thoughts even before Deekie had entered his life. Before his *"Callie"* had returned. But was it perhaps her soul that had sent Deekie? Was it through the Georgian gal's reflection of his wife's looks and manners, that she was confirming his hesitation?

Cord could see in the future of his mind's eye Deekie sneering at him, seconds after he would have just pulled the trigger that killed the gunsmith.

What would she think of me then? That my confession was faked all along just to gain her sympathy? Or that in the decisive moment I had retreated once more into the lonely confines of my hardened heart?

Cord thought he could not go on with the gunsmith's killing, knowing that Deekie would feel the bitter sting of betrayal. *Would she possibly think any less of him than she already must? What does she already think of a man who had admitted his heart's deepest regret? A man who could confess the killing his own wife and child?*

Cord put aside his torment, and sent the reply message that simply said ACKNOWLEDGED STOP DELIVER FUNDS OWED TO THE COMMERCIAL HOTEL FORT WORTH FULL STOP.

He knew the money would be hand-delivered within a few hours. Yet he never considered it blood money, as the rustlers he had hunted for these men deserved every bit of his fury that they had received. But the gunsmith was another deal altogether. What had he done other than turn some cap and ball guns to breech loaders? For this he should die? Then, Cord McCullough, for the first time since coming under the employ of the Exchange, left the telegraph office not sure he could carry out their kill order.

Hours later, Cord McCullough treated Deekie to that steak dinner he had promised earlier. They ate inside the hotel's dining room, having had enough of riding, and for that matter walking, for one day. In reality, Cord sensed that Deekie needed a rest and allowed her as much time alone in her room as he could. Well, at almost alone with River.

They sat over a plain white tablecloth, and when the steaks arrived, they were enormous cowboy cuts. Both Deekie and Cord dug in immediately, and most of the meal was consumed without conversation. Despite the drama of their day, both riders bodies were starved and desperately needed to be fed. When they were done, Cord had nothing left but a picked over bone. Deekie had half a steak left.

"Save what's left for River," Cord said, "he'll really enjoy that. I'll save my bone for him for another day. He 's used to getting my bones, but he'll appreciate all that meat you've left for him."

"River can have his feast," Deekie replied, "cause as hungry as I thought I was, I cannot eat another bite. It was delicious though, wasn't it?"

"Yeah, " answered Cord, "just a hair's bit better than jerky and hardtack."

"Especially after the jerky ran out," teased Deekie. "Ya' went and done took care of yer business down at the telegraph office while I slept, Cord?"

"Yes, I did at that," he said, "they owed me some back pay, and delivered it an hour ago."

"What exactly do these men pay ya' for?" she asked innocently.

The question hit Cord like a round to the chest. He knew he could not lie to her, but neither did he wish to disclose the truth of the situation.

"Let's just say I clean up some situations for them."

"So, ya' round up lost cattle?"

"Not quite." he answered. "It's a little more complicated that that. Let's just say I round up the men who round up their cattle..." His words trailed off.

"I don't understand," she said during his pause.

"... who round up their cattle but aren't *spose* to..."

"I still don't understand," she said.

"Cattle rustlers, Deekie," he said with a little frustration. "I take care of cattle rustlers for them."

"Oh, I see," she said. "And just how, exactly do ya' *take care* of these rustlers?"

Cord hemmed and hawed. "Well, to be truthful, that's pretty much up to them."

"Ya' take them to jail, then?"

"Not very often," he answered. "Usually, they choose otherwise."

"Ya' kill them?" Deekie was shocked.

"Only if they force me to," he said in his defense.

"Ya' kill innocent and defenseless men..."

"I ain't never killed an unarmed man in my life," Cord said with venom in his words, "and ain't nothin' innocent about these types. Ain't nothin' more serious out here in the West than horse theivin' and cattle rustlin'. The men I work for take both extremely seriously."

"And they pay y'in blood money?" Deekie pushed back from her seat at the table and stood to leave. "I can't believe ya' would do such things, Cord."

Cord uncoiled across the table and grabbed at her wrist. "I always give them a fightin' chance," he said taking her arm hard, causing her body to jerk in response.

"Get yer hands off me, Cord McCullough," she barked. The entire dining room was watching them.

Cord released his grip. Deekie pulled away and ran upstairs. Cord paid, grabbed up the bones and followed her.

At the top of the steps, he rapped on her door, but to no avail. Finally he gave up and returned to his. River was still locked in his room from when they had gone down to eat. Cord gave the dog her steak. River settled down on the floor with it and went to work on the remains of her meal.

"Enjoy that boy," Cord said, "cause when she finds out how you help me earn a livin', I doubt she'll ever feed you such again."

The fullness of morning came with Clay and Travis still alive. They were tied up and gagged as the few remaining members of the Stone Canyon Gang argued among themselves. All the while, Clay's Paw continued his servitude, converting more Colt Navies for this gang.

"I say we kill both the bastards," said Garrett, the youngest of the three gang members present. "They sure didn't come out here to wish us well. Hell, that one had that fancy sniper's rifle. They figured to pick off what's left of us, one by one, at long distance. Thank God they were dumb shits enough to walk right into our trap following ol' Hank. Let's get this over with and kill them now.

The fate of the two captives hung in the hot sweaty air. Before the next man spoke, Seth yelled at the chained gunsmith, "Son of a bitch, Enos, you gotta keep that fire up so damn high? My ass is already double roasted in here."

The gunsmith looked up at the three men huddled together. All seemed to be waiting for his response.

"You fellas are free to talk outside. If you want these guns converted that I owe ya, I need to be hammering out breech plates, which means that fire needs to be kept hotter than General Sherman's temper."

With this, Clay's Paw drew a glowing hot disk of metal from the fire with his tongs and began hammering it flat against the anvil that sat in front of the wide, tall hearth. His eyes would flash upward as he did so, to gaze upon his eldest son, shackled in leg chains like a dog, just as he was.

"What do you figure, Warren," Seth asked a second gang member.

"Garrett just might be right, Seth," he said addressing the leader over the gunsmith's hammering. The speaker was another youngster, only a few years older than the nineteen year old Garrett. "I say we take them both out right here and now. Why take any risks?"

Seth ran his fingernails along the bald skin of the crest of his skull, as if parting the hair that long ago given up possession of that parcel. He gave the appearance of great contemplation, but in truth, he had already made up his own mind. He just wanted to figure out the easiest way to get the others to agree to it.

"Look here, Warren, Garrett," Seth countered. "These boys had some five hundred dollars in gold eagles on them. They sure as hell got at least a thousand dollars more back at the safe in their hotel. Damn, they might have five thousand dollars or more in gold coins in that safe. We kill them here and now and we're going to lose all that. We'll have to fight our way in and blow that damn safe just to get to it. Might get one or more of us killed in doing so. We can't afford to lose any more gang members. We done lost six of us over the past dozen or so days, and counting Will up on the bluff, that leaves only the four of us."

"What the hell about me?" ol' Hank protested.

"I keep telling you, Hank," Seth said, "you ain't no member of this here gang. I know you been hanging around the *hacienda* much, maybe even watchin' over Enos here and there, but you are not a full fledged member of this gang. As far as I'm concerned, you never risked your life for the rest of us all."

"But ya' was happy to use my hide to lure these killers out here, wasn't ya?"

"You'll be compensated plenty," Seth replied angrily, "but you ain't getting a full cut of them double eagles. Now, Garrett and Warren, keep in mind this might be our last big score for a while. The gun racket is peterin' out, anyhow. And this fancy dressed fella over here has a card on him identifying him as a Pinkerton. Surely he came to shut us down. Even if they don't, word has it that the Drover Exchange is out for our blood after that rancher Vaughn Anders' son was shot dead with one of Enos' conversion specials. I say we shut this whole undertaking down. Let these two take the rest of the cash out of the hotel safe for us, then we kill them all. We can then move on out West, maybe to the Arizona Territory. I hear that area's rife with cattle rustlin' still. That's my piece."

"Well, I think y'all might wanna reconsider before you go off and kill that Pinkerton," ol' Hank said through his fuzzy gray beard. "They's considered federal agents, same as killin' a marshal."

"So, it ain't like we haven't done that before," bragged Warren.

The leader, Seth raised a hand as he said, "Hold on there, Warren, I'd like to hear how it is ol' Hank has got this all figured."

Young Warren was not amused at ol' Hank getting his say before the other remaining gang member.

"Seth, what about Will's thoughts on this?" Warren objected, "don't my brother figure for nothing in this gang anymore? His say should count more than this old hoot's."

Clay and Travis were listening with great interest to the four figures discussing their fate. Travis was intent on collecting their names. Besides, the old buzzard Hank who had lured them here, there was Seth, the gang leader, the young guns Garrett and Warren, and as he had just heard, the rifleman atop the bluff was Warren's brother, Will.

Yet, all Clay could think of was what kind of life his *Diddy* had been living for the past decade or so under these men. These men, or others like them, had come after him and caught up with *Diddy* and Fanny Belle in Atlanta. Whether they killed the whore or not, they brought his *Diddy* back here to work off the money they had absconded with. That same money his *Diddy* had given his Maw to bring the two converted Colt Navies to him during the war.

"We'll git your brother's thoughts when you go up to relieve him, Warren," Seth said. "I do want to hear his reckoning, but first let's hear how ol' Hank has it figured, as he's been watching these boys in town for us the last couple o' nights."

The three men turned to look at the old geezer, who sat upon a stool not far from the hearth, his old bones seemingly enjoying the heat.

"Iffen that one," Hank pointed to Travis, "really is a Pinkerton, then y'all got big trouble. I watched him go to the telegraph office several times before I moved in on them. If he turns up dead or goes missing, all hell will rain down on y'all. It won't take long before any other feds find their way out here and figur' ya done killed their man."

"Don't listen to him, none," Garrett yelled out. Warren and I say kill 'em, and we both know Will's of the same mind."

"Shut yer trap, Garrett," Seth yelled, "you both had yer say. I done give the soapbox to ol Hank, so let him finish. Or do we need to throw down over this?"

The outburst had caught everyone by surprise, none more than Clay and Travis. The Pinkerton made a mental note that this gang's leader was a volatile man.

"Well," ol' Hank went on, "I know y'all figure you got a great set-up with this here *hacienda* being in the middle of a rocky bowl and with either Will or his brother Warren always up on top that horseshoe watching over us at all times with a rifle. But if the Pinkertons bring out the army troops from Fort Belknap, there won't be enough rounds to fight them all off. The way I see it, yeah, shut down this operation, sure, cause them Colt .45 Peacemakers will soon enough start finding their way down here anyways. Nobody's gonna want old Enos' guns when they can get the real deal. Let the gunsmith go, he's paid off his debt many times over."

"So you figure just let Enos and his son here go?" Seth said. "Just like that? The Pinkerton too? So they can come back to either arrest us, or just out and kill us for what we done all these years to the gunsmith?"

"Ya' said it yerself," ol' Hank repeated. "Take the money from the hotel and run, and let these two free. The way I figure, this game's dun played itself out."

Seth thought for a second on what the old coot had said. Yeah, ol' Hank was only an errand boy, if that term can be used for someone so long over the hill, but he had always been a voice of reason from outside the gang proper, and Seth appreciated his view of things.

"Thanks, Hank," Seth said, as he began his own figuring, "but there's one thing you're forgettin'. Six, maybe seven, members of this gang have shown up dead in the last two weeks. Quincy and Jesse's corpses both got turned in at Caldwell, and nobody done seen nor heard of Emmitt since, so he might be dead too. And then there's our four gang brothers that got taken out in that damn stage coach hold up. Somebody's gotta pay for all that carnage. And I'm thinking we gonna start with these two."

Seth played with the Pinkerton's card in his hand. "The one-armed man over there was sportin' a 1849 Colt pocket pistol in a fancy shoulder holster befittin' a riverboat gambler. And this one *claims* to be a Pinkerton." Seth read from the card, "Travis W. I. Brooks, Pinkerton National Detective. Travis W. I. Brooks, now that's a mouth full. Let's just shorten that, shall we, say to your initials, *TWIB*. Well, let's hear what this *TWIB* has to say for hisself."

Seth slowly pulled his piece from its holster and walked over to the detective. He spoke to the the Pinkerton in a grim voice. "I'm gonna free your muzzle, *Twib*, but if you so much as twitch, it's all over. Got that?"

Travis nodded twice and Seth untied the knot behind his head. He whipped away the bandanna, and Travis flexed his jaw several times to its fullest extension, trying to work out the cramps he had been fighting in it.

"So before we get on with things, Twib, you got my curiosity up. Just what does the W I stand for?"

"Walter Isaiah." Travis said

"Okay. Travis Walter Isaiah Brooks," Seth said as he backed away and trained his gun on Travis. "Man, that really is a mouthful. I think I'll just call ya' by yer 'nitials, *TWIB. So, Twib,* Mr. Pinkerton Detective, speak your piece. And don't go bein' all long-winded 'bout it, neither."

"Y'all pretty much worked everything out," Travis said, "but you got your enemies all confused. Neither the Pinkertons nor I got any interest in your gang, but I do in the man who is out to kill you all. He's the very same man who killed your rustlers up on the Chisholm Trail, then tracked down the three that waylaid that overland coach. We been following his telegraph communications with the Drovers' Exchange for quite some while now. He's been assuming the identity of a Pinkerton at times, and we are out to stop that. We also got our sights set on breaking up the Drovers' Exchange. That's why I was sent here, to arrest their man, this one calling himself Cord *something or other.* We'll take him alive, so we can get what we need out of him on the Exchange."

Travis hadn't said that Cord killed the coach bandits, only that he had tracked them. Not willing to claim their deaths for Clay and himself, he left this misrepresentation by omission to fester within their brains.

"That sounds like a whole lotta hash," Seth said, "being served up to save your own necks, *Twib*. Then, why did you bother to come out here after ol' Hank?"

Travis did not answer right away. Instead he rolled his head in a circle to work out the aches in his neck and shoulders. "See, he's stalling," yelled out Garrett.

Despite this, Travis still took his time in answering both the the question and the accusation. This might be his last chance and he wanted to make sure he got all of his thoughts out exactly as they might benefit him best.

"I ain't got no reason to stall," Travis finally said, "just ain't used to being hog tied and gagged, that's all. I came out here along with Clay, because of this fellow Cord I told you about. This vigilante is trailing a few days after us along with Clay's gal. They should have gotten into Fort

Worth last night or today based on when we know they left Sulphur Springs. We know his name is Cord *something or other*. I figure he'll come out here sooner rather than later to kill the gunsmith, as we know he's been ordered to do by the Exchange. I thought Clay and I could laid low, kept an eye on your camp until he came and I'd arrest him. But I gotta warn you boys, this Cord fella is one bad hombre, and if he's gotta blaze his way through you all just to get to that gunsmith, he will. From what we know of him, he ain't got an ounce of fear in him. If anything, the man seems to have a death wish, but ain't quite willin' to make it easy for us."

"Well, tough or not, we might just make that wish come true for him," Seth said. "Know this man by sight?"

"No, never seen him," said Travis, "but I got no reason to need a description of him. Clay's girl is with him, and I was on the coach with them both, so she won't be hard for me to spot. I bet she can tell us all about him."

"Then tonight, we all ride into the Acre, empty out your hotel safe, then you spot this gal and this Cord fella, and we'll kill them. That'll cinch things up nice and tight." Seth seemed pleased with himself.

"And then the Drovers' Exchange finds another vigilante to come after you all, one you don't know. What'll you do then?" asked Travis. "No, the only real play here is for me to capture Cord McCullough alive so we can get the information we need to break up this Drovers' Exchange. That's best for your what's left of your gang."

"Why are they so pissed at us, in the first place," asked Warren.

Travis saw this might be his last opportunity to stoke the group's fears. He knew that gag would be going back on soon, and he wanted these thugs to really fear the intent of the Exchange.

"You boys been flooding this area with these guns." Travis explained. "The Exchange's ranchers are likely to have lost a few hands to those guns along the way. Y'all are complicating their business. And God forbid if any of these cattlemen lost a family member to one of these guns."

Seth had just about enough from this Pinkerton fellow. "I done told y'all that the cattleman Vaughn Anders lost his boy to one of them pistols Enos converted over," Seth said addressing his crew He then turned to Travis. "OK, *Twib*, we'll ride into town later and tonight you'll point them out and me and Garrett will waylay this Cord fella and bring the gal back here."

Travis knew he had no leverage at all, but decided to play his hand as if he had.

"No, I'll go along only if you agree to let me take Cord into federal custody," Travis said, "and you'll let Clay and his Paw, and the woman, Deekie, all return home back east to Georgia. You boys keep the fortune, we'll break up the Drovers' Exchange so they won't bother you no more and everybody will be well served."

The words hung in the air on the arc of his logic. No one said a word. Finally the silence was broken by Seth.

"Sure, Detective *Twib*," Seth said, trying to hide a snide snarl, "that's exactly what we'll do."

All Stragglin' Dancers Come to the Ball

A chill came over the land, as the trio crawled under its sullen shroud towards the town's salty Hell's Half Acre.

That trio was made of the Stone Canyon Gang Leader, Seth, his nineteen year old gunman, Garrett, and the captured Pinkerton Travis Brooks. They rode eastward along the open trail toward the halfway point - the hamlet of White Settlement. Seth and Garrett trailed behind Travis, whose hands had been freed for the ride. The Pinkerton knew that if he were to break for freedom, he would be shot in the back before his mount could ever reach a full gallop. He could do nothing other than enjoy the quiet of the countryside as the cold front passed through from the West.

Despite the situation he found himself in, Travis thought the ride along the five or so miles of the White Settlement Trail was a peaceful distraction. The overcast clouds stole from its full beauty, although the scent of the sage brush was painted sweetly on the strengthening breeze. He could hear the triumphant yipping of a pack of coyotes that had cornered and killed some prey. Travis appreciated the eerie silence of his two companions, who stalked along just behind him, and refused to talk to each other less they should become distracted in any way.

They soon came into White Settlement, settled in the 1840's in an area that was then mostly comprised of Indian villages. This settlement west of Fort Worth consisted solely of white men and their families. Over the last three decades, the Indians had been forced further west, and the settlement grew to a hamlet, but was still too small to be called a town proper.

Travis knew that despite Seth's agreeing to his plan, great danger still existed. Seth was likely to have figured that even if Travis was allowed to take the vigilante Cord into custody, it'd be months if not years before a case could be brought against the cattlemen of the Exchange. Even Seth could figure that with the ranchers' great funds and their collective herd of lawyers, that no charges of consequence might ever be brought to convictions against them. Not in this town, where they were so feared.

Given this, he thought that Seth already had decided that with his gang as thinned out as it was, they would pull up stakes and head for the Arizona Territory. Before they did, Travis thought that the gang leader would want to get his hands on whatever fortune of gold coins remained stashed in the hotel safe. Seth would then surely kill Enos the gunsmith, his son Clay, and even Travis himself.

As they rode in silence, Travis racked his brain to figure a way out of this situation. He had no gun, and both Seth and Garrett were each sporting a pair of the gunsmith's converted Colt Navies and a rifle to boot. They had left the three others - ol' Hank, Warren and his brother Will, behind to mind to Clay, and his Paw, Enos.

Travis thought if he could somehow maneuver these two traveling with him into a situation where they might be killed or maimed by the vigilante Cord, he could then simply wait until the unsuspecting Exchange enforcer had his guard down, arrest him, and this assignment would be tied up in a nice, neat manner. Sure, that would leave Clay and his Paw in the hands of the others, who would surely take their wrath out on the father and son, but that was not Travis' concern.

Neither was the fortune in gold. Travis knew that much gold would only draw more trouble. His assignment was to capture the vigilante Cord alive so the Pinkerton's could draw out the information needed to make a case against the Exchange. Those gold coins be damned.

Travis continued to rack his brain over just how he might have Cord take care of his two captors as they passed White Settlement and headed on in to Fort Worth. When they entered Hell's Half Acre by crossing over Throckmorton Street, his two captors moved up on either side of Travis. Soon enough they turned north and rode up the stenching stream of mud and horse shit that was Rusk Street, deep in the Acre.

Travis noticed that Garrett on his right kept his gun leveled at him. The Pinkerton knew that if he did anything to escape now, he would be shot down and left for dead in the slop of the Acre's streets, not an uncommon occurrence in the town's notorious third ward.

They stopped in front of an unmarked storefront, hitched the three horses and walked over to enter the building. The crowds were sparse on Rusk at that hour, but a great harangue could still be heard a block over on Main Street. Guns were fired, not in anger, but into the air by drunken revelers. Most wore revolvers, as few were brave, or foolish enough to enter the Acre unarmed. Yet, Travis could discern this was no gunfight by their leisurely pace of the rounds expended, and because there were no return rounds as there would likely have been during a shootout.

Up the block on Rusk Street, a few souls already spilled drunkenly out of Rowdy Joe Lowe's Red Light Saloon, or more likely were thrown out into the street. It was only six in the early evening, as much as Travis could guess, and the bartenders had already become tiresome of some of the drunken patron's rowdier exploits.

"Git inside," yelled Garrett as he pushed Travis harshly inside the vacant storefront. Once inside, Seth had Garrett hogtie and gag Travis until the night fell in earnest.

The few drunken revelers ejected from the Red Light crawled past the storefront window. One had the audacity to lean against it and cup his hands over his eyes in order to peer inside, before his companion pulled him on.

"That Rowdy Joe Lowe really has made the Chisholm Trail his own," said young Garrett with a great respect. "He's got the Red Light down here at this end and another saloon up in Witchita at the other end."

"Naw, I heard he done been run outta Witchita over killin' another saloon owner, one they call Red Beard," Seth said. "I also heard that his woman, Shotgun Kate, ain't one to be fussed with either. She's supposed to have shot dead a client who roughed up some of her whores. Some say she keeps a scattergun close at hand at all times."

"I'm sure that's just tall talk to keep all them drunken cowboys in line - the ones always in the rut," Garrett answered with a smirk, "although I figure her brothel's enforcer keeps a shotgun right close. They all do."

Seth ignored Garrett's comment and looked at the gagged and hogtied Travis. "Grab some shuteye, *Twib*, and don't forget that either Garrett or I will be watching over you with lead in the chamber, so don't try and run off."

Just after Seth, Garrett and Travis had taken refuge in the storefront on Rusk Street, Cord and Deekie rode back from the Daggett & Hatcher Supply House and Dry Grocer. They had purchased dry good supplies for the trail ride back to Georgia. Cord took the opportunity to also get a half dozen of River's favorites, dry smoked pig's ears.

The business had been one of the first ever opened in the city by C.B. Daggett and R. Hatcher. It was widely referred to simply as Daggett's, and many believed it was owned by C.B.'s more famous brother, E.M. Daggett. Captain Ephraim Merrel Daggett was a French Canadian who was generally accepted as the true father of Fort Worth. After coming to Texas, E.M. Daggett had once served in the Lone Star State's War of Independence alongside the legendary Sam Houston. In the Mexican-American War, he had fought with the Texas Rangers under Captain John Coffee Hays. During the Battle of Monterrey in 1846, Daggett fought under the command of William Jenkens Worth, the same general whose name was later posthumously borne by the fort, and now the town itself.

E. M. Daggett recognized the opportunity presented when the fort was dedicated in 1849. He immediately promoted drinking establishments just outside the one mile restriction. By 1873, Daggett had come to own most of the land in the Acre, although it was still somewhat sparsely developed. Later, E.M. Daggett would be influential in drawing the Texas & Pacific Railroad to Fort Worth in 1876, and he would even donate the land on which the new depot would be situated. The new trains made his holdings between the depot and Uptown all the more valuable.

The train depot would come to be at the far end of the Acre along Front Street, and a mule-drawn tram was soon pulled along rails laid on Main Street to carry the train's passengers to Uptown. That tram travelled directly through Hell's Half Acre. Daggett's holdings became extremely valuable as the Acre filled with even more houses of debauchery. While the Acre existed before the railroad's arrival in 1876, it was the arrival of the Iron Horse that kicked the district into the next level of corrupt prosperity. The Acre would continue to prosper in that configuration until the arrival of Camp Bowie nearly a half century later during World War I. Then, the Army would be hell bent on cleaning up the Acre, and so it did .

But even before the 1870's, E. M. Daggett had another reason to be beloved by the citizens of the emerging Fort Worth. In 1856, he along with other civic leaders led the effort to move the Tarrant County seat from Birdville to Fort Worth by promising to build a courthouse at no expense to the government. And this effort eventually proved to be successful, with the first Tarrant County Court House being constructed from 1860 - 1866 on the site of the vacated fort. Its progress had been interrupted by the country's "War of the Rebellion."

Despite all this civic expansion, Fort Worth's population remained very limited. At one point, the town became so quiet that a Dallas attorney famously mocked it when he said that he had seen a panther sleeping on the sidewalks in midday. That comment soon enough ignited the already smoldering Dallas/Fort Worth animosity to a full-fledged feud. Fort Worth soon regaled itself as Panther City. Wherever this attorney claimed to have seen this resting predator, it certainly wasn't in the Acre, as from the beginning of the Chisholm Trail cattle drives in 1866 until decades after the turn of the century, Hell's Half Acre became increasingly rambunctious.

But on this night in 1873, Cord and Deekie rode their horses down Main Street, the courthouse at their backs, although the railroad depot and the tram did not yet exist. They rode through muddy streets of slop, plank boarded with sidewalks for the pedestrians to use. The uptown section of town closest to the Courthouse Square where the fort had once stood was more densely populated, but as the streets increased in number south past Eighth Street, where the Acre unofficially began, there were many tracts still vacant and undeveloped.

"Thank ya' for purchasing all those supplies for us," Deekie said at one point. "Virgil will certainly repay ya' when we find him."

"No need," said Cord, "I've got more than enough stashed away for me and Trouble and River to live off for some time." *More coming when and if he finished his business with the gunsmith,* he almost said, but did not.

"No, Cord," she snapped, "there most surely is a need. I will not have yer blood money paying for them goods to get me and Virgil and his *Diddy* back East, where we rightly belong."

"All right, Miss Righteous," Cord snapped back, "so it's fine to borrow against blood money, as you say, just not take gifts from it?"

"Borrowin's a temporary thing," she said. "Not final, after all, like killin' men."

"They all had it comin'," Cord replied. "Ain't like your Virgil never killed no one, is it? Be thankful you've never been in a situation where you have to decide over whether a man deserves to live or die." Cord was still having that very struggle with regards to the gunsmith.

"But that last comment of Cord's struck deep into Deekie's being. She had, only two years earlier, have to make that very decision with regard to a man herself. It was then that she realized that she had all along justified her own action, just as Cord was now doing. Yes, there was a difference in the quantity of these decisions made, but in the quality of their personalities, they was no difference at all.

"I've said my piece," Deekie finally relented, "and I'll say no more."

Later in the evening, Seth untied Travis and they went to the Pinkerton's hotel to extract the gold coin laden saddlebag. Garrett trailed them with a rifle in case Travis might decide to make a break for freedom. Travis did not, as he knew the young gunman would think nothing of shooting him down in the street. They walked to the Commercial Hotel, extracted the saddlebag from the safe, and it turned over to Garrett, who slung it over his shoulder.

Travis then asked the man working the front desk if he might possibly recognize the description of the man and woman they sought. He could not be sure. After a bribe of a Liberty Head double eagle gold piece was passed to him, his memory improved substantially.

"I'm sure they checked in late yesterday afternoon. The gal was a real looker, with that pretty reddish-brown hair, but it still seemed to be almost blonde around the edges. She came in with a Colt Navy holstered off her hip. All decked out in skin tight riding clothes, which looked good even with that thick layer of trail dust coating her. If she's intent on sticking round to work the Acre, she's gonna be real popular, if you know what I mean."

"Tell me about the man she was with," Travis demanded.

"Big guy, but in no way fat," the desk clerk said. "Stood a little over six feet I'd say. Powerful build. He had that leather duster over his clothes, so I couldn't see what he was packing, but I figure he was. Couple days or so worth of trail beard on him."

"What makes you think he was carrying?" Travis prodded.

"Have to be an idiot to come into town if he wasn't. Besides, what kind of cowboy would travel with a lady who was packin' if he wasn't?"

"Why do you say he was a cowboy?"

"He sure as hell was dressed as one. He wore that trail duster like any drover would have. And his boots and Stetson seemed to have a lot of miles worn into them. His hat was nowhere as pretty as yer's though, mister. And the two of them had a dog with them, can you believe that? I told them to make sure they kept that critter out of the hotel, but I figure that was a wasted breath."

The last comment had his attention. It had been reported that Cord, the Exchange Enforcer, rode the range with a fancy hunting dog of some sort. Someone at the stage coach site had said he came along with a dog.

"They upstairs now?"

"No, they went out about an hour ago. I think they was headed up to Daggett's Supply House. See, I got their two keys right here."

"Two keys?" Travis blurted, then remembered Deekie was Clay's, not Cord's gal. "Anything else?" he asked.

"One thing is for sure, these two draw a lot of attention."

"What makes you say that?" Travis' curiosity was up.

"Oh, nuthin' really," the deskman said as he began flipping the double eagle gold piece.

"All right," Travis said, tossing another double eagle to the man, "but this damn sure best be worth it."

"Last night, just after they went out to dinner, a big galoot of a fella came in to check the register for their names. Didn't do him no good, cause they signed in as Mr. Smith and Miss Jones. This guy was a real bull of a man. Could have been near three hundred pounds or so, built like an ox. He was hot on their trail. I figured he'd been waiting for them to arrive in town, and once he found them, he just waited for them to go out to check the register. He was after something, that's for sure."

"Who was he?" asked Travis.

"I got no idea," the deskman admitted, "but I ain't never seen him around town before. He had a little twang in his voice, I dunno, maybe north side of Mississippi or middle Tennessee?"

"OK," Travis said, "I got what I need. But if I find out that you been spreading round that we been askin', especially to this bull of a fella, I'll be back with my friends to collect more than just them two and half eagle? Got it? " Travis pointed with his thumb to Seth who had stood the whole time over his shoulder during the questioning.

"My lips are sealed, I don't want no trouble with his gang," the deskman said, indicating he had recognized Seth all along.

As they walked out into the windy and crisp fall overcast night, Travis said to Seth, "That's them for sure…"

"…and who's the bull-sized fella?" Seth cut him off.

Travis removed his Dakota and scratched his scalp just as the bald Seth had done earlier. "Likely just some stranger who liked the look of her ass in them tight ridin' britches."

"You'd sure better hope so," Seth threatened.

Travis said nothing, just looked up into the dark clouds collecting overhead.

"Appears we got a storm coming in on us," Travis said.

Seth looked up after he said this. "There's a storm a comin', all right."

The three of them settled in and took drinks in the saloon just across the street where they could keep watch on the comings and goings of the hotel.

"We'll wait for them to leave their hotel," Seth said, "and follow them. Once we have them trapped somewhere alone, Garrett and I will take them at gunpoint and take them back to our storefront."

"At that point," Travis said, "I will take Cord into custody and you can have the girl to release along with Clay and his Paw."

"If she's as comely as that desk man says, I can think of better things to do with her," Seth said. "You forget that this Cord fella done planted some six or seven members of our gang in the dirt. It was the whole reason for us coming back to town. We'll kill him, all right, and you can have the corpse to take back to your Pinkertons."

"There is an investigative procedural issue here. You see, as it is, a corpse does not give up much information under questioning," Travis said. "Who's gonna take down the Exchange? If they're already out to kill your gunsmith, it's only a matter of time before they come for what little's left of your gang."

"With that fortune in gold coins we done collected," Seth replied, "it'll stake us in whatever our next move will be. The Exchange is gonna have to search far and wide for us. We can easily move our operations out to the Arizona Territory. They got plenty of cattle to rustle there. Coaches still run through there as well. We may even take Enos with us. We can sell his conversion works for a few more years."

It was then that Travis knew these men were out for only one thing, the revenge killing of the vigilante, Cord. Travis new after they stalked and killed this Cord fellow, he himself was no longer needed. If they did plan to uproot to Arizona, then they had no fear of either the Drovers' Exchange or the Pinkertons. Travis realized his lifespan had just been reduced to a few hours.

All Hell Breaks Loose

Back at the hacienda, ol' Hank watched over Clay as Enos stoked the fire in the massive hearth.

Standing next to ol' Hank, who sat restively in a chair, stood the rifleman Will. His brother Warren had relieved him from atop the bluff. From that height, either brother could l see anyone coming along the White Settlement Trail to the south, or peer north over the darkened plains for torch lights of anyone coming from beyond Silver Creek.

Inside, Clay had his feet shackled, as ol Hank had found it was too damned hard to tie up a one-armed man, Clay having neither a hand nor forearm on his left side. Enos was also shackled around his ankle to a long expanse of chain to allow him to move between his work tables and the great hearth with its anvil. At that moment, Enos was in front of the hearth at the anvil.

Enos had a bin full of a dozen or so old ball and powder 1851 Colt Navy six-shooters to convert to breech loaders. The guns sat on his bench, useless like tits on a boar hog, as he had neither percussion caps, powder or balls to use in them. He had only a single bullet, from which the gunpowder had been carefully leached out to use as a fit gage for his complete efforts.

Enos' job was to remove the cylinders from the gun, where they would be sent to a local mill to be trimmed back. But the work from the mill was inconsistent, at best, and the amount removed from the cylinders were close but never exactly alike. Enos would have to make up for any differences by custom making breech plates of different thicknesses to offset each cylinder's dimension. This was a very time consuming effort, but also a very critical one.

If a gap was left between the cylinder and the breech plate, firing one round could ignite all six bullets and the gun would blow up in the user's hand. This very fault had been the death of many early gun designs. Who wanted a gun that just might explode when they pulled the trigger?

So, Enos Clay-Harris had spent over a decade at the hearth and anvil perfecting his craft. As Clay now watched, his father measured the trimmed back cylinders and put breech plate blanks of offsetting thicknesses in the roaring fire. The metal discs would glow to a cherry red, and only then would Enos extract them using tongs and hammer them on the anvil to the desired custom thickness.

As he banged away, Will turned to ol' Hank and said, "I can't take anymore of this infernal heat and that banging is giving me a headache. I'm going back up on the horseshoe where it's cool and quiet. I'll send my brother back down."

"Do what ya' like," ol' Hank said, knowing he had to stay to keep watch over the father and son. Just as Will went through the door, Enos called out to his boy.

"Virgil," he said. His son's head, still gagged, jerked up attentively.

"No talkin'," ol' Hank said angrily.

"Ya' remember that game we used to play in the old shack along Petit's Creek?" Enos asked, ignoring the old timer as he hammered on a red hot breech plate disk.

Clay remembered. Hot Potato. His *Diddy* would stoke up a raging fire in the stove, set a stone on the burner, and after it heated a bit, would throw it to his sons to catch. Whoever could catch it without dropping the stone would be allowed to pan with *Diddy* the next day.

Clay's eyes lit up as his memories came alive. He nodded his head as if to say, *I remember, Diddy*.

"I said no chatterin' betwixt the two of you," ol' Hank warned again as he drew his revolver.

"The boy can't talk none, no how, Hank," Enos responded, "'cause ya' got him muzzled and chained like some sort of rabid dog."

"I don't care if y'is doin' all the yappin' and he does nuttin' but looking at yer, it ain't to be."

"Come on, Hank," Enos pleaded, "can't ya' just unchain him and take off his gag for a few minutes. I just want to catch up on some family chatter. Maybe even play a little game with my son."

As he spoke, Enos pounded harder and harder at the glowing red disk of metal that was the breech plate. Red embers sparked and flew with each strike of the blacksmith's hammer. Clearly he was becoming frustrated at the ol' geezer's refusal for him to talk to the son who he had not seen for over a decade.

Ol' Hank sensed Enos' frustration, and slowly drew and cocked the hammer of his revolver. "I ain't neither unchaining yer son nor taking his gag off," ol' Hank said, "And ya' sure as hell ain't gonna play no games with him."

"Then hows about y'and me doin' some playing then, Hank. Here catch," Enos said as he used the tongs to lift up the hot hammered disk. With a flip of his wrist , Enos tossed it directly at the old rustler.

Hank reacted by firing off two shots as the still red-hot disk flew through the air. His bullets hit neither the disc in flight, which he had aimed for out of instinct, nor the gunsmith who had taken aim upon him. As the hot metal disk landed in his lap, ol' Hank screamed out like a skinny-dippin' Texas gal seein' her first ever water snake. An instantaneous smell of roasted cotton trousers filled the dank humid air within the *hacienda's* structure. Nearly instantaneously that smell was overpowered by the putrid, sickening odor of burning flesh that overpowered all other senses. Hank, in shock aas he realized that it was the smell of his own flesh that accompanied the searing, incapacitating pain in his groin, dropped his revolver and jumped wildly out of his chair.

Enos saw the amazed look on his son's face, then broke quickly, dragging his chains behind him. He made a bee-line over to Hank's discarded revolver. Clay's *Diddy* then cocked back the hammer back and took aim at the door, anticipating what was to happen next.

A second or two later, the door swung open wildly, and Will barged in, gun drawn, responding to the sounds of shots of gunfire and ol' Hank's near continuous, terror-laced screams. Will was stunned by the immediate overpowering smell coupled with the sight of the old-timer on his knees writhing in uncontrollable agony.

Will knew in that very split second he must kill them both, father and son. The realization came just a beat late. The young gunman failed to get a single shot off before Enos found him in his sights and pulled the trigger on Hank's borrowed revolver. The bullet exploded into the center of Will's forehead, and he instantly collapsed into a lifeless heap of muscle and bones.

"Hank!" Enos yelled out over the screaming, pointing his gun at the old buzzard, "Git yerself under control, or I'll shoot ya' dead, too. I swear I'll do it. Gimme the keys to Virgil's leg iron. Now, Hank!"

Ol' Hank could stop neither screaming in his high-pitched wail nor writhing in pain. Even though the metal plate had landed on the clothing over his crotch, it had burned clean through to the tender skin beneath.

"Hank, I am gonna give y'one more chance to live," Enos yelled loudly out to him, as if his hearing had been affected by his burns. "Get the keys and release my boy."

There was no response as ol' Hank simply clutched himself in a ball and rocked on the smooth stone floor, as if that somehow could stop the searing pain in his vitals.

The gunsmith then raised Hank's gun and shot him twice in the back from only a few feet above him. He then stood over the old man's slumped body and said, "That'll teach ya' to chain me up like a dog, and worse even, my boy. Even the most tame animal, when mistreated long enough, needs to be feared for its bite."

Enos then moved over to Clay and released his gag.

"*Diddy*, what the hell are ya' doing?" Clay asked.

"Gittin' even, Son, gittin' even," his father said. "Do ya' know how long I had dreamed 'bout doing all that?"

"Ya' better git down before Warren starts shooting down on us from that bluff overhead," Clay warned.

"Let 'em go ahead and waste his ammo," Enos said. "This shack has stone walls and a *terra cotta* roof. He can waste his bullets shatterin' tiles. But if he comes through that door, I'll drop him just like I did his brother."

Enos then walked over to the hearth and put the tongs back in the fire until they glowed a bright cherry red. He took the tongs, and dragging his chains behind him, hobbled over to Clay's chair. "Can ya' scoot yer chair around, Son? So's I can gits to yer shackles before these irons cool. "Here, put this thick leather cloth over yer feet so the splatter don't maim ya none."

Clay did as Enos had said. The gunsmith merely touched the red hot tongs to the bolt securing the shackles before it melted through and fell free in two pieces. Enos then reached out and embraced his son, in the process feeling the stump of his left arm through his sleeve.

"Son," Enos said, "it kills me to see ya' crippled as y'are. I had always hoped to get those guns to ya' so ya'd come back from the war in one whole piece."

Clay then whispered in his father's ear, "*Diddy*, if I didn't have that pair of Navy Sixes, I wouldn't have come home from the war t'all. They not only saved me, but Willet as well."

As he had said this, Enos ended his short embrace, stood and returned the tongs to the hot ember bed of the raging fire.

"Can't wait to hear about it all," his Diddy said, "but right now we gots other things to do. Go ahead walk over and grab yer gun."

"Why'd ya' tell them I had that Colt Pocket Pistol, Diddy?"

"Cause Seth would have killed ya' when they found it. He's one mean bastard. I couldn't let that happen."

The gun they talked about was just outside Enos' length of chain on the table nearest the door. Clay picked it up, opened the loading gate, and spun the cylinder to reveal the four bullets he always kept loaded in it. The fifth chamber he kept empty when traveling for safety. He then loaded it.

"What about that chain they got around yer ankle?" Clay asked.

"It t'ain't nuthin', Virgil," his Paw said as he wrapped the thick leather cloth round his foot before he pulled the red hot tongs once more from the hearth. He again pressed it onto the bolt and soon the shackles around his leg fell free.

"They kept ya' chained up like a dog that way for the last decade, *Diddy?*" Clay asked.

"No, not at all," Enos said. "Most times I was free to work here unchained. They almost always had someone with a gun on me. When they had to leave me alone they'd chain me up, like ya' seen. When they heard ya' were in town, they took no chances. I been chained up for several days now. My ankles are raw from the chaffin' somethin' fierce. But this here ain't the first time I've done this, boy. That's how I was able to give myself a break whenever they done left me alone."

"Why didn't ya' just free yerself and run, *Diddy?*" Clay asked.

"I was afeard to die, I reckon," his *Diddy* said. "How far could I have got? But this here was the best chance I am ever gonna have to escape with their numbers bein' down and two being off to the Acre. Now we just gotta take care of Warren up on the horseshoe overhead. He's easily the most excitable boy in the gang, especially as he's likely to figure his brother done bit the dust."

"I ain't sure he would necessarily know that Diddy," Clay reasoned. "So don't go spillin' the beans as such."

It was just then that the faint voice of Warren from atop the bluff could be heard outside the *hacienda*. "Will? What's going on in there, Will?"

Enos sat and massaged his bloody ankle from where the shackle had continuously rubbed him for so long. He then rose and walked stiff-legged over to the door, opening it slightly and yelling out.

"Yer brother's wounded a bit and gagged, Warren. So is ol' Hank. An we will take it easy on ya' too if ya' lay down yer guns and come on in. My boy's a trained sharpshooter and he's got this fancy sniping rifle, so ya' don't likely stand a chance."

Enos closed the door, turned to his son and said, "Let him chew on all that for a minute or two."

"Ya' bastard, Enos, ya' best not have killed Will?" screamed Warren from atop the horseshoe. "I don't care about yer boy and his fancy long gun, I got the high ground. Any of y'all come out that door and I'll lay yer low, I will. Seth and Garrett will be back soon enough. We'll set this straight."

"Well, so much for plucking Warren's last nerve!" Enos said as he walked over to get a closer look at the Whitworth Rifle. "Where'd ya' git this fancy gun, Virgil?"

"It's a damn long story, *Diddy*," Clay answered.

"Well, we got plenty of time cause that door is the only way in or out. We got ourselves a real Mexican standoff here. Just keep yer revolver at the ready in case of any visitors."

Just then a crack of lightning lit up the night sky. A front was rolling over the prairie sky and the temperature dropped like a loose canyon stone.

"Come on, son, tell me the story," Enos pleaded.

"'Bout what?" Clay asked his Paw.

"About all we're going to do with that fortune of gold coins Seth and Warren are bringing back to us."

"*Diddy*, that money ain't brought us nothin' but bad luck since we laid hands on it."

"Strange," Enos said, "I can't imagine it bringing nothing but a mountain of pleasure."

Evening crashed into night with a tremendous arcing of spider like lightning, but released no cleansing rain over the Acre. Instead of night falling softly like the last of seven veils, the skylit fire fall made it feel more like the tearing of the seventh seal. The lightning was seen by many to be an omen of just how much evil the coming hours could hold.

However, even this did not dissuade the cowboys who drifted along Main, Rusk, and Calhoun Streets looking for just the right venue in which to flitter away their earnings and hopefully any innocence they might have left. The trail drives had ended for the year, but there were still enough locals to light up the Acre. In fact, even in this early year of the Acre's existence, there were palaces of sin such as The Two Minnies Saloon, where patrons, upon throwing back a shot of whiskey, would discover the glass ceiling through which they could watch buck naked women on the floor above undertaking various activities, including ten-pin bowling. The Acre held so many such attractions that neither lightning, hellfire nor brimstone could scare off the clientele.

Before beginning their search for Clay in the Acre's saloons, Deekie and Cord had lured River into the hotel room with one of the smoked pigs ears procured from Daggett's. They dared not allow River to trail them into the Acre, where drunken cowboys might attempt target practice on him. So, after locking the dog in for the night, they decided to begin in some of the more "refined" saloons. They started out at the Emporium just outside the Acre, and after having no luck there, wandered deeper into the district. They ended up late that night completing their rounds at Rowdy Joe Lowe's Red Light Saloon.

They were not aware that they were being followed by Travis, along with Seth and Garrett in tow. Garrett carried the saddlebags of eagles over his shoulder like a gold-lined Mexican poncho. Its weight bore heavily on Garret's frame, but he was young and took this golden yoke in stride.

The three men had followed Cord and Deekie until they dipped into Rowdy Joe's, only a few hundred feet from their storefront and their tethered horses.

"This is where I'll approach them," Travis said to Seth. "You and Garrett can cover the door, as I am sure you don't want him lugging that loot into a saloon full of drunken drovers. There's several thousand dollars worth of double eagles in that saddlebag. I suggest Garrett stay out front, and you can position yourself where you cover the back and still keep your eyes on him, less he should decide to take off with it all."

"All right, *Twib*, but just remember, I can cover the back door and still keep an eye on Garrett and all that gold and still gun down any of ya' trying to run off. We'll give you ten minutes before we come in after you. Any funny business and we'll find you and kill you. Got it?"

"Yeah, I got it, Seth," Travis replied. "Just give me my full ten minutes to talk them out."

Travis then slipped inside Rowdy Joe's Red Light, where Cord and Deekie had a verbal battle ongoing with the bartender.

"I don't give a damn how much you dress her up like a some high plains rider," the barkeep said, "no women are allowed in this here joint."

"What about them?" Deekie countered as she pointed past the poker and Faro tables to the women milling about seductively, pressing themselves as tenderly against the drovers as them cowboys might handle a calf strayed from the herd.

"They work here," the barkeep said angrily, "and if you want to come by for an interview to do so, that's done in the daylight, not in working hours. Come by tomorra', and I'll interview you myself," he said with a piggish snort.

"You son of a bitch," Cord reacted just before a well dressed figure stepped up to the bar.

"Friend," Travis said to the bartender, "lets call this consideration for your looking the other way this night." He slapped down a Large Head Gold Princess Dollar on the bar. "Give us three beers and we'll disappear quietly into a corner and no one will know the better. If we are not interrupted, there's another one of these awaitin' ya, friend."

"Huh!" said the bartender, as he inspected the gold coin. Then he walked away and began pulling the three draughts. He slid them down the bar, one by one, to Travis. True to his word, Travis passed the first two to his new friends, grabbed his own and led them to a corner not far from the front entrance.

"I reckon one don't see that many big head Princess Dollars no more," said Cord. "Where'd you get that?"

"Forgive me for interrupting your little conversation with that ape of a man," Travis said, extending his free hand toward Cord. "I'm Travis Isaiah Brooks." He left out the Walter from his name, for he felt that name was a bit too mundane."

"That's a might fanciful name," Cord said.

"I'm Deekie and this is Cord," she said, taking his hand that Cord had delayed in accepting. "Thank ya' for yer helping us out."

"My pleasure, indeed," Travis said doffing his Dakota, drawing a smile from her. "Actually, Miss Deekie, I believe we are already acquainted. We shared a coach from Fort Smith together. And to answer this gentleman's question, I believe that gold piece, as well as all the others in my pocket belong rightfully to you. Or your man, Clay."

"Oh my Lord! You're the one who took out them robbers on that Stage Coach with my Virgil. You're the one done got us to that Sulphur Springs place. Ya' may have saved my skin."

"He's also the one that went off with your Clay," Cord said. "That explains the gold pieces. He likely killed yer man for them."

"I don't care about all that gold," Deekie said. "Where is my Virgil?"

"Your Clay, that is Virgil, has already been reunited with his Paw. And as far as that shootout at the stage coach, that was almost all of Clay's doing. I merely helped out a bit here and there. And the gold is all his, that is yours, except for the pocketful he gave me to come find you."

Travis' rushed delivery caused both Deekie and Cord to be suspect. They looked at each other, wondering if they could trust this man. In near unison, they drew gulps from their glasses of beer.

"There is one other thing we all need to discuss," Travis said over the din of the saloon.

"What might that be?" asked an untrusting Cord.

"This killer you're traveling with," Travis said turning to Deekie. "Did you know he killed two rustlers, maybe three, a few days before that coach robbery."

"Watch yourself, partner," Cord warned.

"I know Cord here is a killer," she said plainly. "Ya' just said y'and my Virgil killed those men attempting to rob the stage coach. So that makes y'all about the same."

"This man, Cord, was trailing them," Travis said.

"They were rustlers before they turned bandits," Cord added. "So, hell, yeah, I tracked them."

"So, it looks like, perhaps, I prefer the company of men who rid this world of other bad men," Deekie said. She was pleased with her answer, and wished it to be true.

"Well, you just may have a little conflict about to crash into your well structured world, Miss Deekie," Travis said. "Go ahead and ask your man Cord here who his next mark is. Who the Drovers' Exchange that he works for has ordered him to kill next. Just, go on now and ask him."

Deekie turned her head slowly to study Cord. His jaw tightened, his face became flush with anger.

"Cord," Deekie asked, "what is this man talking 'bout?"

"Look, mister," Cord snapped, "I don't know who you think you are, but you best watch your step. I am armed to the teeth and best I can tell, you ain't carrying no sidearm."

"Now, Cord," Travis replied, "would you be holstering them cap and ball sidearms or one of them breech loading revolvers converted by one Enos Clay-Harris?"

"Oh my God," Deekie gasped as Travis mentioned her Virgil's Paw. "Cord, tell me y'are not out to kill Virgil's *Diddy?*"

"Deekie, I have never lied to you," he said vehemently.

"I know, Cord, so tell me y'ain't out to kill Virgil's *Diddy,*" Deekie repeated.

"That is exactly who he is to kill next," Travis interrupted. "Seems one of Enos' guns was used in the killing of the son of Vaughn Anders, one of the prominent cattlemen in the Exchange. They are out for old Enos' blood, nothing less."

"And what are y'out for, Mr. Travis?" Deekie said sharply. "Where do yer fit into this whole mess of things?"

"Ma'am, as it turns out," Travis said, "I am a Pinkerton Detective from Chicago."

Deekie watched the confident expression on Cord McCullough's face fall upon hearing these words. "That explains the finery of yer clothes, all right," she said. "So you're here to arrest Cord, is ya'?"

"Yes mam," Travis answered, "so he can help us bring down that Drovers' Exchange outfit. No harm will come to him if he cooperates. He may not even have to go to prison. But sure as tomorra's sun's gonna rise, Cord here is only using you to take him to your Virgil's Paw. He still ain't answered your question, you'll have noticed."

Deekie looked at Cord. She thought he was fuming like a penned up mustang, a wild thing cornered.

"So I guess all that ya' said about yer wife and little Sean was just all lies to soften me up? Make me feel sorry for ya?"

"Deekie, I told ya, I've never done lied to you," Cord said, "but you best wonder if this Travis fellow is…"

"Say it Cord!" she all but screamed at him. "Say yer not out to kill Enos Clay-Harris next."

"I can't," Cord answered, "because as I sit here I am strongly thinking Mr. Travis Isaiah Brooks, Pinkerton or not, will be takin' that notch on my belt."

"Kill an unarmed man, would ya', Cord?" Travis accused him, "I am not surprised that you are capable of it. But as it is, I am indeed unarmed, but not alone. Outside this establishment are waiting two members of the Stone Canyon Gang, fully armed, mind you, just waiting for us to emerge. They got front and back covered, so slipping out through the whore's cribs in the rear will not suffice. I figure if we up and kill them both off, I can take Cord here over to the jailhouse for safekeeping before taking you, Miss Deekie, out to be reunited with your Virgil. Everybody in?"

"Cord," Deekie moved in close to him, "I know y'ain't lied to me none. I believe y'about *Callie* and little Sean, about them Jayhawkers. But there sure as hell is another kind of lie, the kind ya' tell by what y'ain't said. Ya' never said ya' were out to kill my Virgil's *Diddy*, but now I am asking ya' straight out to tell me that ya' won't. Don't ya' see that this may just be yer chance to change that life of riding the trails as a hired killer. That's what's been eatin' at yer hide from the inside out. Don't ya' see it's so?"

He looked at her, but could not bring himself to answer in the way she so badly wanted.

Cord then looked at Travis. "Just two you say?"

"Yeah," Travis answered, "they brought me here at gunpoint. One is a young fella with a saddlebag slung over his shoulder like some sorta leather poncho, the other is a gimpy bastard staked out back."

"Rifles?" asked Cord.

"Yeah, the both of them, and the gunsmith's revolvers," Travis answered. "A pair on each of them. Way I figure it, you give me Deekie's gun, and I'll take out Seth, he's the bald headed hobbler out back, and you take out the other out front."

"There ain't no way in God's creation you are getting a weapon in your hand, Travis," Cord said. "Now I'm in for this, but if you ain't telling the truth about their numbers or weapons, so help me, I'll take you from this life before they can kill me. Understood?"

"Understood!" Travis said.

"No," Deekie said, "No one goes anywhere, until you, Cord McCullough, answer me. Are ya' fixin' to kill Clay's *Diddy*. Answer me or I'll draw my weapon and all hell will break out in here."

"Okay, Deekie, enough already!" Cord said. "I promise you I won't kill yer Virgil's Paw."

"Swear it, damn it!" she demanded.

"I swear it," Cord answered, "on the souls of Cassie and little Sean, such that they may rest in peace."

She let out a sigh of relief. She trusted him to his word. All the while Travis could only think of one thing. *McCullough. Cord McCullough. Now I know for sure who I'm hunting.*

Gunfights and Gitalongs

The cold front rolled in as the dry sky flashed overhead with crackling pulses of an angry blueish-white light.

The standoff with the rifleman, Warren, on the bluff overlooking the *hacienda,* had been going on for about an hour. Neither Clay nor his *Diddy* had any ability to detect exactly where Warren was up on that rocky ridge.

"Maybe he up and left," Clay's Paw, Enos, said.

'Not with all that booty coming back here," Clay pointed to the table that bore just the small taste of the gold coins he had carried in his pockets. "What's coming is that many, many times over, *Diddy*. Besides, he likely has hopes ya' was tellin' the truth about his brother only bein' wounded. He'll be pissed when he finds out otherwise."

"Ya' don't say, son," Enos said with a gleam in his eyes. "Then yer right. That young buck Warren is sticking around thinking he's got a cut coming his way."

"Even if he don't want to risk his life for it," Clay said, " Warren knows that Seth and Garrett will kill him for giving up on us so easily. He'll stay up there until they get back from the Acre. Then we's trapped. One thing's fer sure, though, that boy's got his dander all riled up knowing that we brought harm down on his brother, Will. "

Clay's Paw had a flicker of pride come over him. "Virgil, I always said ya' had a way of seeing things for what they are. Ya' may not be book smart like yer brother, Truitt, but ya' sure got a way of figuring out what drives men, be their nature good or bad. How's yer brother, anyway?"

"Ya' was right all along about him, *Diddy,*" Clay answered. "He's smart something special. He's finished up his schoolin', and Truitt's now the county's Clerk of the Court," Clay said with pride.

"I always told yer Maw he was sharp in a way I could never explain," Enos said. "Even as small as he was when I left, I could see that in him. Clerk of the Court? Well, I'll be. I'll bet yer Maw is bustin'!"

The drop of Clay's eyes gave him away. Instantly, his Paw knew that his wife was no longer of this world.

"Damn it. How?" Enos simply asked in a flat toned voice.

"The Consumption." Clay answered, "two years back."

"I see," his Paw said. "She never forgave me, did she, son?"

"I reckon not," Clay said. "Might have been that whore ya' brought to town with ya' while I was off at war."

"Ya' mean Fanny Belle?" his Paw asked, as a broad smile overtook him. "She was a true blessing to me. Ya' know, I come down here to make some money for the family by convertin' these pistols, and this gang set us up with all we needed out here. They built this *hacienda*, as they took to calling it. Fannie Belle gave up her whorin' and moved in with me here. We made a mess of money converting them cap and ball guns. I just figured that money was mine to take back to Cartersville along with yer two Colt Navies. That Stone Canyon Gang never quite saw it that way. They figured that money was theirs. Fanny Belle just reckoned it was a good chance for her to git out of her life of sin. So she came back East with me."

"Only to be followed and caught again by these fellas," Clay said, before asking, "Did they really cut her up and toss her body parts out of the train back to Texas?"

His father started to chuckle. "Naw! That was just a story made up by that fool they sent after us. His name was Quincy. They picked me up at the Atlanta train station just a few hours after I had put Fanny on a train to git on to her sister's place in South Carolina. Quincy didn't want to git cross ways with that hot-headed son of a bitch Seth. Even then he was leader of the gang. So Quincy just made up that whole tall tale. I was happy to go along with it, cause it meant no one would be goin' back after her no more."

"I never met the woman," Clay said, "but I sure am tickled to hear that the train story t'ain't true a t'all."

"Ya' know, son," his Paw's heart lightened each time he called Clay that, "that bluff encircles nearly this whole building in a horseshoe. But there's really only one part of it, at the left tip of the horseshoe, that has a clear line of sight of that door. Maybe we could draw Warren out to it. Might give ya' a clean shot at him. I got's an idea."

He whispered his idea in a hushed voice, even though there was no possible way Warren could hear them.

"That might just work, *Diddy*," Clay said.

Seth and Garrett had fanned out to cover the front and rear doors of the saloon. Both had their revolvers drawn. Garrett was across the street from the saloon, directly in front of its main entrance. His rifle propped up against the storefront behind him. Seth was standing wide of its rear door in a vacant adjacent lot. That spot also gave him a full view of Garrett and the gold fortune in that leather saddlebag.

The Red Light Saloon's doors swung open and the sole figure of Cord McCullough burst out walking at a brisk, determined pace.

"You hold it right there, fella," Garrett called out just before he yelled out at the top of his lungs, "SETH!"

Cord did not falter. He walked into the wide muddy street and right towards Garrett. Then he suddenly stopped, about fifteen yards from where the young gunman stood above him on the wooden sidewalk.

Behind Cord the lightning's flashes betrayed the night's shadows, exposing the hobbling figure of Seth in their afterlight. It was just enough to allow Travis and Deekie to detect his distinctive gait as they slipped out into the stormy night behind the gang leader. The two had waited till he moved forward, then quietly slid out the back through the whore's quarters. They followed Seth as he moved parallel to the saloon, toward the street, hoping to sneak up behind the tall figure of Cord standing in it.

From the center of the street, Cord called out to Garrett, "Mister, I got no beef with ya, but ya' move back to that rifle and yer dead. I'm also telling ya' if you don't lower your revolvers and walk off, I'm taking y'out, here and now. Ya got maybe one shot, best make it a good one, cause I don't figure to miss."

Just then came Seth's voice from behind Cord. "I got him, Garrett. Don't let this fella rattle ya' none." The distinctive cocking of the Colt's hammer came next, but it was as much a surprise to Seth as it was to Cord.

"Ya' so much as draw that hammer back on yer weapon, Mister, and I'm saltin' yer hide with lead," Deekie said.

Seth turned slowly to see the gal and Travis behind him. "You done double-crossed me, *Twib*. You're gonna live just long enough to wish ya' hadn't."

"I'd advise you to pay attention to the girl, Seth," Travis said. "She claims to have killed one fella back East already. I'm inclined to believe her."

A crash of lightning arced across the sky. Tension ratcheted through the five figures. The danger of the situation was coiled like a viper just waiting for someone to make the first move before striking.

"Well," Seth shouted, "I bet that fella she says she killed wasn't looking her in the eye when she done so. Little gal, I've done turned around so you can see my face when ya' pull that trigger."

As Seth had turned to look her eye to eye, Deekie could feel her innards stiffen. She knew she had to suppress this fear, and she prayed her voice would not betray her.

"Well, mister, thank ya' for turnin' bout so," Deekie said after a pause, "as I don't much like shooting any fella in the back."

Just as she finished saying this, Seth quickly cocked back the hammer of his revolver as he raised it to shoot. Deekie without hesitation pulled the trigger of her already cocked and aimed gun. The bullet that blast from her barrel set off the chain of mayhem that night. Its flight was true, catching Seth in the chest just as he fired his own gun, which yanked upward. His round sailed high over her head.

"Son of a bitch," he muttered through clenched teeth as he fell forward to the ground.

When Deekie's shot rang out, it snapped the tension like the yanking of a hangman's trap. Everything went into chaotic motion all at once. In the Acre, once more, all hell had broken loose.

Garrett fired two shots from his revolver in a rapid succession. The first whizzed by Cord's head, just over his left shoulder. The second ended up in the mud ten feet in front of him because Cord had already fired a round that struck true to Garrett's stomach. Cord fired another to the same area and that sent the young man crashing into the storefront behind him, knocking over his unfired rifle. Then, Garrett slid down into a still heap on the boardwalk.

Cord moved forward, gun still drawn and up on to the elevated boardwalk. He quickly took the gunman's two revolvers. Then he removed the saddlebag the young man had been wearing across his shoulder. In the darkness Cord could not assure that he was dead. Then, just as he began to reach for Garrett's rifle, he heard a scream from behind him. He could heard the terror in Deekie's voice.

Deekie had moved toward Seth, figuring him to be dead. To her surprise, the bald marauder raised himself to his knees and aimed his revolver at her. She could see he was bleeding badly and might last just long enough to take her life. It was then that she screamed.

Cord forgot the rifle and moved with purpose, leaving the dropped figure of Garrett behind. He walked at a brisk gait, aiming his gun at the back of the strugglin' figure of half-dead Seth. Cord squeezed off shot after shot after shot as he walked closer and closer, all finding the gang leader's back. Seth never did get off another round before he collapsed into the slop that was Rusk Street.

Deekie ran past the dead man into Cord's arms. "Oh my God, thank ya, Cord,'" she gasped through tears as she squeezed him tight. "I thought he was gonna kill me."

Cord looked down at Seth's dead body, flopped over on its back. It stared up open-eyed. "Thank whoever taught you how to shoot," he said, "your bullet was just below his heart, maybe punctured clean through a lung. Otherwise he likely would have put you away. Gave me just enough time to git over here. Besides, I wasn't about to watch another half-dead fella take you from me, *Callie*."

Deekie was about to comment on his calling her by this name when she looked over to the board wallk and said, "Where did he go? I saw ya' kill that boy."

"Huh?" Cord said as he turned briskly around to look behind him. Across the street, the wooden sidewalk was empty. No sign of the gunman Garrett's body.

Deekie ran her hand across the leather of the saddlebag that hung from Cord's shoulder. Her nail snagged on two holes, ripped open violently by Cord's bullets. She could feel the gold-rimmed splatter from them.

"Looks like he was wearing some pretty expensive armor," Deekie said, showing the two bullet holes to Cord and Travis. "Yer shots never went all the way through."

"Bastard played possum on me," Cord said. "His rifle's gone too. Even with it, he didn't seem too interested in rejoining the fight. I figure we seen the last of him."

"Come on, you two, we gotta get out of here," Travis said, "we've already drawn a crowd. Best we clear out and quick like."

"We're going back to the hotel and getting Trouble and the other mare and headin' out to find Clay and his Paw tonight," Cord said. "We'll take River along too."

"All right, but rememba' ya' swore not to kill Virgil's *Diddy*, Enos" Deekie demanded. "Say it to me, Cord. Promise me on *Callie's* soul."

"Deekie, I done already promised you," Cord said, "but one more time over *Callie's* soul, I won't kill that son of a bitch gunsmith. Ya got my word."

Warren sat upon the horseshoe-shaped rocky bluff overlooking the *hacienda*. He stayed off on the left side, but away from any direct line of sight from the building's door, its only opening. He recalled far too clearly that Enos had bragged about his son being a sniper during the war.

All of a sudden a loud ruckus came from within. There was hollering' followed by shots fired. Then the front door swung open and the gunsmith, Enos, ran out in a terror, yelling, "I done told ya' he weren't dead…"

Just as Warren took aim in the darkness at the fleeing figure, three shots rang out from inside the still open doorway and the gunsmith fell to the ground, where he lay motionless. Finally two more shots came from inside. Then he saw his brother's body fall wounded against the open door's frame, before it slid slowly down to the ground. Will fell face down onto the stone threshold.

Warren's heart raced within him. Not a sound came from within the house. He stayed put, knowing this must be some sort of a trap. Or could Will have actually played possum long enough to have mustered the strength needed to shoot down these two unsuspecting holdouts? It was too unlikely to be true, but what if it was?

"Waarrnnn," a muffled voice moaned. *"He'p me, Warn."* It didn't quite sound like Will, but he was certainly badly injured. What if it was his brother?

No, it was a trap, Warren decided. He waited for what seemed an eternity. Then the sounds of the night that had been silenced in all the commotion began slowly to come alive once more. A hoot owl found his voice, and joined the night chorus of coyotes yipping off in the distance. Minutes passed by with nothing but this nocturnal serenade. Finally, Warren heard another muffled moan coming from the direction of the doorway.

His brother Will still lay face down at the base of the open door. The shallow moan continued. Warren could not see any movement coming from his brother's body, but also could not rule out that the moan was not coming from him. Warren watched the flicker of the hearth's firelight from the open doorway for any trace of a telltale shadow. No such shadows were cast, all was still but not completely silent. Then the moan sounded as if it were a single slurred word.

"Wwaaaarrrrnnn," dragged through the night air again, but this time on the shallowest of breaths.

Warren still thought it to be a trap, although he wanted it desperately to be true. Each second ebbed away at his staunch reason, till the threshold of hope was crossed.

"Will, is that you, brother?" He called out on a nearly equally soft breath.

"Gottthhhemm," then came the soft moan in response, *"Ahgotttallemmbastahhhds."*

"Will," Warren called out, "move something, so I know ya' hear me." Nothing moved, but Warren couldn't quite see all of him from his position atop the horseshoe.

"Caaaiiinnnntt," the moan bellowed, almost too low to be heard. *"He'ppp me."*

No further sounds persisted, only those of the night.

Warren felt torn between his suspicions and his hopes. He moved out closer to the tip of the ridge's horseshoe to get a better view. The body of Enos below still had not moved, but neither had his brother's.

Then, Warren yelled out in a slightly higher voice, "Will, tell me our Maw's name so I know…"

Warren heard the shot ring out just a split second before it slammed into his forehead. Then, everything went black.

The sky had morphed from a violent night to a passive onset of dawn as they rode west along the White Settlement Trail. The hamlet was behind them and the trail was the only scar on the dark open prairie surrounding them. The temperature had dropped, resulting in a heavy dew's frost.

Cord, Travis and Deekie wandered further west with River well out in front of them all. Travis rode point, ahead of the others slightly. He was unarmed, and neither Cord nor Deekie felt compelled to keep a weapon drawn on him.

"Lucky for y'all that I remember this trail and the way to the gang's *hacienda*," Travis boasted.

"More like it's lucky for you," Cord said, "otherwise I'd have no reason to keep alive a Pinkerton who only wants to see me behind bars. You best not be taking us on some wild goose chase."

"I might be many other things, Mr. McCullough," Travis said, "but I am a man of my word."

"I can't wait to see Virgil again," Deekie said.

"So you can run to his arms?" Travis asked before adding, "or is it more proper to say arm?"

Deekie made a snared face at the Pinkerton. She had certainly heard those lame cracks many times before.

"Neither," Deekie snipped, "I can't wait to give him the business for abandoning me back at Sulphur Springs."

'Well, Deekie, to be fair," Travis went on, "I was with you when we got there, and you sound one hell of a lot better now."

"Don't matter none," Deekie said, "he should have waited for me instead of rushing out here to his useless *Diddy's* side and getting wrapped up in all this trouble. How many men ya' say guarding him and Enos out there?"

"Three," Travis answered, "unless that young Garrett, the one Cord let get away, somehow got ahead of us and went there while we was fetching the horses."

"No, he's actually behind y'all" yelled a voice from their rear amongst the frosted white trailside scrub. Out walked Garrett on foot with his rifle aimed at them. "Nothin funny now, or I start shootin'."

"Where'd you come from?" Travis asked. "You were behind us,"

"No, I was far out in front of y'all along. Ya see, I knowed y'all'd go back for that gunsmith. So I came out and hitched my mare off the trail, before I tucked back in to the scrub. Then, I let y'all pass by to get the drop on ya."

The dog, River had raced back to the rear, barking at the young gunman. Every time Garrett tried to get a shot off in his direction, River skittered away from in front of its barrel. The dog never stopped barking, and made for a great distraction. Each time Garrett failed to aim up on the dog, he quickly returned his aim back to the three of them.

"Now, Mister Cord, or whatever ya' call yerself, throw down that saddlebag. I've come to be fond of it, it having saved my life tonight and all."

"As soon as I do, your just gonna kill us all," Cord said calmly, "so, I think not."

"All right," young Garrett answered, "we'll just do it in the other order. I don't mind."

Cord awaited the first shot. He thought that if he could draw his revolver before the boy was able to lever the next round into the rifles's chamber and fire, then he could get a shot off at Garrett. But Garrett's first round was surely going to kill one of the three of them. *If the first shot takes me out,* Cord figured, *then we're all good as dead.*

River was, by then behind Garrett and barking incessantly. Then the dog skittered to one side and barked even more frantically.

"Cord," Deekie whispered, "do ya' see what I'm seeing behind him?"

A second shadow had emerged from the brush behind the boy. It was huge, and still dark in the spreading morning light. It crept toward the young gunman. The falling of its steps were covered by the dog's barking.

"Don't say a word, Deekie," Cord replied loud enough so Travis could also hear him, "It might be our only way outta this."

The dawn's light slowly crept across the face of the stealthy shadowed figure.

"He's a bad, bad man Cord," whispered Deekie.

"Let's get out of one fix at a time," Cord said flatly.

Garrett could hear their voices, but not make out their words. "What's all that muttering about over there?" He yelled, oblivious to the hulking shadow behind him. "Not that it matters none. Time's arrived for the three of y'all to meet yer maker."

As the young gunman raised his rifle, the massive figure of Orrin Fletcher James came up behind him. He punched Garrett with all his might in the lower back. Garrett dropped to his knees and Orrin quickly reached his massive arms around the boy and grabbed the rifle, one hand on its stock and the other holding the metal barrel.

The dog River had gone into a whole other level of blaring out danger. He circled and barked and skirted from side to side, awaiting his master's signal to attack. That signal never came from Cord, who thought it best to let one man kill off the other.

Garrett, despite being surprised by the attack, fought Orrin for control of the rifle. He pulled the trigger and fired off the round in the rifle's chamber. Its explosion cleaved the calm of the frosty morning air. The searing heat of the barrel scalded Orrin's right hand, but he did not release the weapon. He violently yanked the gun back against the throat of the young man, crushing his windpipe instantly. He then released the barrel, and windmilled the Spencer around the kneeling, choking boy. Orrin then kicked him to the ground and half-cocked the Spencer to clear the empty casing before fully cocking it to load another round into the chamber. Everything had happened with a speed that seemed unnatural to the girth and mass of the big man. Orrin then pointed the rifle at Garrett who was still sucking for air as he writhed on the ground.

The strong man pulled the trigger and the blast splattered the young boy's head like a dropped summer melon. Deekie had to turn away from the grotesque sight. Orrin then pointed the Spencer up at the three of them, all still on horseback.

"It's a good thing none of y'all tried to run off," Orrin said, "cause with this Spencer I would have dropped y'all before yer got very far. Now throw down yer guns. And somebody call off that damn dog."

"River, down, hide," commanded Cord, and the dog instantly stopped its barking and ran off into the brush.

"I can't believe the way ya' executed that boy," Deekie said.

"That boy was gettin' ready to kill the three of y'all, so ya best be glad I done did it," Orrin replied. He was flexing his right hand, trying to work out the pain in his scorched palm from the heat of the barrel blast. "These two I could care less about, Miss Deekie, but y'and me got unfinished business ahead of us. Now, throw down that saddle bag, mister, and all that gold in it. I come a long way and spent a lot of precious time searchin' for that fortune."

"Half fortune, you mean," said Travis, thinking fast. "The other saddlebag full of gold is already at this gang's hideout. We were just goin' there to collect it."

The big man looked at the Pinkerton, measuring just how much truth hid amongst his words, if any. Finally he said, "Then let's go get it. I lost y'all in town, but I knew if I followed this here boy," Orrin pointed with the rifle barrel down to the nearly headless corpse at his feet, "then yer'd all be along soon enough."

"I assume you got yerself a horse tied up nearby," Cord said, thinking through when he might draw the Baby Colt hidden in his duster.

"Yeah, and he'll stayed tied up there," Orrin said. "I ain't giving any of y'all a chance to escape by my going back for it. No, I'll just walk the rest of the way with this Spencer behind y'all until we get to their camp."

Travis lead them on. As Orrin walked behind them, he collected the revolvers that had been thrown down on the trail. Yet, one gun that he did not know of still lay hidden in the secret pocket at the bottom of Cord McCullough's leather trail duster.

River allowed them to pass and then trailed the four figures and three horses from a distance.

Showdown in the Morning's Mist

The rising sun eerily backlit the mist rising from the frosted heavy dew.

Clay climbed atop the horseshoe-shaped bluff just in time to witness the sun casting across the white coated landscape. It was a pure sight he thought, pure as the veil of a virgin bride. But like that image, its purity could not be taken and kept at the same time, and a thick mist rose as the sun slowly warmed the lovely white blanket of frost.

Clay then raised the scope of the Whitworth to take in the surroundings. Behind him in the rising mist, he could make out the trail that split off from and descended down from the White Settlement Trail. There was no sign of life along it. Clay then swept the landscape forward and below him. There was Silver Creek just as his *Diddy* had said, and beyond the trees along its banks was an open plain.

Clay then could see under the barren branches of two trees along the creek what seemed to be an old springhouse. *Odd,* he thought, *why would there be a springhouse with no farmhouse nearby?*

Clay then used his gun's scope to pan the full circular vista. He would be able to see anyone coming from all directions, including the approach from the White Settlement Trail behind him. He thought about what the Pinkerton had said, that another man was coming to kill his *Diddy*. He knew he needed to get Enos into a safe location, and he reckoned that lonely springhouse was as safe as any thing nearby. With the range of the Whitworth, he could even provide him cover from up here on the horseshoe.

Clay waited and fell into a rhythm of checking first the White Settlement Trail, then the open range across Silver Creek, and finally any other advances that led to the *hacienda*. The rising mist made his scouting all the more difficult, but Clay persisted. Finally, Clay could make out some figures off in the distance coming towards him from off the White Settlement Trail. As they neared, he could make out four images, three on horseback, and one walking behind them with a rifle at the ready. He waited until they came closer, at which point he could clearly make out Deekie and Travis, but the third rider he had never seen before. And damn if not too far behind them they were trailed by a mottled hound of some sort.

Then he focused on the walking rifleman. It did not take him long to recognize the massive outline of the strong man from Tennessee, Orrin Fletcher James. No Seth, no Garrett. He didn't know what exactly to make of this, but he knew despite the changes, the overall picture was no brighter without the two gang members. Orrin Fletcher James was just plain bad news.

Clay had but two options. Wait until they came closer and kill Orrin, or get back below and get his *Diddy* off into hiding. He did not have enough time to do both. Clay decided that even with Orrin dead, the third man was likely the one sent to kill his father. He would git below and send his Paw off to the springhouse. He decided to leave the loaded Whitworth, along with the remaining four hex bullets atop the bluff. He just might need to come back up to take out somebody or other. Clay reckoned the sniper rifle would be safe left up there.

Clay had thrown Warren's body over the side of the horseshoe when he first had scrambled up its height, and it had landed in almost the exact location where his Paw had played dead while they baited the gunman out of his hiding. Clay then scurried down the bluff to rejoin his Paw inside the *hacienda*. Enos by then had dragged the bodies of Will and his brother Warren inside, leaving a large swath of blood smearing the frosted grass as well as the stone walkway. He placed them next to ol' Hank's corpse.

"We got company coming, *Diddy*," Clay said excitedly. "Maybe fifteen minutes out, twenty if we're lucky. Ya' gotta move, I wan't ya' to git on down to the springhouse along the creek."

"The German farm springhouse?" Enos asked.

"I didn't see no farm," Clay said.

"Cause the gang burned them out of it years ago," Enos said, "for building too close to their *hacienda*."

"They got away with that?" his son asked.

"They made it look like Injuns done it," replied Enos. "Nobody ever bothered to come back out this far since."

"Just git yer carcass down there, quick like," Clay said.

"I never understood why they never torched that springhouse, though," Enos said.

"It don't matter none, *Diddy*, now just git along," Clay said.

"I'm taking these here wit' me, son," Enos said as he collected up the few gold eagles and double eagles left on the table. "I haven't so much as even seen a gold coin for a decade or more, let alone held one."

"Take 'em," Clay yelled at him, "just git along now, we're running outta time."

Enos made his way out of the *hacienda* and through the opening of the horseshoe-shaped bluff. Clay took the rifle that Warren had used, and hid himself in the tall grasses growing at the horseshoe's base.

Orrin and the three riders arrived at the natural opening of the horseshoe that surrounded the *hacienda*. The dog River held back, somewhat between the bluff and the creek at the bottom of the downslope in front of it. River appeared tentative, and knew not to get too close to the big man.

"You, Fancy Man," he said, pointing with the Spencer at Travis, "go on and stick your head around that corner and tell us what ya' see. If someone blows it off, we won't be missin' nuttin' since ya' done already got us here."

Travis did so, ever so cautiously, fearing his face could be met by a sniper's bullet. He instantly noticed all the smeared blood. He thought he smelled gunpowder in the air. "Looks like a battle took place here, and likely very recently. I can't tell if there's anyone alive inside or not, so you'll need to send one of us to walk on in."

"Deekie, yer up, sister," Orrin said. "If yer Virgil was the winner here, then ya' got no worries. If he lost, then ya' best hope whoever did won won't stoop to shootin' an unarmed woman in cold blood."

"This gang's got no scruples," protested Cord. "I'll go in her place. You may need her to barter for the gold you've come for." He said this knowing that second saddlebag of eagles was a myth.

"You can't send Cord!" protested Travis. "That man should be mine for leading you here. They know he's come for Enos. They'll shoot him for sure. You owe me, Orrin."

"I don't owe ya' shit nuthin', pretty boy!" Orrin said. He thought through his options, before placing his large, meaty hand in the center of Deekie's back. He pushed her out into the open and said, "Looks like yer up, girl. Just walk yerself up to that door and peek inside and yell out what ya' see. If anyone's pointing a gun at ya', just holler out the number of how many of them there are before they shoot yer pretty face off."

Deekie then walked ever so nervously toward the door of the *hacienda*, her senses tightening within her as she took each step. Clay watched from his position behind cover at the base of the horseshoe. He decided he'd wait until he got the four of them all trapped inside and then he'd make a play. He thought he stood a better chance with everyone contained within the structure, in close quarters. As far as he had seen, only Orrin had weapons.

Deekie had not yet made the doorway when she clearly smelled the metallic scent of fresh blood, and lots of it. It rose off the grass and from the smeared stone walk under her feet, as well as the threshold of the doorway. Somehow, in the most perverse way, it settled her, for she thought it reminiscent of some carnage Clay would make of his enemies. She made it to the doorway and gently pushed it open, slowly tilting in her head inside.

"Three," she yelled, "all dead!"

Orrin, Cord and Travis came out from behind the bluff's hillside. Then they walked double time to the door.

"Is the gunsmith one of them?" asked Cord. He was even then still torn between his duty to the Exchange and his promise to Deekie. Finding Enos' corpse would mean he satisfied both, but this easy way out was not to be.

"Naw, no *Diddy*, and no Virgil either!" Deekie called out. The three men behind her rushed forward, the last being Orrin with the Spencer.

As Travis entered, he recognized all three dead men. "These are the other gang members we left behind. That would leave only Clay and his Paw still alive."

"Where's the gold?" Orrin asked aloud, almost to anyone who might have any inkling of an answer. "Where's the damned gold?"

"I guess they took off with it," Travis said. "Looks like Clay and his Paw somehow overpowered these fellas and took them out. They can't have been gone very long. This blood is still fresh."

Orrin Fletcher James' face brightened to a visible red as rage overcame him. He said, "There never was any other gold, was there? I should have killed y'all back on the trail when I had the chance. But I got this here saddlebag and her. That's enough, I figure."

Orrin patted the saddlebag slung over his shoulder containing the gold eagles, and then pointed at Deekie. "Looks like yer one-armed Clay done deserted ya', girl."

Orrin, Spencer rifle in hand, stood between the three of them - Cord, Travis and Deekie - and the doorway. Travis then responded for her.

"First of all, Deekie, your Clay likely still thinks you're back in Sulphur Springs healing up from your episode of Yellow Fever. He would have no idea that you had left there with Cord. I knew from checking the telegraph messages that you had, but I sure never told Clay that. As for your gold, Orrin, there's a double eagle coin on the floor near your foot. I told you there was more gold here. Clay and his Paw likely took it all with them on their way back to Sulphur Springs."

"I don't think so," said Deekie, "as far as finding Virgil, Orrin, if I were you, I'd turn around, but real slow like. He's got the drop on ya'."

Orrin did just that to see Clay in the open doorway with Warren's rifle trained on him. His only hand was on the trigger, the stock bumped up against his shoulder.

"Where's the gunsmith?" yelled out Cord.

"Where's the rest of the gold?" demanded Orrin Fletcher James, as he glanced at the single gold coin at his feet. Once more the big man had become hopeful that a second saddlebag of fortune did indeed exist.

"All yer questions will be answered in due time," Clay said, "but first how about ya', big man, dropping that rifle and kicking it slowly over to me."

Clay kept his rifle trained on the Tennessean. Holding it with only his one arm was tiring, and it began to sway ever so slightly. Clay knew Orrin was the greatest threat to him right then, and he watched him carefully.

Orrin dropped his rifle slowly to the ground,nestling it on his foot. When Clay's rifle stock slipped slightly on his shoulder, Orrin kicked his weapon up with all his might. The Spencer flew like a rattler's strike through the air, smashing into Clay's rifle. By the time Clay was able to squeeze his trigger, the guns had already struck each other. Clay's shot was driven high into the roof overhead. Shards of terra cotta tile rained down behind them all.

As Clay struggled to cock the rifle to load its next round to fire, Orrin was all too quickly upon him. The Tennessean drove the rifle aside with his left arm. Clay knew he was in great trouble as the man soon had him pinned against the door frame, with Orrin's powerful right hand squeezing at his throat, the other wrapped around his gun hand. Clay had no way to defend himself other than to attempt to strike with the lifeless stump of his left forearm, a uselessly wasted effort against the strong man.

As Orrin strangled Clay, Cord McCullough dropped to one knee and reached for the weapon inside his leather duster. Yet as he did, Deekie yelled out, "Fer mercy's sake, we gotta do something," and pushed him aside, knocking Cord off-balance to the ground before he could draw the hidden weapon. Deekie then ran past the fallen Cord, went to the fireplace and drew the red hot iron rod used to stoke the ember bed.

With his left hand wrestling for control of the rifle, Orrin tightened his other hand's grip on Clay's throat. That right hand was already scalded from the rifle blast on the trail. Clay felt as if the bones in his neck were about to snap under Orrin's grip. He concentrated as much as he possibly could on not allowing Orrin to pry the rifle out of his hand, but knew he was fighting a useless battle. It was when his vision darkened and he knew he was about to pass out.

Suddenly and unexpectedly, Clay felt the weight of the big man slam into him, and at the same time both Orrin's hands unexpectedly released their grip. Clay felt the doorframe jam hard between his shoulders. It felt like a train rail as his body followed and he slid to the floor, coming to rest in a wretched heap on the stone threshold. Clay grasped at his throat with his now freed hand. He wheezed uncontrollably as he attempted to draw any air he could inside his lungs. He fought to calm himself, but the fear of impending death at the Tennessean's hands had already sparked a panic throughout his body.

Deekie lashed with all her might, blow after blow of the red-hot stoker across Orrin's broad back. Then, with one mighty turning swat of the blacksmith's arm, he sent her reeling backwards. Orrin was soon upon her and pulled the stoker from her hands. He raised it to strike her with it, just as she had done to him. She dropped herself to the ground and curled in a fetal ball, braced for its impact. That was when Cord McCullough threw himself upon Orrin. The two giants wrestled for control of the fireplace stoker. Cord's gun was still in his duster, because in all the commotion, he had not enough time to draw it and still protect Deekie. The two men were thus cast in a battle for control of the stroker. Cord knew if he lost it, Orrin would kill him with it. But he could also see that the Tennessean's scorched right palm was split open and bleeding profusely.

Deekie's eyes left the battle above her to gaze upon her Virgil, who lay gasping for breath only a few feet away. She could not get to him. She had never seen him so helpless, so in need of her. He certainly was in no state to fight anyone. Travis Brooks pulled Deekie to her feet, but the Pinkerton made no attempt to join the fracas of Cord and Orrin's death struggle.

Travis was still unarmed, but caught sight of the two rifles just beyond the men on the ground, not far from Clay, who was still struggling to regain his breath.

Outside the bluff, the excited renewal of barking by the dog, River, echoed through the hillside.

"The gunsmith," grunted out Cord to Travis and Deekie as he struggled with Orrin. "He's barking at the gunsmith."

"Then there was more damn gold after all," said Orrin Fletcher James, abandoning his attempt to free the stoker from Cord's grip. Instead he pushed it with all his might and let it go, driving Cord back against Travis and Deekie, falling back onto them. Orrin stepped over Clay, grabbed the Spencer and raced out to find the gunsmith he once again knew had the rest of the gold.

"Aw, hell," cursed Cord, slowly getting a hold of himself after the struggle. "Damn, that bastard is strong."

Travis stood aside Cord, while Deekie had dropped to her knees to care for Clay, who was still struggling to draw any breath he could. Travis then stepped around them both to pick up the other rifle from the ground.

"Cord McCullough," Deekie cried out, "Thank ya' for saving my Virgil."

"Cord McCullough" repeated Travis Brooks, then waited a beat to say it again for dramatic flair, "Cord McCullough, you, sir, are under arrest, and as such, are a prisoner of the Pinkertons."

Cord looked to see Travis aiming the rifle at him. Travis made no effort to go after the fleeing Orrin.

"OK, pretty boy," Cord smirked, "now I gotta worry about yer runt ass? I don't think so. I'm sorry, mister, but you're gonna have to stay here with her and her man while I make after that Orrin bastard."

Travis fired a shot over Cord's head into the ceiling. "You are coming with me, Cord! The two of us have no further interest in this sideshow. I'm taking you back to Fort Worth. The gunsmith, the girl and the cripple are no longer our concern. Nor is that Orrin fella. I have a singular purpose, and that is to bring you in. You will come with me or you will force me to show you that I mean business."

Cord still had not drawn his own revolver from the hidden pocket inside his duster. He could tell that the Pinkerton did not realize he carried it.

"Go with him, Cord," Deekie said, "Clay will look after me." Cord looked down at her attending to her gasping man and knew this was wishful thinking. Clay needed a hell of a lot more looking after than she did.

"Let's go," Travis said, "get on out to the horses."

They marched out of the *hacienda*, leaving Clay and Deekie behind. Travis followed closely behind Cord, rifle at the ready.

As they cleared the bluff's opening, Cord could see in the distance Orrin wading across Silver Creek in pursuit of the gunsmith as River trailed him, barking excitedly.

"Mount up, McCullough," Travis ordered, the rifle still aimed at him. Cord stepped up into the stirrup and threw his leg high over Trouble's saddle. He allowed the momentum to carry him far to its other side, where he leaned forward on the pommel in an awkward position, but one which allowed him to fish out the hidden gun from his duster while momentarily out of Travis' sight.

The Pinkerton then raised the rifle to the sky to walk aside his own mount. As he did, Cord fired two shots over his head from the pistol he had drawn. Travis' mount bolted away in terror. Cord leveled his pistol at the Pinkerton, and forced him to carefully hand over the rifle.

"I got some unfinished business across that creek," Cord told him. "And I don't need ya' rustlin' up another weapon and coming after me none, Pinkerton."

Cord pointed his pistol at the calf of the Pinkerton's left leg and fired a ball into its flesh, ripping through the top of his boot. Its leather exploded with a crimson burst. Travis went down immediately, writhing in pain. His face became distorted by a grimace of severe agony.

"There, Pinkerton, that oughta keep y'out of my hair for a bit. I gotta go after that other fella. But if I'm able to do so, I'll come back fer ya'." Cord took off on Trouble toward the creek. Travis Walter Isaiah Brooks, Pinkerton, was left to roll in the dirt in an unending torment of pain.

Deekie never left the *hacienda*, instead she hovered over the collapsed Clay as he attempted to regain his wind. He had thought his throat had been crushed by Orrin, and could barely work up the ability to speak. But he soon realized he was slowly recovering as Deekie calmed him.

Deekie hid her tears as she realized just how injured her Virgil was. She told him how brave he had been while stroking his blood red face. All he could do was to make a symbol with his hand pointing to the heavens.

"No, Virgil," she pleaded, "don't get up just yet. Stay on the ground and rest. Catch yer breath."

He opened his mouth to speak, but seemed unable to draw any breath on which to form even the simplest words. Finally, he squeezed his gut tight as a fist, and forced through his raw, swollen throat a painful garble.

In a voice rougher than a roadbed of gravel, he struggled to force out only a single word, *"Diddy."*

Deekie helped him to his feet, on which he was unsteady. Clay motioned out the door to the path that led to the top of the bluff. He moved slowly to it, with Deekie serving as his human crutch.

Deekie steadied her Virgil as he used all his might to climb up that path to the horseshoe's flat top. His exertions only compounded his troubles as they forced him to draw deeper breaths. The stabbing pains returned to his bruised windpipe. He stopped several times, with Deekie holding him, before he could push on further. It took a few minutes, but Clay and Deekie reached the top. He was thankful that he had left the loaded Whitworth sniping rifle atop that bluff, for he would not have made it otherwise.

Clay lowered himself alongside the Whitworth, which Deekie at first thought was his needing a rest after the hard climb. Then she remembered the supine firing position, and recognized that Clay was preparing himself to snipe with the Whitworth from it.

Deekie looked out over the grassy plain that opened up before them. The mist that had risen from the sun's warmth of the frosty dew was just beginning to burn off. It yielded glimpses of what was going on just beyond Silver Creek. There, not far from the springhouse, in the open field, she could made out Orrin Fletcher James standing with his back presented clearly to Clay's aim. The saddlebag full of gold double eagles was still slung over his shoulder, and she wondered if he had come to know by then that there was no second saddlebag of plunder.

In front of Orrin was Cord McCullough atop Trouble. His face was clearly visible to Clay's scope. But something appeared to be badly out of sorts to Deekie.

She could see Cord was leveling the rifle that Travis had used to take him captive. He had it aimed at Orrin, but for some reason wasn't firing it.

Clay took aim on the center of Orrin's back. "*Diddy?*" he asked wheezily through his throat. He honed in on Orrin through the sniper's eye scope, and as such he did not have the broader field of view that was available to Deekie's naked eye.

"No, Virgil," she answered, "I don't see him nowhere." She felt something was wrong, but couldn't put her finger on it. Something was terribly wrong, she thought.

"G'bye, Orrin," Clay wheezed. The words ripped from his bruised throat as if they were wrought from razors.

"Wait, Virgil," she gasped, "don't shoot!"

"Deeks?" Clay was stunned, his voice still hoarse and raspy, almost to the point of being unrecognizable.

She reached around her neck and removed the crucifix Cord had given her. She kissed it, held it high to the heavens and then bent over to touch it briefly against the barrel of Clay's Whitworth.

"OK, Virgil, now," she said, "let him have it."

Cord McCullough faced Orrin Fletcher James, in whose embrace was wrapped Clay's father, Enos. The Spencer lay on the ground, discarded nearby. By the time he arrived, the Tennessean had just run down the old man. He had him by the throat, apparently the brute's favorite method of killing. He seemed to crave squeezing the life out of men with nothing but his bare hands.

"I'm tellin' ya', there ain't no more gold coins," Enos gasped as Orrin eased his grip.

"Where the hell is the other saddlebag, y'old geezer?" Orrin demanded. "You best think hard on it, now, cause if ya' keep tellin' me there ain't none, then I got no good reason to keep yer ass alive."

"That's enough," Cord said, as he halted Trouble a short distance in front of them. He pointed the rifle at the strong man.

"Go on," Orrin said, "ya' can shoot him for me."

Cord knew he was right. Even with this rifle at this close distance, if someone moved it would be possible he would shoot the gunsmith who Orrin used as a shield.

"What do I care? I was sent to kill this Enos anyway." Cord answered. *But,* Cord thought, *if I do nothing, Orrin will kill the man for me, and I will have kept my promise to Deekie. I only said, after all, that I would not kill Enos. And I'll stay in the Exchange's good graces.*

Orrin struggled with his bloody, scalded hand to strangle the old, but still wiry, gunsmith fought who against him. The mist was parting in the warmth of the rising sun. Through it came a reflected glint of sunlight from high atop the bluff surrounding the *hacienda.* Cord looked past Orrin's shoulder and made out Deekie's image standing atop the horseshoe raising something high. Somehow, Cord knew it could only have come from the silver German crucifix he had given her. *Or was it Callie, come back to assure I would do the right thing? After all, I had made my promise against her soul...*

Cord then realized that Clay must be lining up a shot to take down Orrin. He held the rifle with his right hand, and waved his free arm frantically, trying to get their attention. *Don't Shoot!*

Cord knew from his vantage point that Clay could not see his Paw through Orrin's bulk. It was the same situation as with little Sean and the Jayhawker, but in reverse. *Callie has switched places with me. She's letting me feel exactly how helpless she was that day when she and our little Sean were lost forever because of me.*

Cord knew at that point he could not let either his *Callie* or her reincarnation of Deekie down. He could not allow Clay to take the life of his own father.

But what could he do? If Cord fired his rifle at Orrin he might well kill the gunsmith himself. If he did nothing, the gunsmith would have the life choked out of him. Cord McCullough then took the only choice left to him in that moment. He whistled for River to attack.

"Hold yer shot, Virgil," yelled Deekie atop the bluff as she saw River break into a full out run across the frosted white tips of the grassy field. The animal was as graceful as anything she had ever seen. "Hold it, Virgil, hold yer shot!"

The dog ran at a pace that seemed more like a sprinting deer. It covered the distance in bounding, arched strides. As it neared the big man, it leapt through the air, clamping its jaws around the massive, already bloodied palm that Orrin put out to stop it. River's jaw ripped forcibly into it, opening the skin amidst a crimson spray. Orrin screamed in pain, as the dog clamped its jaw down in the lock of an unyielding vice. For the first time, the Tennessean showed that he was indeed mortal, that he could be brought down by pain same as them all.

The net effect of River's momentum and his refusal to release Orrin's hand was to swing the big man around, such that Clay and Deekie could now see that Orrin held Clay's father in his clutches.

"Diddy!" Clay exclaimed.

Just then the old man fell free from Orrin's grasp as the dog and the Tennessean spun around in unison. This left an open shot for Clay.

"Now, Virgil, take yer shot," screamed Deekie.

Clay had the scope centered on Orrin's chest. He squeezed the trigger as smoothly as he could. The six sided bullet screamed out of the rifle's barrel, and raced the nearly three-quarter mile distance across the creek and into the shoulder of Orrin Fletcher James. Or rather it would have, if his shoulder not been covered with the saddlebag full of gold.

Despite the round not penetrating the saddlebag, the big man was spun back in the opposite direction by its impact and he spiraled down into the grass. The saddle bag flew free and away from him.

Orrin lay on his back as River lunged again at him. The two figures were obscured by the tall frosted stalks of growth. From their vantage point, Deekie and Clay could only see that both dog and man were locked in a mortal battle.

Clay frantically reloaded the Whitworth, which was a tedious undertaking for this one-armed sniper. Even for a fully capable sniper, it took near a full minute to muzzle load. By the time he had resumed his supine firing position with the weapon, Clay could see Orrin with his massive hands, covered in blood, around River's neck. The dog fought frantically to free itself, but Orrin was clearly choking the life out of it.

"Damn it," Clay cursed hoarsely, looking through the restricted field of view of the scope.

"Don't ya' dare hit River, Virgil," Deekie said. "Hold yer fire, Virgil, Cord has it under…"

In the distance, they had heard the rifle shot. Its sound seemed to echo out across the land before it reached them like a ripple on the surface of a pond. Cord McCullough had lined up his shot on Orrin Fletcher James as he knelt on the ground choking River. Cord simply sighted on the only part of the man where he was sure not to harm River - his head. Cord squeezed the trigger and the strong man's skull exploded, his bulk instantly dropped lifelessly and disappeared into the tall white-tipped grasses.

Even in the distance, Deekie could next make out Cord dismounting and racing over. He reached down and picked up River with both hands. The dog, covered in blood, was hurt, perhaps badly she feared, but was clearly alive. Deekie was very much relieved.

"Oh, thank the Lord above that River's done survived," she said, although unsure of the extent of the animal's wounds. "He's all Cord has left."

"*Diddy?* My God!*"* Clay rasped out, still watching through his scope and following Cord's every movement. He gazed on as Cord walked over through the tall grasses and stood over where Clay's father had been thrown. Cord held River over his shoulder with his left arm, as he extended his gun hand with the rifle pointed at Enos.

"No!" screeched out Clay. The word seemed to whistle painfully from his scarred vocal cords.

"He won't hurt yer Paw, Virgil," Deekie said.

"No!" Clay repeated defiantly and lined the crosshairs on Cord's chest. Clay had no voice to say, could only think, *He was sent to kill Diddy. I'm dropping him!*

"I said *No!*" Deekie objected, already sensing the fear racing through him, "Cord will not hurt yer *Diddy,* Virgil. He promised me. He promised *Callie*. So trust me and old yer damn shot!"

Clay had just started to squeeze the trigger, but instead, at Deekie's insistence, he relaxed his finger. What he saw next through the scope was Cord's extending the rifle, butt stock first, to the old gunsmith, who reached out to take it to pull himself up to his knees. Cord McCullough then put the weapon in his left hand, balancing River on his forearm and shoulder. Then Cord reached out his empty gun hand to assist Enos Clay-Harris to his feet.

"I told ya' he wouldn't hurt yer *Diddy*," Deekie said, breathing out a sigh of relief. "I knew he'd do the right thing all along."

Clay lowered the Whitworth and collapsed onto his back. It was all over. He closed his eyes and breathed as deeply as he could. He felt the tension and danger drain from him. He had come so close to killing his own Diddy, he thought. Had it not been for Deekie, he surely would have made that terrible mistake.

When he opened his eyes, he looked up at Deekie who stood over him. She was worried about him, but he himself knew then that with time he would be all right.

"Callie?" Clay finally found the strength to ask her.

"It's a long story, Virgil…" she said as she knelt by his side. She stroked his face as she said, "… a very long story that begins with a jack ass of a man abandoning his gal just to sneak off to find his good for nuthin' *Diddy*."

Goin' Home

The note started simply by saying,

"I'm Truly Sorry, Son!"

Clay, Deekie and Enos had been on the road about a week. The trio had stopped overnight in Shreveport, Louisiana. In the morning, their party had been reduced by exactly one third. Enos was gone, and with him the saddlebag of gold coins. But Clay's *Diddy* had been kind enough to leave them a small stack of gold double eagles, saying this should be enough to get them home to Cartersville.

"Ya' want me to read the rest of it, Virgil?" Deekie asked.

"Not really, but I need to know what it says," Clay figured, his voice still rough like gravel. "So, ya' go ahead."

Deekie read it out in a clean voice, but Clay could only hear once more the excuse-laden ramblings of his *Diddy*.

"I really wanted to git on home with y'all and see yer brother Truitt one more time. But while Deekie and ya' was sleeping in yer hotel room overnight, I come to think that I had not been to N'awlins in some time. After being held so long 'gainst my will, I reckon I owed it to myself to live a little. And since ya' was intent on turning this fortune over to Sheriff Alpheus T. Goff on yer return, I thought I'd save him from the temptation of pilferin' from it. Ya' said this mountain of money only brought ya' nothing but sorrows, so I figure I'd lift the burden from yer shoulders. Please don't be too cross with me."

"That's it?" Clay asked.

"Every last word" Deekie answered. "Did y'expect anything else?"

"Well, maybe a simple, *'Was sure good to see y'again'* would have been nice," Clay said.

"Them kind of niceties are few and far between from the Clay-Harris men," Deekie said. "It's just the nature of the beast."

"Who the hell wrote this note? *Diddy* cain't write, not so good as that, anyhow…"

"Well, Virgil," Deekie said softly, "Maybe your *Diddy* learned a lick in all them years he was bound up."

"Or maybe," Clay proposed, "*Diddy* found hisself a whore after we turned in. Someone to git down to N'awlins with. Had her write it up. Should we go after him?"

"I think yer *Diddy* can handle a whore on his own. He ain't forgot that much!"

"Seriously, Deeks, he could be in danger…"

"Hell no, Virgil!" Deekie said forcefully. "Old Enos already done 'nuff to us. Nearly got us all killed. We go home, and ya' can feel good that ya' got him outta that gang's clutches, then we forget this whole helluva mess."

"I feel like we should let Cord know…" Clay said.

"Why, Virgil?" she said. "Cord was preparin' to kill yer Paw at one point, and now ya' want to keep him up to date on where *Diddy* is heading? Makes no sense at all. We just need to forget both Cord and yer *Diddy* and head on home."

"All true," Clay said, "but in the end he did save my *Diddy's* life. I still feel as though we owe it to him."

"I will have no more of this talk," Deekie said, "Cord is in our past and, as I see it, he'll stay there."

They both knew what she was doing. Deekie was hiding her real feelings for Cord McCullough, who she had come to know a bit too closely. She was, despite the show of bluster, having a terrible time leaving him behind. That much was evident to Clay.

Only a few nights before, Clay, Deekie and Cord had been forced to stay in Fort Worth to clear up the whole course of events with the town's marshal. No charges were brought against any of them, as the town was more than happy to be rid of the gang. That last night, Deekie and Cord said their farewells as they walked along Main Street.

"You know, Deekie," Cord had said, "I gave a good bit of thought of askin' you to stay on here with me. Then I realized you could never leave yer Virgil."

"No," she answered, "I couldn't. Besides, ya' don't have a *here* for me to stay on to, do ya'? Ya' certainly won't stay in Fort Worth, where the Drovers' Exchange can hunt ya' down so easily."

"It's true, I got no place to call my own," Cord said.,"as true as when I told you I could never lie to you."

"Ya' mean ya' could never lie to *Callie*…"

Cord knew she was right, that his feelings for her were merely reflections of the lost love of his wife.

Cord pulled her gently by the hand until they were a few steps into the privacy afforded by the darkness of an alleyway that ran between buildings.

"Well, Deekie, I did tell you at least one half truth along the way," Cord admitted.

"And what exactly was that?"

"I said that me and Trouble and River just wandered the trails all our days," Cord said, "but the truth is, we always do manage to find ourselves some where to bed down for the winter months. The trail is just too bitter cold then. So we'll be headin' down to San Antone to stay with a lady friend o' mine on her spread there until mid-March."

"I didn't figure ya' for having many lady friends, Cord," Deekie said, as a small bolt of jealousy rose within her, "I mean, other than the ones ya'd paid for."

"As it is," Cord replied, "I had paid for Lucia once."

"Lucia?" Deekie repeated. "What a lovely name for that type of girl."

"Well, Deekie, it turns out she really is a lovely gal. Lucia has decided to give up the sportin' life. She offered me to stay with her down there until she gets her feet on the ground…"

"Ya' mean cause she's so used to them bein' up in the air? I guess ya'd be helpin' her through her changin' into being a woman of honor?"

"Come on, Deekie," Cord said, "don't be this way. Lucia knows that some of her former customers are likely to come a callin', and she just wants me around to run them off. Convince them that she was serious about giving up that life."

"And what are ya' goin' to do when the Drovers' Exchange comes callin' on y'about giving up yer past life?" Deekie tried hard not to show her concern for him.

"I figure I can just lay low with Lucia for the next few months. I'll deal with them iffen' when they find me, but likely by the time they do, me and Trouble and River will be on the move amongst the buds of the spring trails."

"And the Pinkertons?" Deekie probed further. "They're likely to find ya' first. They won't be too happy about what ya' done to that Travis Brooks fella."

A glimmer of pride came over Cord. "What? I done right by him. I took him to White Settlement for treatment of his wounds, didn't I?"

"Cord," Deekie said incredulously, "it was ya' who shot him up with them wounds in the first place."

"The man had a loaded rifle on me," Cord said, "I was justified in defending myself. Even the marshal said it was so."

"Well, ya' know he'll come after y'again, for sure," Deekie reasoned.

"It's all right," Cord replied, "by the time his leg heals up, I am most certain we'll all be back safely on the trails again. Even after his healing, he'll likely have that hobble I gave him for the rest of his days. It will surely slow him down quite a bit."

"Well, Cord," Deekie relented, "I can only hope that everything works out for ya' like ya' got it all figured. I'm sure gonna miss hearin' from ya'."

"Well, I bet that even a little backwoods town like yer Cartersville gots itself a telegraph these days. I may just drop you a line or two from time to time. I mean if it wouldn't get Clay too upset."

"I'd like that," she said, smiling broadly, "and Clay will just have to make do with it. T'ain't like nuthin' ever really happened between y'and me."

She said this last line with a blush of remorse.

"Not because I didn't want it to," Cord said. "and yer Virgil's a smart enough man to know that I sure wished it had. By and by, I am more than happy that you brought my *Callie* back to me. Even if just for a short while, it was a blessing to have her close again."

Deekie then took his hand and pressed something hard into his palm. "And ya' need to keep yer *Callie* close, always. Just as I had promised, I am giving ya' back the silver crucifix that ya' give me. Ya' gave it to her, the woman that was always closest to yer heart. And it hung close to mine, until she called on it for me to signal ya' from atop that bluff. So, anyways, I bought ya' a proper manly chain to go round yer neck, of a length so it should hang aside the heart that still loves her."

Cord began to object, but before he could, Deekie stood on her tiptoes and gently pressed her lips to his. He slid his hand behind her back and pulled her close. His coarse weathered lips explored the softness of her own one last time. He kissed her passionately. She did not resist. For that last extended moment, she was again his *Callie*.

Then, after the moment had lingered, she pulled gently away from him. Deekie knew that Cord was the one desire, the sole temptation that she could never allow herself to fully give in to.

When they physically separated, Cord could find no words for the moment other than, "Come on, River, time for us to go." The man and his dog left her there alone, just a lovely shape in the shadows, but only a few steps away from the busy, illuminated street. Cord and River walked away deeper into the darkness to find Trouble.

"I still think we should go after *Diddy*," Clay said, snapping her from the sweetness of her reminiscing.

"No, Virgil," Deekie said, "I'm through chasin' memories. Let him go off and find out just how much trouble that gold can bring on. We sure as hell did. We'll just git on home, it's well past time we done so."

"Even so, Deeks," Clay said, "we still got enough problems of our own."

"Like what, Virgil?" Deekie asked.

"Well, for one thing, are these few gold coins Diddy left us really going to be enough to get us back to Cartersville?"

David and Marie Trawinski

David and Marie Trawinski are graced to be citizens of Cartersville, Georgia. That wonderful north Georgia town had long ago captured their hearts, enough not only to draw them to retire there, but also to publish their first joint historical novel, *"Ever Blooms the Rose."* That story is set in Civil War and Reconstruction Era Cartersville, and introduces the characters of Clay and Deekie. This novel, *"Guns of the Yellow Rose"* is *"Ever's"* sequel, and hopefully the second in a long line of Clay and Deekie adventures. Dave and Marie are both members of the Booth Western Art Museum Writers' Guild, and also of the Etowah Valley Historical Society.

AUTHORS' NOTES

The first draft of this story was completed by Thanksgiving 2021. The revisions and editing process that commenced thereafter did little to alter our storylines or historical factual content of this work. This is important to us, because we are dedicated to keeping as factually true to the period as possible. This includes insuring that any of the institutions that we mention were actually established on or before the fall of 1873. As much as we possibly could have, we kept this story true to the time.

When it came to Cartersville, the details of this story were readily available. As we noted in *"Ever Blooms the Rose,"* the fictional characters include Clay, Deekie, and Truitt, as well as those of Horace Woodard, Sheriff Alpheus T. Goff, and the widow Rebecca Howell. The latter's porch-fronted abode is also fictional. All other details regarding the town, the Gilreath cottage and lawn, and even the Park Hotel are, to our knowledge, accurate.

The representations of Nashville and Memphis are as we have researched. Nashville was indeed a thriving metropolis after the war, and through it much trade between the North and South was conducted. This was thanks to the influence of the business magnate Cornelius Vanderbilt. This book is set some twenty-two years before the Commodore's grandson, George, would go on to open Biltmore House of Asheville in the neighboring state of North Carolina on New Years' Eve, 1895.

Memphis was a thriving Mississippi River town, and as such was prone to recurrences of Yellow Fever, spread by infected mosquitoes by the riverboat traffic. In the fall of 1873, it suffered its worst outbreak to date, only to be later surpassed in 1878. Entire cities would empty out during these outbreaks - at least those that could afford to leave - and this was true in Memphis. It is also accurate that this city's Peabody Hotel was then in its fourth year of operation at its original location on the corner of Main and Monroe, not yet at its current address of Union and Second Street. The Peabody being one of our favorite of the great Southern Hotels, we wished to include it in this tale, even if it was long before the legacy of the March of the Peabody Ducks was initiated in 1933.

The history of the various renditions of the Old Butterfield Stage Coach routes is as accurate as we could research. While there is a tremendous amount of detail regarding its routes and stops in the pre-war years, there is much less in its post-war configurations. Surely the stage coach ran into Fort Worth, we know, in 1873, as their was no train service to the town until three years later. Robberies had become so commonplace along these routes, that as soon as train services reached a town, stage coaches quickly terminated operations there.

Having lived in Fort Worth for the better part of a decade, we were pleased to include the town in our tale. During 1873, the great herds of longhorn cattle were still driven right through the town on the way to the Chisholm Trail. The fort the town was named for had been abandoned by the army for over a decade. The town's *Hell's Half Acre* district was a notoriously lawless sprawl of saloons, gambling parlors and houses of prostitution in their various forms. *"The Acre"* catered to a most unruly clientele.

While we were excited to include some of our favorite establishments and historical figures, it turned out some just didn't fit our timeline. The White Elephant Saloon did not open in town until 1885, as best we could research. "Longhair Jim" Courtright, the brassy gunman, did not become marshal of Fort Worth until 1876 (through 1879), and his famous duel with the White Elephant's Luke Short would not result in the taking of Courtright's life until 1887. All sadly outside the arc of our story's timeline.

That said, the Acre, even in 1873 proved to be a financial boom to the city. Saloon licenses alone brought in great revenue. The steady stream of drovers coming through town proved to be a source of revenue to many enterprises, both legal and not. We were grateful to have the electronic resources of several Texas historical societies to consult, as well as historical reference titles dealing with the history of "Hell's Half Acre". Other Texas history included in our tale, specifically that of Sulphur Springs and White Settlement, is accurately presented.

We noted earlier that the Drovers' Exchange is fictional, as are the Stone Canyon Gang, and the gunsmith, Enos Clay-Harris. However, the illegal conversion of cap and ball revolvers to breech loaders was still an ongoing criminal enterprise at that time. While the Colt company introduced the breech-loading Single Action Army Revolver (also to become known as the Peacemaker, the Colt .45, or simply as the SAA) in '73, it was not readily available. The US Army bought up as many of the SAA revolvers as the Colt Company could produce initially. The Colt company even continued to convert their stockpile of old Colt Navies and other cap and ball pistols for sale to the general public.

While we are discussing guns, all other weapons discussed within this story are indeed factual. Griswold and Gunnison Revolvers were copies of the Colt Navy Designs. Cook and Brother long guns were highly sought after. The Whitworth Sniping Rifles from Britain were the most highly prized of guns for both their accuracy and rarity.

We had some fun with the names of the madams throughout the Acre, and all are fictional. There never was a Fanny Belle or Momma Mary Lee Parker, but there were many women entrepreneurs making fortunes in "The Acre."

The storyline of the fictional gambler Jefferson Calhoun Armistead running counterfeit guns emerged when we began to research these Confederate weapons. For the counterfeiting of Dixie weapons was so rampant after the war, that today, over 150 years later, these guns are nearly indistinguishable based on age alone from the guns they counterfeited. We suspect many a collector has purchased a fake Confederate weapon believing it to be authentic. It was the uncovering of these warnings even in today's markets that gave us the seed of that particular storyline.

We greatly enjoyed developing and writing this tale of the Old South meeting up with the Old West. Revisiting the characters of Clay and Deekie, as well as developing those of Cord McCullough and Travis Walter Isaiah Brooks, was truly a delight for us both. Who knows if their four trails will cross again in the future, but who's to say that each pair might not have future adventures of their own? In closing we thank you for coming along on this adventure with us. It was great to have y'along!

David and Marie Trawinski

Image Credits

Front and Back Cover Design by David Trawinski
Stage coach image used with permission of the
Booth Western Art Museum of Cartersville, Georgia
Background of edited Adobe Stock Images
Yellow Rose #189515881 Ekaterina
Texas Sunset #217819820 donyanedomam
Three Cowboys # 5831303 outdoorsman
Dog Silhouette # 88331086 Majivecka
Crossed Gun Images by Davis Trawinski

Figure 1: Frank Leslie's Newspaper, Public Domain Image
Figure 2: Gilreath Cottage used with permission of
Rose Lawn Museum of Cartersville, Georgia
Figure 3: Chisholm Trail Map 1873, Public Domain Image
Figure 4: Guns of the Confederacy, Compiled by David Trawinski
Figure 5: Lee & Gordon Mill photo by David Trawinski
Figure 6: River by the Cimarron, Edited Adobe Stock Image
 # 19192238 eAlisa
Figure 7: Original Peabody Hotel, Compiled by David Trawinski
Figure 8: Memphis on the Mississippi 1870, Public Domain Image
Figure 9: The Mighty Mississippi, Adobe Stock Image
#125702104 johnsroad7
Figure 10: The Butterfield Stage Coach Map, Public Domain Image
Figure 11: Butterfield Stage Coach Image used with permission of
Booth Western Art Museum of Cartersville, Georgia
with edited background of Adobe Stock Image
 # 863277234 Microstocker
Figure 12: Butterfield Stage Coach Interior Images
used with permission of The Booth Western Art Museum
of Cartersville, Georgia
Figure 13: Fort Worth Town Map 1876, Public Domain Image

Guns of the Yellow Rose
Proudly Published by